WORLD WAR III
TOOK PLACE ON A HOT FRIDAY
AFTERNOON IN JULY

But most Americans never even knew it

On the entire continent of North America only 14 humans survived . . . only 14 heard the news that . . .

"The United States of America has been obliterated and burned to death . . . There is no USA!"

Now deep in the earth, in the fantastic shelter of a Connecticut millionaire, the survivors face the beginning of an underground nightmare that threatens what is left of their sanity.

TRIUMPH—THE MOST FRIGHTENING NOVEL YET TO APPEAR ON THE AFTERMATH OF WORLD WAR III . . . "HAIR-RAISING."
—*Newsweek*

"TERRIFYING IN THE TRADITION OF ON THE BEACH . . . THE BEST AND MOST THRILLING OF WYLIE. . . ."
—*Christian Herald*

TRIUMPH

BY PHILIP WYLIE

CREST
BOOK

A CREST REPRINT

FAWCETT PUBLICATIONS, INC., GREENWICH, CONN.
MEMBER OF AMERICAN BOOK PUBLISHERS COUNCIL, INC.

For Ted and Mike and Gale Pryor

1

THE YOUNG MAN driving the car interrupted a question about mathematics to whistle. "Brother! Is that the one?" He nodded at a private, ten-place jet plane standing in slack-winged silence at the head of the airstrip.

Ben Bernman grinned and, characteristically, answered the math question before he spoke of the plane: "Belongs to Vance Farr, my weekend host."

The pale, intent youth whistled again, but softly. "He must own all the tea in China *and* the coffee in Brazil!"

The other man chuckled. "Maybe he does. He's in the import-export business."

"Oh." The driver braked his secondhand vehicle as it neared the jet. "*That* Farr!" He remembered something. "Wasn't it his daughter you rescued, last winter?"

The older scientist, who was not really old, busied himself with two items of luggage, a brand-new airplane suitcase made of reinforced magnesium and a second item that invariably went wherever Ben went, and invariably in his hand or at his side: a locked, leather briefcase. With these extricated from the rear seat, he answered. "Faith Farr. Yes. I happened to be the first person to pass the place where she'd skidded off the road, in a blizzard. So naturally I stopped and went back and found the lady."

The other scowled briefly, then smiled in recollection. "Not the way I read it," he said, admiration in his voice. "I remember that plenty of cars had passed and not noticed the drifted signs of that wreck. It took—and I more or less quote—the brilliant Dr. Bernman to make the scrutiny and deduction, stop, wander with a flashlight in the blinding snowflakes till he found the damsel, hoist her near-freezing and unconscious form to his brawny shoulder, and roar to a hospital."

Ben cuffed Dr. Swenson lightly.

But he went on, eyes twinkling. "She was exceedingly beautiful, judging from the photographs appearing at the time. About—roughly—as attractive as you are homely, Doc. A coppery-haired blonde, right? Angel face. Brains, too, if I

7

recall the stories. Or was that brains item just press-agent stuff?"

"Faith's plenty bright," Bernman answered. He picked up his luggage and, for an instant, eyed his assistant with an expression that was sad, regretful or, perhaps; meek. For a man of his reputation, a man who'd won the Fermi Prize at twenty-six and now, ten years later, one who headed a department at Brookhaven, Ben Bernman was far too modest, his assistant and chauffeur felt.

Swenson watched his chief move toward the plane in the staggering heat of the last Thursday of that July, wondering if any very rich girl was bright enough truly to appreciate Doc Bernman. He decided not, and turned the car.

The pilot of Vance Farr's plane came hurriedly and the two men argued a little absurdly about carrying the luggage. Ben gave in with a slightly embarrassed laugh and, sweating, followed the muscular pilot—Al, he'd said his name was—to the jet.

Minutes later it was airborne.

Ben watched the atomic-research facility at Brookhaven as it diminished in the shimmering air to a toylike marvel: bizarre buildings that contained reactors and particle accelerators, lead-walled gardens where experiments went forward in the effect of radiation on plants, red-and-white stacks and shielded earth-rises beneath which plasmas, sun-center-hot, stormed in magnetic "bottles" as the search was continued to find a means of transforming the energy of fusion bombs to a practical power source.

They'd been at it for almost twenty years now, and during the past six he'd worked on the theoretical end, at Brookhaven. When the distant toy-town and its Martian aspect were replaced by the blue of Long Island Sound, Ben perceived the speed of this luxurious plane; but the quietude of its blue-and-gold interior surprised him only when the pilot, Al, spoke: "Be over the Connecticut shore in a sec. Then it's only thirteen—fourteen minutes to Uxmal."

"Ooshmal?"

"The Farr place. Spelled, 'U-X-M-A-L.' Mayan town in Yucatán."

"Oh, yes!" Ben had never seen Uxmal—or Chichen Itza, either; but he knew about them.

"Ever been there before?"

"Never have."

"Quite a sight. If you like, I'll take a turn around the place, Doctor."

"Sure. *Uxmal*. Mrs. Farr told me it was modernistic, with what she called a Mayan-Toltec 'feeling.' But I didn't know——"

"She just picked a name for it last month."

"Oh."

Al listened to talk from some control tower or other, in the headphone covering his opposite ear. His nearer ear was free of its disc for in-flight colloquy. He nodded to himself and went on talking about the Farr "place" in Connecticut:

"It's on a hilltop—young mountain, comparatively, for these parts. Called Sachem's Watch. The Farr family have owned it since before the Revolution. One of those Victorian jobs stood on it—all gables and porches with fret-work. Iron deer in the gardens. Shrubs clipped to look like birds and animals. Mrs. Farr decided to build the new place maybe ten years ago. About when I signed on as Farr's pilot. They had a turboprop Panther then, and a couple of chop-pers. Helicopters." The blue-eyed, extraverted man saw Ben had understood "choppers," and grinned. "You probably fly a lot, being in the H-bomb business, eh, Doctor?"

"Some. Though I'm not, really, in the bomb end. Was, for a while. But back there at Brookhaven, we're trying to turn H-bomb power into cheap electricity."

"Hope you do! Anyhow, they tore down the Victorian job, gazebos and all, and had one of that—what-was-his-name— that Frank Lloyd Wright's students—man of fifty, now —design their new house, so-called. Cut a road to the top —the old road was for buggies, I guess—round and round the hill. Going up it dam' near gets you dizzy—a real spiral climb! Mr. Farr sold off a hunk of the hilltop land and some developers built a bunch of cooperative apartment houses there. Mrs. Farr raised hell about that, and planted full-grown white pines and spruces, oaks and maples, all around the new house, to cut off any sign of the development. Candlewood Manor, *it's* called. The Farr place has a lot of history. Big caves under Sachem's Watch. Farr's great-grandfather used 'em, so it goes, to hide slaves in, over a century ago. Thing called the Underground Railway."

"Yes," Ben said.

"Don't suppose your folks had reached America yet." Al said that casually, not meaning to be hurtful and hardly aware he had indicated the evident fact that Dr. Ben C. Bernman was a Jew.

"Still in Germany," Ben replied pleasantly. "And points east. Estonia. The Ukraine."

"Sure. Well, the Farrs hid slaves that got from Dixie to Long Island Sound as stowaways in ships, before the Civil War. And there were Farrs living on Sachem's Watch before the Revolution. Men who went to fight it with Israel Putnam. Big family, once. Funny, how those big families can dwindle down to—well, even to just one person. And that, a girl. Faith."

Ben said nothing.

Al shook his head. "Imagine! Imagine having your name as celebrated *and* historic as 'Farr' and then realizing it is going to disappear, the minute a lone gal becomes Mrs. So-and-so!" He glanced, innocently, at the scientist. "Say! *You're* the man saved her, last winter!"

"Mere chance."

"Saw you on TV! In the papers! Be damned!" Al meditated a moment. "Didn't mean anything by that crack back there about when your folks reached the good old U.S.A."

"Of course not."

Al relaxed. He listened again to the phantom talk from the unknown source and hooked a throat mike to a blue collar open over red hairs on his chest. He spoke briefly and almost inaudibly insofar as Ben was concerned. Numbers, mainly, and a final, "Roger!" Then the jet tilted for a slow turn and Al pointed. "Uxmal," he said.

Ben looked down with absorption. The house—if a rectangular set of buildings with a flashing moat, surrounding an interior "patio" so extensive that its flagged areas, gardens, and terraces dwarfed a tennis court, could be called a house —lay ahead of and below the slowing jet. A spiral highway, visible here and there through giant trees, gave the hill a terraced look, suggesting, at least, the step-pyramids of ancient Mayans and Aztecs. The low buildings, flat-roofed, glass-walled, stone-supported, here and there sustained by squared timbers, did resemble pictures of the temple-surrounded playing courts of their barbaric ruins in Yucatán.

"Uxmal" was a good name for the place, Ben thought.

He also noticed, as the plane held its arc, the white, numerous, and many-angled roofs of the cooperative apartments—of Candlewood Manor, he repeated to himself. And he saw the massive tree-plantings that separated Uxmal from the common herd at Candlewood—a nevertheless expensive abode. His attention moved to another phenomenon.

One side of Sachem's Watch had been sheared away—by man or nature, he couldn't be certain in the brief view he had. But he saw a cliff-face that began some distance downhill from Uxmal and then, to his faint surprise, as the plane unfolded it, a mighty slope of raw limestone that had evidently been quarried from the area in recent times, for it lay in glittering beige blocks of enormous size, below the cliff. That evidence of Brobdingnagian blasting vanished as trees intercepted it. Next, for instants, Ben glimpsed the white clapboard sides and slated church steeples of as much of Fenwich Village as tall trees allowed airborne viewers to behold.

The plane straightened, descended, bumped. Ben had a flashing sight of a tall young woman with copper-gold hair, in a light-brown dress, standing beside a cream-and-scarlet automobile. *Faith.*

The jets thundered into air-scoops that threw their power forward; with a gingerly foot, the pilot braked, thrusting Ben forcefully against his safety belt. It was a short airstrip for such a craft, the scientist thought. But long enough.

Ben said, in the sudden diminishing of that final sound, "Nice trip!"

Al grinned. "Poky! Never did over five hundred miles an hour. No time for climbing, to go supersonic." He increased the sound again, swung the plane around, and blasted grass alongside the paved strip as the plane rushed back toward the other end of the field. There, he cut the two jet engines.

Doors opened automatically, their click amazingly sharp and specific. Hot air rushed in from the wilted field, air bringing the aroma of baking concrete and grass perishing. Al made to unhitch himself and Ben shook his head. "Stay right there, friend! When the day comes that sees me unable to lug a suitcase and a little locked sack a hundred yards across a field, I won't *be* riding jets!"

"Have it your way! Pleased to meet you."

Faith ran toward him from the shade. He realized the motor of her Jaguar was running and thought it wasteful till he saw its windows up and understood: it was air-conditioned and Faith had not wanted it to heat up inside, as it would have, in minutes, without cooling on this torrid afternoon.

"Welcome, *Ben!*" she called.

"Hi, Faith!"

They were almost within handclasp distance when he saw the flare on her ring finger. Not aware that he did so, Ben stopped. So did she. Faith seemed surprised, then understood. "You should read the society pages, darling," she said softly. "Happened a week ago. Kit Barlow. I'd assumed you knew."

He smiled then, and strode forward. "Lucky guy!" he said, and dropped both pieces of luggage. His long arms went around her and his ugly-solemn face bent down. He kissed her firmly. "I'm glad for both of you," he said.

She looked at him, brows winged, her gold-dappled, hazel eyes alive and truthful. "The hell you are!"

He kept his smile. " 'Have it,' in Al's words, 'your way.' "

Faith shrugged.

It was cool in the car, so cool he felt cold. But the thermometer on the dash showed seventy-five degrees. Outside it was probably well over a hundred in the shade. Which made the contrast.

For the first part of their journey she was occupied by driving. A sweep of paved access-road took them onto the Yankee Turnpike. There, men driving alone in big cars, medium cars, and small cars, along with whole families in cars that sometimes sprouted children from every steaming window, swept north in all three lanes. *Only Thursday*. But every businessman who could, and every family able to do so, sped outward to escape the brick-kiln walls of Greater New York, to get clear, even, of Bridgeport, in this heat wave, or of any and every city, and to move out into any countryside beyond suburbs. There, still, an excessive glare fell on hamlets and farms and penetrated trees, hot as the pointed fire from sun-aimed magnifying glasses. Even the countryside panted. Its lakes were warm, its ponds hot, and some brooks had vanished, for the midsummer while.

The Yankee Turnpike, where Faith fought out a series of accelerations to gain the opposite lane, led to a cloverleaf that took them onto a blazing stretch that became asphalt and dived under trees and had a new name: Wandering Hills Road. The Jaguar slowed on a bridge beneath which water charged and foamed. Faith said, "The Lute River."

"Lovely name!"

"Isn't it!" The car moved ahead. "When I was little, I thought that lute meant 'flute,' or something like it. So I used to listen for whistling sounds. It never had any. Winter or summer, nearby or in the distance, it always either tinkled or jangled, sort of, in deep tones. *Like* a lute." She smiled.

He saw her momentarily a child, pert-nosed, wide-eyed, each metallic filament of her hair disordered by play—sweaty, perhaps, in summer—her then-flat chest bared (or, in winter, wearing ski pants, probably) listening for a river to make sounds it couldn't, or didn't, or wouldn't. He banished the picture, almost as an angered man might douse the fire of a cigarette.

The Jaguar now rose on the spirals that terraced Sachem's Watch: sheer stone on the inside of the rising turns with, soon, treetops, opposite and below. They both noticed, when a random sunray set spinning color flying about the leather-upholstered car from her ring. Both looked at the ring.

"Mother," Faith said, "is ecstatic. Naturally. She's plugged Kit since he was eight and I was six—when the Barlow family built their place. On a slope of this hill. We'll pass it, soon. Dad's indignant."

"Indignant?" Ben's voice showed surprise.

She laughed. "Why not? He knows Kit and I have bored each other, off and on, for ages."

"People do," he responded gently. "Married people. Always. From time to time."

"Oh . . . that. Sure. But Dad thinks Kit is a 'lightweight,' mentally. A Little Leaguer, Dad calls him, who never grew. Dad sometimes refers to him also as"—she giggled—" 'what you find on the other end of golf clubs.' Still—" she didn't sigh, though she would have, if she'd been given to self-dramatization, "Kit's big and easygoing and comfortable and familiar and *very* tolerant!" The wide eyes cut toward him.

He ignored them. "I'm anxious to meet Kit."

"I'll *bet!*" Faith's laughter was short and she followed it with a question. "Why didn't *you* ever ask me to marry you?"

A joke? Sadism? Did she *mean* it? Ben felt twenty billion electron volts could not have shocked him more. But he felt he had to hurry with some sort of reply. He took an attitude seemingly, at first, very solemn:

"Let's consider that question, Faith. First, the man's looks. Mine. I have been called a bean pole. Even, 'the Israelite Ichabod Crane.' My ears have been described as squashed paper cups set at right angles to a head that is often said to be more equine than human. Horselike. This beaky and elongated nose has been claimed as the equal of anything Modigliani ever painted. My eyes are held to be the same 'blue-clay blue' that the pre-Roman cannibals of Britain daubed themselves with."

She gurgled with mirth. *"Homely,"* she finally agreed. "But *how!* Yet, when you smile, it's like a Christmas tree coming on in the dark! Next fact. All the people who work for you, with you, over you—everybody I ever heard of who knew you—loves you. Including me. So *there!"*

He nodded soberly but went on. "You are Money, Miss Farr. Also, Society, Café Society, *and* Blue Blood—*not* mud-blue, either. The McCoy. My old man is a Jewish shop-owner in Newark. I'm exactly one generation from going to church in a yarmulke."

"Oh, fiddle! You're as religious as Dad. Nil. Nix. None."

"Then there is the matter of my métier."

"Math? Physics? I was damned good at math in college! Our prof literally implored me to go on, after calculus."

"But you studied opisthotonos dancing, instead."

"You fool! Wait a sec! *Opisthotonos.* That's the spinal backbend you get in your dying agonies if you take strychnine. Or if you die of tetanus."

He nodded, his expression unimpressed. "Next on the agenda. My present plans. Along about mid-October I'm scheduled to leave for Antarctica——"

"But! You're *not!"*

"—a thing you'd know I recently agreed to do, if you read the *science* news. Some special studies to be conducted down there, of the magnetosphere, certain new missiles, and communications. Some low-temperature work: laser phenomena at near-absolute zero."

"Near-absolute zero is right! How long will you be gone?"

"Two years," he said quietly.

She accelerated so savagely she had to brake hard and instantly, afterward, to keep from leaving the road and flying onto the roofs of Candlewood Manor Apartments, visible below. She flushed, then grew slightly pale, bit her lip, glanced at a vast mansion set far back from the road, and did not tell Ben it was the Barlow home—did not need to. Finally, she said, "Do—are you—allowed visitors?"

"Like in penitentiaries?" He chuckled. "Sometimes."

"Women?"

"Sometimes. Wives, at least. After all, it was—oh, in the Kennedy Administration, I guess—second term, I think—when they started building a genuine, domed city in Marie Byrd land—and it's as comfortable as your family's Park

Avenue penthouse, indoors, even at minus seventy outdoors."

"Goody! Then the very first time Kit and I fight—after we're married, I mean—I'll come down and see you!"

"Do that! You'd really be an ornament—in a military jail!"

She responded forlornly, "Oh, *Ben!*"

Then the trees under which they'd climbed opened up. Ahead he saw a stone gateway. On its summit stood an exact replica of the "tiger" god found deep inside the largest pyramid at Chichen Itza—complete, even, to glowing green eyes of Chinese jade that somehow the Toltecs had imported centuries before the Spaniards had crossed the Atlantic to smash their idols and steal their treasure in the Holy Name of a different deity.

This great cat—a panther, Ben thought—was beautifully modeled in what would be accepted as a most "modernistic" style.

Beyond the gate lay a sort of plaza—as big as the game courts of Uxmal or Chichen Itza, Ben thought—surrounded by the temple-like edifices of stone, timber, and glass which were living rooms, dining chambers, and guest quarters, connected by closed passageways and looking out, on all four exterior faces, across a moat swimming pool where cool-looking water shimmered in sun or drowsed in shade. The car stopped on bluestone beside a building where half a dozen other cars glittered in the shade, and there was room for many more.

From a door came a slender, white-uniformed Negro of middle age. "This," Faith said, "is Paulus, Dr. Bernman. Paulus Davey, our butler. *Lord!* It's *hot!*"

To Ben's great surprise, the butler held out a confident hand. Instantly, Ben took it, aware that Faith had watched to see what he would do. Paulus Davey said, "Pleased to meet you, Doctor," and picked up the luggage.

Faith had already started for a near door. She turned. "Wear shorts, if you like. A bathing suit'd be even better! Swim down to the terrace. Mama'll be in the front room—" she pointed—"and I'll meet you in a mo'."

Ben studied the man at his side and said, "She has no imagination."

Paulus Davey protested. "Miss Farr? She has *too much,* if you take some of her friends' attitudes."

"None at all," Ben argued calmly. "Otherwise she'd never have suggested shorts for me. If the girl had imagination, she'd even have realized I brought no such garment! Shorts, indeed!"

The butler laughed with a deep sound and in agreeable amusement. Then, quickly, he moved toward a different door. Ben followed. It was cool, mercifully so: air-conditioned—even the passageways. They went up a short flight of steps, along a flagged corridor, and were about to descend a longer flight when Paulus Davey halted, set down his burden, whipped open a door, and called, "Glyph! Get out of there!"

Looking over his shoulder, Ben saw a large collie stop its bemused swim in the moat and turn, reluctantly, to the stone edge only inches above the water surface. The dog heaved itself out and shook, filling the air with brilliance and marking the stones with falling spray. Davey went on. Ben repeated, "Cliff?"

"Glyph," the butler replied, and spelled it. "He has a funny patch of white on his chest——"

"I noticed."

"—that Mrs. Farr says is exactly like a Mayan glyph."

"Oh."

"Here we are."

Ben had been ready for anything in the matter of guest accommodations at Uxmal: an Egyptian room, say, or something with a roof of corbeled arches, all stone, with feather decorations that might even have actually once been the cloak of some cruel, gaudy Aztec. Instead, he was led into a suite —living room, writing alcove, library alcove, bedroom, and bath. It made him think of the "best" suites in the newest motels. The prevailing color scheme was yellow and brown; but blue-green ornaments, bath towels and mats, curtains and small rugs cooled that rather too-warm combination.

It was the sort of place that, save for variation in color scheme (and a book-lined anteroom), one could enjoy everywhere in America—at a price. Living quarters in which you knew exactly where to find the phone, extract ice cubes, turn on lights, press the switch that would cause a panel to slide back and expose the fifty-inch screen of a color television set, and where you'd know how to operate the light-dimmer and the electric blanket—not needed, now.

Paulus Davey adjusted an air-conditioning control after glancing at a thermometer. He had put the briefcase and the shiny, magnesium suitcase on two luggage racks at the feet of twin beds. After Ben had thanked him and said he needed nothing more, the butler departed.

Ben walked to the exterior wall and pulled cords which

drew back yellow traverse curtains lined in brown. He had expected a vista but not so grand a one.

From his position in the center of a glass wall he could see far, far away a black-brown opacity where the air was smoky, and, vaguely, in that, verticles which were the faint, sun-illumined edges of Manhattan skyscrapers. In front of the floor-to-ceiling, crystal-clear plate-glass wall was a table which, he thought, had been placed there to prevent people from bumping into the invisible surface. Looking down at it, however, he saw a map under glass on the table top, a map marked with ruled lines pointing from Sachem's Watch to the old Empire State Building, the new Pan-American Building, Bridgeport, and other objects and places.

Distances were marked on the lines:

Forty-three and seven-tenths miles to the Empire State, a mere shimmer in the heated smog now; forty-two and three-tenths miles to the Pan-Am tower; a bit less than forty to the bluish haze that in clear weather would be Long Island Sound.

His eyes lifted and moved among the steeples and trees and flashing clapboard walls of Fenwich Village. Five and three-tenths miles to—apparently—the steeple of the Congregational Church. In that drooping, dusty greenery he caught sight of a frothy rainbow where the Lute River splashed down a short falls. Nearer still was the titanic tailing, the down-slide of boulders new-blasted from the cliff on Sachem's Watch.

What were they mining? Mining, because this was not evidence of quarrying. This colossal slide of limestone had not been taken from the hill for itself: the rock lay unused and there was no sign of machinery to cut, trim, or otherwise work the vast stones. Still, perhaps he was wrong. For he noticed a railroad spur that went, evidently, to the foot of the cliff. The rails shone in the sun, blue and recently-used. He gave up. Probably they hauled off the stuff, after dynamiting it again into manageable size.

His thoughts turned to Faith.

Her stunning question echoed in his mind. He wondered how long it would go on echoing there. And he could not quite explain it. Faith was impulsive, but not mean. She enjoyed jokes, but it hadn't been said in jest, exactly. She was curious, yet not idly and inconsiderately curious. So, *why?*

He began to unpack. Then to change into slacks, a sports

shirt, and loafers. He thought of the Priscilla-John-Alden-Miles-Standish classic: *Speak for yourself, John.*

He grinned, and without realizing it, said aloud, "Pfui!"

2

WHEN HE ENTERED the Farr living room he heard Faith's mother but, at first, could not see her. She was talking on the phone. A fountain was busy making muted cascade noises somewhere, too. And music was issuing from an unseen loudspeaker.

"Too bad, Vance!" Valerie said. "Of course, I understand. You'll be late. And bring Mr. Lee with you. What's that?"

Mrs. Farr's voice was a good deal like her daughter's: deep and deft and broad-A-ed. But she talked more rapidly and she now slurred an occasional word slightly.

It was, Ben reflected, after five. And the sun went over the yardarm, for Mrs. Valerie Farr, about four, he knew. All day long the tall, dark woman who didn't look her fifty years and did look attractive would be integrated, busy, sober. But by six o'clock she would be a bit squiffy. By eleven or twelve, every night, plain drunk. Faith's mother was an alcoholic, a fact he'd learned in the days when Faith had been mending in the hospital on Long Island, not far from Brookhaven National Laboratories or from the spot where he'd found the young woman under the snow.

He knew Mrs. Farr that well, and her husband, too, for they had liked him, he was certain, from the first. But he had not presumed. After Faith had been discharged—limping, still, for a while, but healed—Ben had seen her several times in New York City. He'd had a lunch or two with Vance. However, this invitation to the Connecticut place was Ben's first, of its sort, and the first time he'd seen any member of the family since late May. Still, he knew about Valerie Farr . . . and her drinking.

She now repeated, "What's that?" And paused. Then she said, lightly, amiably, "All right, dear. We'll expect Miss Lee for dinner. And I'll have a guest room ready for her, and one for her father, whenever you both come in." She added, not quite sincerely, "Have fun, you and your Mr. Lee!" And hung up.

Ben had located her by then.

The living room in Uxmal had a deeply-recessed "well" in one end, an oval pit of the sort that had grown increasingly popular in the past dozen years among those who built new houses and could afford such, to Ben, incomprehensible innovations. Black, gray, robin's-egg-blue and gold, this long room had magnificent glass walls now half-shaded by an outside awning. Like the window in his suite, it faced south. Valerie Farr was sitting on a banquette that ran around the depressed part of the room, with a plug-in telephone in one hand and a drink in the other, a greenish-yellow potion in an old-fashioned glass.

After replacing the phone she finished the drink; ice tinkled, jewels on her fingers flashed, and a ray of sun leaked through an awning aperture. It set the red in her nearly-black, wavy hair gleaming with a beauty that, Ben thought, was probably natural, though carefully nurtured.

She saw him. "Ben, darling! Join me!"

He approached on a carpet so deep it almost seemed to require a balancing effort. She added, "Mind the stairs! Five of them, down to here! If you trip—and people have done it —you can land in the goldfish pool."

He laughed, lightly came down the steps, took her hand. "You look marvelous, Valerie!"

She surveyed him, holding his hand, standing—tall, graceful, and glad to see him, plainly. More glad, he thought, than usual. And perceived the obvious reason: Faith was engaged to Barlow so he was no longer a potential peril. He noticed that her dark eyes had a too-wet glitter not from tears but owing to her sad affliction. Her addiction. He wondered how many hundreds of thousands of women like this one "had everything" and also had the same disease. Women similarly shielded in their illness by friends and family and by their own refusal to acknowledge that they were alcoholics.

"*You* look, Ben," she finally said, "as pale as an oyster; and you seem to get more round-shouldered every month. You need to get outdoors more, take some exercise! Meantime, how about a slalom?"

"Slalom?"

Valerie lifted her glass and rattled the ice. "A little drinkee I concocted, and named. 'Slaloms' are those tricky zigzags in skiing that make so many people fall down!" She laughed, a bit too heartily.

Ben shook his head. "Not cocktail time for your round-shouldered, pallid, physicist friend. But, iced coffee?"

Valerie nodded, pressed a button, spoke into something invisible from his angle, and ordered another slalom with his iced coffee.

Afterward she chattered. "Vance just phoned. He's still in New York, at the office. He had expected to come out for dinner but he has a meeting." She paused. "Meeting," she repeated, rather dully. "With his Far East manager, he says. Who was to be out here also. And has a daughter. Charming, Vance says. The girl was in Maine but she's driving down and expects to reach here any minute. I haven't met these Lee people." She waited while Paulus Davey brought the two beverages and until she could take a few slow, multiple swallows of her slalom. Her ensuing, "Thank you, Paulus!" was a trifle too stiff and at the same time too vigorous. The Negro bowed—sadly, Ben felt—and left.

Valerie mused, "I wonder if they're related to the Robert E. Lee family. I know half a dozen people who are."

He sipped his sugared and creamed cool coffee and reflected that he had never before considered the probability of living relatives of the Civil War general, either direct descendants or collateral. No doubt there were many, and no doubt the Farr's knew those who were illustrious, wealthy, or social—or all three. He also reflected that, as a Bernman, he was related to sundry other Bernmans, to Koviskis, a Cohen, certain Steins, and one Walters family that had once been Wildenbeiter.

Faith appeared, then, in a dress like amber mist, and when she crossed a ladder of sunbeams he had a momentary glimpse of most of Faith. She was smiling and her eyes danced. "Imagine!" she exclaimed. "I've just had a long, long talk with Kit. And he's not coming for dinner! Because why? Because he's down at the Yacht Club and he made a bet he could swim from the dock there to Savin Rock—must be a dozen miles. The idiot is starting right now!"

"We're being abandoned right and left," Valerie said to Ben, somewhat irritatedly; she carried that tone in her subsequent words to Faith: "You seem to be totally undismayed."

"Why, of course! Because now I'll have Ben to myself all evening!"

Mrs. Farr's eyes gleamed briefly with temper. But she

controlled it. Or perhaps a new thought erased it. "Maybe.
But a Miss Lee is due here soon. And she may find the Great
Scientist as fascinating as you do, dear." Valerie explained
about Miss Lee.

Faith seemed interested, but not worried. She rang, if that
was what happened, and ordered a martini on the intercom,
which eventually Paulus Davey brought. He had changed to
a mauve dinner jacket, black silk trousers, pumps, and a dark-
purple bow tie. Whether that was his own idea or Mrs.
Farr's, Ben could not guess.

The faint sound of door chimes made Paulus change his
course. Presently they heard his gentle voice say, with an
undertone none of the three people in the living room could
interpret but all three caught, "Oh. Miss Lee. Of course! I'll
take your luggage and put your car away. You'll want to greet
Mrs. Farr."

A voice that had a strange quality and yet was without
accent, an alien but American voice which, to Ben, seemed
enchanting, said, "Yes, of course. I'll unpack and change
soon, though. So——"

Then she appeared. She had black, shining hair and dark,
dark eyes. She was exquisitely made and dressed in a soft,
rosy suit of some sort. Her lips were a rosy-red of the same
hue but with a heightened intensity. She came in smiling a
little, walking with a very straight and yet not self-conscious
carriage. She was—at Ben's guess—a little younger than
Faith Farr. Her cheekbones were high, her eyes sloped and
almond shaped, and her skin a golden-tan color . . . the
ensemble, Ben thought, beautiful as water lilies. Miss Lee,
he also thought, and turned to see Valerie react, was not a
relation of Robert E., or any such Lee. Indeed, it proved
that the lovely young woman spelled her name in a different way: not L-e-e but L-i. Lotus Li.

She was Chinese, a fact Vance Farr had either neglected
to tell his wife or deliberately omitted. Ben wondered which.
Overlooked, he decided. Farr wasn't the sort of man who
would risk embarrassing a girl to play games with his wife.
Besides, the Farr family was cosmopolitan beyond the American norm.

Valerie exhibited that quality almost instantly. After a sub-
audible gasp, her face broke into a smile and she actually
went up out of the recessed area to greet the girl. "You're
Miss Li! How perfectly charming, my dear! We're delighted
to have you—though we're also a bit disappointed! Did you

know your father and my husband won't be here for dinner.
Not till late, in fact."

Miss Li was bowing slightly. She took Valerie's hand. "Yes,
I know," she said. "I have a phone in my car. I talked to
Daddy—oh, a half hour ago—while I was stuck waiting for
the police to clear up a wreck on the Turnpike. I do hope
I'm not delaying you?"

"Of course not."

Introductions. Faith was first. She said to Miss Li, frankly,
"I think the Chinese are the most lovely women on earth—
and you are one of the loveliest I ever saw!"

At dinner they were to find her first name was Lotus but
everybody at Radcliffe, from which she had just graduated,
called her "Lodi." Now, she flushed faintly at Faith's words
and then, realizing they were frank and intended, she smiled
with a vividness that Ben found breathtaking.

"Thank you," said the Chinese girl, and, looking straight
at Faith, *"You* can easily afford to say such a thing!"

Whereupon they both laughed.

Everybody did.

Lodi Li soon departed to change for dinner. Faith and her
mother waited till the footfalls died on distant flagstones and
then both said, though differently, *"Well!"*

Ben supposed Mrs. Farr meant, "What a surprise!" and
Faith, "What a beauty!" In any event, he said, "Exactly."
And that seemed the right word, for Valerie smiled at him
and Faith, after an appraising glance, gave him a sudden,
almost undetectable wink. . . .

Ben sat on a terrace after dinner with Lodi and Faith, in
sling chairs, beside coffee cups on low tables. Valerie had
made her apologies at the end of the meal and vanished, not
quite steadily but unaided.

The last sun fell on the upper leaves and structures of Fenwich Village and the long, sloping, hazed land that led to
the sea, the Sound, Long Island, and the Atlantic beyond.
Ben mused absently over Lodi Li's slight reaction to Valerie's
going.

The Chinese girl had watched, of course, then turned
to Faith and said, with the utmost quietude, "Does she
often——?"

Faith had replied softly, "Always."

Lodi Li had finished the conversation insofar as that topic
went: "Oh, dear! How pitiful."

The terrace was shielded from the near-horizontal sun, a

red ball, about to set behind the lesser ridges west of Sachem's
Watch, which dominated them. A hazy sky began to ac-
cumulate tints: salmon-pink, orange, meringue-tan.

Far to the south a darker darkness emitted occasional
flares of pink light. A thunderstorm, there, moved toward
Connecticut and then retreated, leaving them in sultry calm.

"Which do you like better?" Faith asked. "Sunsets or sun
rises?"

Ben waited but Miss Li didn't respond. So he said, "Why,
I don't know. Both, equally, I guess. Some of my scientist-
colleagues probably take the same view, on different grounds.
The grounds that both phenomena are merely the result of
light rays being reflected by dust, and absorbed, too—and by
water vapor, of course. This, with the rotation of the planet,
causes sunrises and sunsets—misnomers, they'd also doubtless
point out—optical effects readily explained and of no special
novelty or import."

Miss Li laughed. "Perfect! For a scientist."

Faith said, "And you?"

Ben chuckled, sipped coffee and let the cool air that eddied
from some silent but potent source flow over him, gratefully.
Finally he said, "As for me, I am a good scientist only when at
work. As of now—digesting filet and a lot of other delicious
things—I feel more inclined to the poetic view than the
physical. Sunrises and sunsets, even though explicable, always
have a mystical effect on me. And I never inquire why I
feel any mystical sensation, unless I'm in a lab. They're too
rare and valuable to analyze."

"Me, too!" Faith nodded. "Sometimes when I watch the
sunset, I'm almost angry with education. I wish I didn't know
about the diffraction of light and the rotation of the earth
and so on! It must have been far more fun to be alive when
everybody didn't know everything!"

"Everything?" Miss Li murmured.

"Too damned much, anyhow."

"Oh, yes!" The Chinese girl agreed with that. She was
looking at something that had caught her interest.

Another girl—as different and, in her way, as lovely as
Lodi Li—appeared, briefly. A Negress. Tall, tawny-skinned,
lithe, and striding, almost—yet with feral smoothness. In white
shorts and sneakers, with a white halter, carrying a tennis
racket which made Ben realize he'd been dimly aware of the
thonk of tennis balls ever since they'd come out on the
terrace for coffee. The girl's black hair was wavy and long

and worn now in a pony tail. She looked toward the house
and raised her tennis racket. "Hello, Faith! Evening, people!"
She laughed in saying that—calling it, really, over green lawn
and the hedges silently busy pushing out their shadows.

"Hi, Connie!" Faith's response was warm and clear and,
otherwise, unexplained.

Lodi Li had murmured something when the dark girl had
appeared, but Ben hadn't caught it.

Now, Faith said, "There's the first star."

Ben looked up in the darkling azure where overhead, and
only overhead, the smoggy mist of the heat wave had not
faded the sky's blueness. He was on the point of correcting
the word "star" to "planet" and decided it would be too
damned exact. Too Brookhaven. He nodded. They sat in
silence and peace.

By and by Lodi Li stood up. "If you two will forgive me,
I'm going to my—" she smiled at Faith—"*very* elegant rooms.
They gave me a farewell party up in Maine last night. And
I packed afterward. And then I started driving. So——"

"You mean, you didn't sleep at *all?*" Faith exclaimed.

Lodi Li nodded. "Not any. So——"

"Lord! You must tell me how you managed not to show a
trace of it!"

"That's easy! I managed by telling myself, the whole afternoon and so far this evening, that I'd soon be asleep!"

"Zen!" Faith cried, pleased and not mocking.

"Yogi," the Chinese girl chuckled. "But it doesn't work
endlessly. If you'll forgive me——?"

When she'd gone, the two people on the terrace were
quiet for so long that each began to wonder, in the deepening
dusk, if the other had dozed off. But just before Faith rose to
make a close inspection, Ben, seeing the preliminary movement, said, lazily, "What's that giant rockslide that looks
fresh-blasted, down below Sachem's Watch? You quarry
limestone here?"

"Papa's Panic Palace," Faith answered—sharply, he thought.
"Hasn't he told you about it, by now?"

"Panic Palace?" he repeated. "No." He sounded puzzled
and then, not. "You mean——?"

Faith nodded and he saw that clearly, because just as her
bright head moved, she turned on lights which, though wan
and indirect, momentarily almost hurt his dark-accustomed
eyes. "He'll take you on the grand tour tomorrow, that's for
sure. However, I'd rather talk about almost anything else in

the world than that! It's so dull, and so interminable. I'd even rather talk about Antarctica."

He grinned. "Okay. Let's."

From Antarctica their conversation fled the world over, but rested mainly upon themselves and their agreements and differences on more subjects than either would have guessed they could or would summon in an hour or two of random talk at twilight, subjects that ranged from sleeping "raw" (they both did, they found) to junk jewelry (neither one liked it, as a rule), and from French cigarettes (another point of mutual distaste) to horseback riding (she did; he didn't).

When the phone summoned her, he sat alone watching the stars overhead, and trying to find the planet, but failing, as it had already descended into the murk that rode above this heavily-populated and largely-industrialized portion of New England.

Faith reappeared finally, but did not resume her lounging seat. "It was Kit. He won his bet. He's going home and says he'll show up in the morning. Want to know something?"

"What?"

"I'm pretty sure Kit made that bet and took that long swim on purpose." She saw he failed to comprehend. "I mean, so you and I could have this evening together. He's nice, a lot of ways. See?"

"Yes. Guess I do. I'll remember that degree of niceness. And I appreciate it, too!"

She smiled gently. "I hope. But the appreciation hour's over. I'm going in. Letters to write—then, bed."

She came nearer. He had risen and he had the sudden thought that she expected, or hoped, he'd kiss her goodnight. Like a pretty tot offering herself, hesitantly, to a new-met but approved-of uncle. *Maybe.* He held out his long arm, its long-fingered hand.

When she'd gone, he thought a stroll in the gardens would be appropriate. Thought that until, stepping from the air-conditioned outdoor area of the terrace, he rediscovered the heat of the dark. Ninety-five degrees, he guessed; and like hitting a good line of an opposing football team. It virtually halted him, nearly threw him back for a loss. So he went to his room . . . and, at last, to sleep.

3

AT 4:15 A.M. on that hot end-of-July Friday a phone rang in the bedroom of the President of the United States. He woke instantly. Lights went on automatically with the phone's jangle. The President saw—indeed, already knew from the sound— it was not the red phone. The dreadful one. The phone that was the last thing he looked at every night, and the first subject of his nightly prayer, a reverent entreaty that the red instrument would never ring. This was the less-loud but still-portentous green phone.

"The President"—he had to clear his throat—"speaking."

"Ralph Hager, here." His Secretary of State—and, as the President knew, the phone he held would also be connected with others: his Chief of Staff, the Missile Center Commander, General Torrence, the Vice-President.

"Yes, Ralph?"

"Sorry about waking you. But it's pretty bad." The Secretary of State seemed to have trouble with words, as if he'd been drinking. But President Conner knew it wasn't that. If Hager had lost his seemingly indestructible poise, this crisis call was more serious even than those other, often-appalling night alarms he and his predecessors had so often received. As they had done in their time, Conner now tried for an initial easement.

"I suppose," he said, rubbing an eye with his free hand, then using it to rake his now-white hair, "Costa Rica has just tested a neutron bomb?"

The chuckle of the listening men ran from hollow to admiring. The Secretary of State then put it bluntly: "A so-called 'volunteer' army is crossing the borders of Hungary into Yugoslavia. With Tito gone the Reds have apparently been setting this up for years."

"What's the NATO reaction?"

"To wait for word from you. Because this one's tough! Moscow and Peking have sent a joint ultimatum to London, Paris, and us. If NATO, or anybody, tries to prevent this 'liberation' of Yugoslavia, Grovsky's threat is to use two shots on two cities. Wipe out Paris and London. Of course, both capitals are frantic. We have two hours—less about ten minutes, now—to decide."

The President did not know he had stood up. Did not know he was breaking out in sweat. All he knew was that he had to concentrate his whole being—brain, heart, soul, and body —on this sudden and not wholly foreseen situation. He thought for a moment.

"Okay," he said to the breathing men who waited. Said that, because it was a relaxed response. He added, "Get Moscow and Peking right away. Tell them we have to have *six* hours. Say that I'm taking a secret rest-up and can't be reached except by helicopter—better yet!—by *horseback*. A couple of times in my first years, you'll all recall, I *did* put myself in such a position! Just to *establish* it. In case we ever needed to gain time. We do *now*, God knows!"

General Eade McClung, Chief of Staff, said in his deep, roaring tone, "We won't *get* six hours, Mr. President."

"No. But we'll get four. Better than two."

Another voice entered the discussion, light, effete, not at all indicative of the mind that was its master: the voice of Purdy Smythe, Intelligence Coordinator: "It is possible, Mr. President——"

"Oh, 'morning, Purd!"

" 'Morning, sir." Reluctantly, it seemed, the Coordinator obeyed some standing recent presidential order: "I mean, *Dave*. Certain information makes us wonder, here at Intelligence, if *this* time they really mean to pull the plug."

"The stuff you sent over yesterday? Subs sneaking around? The presumed 'wreck' the Navy just located off Boston, near one already on their charts? The *new* wreck? Have they looked it over?"

"No, Mr. Presi——Dave. The Navy feels that even an undersea approach might—well——"

"Detonate it? Providing it's what they fear?"

Smythe breathed a relieved, "Exactly." David Conner, President of the United States, caught on fast, Smythe thought —and that, from a man as eclectically educated, as traveled, as accomplished in fifty diverse ways, was a great compliment.

The President then spoke to all his auditors. "Right, gentlemen. Try for a six-hour delay. Get the London-Paris latest reactions. Remind Moscow and Peking we are ready and—if we must be—willing. Say that Yugoslavia *recently* chose, in a free, UN-supervised election, to side with the West, and the West stands for that freedom of determination, *with or without* London and Paris. Say I am adamant, but willing to confer—given six hours, *not* two. You'll know the distribution of other essential calls. Alert the retaliatory and defense system. And for the love of God, you who will talk to the Reds—sound *calm! Lazy.* Even *bored!* The way you're panting over your phones now is *not* how to do it! If Grovsky in Moscow, or any of his top men—or if Tsin-tsu in Peking—wants to talk to me, put them through . . . *after* you've arranged a longer stretch of time."

Admiral Boone's worried voice came then. "You, Mr. President, and Mrs. Conner, and the children ought, I think, to fly at once for the Maryland post. I mean—if this thing warmed up——"

The President said, "Fooie! I'm going down stairs for some breakfast. I'm hungry!" And he hung up, grinning at the faint sounds of dismay he'd overheard.

His grin faded the moment he set down the phone. It had been the best he could do. Was it good enough? It had always worked before.

Threat, counterthreat, compromise, and—usually—some slight retreat of the free world that, as time passed, showed itself to be greater than it had first appeared. . . .

4

BEN WOKE IN the predawn hours surprised that he had already slept deeply. He had not expected that. Undressing alone in his guest chambers, he'd anticipated a night of nervous insomnia. One small question had altered his insight and even battered his basic concept of himself. . . .

Why didn't you ever ask me to marry you?

Faith had meant that . . . almost. Faith had meant, anyhow, that her engagement to Kit Barlow was not the whelming joy an engagement ought to be. She had meant she found him—Ben Bernman—attractive . . . at least, interesting.

With that he had realized how his feelings for her had grown, unknown by him, like the crystals that create a complex beauty inside a geode. Feelings that had begun

with his first, startled grunt as he'd brushed snowflakes from
the face of an unconscious woman and seen in the steady
beam of a flashlight that she was beautiful. Feelings that had
become clear and sharp and urgent . . . but stifled . . . in
the weeks he'd seen her during her convalescence in the
hospital on Long Island. Feelings that had exploded into
his awareness only when she'd asked that strange question
. . . asked it lightly yet with an undertone of urgency, or of
—perhaps—irony; even bitterness.

Then he had known, of a sudden, and known in the next
flash of thought that it was too late to know, to count, to
matter. Known—or at least presumed—that Faith's words
rose from her version of represented reaction. Not love necessarily of him, but an expression of the small and uneven
affection she held for Barlow. So he thought.

Still, being honest—scientific as well—and a kind of
brave gambler where his person and destiny were concerned,
Ben wished he *had* asked her . . . wished he'd had the insight earlier, because it might have led him to ask . . . wished
he'd taken the chance even though the outcome would have
been . . . *what?* The yet-more-brutal thing of Faith's dis-
illusionment in being engaged, or promised, or whatever, to a
Jew, with all that signified? A love affair, maybe, broken off
eventually? The mere idea stirred him to a degree he'd never
experienced.

Or would she just have laughed at him, supposing he had
known he loved her and said so? Worse, would she have
tried to play up to such a statement and then gently let him
down . . . because she would have felt she owed him the
(accidental) debt of her life?

With his mind in a furnace of retrospection, of premises
cast down as quickly as they were devised, Ben had anticipated a restless night. Yet he'd slept from about eleven until
now. And now, his watch said in chimed code, was close to
daybreak. He lay still, wondering what alarm had aroused
him, and then why he felt his awakening had been caused
by alarm.

The hot dark outdoors was silent.

Not even a rooster crowed anywhere yet.

Was someone in danger? Had there been some devilish
calamity at Brookhaven? Had some stealthy hand tried his
door? *Why* did he feel, for an instant, a cold surge of fear
that, as he examined it, became baseless?

Ben didn't believe in telepathy. Didn't believe in the

possibility that he, or anyone, might catch a winging wash of dread like this, that grew in intensity minute by minute on waves of unknown lengths from random epicenters. No physicist had detected any electromagnetic pulse related to such phenomena—hence, none existed, in all likelihood.

Since his nameless dread ebbed as rapidly as he searched for its source, Ben gave a mental shrug and shut his eyes again. It was a long time afterward when he would recall that just before he fell asleep, for a second time, his mind did fix momentarily on the hazardous circumstances in which modern men had lived, decade after decade: the madness of civilization that had reached a peak at which it could eradicate itself. But that fear, almost a generation old, was not then connected by the physicist with his awakening or its sensed cause: an undefined anxiety.

When he opened his eyes again, it was light. He thought he heard splashing sounds beyond his curtained glass wall and wondered, hopefully, if it was raining. He rose, donned a dressing gown, and drew the traverse curtains.

Vance Farr was swimming in the moat, his short, sturdy body in easy motion. Moat . . . or pool. Or whatever they called it. Farr's red hair was darkened by the water, and his face, square, solid, amiable, turned toward the watching man with every other stroke. Its blue, open eyes must have seen the curtain draw, for Farr stopped swimming, began treading water, and beckoned.

When Ben smiled, nodded, Farr grinned back and waited.

In a matter of a minute Ben stepped outside. The flagstone rim of the moat was already hot on his bare feet. Farr waved.

"Hi!" Ben felt cheerful. Liked Farr.

The tycoon had an astonishingly versatile brain. He was genial and congenial. Thinking about him, as Ben often had done, he'd felt Farr did not quite fit the big-business mold. He was too imaginative and too learned. Too unconcentrated. Above all else, too observant. For it had always seemed to Ben that Farr was the most *noticing* man he'd ever met.

Ben's greeting brought a challenge from the swimming man: "I always go clear around the place, mornings, if I have time." Farr chuckled, spit water, and added, "And if the moat has water in it and the water doesn't happen to be frozen."

"How far is a lap?"

Vance replied as only he would, "Nineteen hundred and

sixty-two yards and three inches—outside dimension. Bit over a mile. But I've done about a third of it. Game?"

Ben nodded. "Race you." He dived.

It wasn't a fair race, Ben realized, after they'd covered a hundred yards. The older man had energy and endless courage but he couldn't keep up with a competitor who was not only a foot taller but an ex-water-polo player and one, besides, who took a workout daily in the water—the pool inside the apartment where he lived, or on one of Long Island's beaches.

There, Ben now reflected, slowing down to keep even with Farr, this very Friday, some of his Brookhaven colleagues would beyond doubt soon be ranged along an Atlantic-facing beach and, certainly, talking physics or math while they drew diagrams in the sand. As he swam—almost languidly, for him—Ben recalled a scalding afternoon in August, two summers ago, when Kleinschmidt had suddenly hit on a new concept that explained how and why low energy particles failed to obey the laws of parity that the other particles followed precisedly.

Sitting on the sand, drawing diagrams and scribbling equations in it, while the girls accompanying the men watched, bored but unable to stop the demonstration.

And, Ben mused on, at noon this very day Kleinschmidt and whoever else was hanging around the labs at Columbia University would hold their immemorial "Chinese lunch"— the weekly meal-and-brains gathering that might continue a noon session through dinner or even far into the night. Even all night, if what was "started" over the soups, the dumplings, proved sufficiently interesting.

Both men pulled themselves out of the moat at the terrace, where Farr had started. Ben wasn't even panting, which Farr noticed with no comment.

"Get in last night?" Ben asked.

"Around two this morning." Farr took a huge towel from a waiting stack and tossed another to Ben. "Miss Li arrive?"

"She did. Charming girl!"

"M'm'm'm! Her dad's quite a guy, too. He stayed in town, though. Be out here early this evening. Business kept him." Farr laughed, for some undiscernible reason, and then eyed the scientist candidly. "What fools men are! 'Business,' I said. Actually Sam Li had a girl friend he wanted to visit. His wife—Lodi's mother—is still in Hong Kong. I wouldn't divulge Sam's pleasure to my wife. Or Faith. But why should I push alibis with you?"

Ben smiled but never made a reply; Paulus Davey appeared soundlessly and said, "Telephone, Mr. Farr."

The redheaded businessman excused himself. He was gone for some time—time enough for Ben to decide, after Paulus had made the suggestion, to have breakfast on the terrace and in the garment he wore—bathing trunks. He was eating an omelet with strawberry jam in its fluffy middle when Farr returned.

A different Farr. Pale. Stiff. Remote. Silent.

A Farr who rang for the butler, said, "The usual," and then sat in silence broken only by sudden exhalations from his puffed-out cheeks . . . the half-comic but seriously-intended antic of a man preoccupied by something very disturbing. Finally he gave Ben a partial explanation. "Friend of mine, a senator, phoned just now from Washington. New crisis blew up last night."

Ben's calm eyes met the other man's blue gaze. "Serious?"

"Aren't they all?"

"Potentially." A long pause. "What happened? Or is it a confidential thing?" Ben asked.

Farr was scowling with inner concerns and he looked at the scientist now almost as if he'd forgotten he was there. Forgotten—in seconds. But remembering, recognizing, he smiled faintly. " 'Liberation army' marched into Yugoslavia, yesterday. Still under wraps, Ben. But, I daresay, you're a bank vault of much greater secrets."

"A few," Ben agreed. "Though since I left Los Alamos, since I gave up weapons work, I——"

Farr nodded rather curtly and excused himself. "Think I better put in a call or two."

Ben was left facing an empty chair, a half-eaten croissant, and a partly-drained coffee cup.

By and by he completed his solitary meal and entered the house through a "sunroom" adjacent to the terrace. Covered walks led to his quarters; Ben dressed quickly in his coolest slacks, lightest sports shirt, and loafers without socks. From the library corner of his chambers he selected a book, after deciding his initial impulse to pick a volume from one of the many, leather-bound sets of classics would seem ostentatious. Too academic. Antiweekend in spirit.

So he scanned the shelf of recent novels of at least some importance and chose the first attempt at fiction to be made

by William Percival Gaunt, the popular philosopher. It had
proven already that he was even more popular as a novelist.
The book was called, *The Laser of Lemuel Lett*. It concerned, Ben knew, the imaginary events that ensued upon
the establishment of communications with an earth-bound
space ship coming in from one of the planets in a system
known for some years to exist around Proxima Centauri. The
tale was, essentially, a spoof of the current, wasteful, hostile, and emperiled societies on Earth.

Ben went back to the terrace and read until half-past ten.
Nobody, the butler excepted, appeared there. Music from
somewhere in the house suggested that others were awake
and, perhaps, breakfasting in bed. A sensible way, Ben
thought, of starting a day that was, according to all meteor-
ological predictions, sure to break the all-time Weather Bu-
reau for heat records for the date, in New York City and
south to Philadelphia and Washington, as well as through-
out most of New England.

When the moving sun touched him, Ben pushed his chair
into the remaining shade. He was eventually relieved by the
starting of the terrace air-conditioner, which soon reduced
the terrace temperature from a (guessed) ninety-five to a very
comfortable eighty—again, at a guess.

In the distance he did see or hear signs of life.

A station wagon, driven by a man in a white coat, was
visible, serpentining down Sachem's Watch. Beside the man
was a gray-haired colored lady—the butler's wife, Ben surmised.

Later the sound of tennis reached him and, faintly, the
voices of a woman (Connie?) and a man, calling scores.

He also heard a motorcycle approach the premises, but
did not look up from his book in time to catch sight of its
rider.

Eleven o'clock.

The novel had now captured Ben. He scarcely noticed as
the butler made quiet trips to clear the breakfast table. He
did notice, however, on two or three occasions when Paulus
Davey went through the door, that Farr, by the door-hushed
sound of his voice and by its intervals, was still on the phone.
And, plainly, still agitated.

Eleven-nine.

The tennis had stopped. There was relative silence: only
a very faint, incessant hum from the distant Turnpike; the
chirping of birds in the shrubbery and trees of Uxmal; the

remote sky-scuffle of a commercial jet carrying passengers on a course which, if Ben had given it his attention, he might have guessed would take it east and north toward Ireland. Toward Shannon Airport. Aside from that, almost nothing. The hottening, whitening sunlight, that made shadows constantly blacker and sharper; and haze transpired from reluctant leaves that half-obscured the white walls and gray steeples of Fenwich Village.

Eleven-ten.

Some further seconds.

And hell broke loose.

Ben leaped to his feet, dropping his book, as an ear-splitting scream blasted over the lawns, gardens, and the hilltop. It stopped, and came again, migrainously, enormously. In the interval Ben had heard the unmistakable wail of Fenwich Village sirens.

For seconds, he stood still, startled, uncertain.

For seconds, he insisted this instantaneous clangor could not possibly be what it seemed. And when he acknowledged the potential meaning, he still told himself it must be a mistake, or at most a practice alert.

But then he saw people streaking toward the place where he stood galvanized, half-crouched, with a dropped book at his feet.

A moment later, eyes dilated, skin a strange yellow, voice hoarse, Paulus Davey appeared. He said repeatedly and with a sort of crazed urgency, "This way, Doctor Bernman! This way, please!"

Ben finally understood. Understood the words, at least. He croaked, "Shelter?" The butler nodded, took his arm, made him run.

The ensuing ten or twelve minutes were perhaps the most mixed-up and forever impossible-to-unscramble of any in Ben's life.

He went, with the shaken and shaking butler, through the house—the sunroom, the great living room with its recessed sitting area, and the hall. Outdoors, next: the quadrangle. Thence through a geometrical rose garden brilliant with early-watered blooms, toward a paved area beyond the open garage.

Arriving there, he was told to wait, by the frantic butler. "Don't under any circumstances go *anywhere* else! Just *wait*." Paulus Davey then ran back toward the door through which they'd emerged.

Ben waited.

But not alone for long. The courtyard rang and bellowed with the electric alarms, a battery of hooting horns. In the middle of the concrete area beside which Ben had been ordered to wait, two portals rolled apart. They were, Ben saw in a sort of pop-eyed wonder, *steel*. Thick steel. Very thick steel—like heavy battleship plating or submarine-hull steel. And huge. They opened to reveal a vertical shaft that went —Ben walked nearer, his muscles leaping—down and out of sight: bottomless, it would seem, and big enough to swallow a house.

Then, people.

Mrs. Farr first, in a morning coat and slippers, clutching a large, lavender case to her bosom, dough-pale and sweating.

Then Lotus Li, looking almost calm, sprinting lightly, carrying nothing at all but wearing a rose-beige tennis dress. Behind her, running hard and also empty-handed, Faith. She saw Ben and rushed to his side. "I looked in your rooms but you weren't there!" She said that, smiled, and took his hands. "*God!* I'm scared!"

She looked at the sky apprehensively. So did he. There was nothing to see but the steamy azure.

The girl called Connie ran into view half-dragging a tall, apparently dumfounded young man whom Ben had not seen. He carried a small, cheap, and obviously heavy satchel; his trousers were clipped to his ankles; he wore no jacket and his blue shirt had an open collar. But though Ben noticed the clips he failed to think of the motorcycle he'd recently heard. Paulus Davey was next, sobbing. And carrying a light, automatic rifle. Then Farr, also with an automatic weapon and a belt from which grenades bobbed. Nobody seemed to think this sudden-appearing arsenal was strange, except Ben, who winced a little.

Farr stopped in their midst and called their names. Then he turned raging eyes on his wife and half yelled, "*Maids? Sam Hyama? Mrs. Davey?*"

Valerie answered in a moan. "Gone to Fenwich."

"Good God!"

Ben heard a rumble of machinery and turned. A railed platform, an elevator bigger than Ben had seen anywhere, was slowing to a stop at pavement level. Nobody stood on it, so plainly it ran automatically. None of the group moved until Farr bellowed, "Get aboard, damn it! Everybody!"

They got on.

Tires squealed outside the buildings and a sports car thundered into view, crashed through the rose-bed and halted. A handsome, big blond man vaulted out and said, "Cheerio, people! It's *it!* Right?"

Vance bellowed again. "Didn't you *bring* anybody?"

"Tried to. My folks are in Maine. As you know. I let the servants take off the weekend, starting early this A.M. Saw some women and kids as I came up. Stopped. Offered 'em shelter. They didn't even speak. Just kept running. Panic."

The hoot of Farr's sirens suddenly stopped. In a shuddery aftermath the Fenwick Village sirens sounded plainly. Davey stepped off the elevator, saying, "Guess I'll wait for Mother."

Vance yanked the thin, light Negro back on the platform. "No use! They'll find shelter where they are. Listen, people! It's eleven-nineteen! If there's nobody on the premises—if you're *sure*—down we go!"

He waited and was answered only by far-off sirens and the butler's sobbing.

Farr moved a lever on the elevator rail and Ben, like the rest, felt it begin to sink into the earth. Like the rest, his eyes raised as the descent accelerated and, like them, he took a final, though unconscious look at the sky, swiftly narrowing to a slot and soon wiped out, as two portals of incredible size closed together along a horizontal plane. Running, Ben thought, on heavy-duty and, doubtless, multiple tracks, recessed in the shaft.

The platform went faster and faster, down and down, not quite in darkness, because dim lights came on, above the railing, as the first portals crashed together.

Vance Farr, near Ben, murmured, "Five thousand psi." And when they passed a second, yard-thick slot that extruded another pair of doors, the same figure was repeated. "Five thousand psi."

It happened a third time, with a third pair of doors. Ben had by then noticed that each pair of the doors met at right angles to the pair above. The elevator kept dropping. Without any special reaction Ben found that Faith was holding his hand. He did not notice she was holding Kit Barlow's hand, too. He saw Farr unbuckle the belt from which his grenades hung and in a gingerly fashion set down the load.

Ben was on the verge of asking how much farther into the limestone mountain this shaft would take them, when he felt a slowing of the flat, vast conveyance.

5

ON THAT HOT last Friday of July, America was on vacation, in millions, and at work in towns and cities—again in millions—on its streets and in its offices, stores, restaurants, subways, buses. Americans were busy outdoors in suburban yards and at work on farms and on weekend junkets to the seashore, lakes, mountains.

The President had thought, earlier in the morning, that the new menace would, at worst, become negotiations which, if the alleged Red "volunteers" had managed to occupy and panic Yugoslavia, might end up in the loss of that country and its people to the West. He'd requested an extension of the "ultimatum" and a halt of the invaders for six hours expecting to gain at least something more than the proffered two hours. He was, to his initial surprise, granted his request.

In Washington and in New York political and military leaders began, before dawn, a telecast "conference" with their opposite numbers in London, Paris, Moscow, and Peking. Satellite-repeaters enabled all participants to see as well as hear each other. The talk dragged on till the six inconclusive hours of "armistice" had passed. President Conner had received, meantime, reports that the invading "volunteers" were swiftly fanning out in Yugoslavia and, though dressed as civilians, their hordes were equipped with the latest conventional weapons and mobile arms. They had shattered all Yugoslavian military resistance.

Charging Grovsky, the Soviet Premier, with treachery, he received a not-unexpected reply:

"These freedom fighters, Mr. President, are not to be controlled, I regret to say." He stroked his waxed and elegant mustache and gave the free-world leaders his familiar, panther-like smile. Grovsky was the first Russian Premier to be an out-and-out dandy—a tall and handsome man who wore Bond Street clothes; his mustache had endlessly beguiled cartoonists and was compared to the similar adornment of a renowned, if unfathomable artist, Salvador Dali.

37

Grudgingly, at a quarter to ten, A.M., Grovsky agreed to send Red troops into Yugoslavia to check the "volunteers" so that a new "free election" could be held. The pledge was considered empty. For the Soviet boss had insisted this was not a "take-over" but represented the "inevitable march of free Communist hero-volunteers" on a step toward the eventual liberation of the entire "capitalist-imperialist" world. But he would not, Grovsky had said—to the exhausted joy of the long-distance conferees—"annihilate London and Paris," so long as no outside power interfered with his promised Soviet endeavor to "restore order in Yugoslavia." His troops, weapons, navy, and so forth would nevertheless engage in practice alerts "just in case" the Western powers, or any one of them, *did* start "meddling." This decision was hardly ideal but, to the President of the United States and to the heads of government in England and France, it was welcome.

With it the long, trans-TV conference ended. Reporters everywhere, aware of some new but as-yet unannounced crisis, were given a general account of the situation and, at about ten-thirty, Eastern Daylight Time, they began to file their stories and to broadcast an outline of the new Red "Push."

A little later the giant radar receptors in Greenland, northern Canada, and Alaska began to show ever-increasing numbers of blips that indicated planes winging toward North America, and, minutes later, the upsurge of swarms of what seemed to be missiles. In Nebraska, where the information was collected and computer-analyzed, there was a period of hesitancy, owing to the fact that Grovsky had asserted some such "maneuvers" could be expected. Many precious minutes were lost before the warning system made its electronic knowledge certain:

This was an attack aimed at America.

And now, as the red phone did ring at President Conner's White House desk and as the nightmare of three Presidents became imminent reality, he gave coded orders in a steady voice, while tears ran down his cheeks. Then, impulsively (and disastrously) he phoned his mother in Seattle to urge her to take cover. After that, with his wife and three daughters, who had been waiting outside his door, he proceeded to the helicopter on the lawn. It took off, swiftly, toward the cavern carved in a Maryland hill provided for just such danger.

The helicopter did not reach it.

The delaying confusion as to whether the Soviets were merely staging maneuvers or starting assault—and the call to Seattle—had cut the time left to a margin not quite sufficient.

Still, the President and his family, their pilot and co-pilot, were fortunate, in a fashion—more fortunate than scores upon scores of millions of their fellow citizens. For they, at least, never clearly knew the cause of their swift obliteration.

Of the salvo of twenty-three, five-megaton missiles launched at the Washington-Baltimore area, seven were precisely on target and eight burst within twenty-five miles of their aiming-place. Most, as intended, went into fission-fusion-and-fission on or just above the ground, with a burst-altitude variation of some twenty thousand feet. One of them opened in the hot, clear sky almost directly over the green field where the President and his party were about to descend in order to reach the fortified cave, mere yards away from the landing field.

Father, mother, daughters, and two fliers neither saw nor heard and probably did not even have time to feel—what happened.

The missile exploded at eighteen thousand feet. Its nature and effects were characteristic of most intercontinental warheads in the current Soviet arsenal. . . .

The burst of a nuclear weapon is curiously different from an ordinary explosion. An observer, providing he has adequate protection for his eyes and is far enough away to survive, at first merely *senses* some tremendous event in the air. There occurs a not-really-seen but shocking awareness, as if of an invisible leap, or as if the air itself had been smitten by a colossal but unseen fist.

This, in the case of a weapon such as annihilated the presidential party, swells, to engulf between two and three miles of whatever surrounds it. For seconds, with unholy glare, it grows. Where it touches the earth, it melts it, rends it, converts millions of tons of it to gas, and only then, heaved upward by a rebound force of its own making, the fireball climbs and flickers, in vast churnings of white light mixed with enormities of darknesses, until, free of earth, it gradually billows out as pure light, and still ascends steadily, a torrent of interwhirling luminosity of every hue, composed from the intermixed and sun-hot elements of itself and the air and the cratered earth beneath.

So it is not like the shuddery thump of a land mine or the geysering bang of a torpedo or the boom of shell. There is no sudden noise. When the noise comes, it is infinite, enduring, and more a *compression* than thunder—thunder augmented beyond belief.

Radiation, however, will already have sluiced in every direction at light's speed from the first instant of burst. That, alone, will have destroyed all life and all semblance of livingness in all creatures within the closest miles. Heat, too, hundreds of thousands of degrees of out-charging temperature, will have reduced everything to gases, alive or not, within a comparable range.

In a roughly circular area, miles across, underneath this thing, all buildings will have been vaporized. Farther out, for more miles the thrusting ram of steel-hard air will topple the mightiest structures and sweep all lesser edifices to earth, as if their brick and stone, girders and beams were tissue paper. Locomotives, even cathedrals, will be torn from the ground and pitched perhaps a far, far way, in hundreds of square miles of further-out regions where, still, the blast marches, tearing, rending, breaking, and splintering. If a million people happen to be behind a million windows in any such enormous area, glass alone will carve them up in the way of ancient Chinese torturers.

And still the capacity for ruin of just one such weapon is but fractionally spent.

Its light, alone, has peculiar horror. In clear weather all persons with unprotected eyes who are in a position to look will do so involuntarily, before they have time to think they must not look. These, upon staring with naked pupils at the white expansion, will be blinded—their retinas scorched—and they will remain forever blind if they even glance at such a thing in such lucid weather from twenty miles away, or thirty.

So all the men and women and children who look, without any chance of not doing so, will experience dazzlement and pain and turn away reflexively, but too late. Then all of them who looked, even though they are not otherwise injured, will cease to see. These will everywhere probably be tens of thousands, driving cars and trucks and buses; they will be locomotive engineers and the pilots of commercial planes

. . . struck blind, in an area of a thousand square miles or more.

Hence, myriads of cars and trucks and buses in a populous area where one weapon opens the sky, though beyond the range of other immediate damage, will stop, collide, skid into each other, and roll off bridges. Planes in hundreds will crash, no matter how long their blind pilots can keep them hopefully aloft. Trains will run through signals and be wrecked. Hence people hoping to evacuate cities, and people who merely happen to be leaving or approaching struck areas, even if they are shielded from each such sky-glare, will be trapped in miles of vehicular disaster, of fire and blood and blinded agony.

Next, the *heat* of the thing will set alight every desiccated, flammable object—leaf, bit of paper, shingle roof, telephone pole, barn, fence, tree, and wooden box—in *instants*, and over an area, again, of a thousand square miles or more. The wave of the city-toppling blast that follows will surely blow out multitudes of such millions of instantaneous fires; but not all; thousands will continue to burn. Near the hot vortex of the phenomenon, if a city lies there, it will now be ruins. Within its jagged shambles other fires will start, where pipes leak gas, wires spark, blow-torches fume under the rubble, electric stoves glow, gasoline-station hoses meet cigarettes, and where all similar flame-points find any fuel.

Soon those fires will coalesce and become one great pyre, city-wide and suburbs-wrapping. This blaze will rise from each area of urban residue for miles into the sky. And air will come hurtling to supply oxygen for that firestorm—air to feed the appetite of this giant crematory—air sucked at a speed, around the unlit perimeter, of a hurricane. Men and cars and implements for fighting fire will hardly dare approach the incandescent edge; if they do so, they will be tornadoed, bodily, into the roaring, miles-high blaze of a city afire in its wrecked totality where rushing wind would snatch even the heaviest fire trucks into the appalling mountain of flame.

People in shelters under these holocausts, people in subways, even miners, if their mines run beneath these H-hit areas in firestorms, will soon die hideously, deprived of oxygen, as every breath of underground air is pulled out to hotten every Everest-tall blaze. Or else the sheltered will be smothered, or baked alive, with the replacement of subterranean air by carbonic gases heated to such temperatures as wilt steel.

By that time each mushroom cloud will have lofted itself to the upper atmosphere and commenced to dissipate on whatever wind prevails at the moment, hiding the sky as if a dirty banner had replaced the blue vault: a banner moving outward and downwind, a bunting of many, darting hues, each miles-long and sullied by its burden of vaporized buildings and earth and rock that was heat-stolen from the crater left behind.

In an hour or so, from each such "banner," the heaviest particles will fall, then the finer particles, so that a seeming "snow," and soon an invisible "snow," will gently descend on a great oval tract, downwind. That is "fallout," highly radioactive, even if invisible, and it may cover an area of some five thousand square miles per bomb. In each average square foot of such region, for a day or so, the earth, however unaltered it appears, and all streets, roofs, walks, tops of trees, and every place where the hot dew rests, will emit so much radioactivity that a man exposed for fifteen minutes, anywhere, will likely die in days, or a week, or perhaps two.

Fifteen of such warheads, then, exploded over and around Baltimore and Washington within a period of nineteen seconds. Eight others, also aimed at those targets, were either intercepted by American defense rockets or—in four cases—detonated over or pitched into the Atlantic, miles from the coast.

But there were two areas only, of hundreds under attack.

Weapons aimed at hardened missile bases in America destroyed sixty-five per cent of such retaliatory installations before they could be used for a single launch. From a merely military viewpoint that was not of great moment: the remaining thirty-five per cent of bases flung up missiles that did, as calculated, approach the Soviet Union in their outer-space trajectories. The U.S.S.R., like the United States, intercepted only a third of them. The rest were sufficient to accomplish their retaliatory intent, and more.

In all, during the initial hour of attack, approximately one thousand enemy missiles of an average caliber of five megatons reached their targets, or a nearby area, in the United States.

Few airfields were left, fit for launching supersonic bombers. But many American planes, at that time, were already on the way to the enemy. These carried twenty-megaton bombs, three or four to a plane. When their long-trained pilots drew within range of the calculated borders and enemy rockets rose toward them, they followed their gallant, necessary procedure. They launched their own, aimed, long-range missiles. Then, one by one, like giant descendants of the kamikazes of another war, the planes dived in the twilight, toward their attackers, and set their triads and quartets of H-bombs hurtling, under separate rocket power, toward the enemy bases. The first dozen, of most of the many invading files of planes, missed some of their targets and were themselves blown to sun-hot gas by A-weapons, or in a few cases were destroyed when their own weapons were detonated by the defenses of a still-distant foe.

But each invading American plane was able to approach closer to the enemy frontiers than its leader and each, in perishing, shook the defenders more savagely and made possible a nearer strike for the plane behind. So, plane by plane, as crews died in the prodigious burst of enemy weapons and their own, corridors were cut through the Soviet defenses until planes somewhere in each strung-out squadron and all those beyond were able to penetrate the last defenses and reach the Red military bases and Russia's cities.

These, for the most part, had by then already been turned into separate mountains of fire by American missiles, launched from far and near, land and sea. The subsequent bombers blasted fire deeper into the gigantic nation, seeking out the hidden industrial complexes in Siberia and leaving them in conflagrations that towered higher than the night-hung Ural Mountains. They flew on then to hunt for lesser targets if they had unspent bombs. At last the surviving planes turned, but not back to America. Their crews knew that what they witnessed on Russian earth was happening at home. They had not actually expected or intended to return. There was nothing to go back to.

By midafternoon that Friday two-thirds of the surface of the United States had become—irregularly and unpredictably —so radioactive it might as well have been molten rock. Not one major city and few suburban areas of any size remained standing; and nearly all were in firestorm.

In those command posts undestroyed by nuclear fire, in many naval vessels, and in certain far-flung, deep-secreted, retaliatory bases—secure, still, because enemy agents had never learned of them—haggard commanding officers waited, aware, even where their communications had failed, owing to a thousand factors, that their nation had been reduced, in hours, to a fraction of its population. Reduced to a scattered minority who, even if they lived through the weeks ahead, would generally be in shock or madness and beyond sensible reorganization, for an unguessable time. They would also lack the most rudimentary means of sustenance, nearly everywhere.

Most commanders (who thus waited for anticipated orders) had come to share the commonest military view of any potential thermonuclear assault: that it would be designed to limit America's reaction and, at the most, to destroy a large enough part of America's industrial power to prevent speedy recovery.

No other enemy intent had seemed sane. Mere city-smashing had been semiofficially declared senseless, since the population and their facilities would expectably be spared to serve as productive agents for the conqueror. Because no method could be devised for assuring the safety of city populations under thermonuclear attack, the military effort had been concentrated upon hardening and dispensing ever more "sophisticated" systems of defensive and retaliatory weapons.

American military "assumptions," furthermore, had always envisaged as the most appalling possible form even of a "first strike," enemy use of mere hundreds of megaton weapons. The fact that the United States had made it known, as long ago as 1961, that it had in being and ready for use "tens of thousands" of nuclear weapons, had not impressed upon the Pentagon another obvious fact: that the U.S.S.R. doubtless possessed near-equal numbers, even that long ago. One additional datum had been long known even to that part of the American public interested in such matters and informed enough to comprehend its implications. That datum, announced in the mid-Fifties, when the earliest practical H-bombs had been tested, revealed such weapons were "open-ended" and so could be built in any megatonnage desired. But again the official American view had been that a twenty-megaton weapon—large enough to wreck a city, set it and its environs into firestorm, and powder ten thousand square miles downwind with radioactive death—was large enough for any military purpose.

The American war planners had not revised such ideas even after the U.S.S.R., in 1961, had exploded a bomb of one hundred megatons tamped to yield fifty-eight and, even so, three and more times the caliber of any weapon stockpiled by the

United States and the free-world nuclear powers. The giant
Soviet "device" had been simply dismissed as "fit for no
military end," and so, a "useless, air-contaminating gesture,"
intended to arouse mere terror and to create, among less-
advanced peoples, an "untrue sense of Soviet might." "Anybody," it was also noted scornfully at the time of the giant-
H-bomb test, "could do as much"—if any other nation was
that "foolish."

What, fundamentally, the free-world leaders—military and
political—had never understood was that the Russian Communist leaders had always been willing to pay *any* price
whatever to conquer the world, so long as *some* world remained to be ruled in slavery, and so long as some of the
Soviet elite survived to be its rulers.

So, as that lethal Friday night fell over a Russia illumined
everywhere by the miles-high towers of its city-flames, in
certain long-planned and meticulously-selected areas thousands of Soviet men and women and children, hand-chosen,
screened in a hundred ways, waited in safe shelters both
amid and outside the holocaust. Top political echelons waited
in safety. The most versatile, talented, and politically "re-
liable" scientists and technologists, along with metalworkers,
agriculturists, and other essential cadres, waited. Even certain
authors and artists, chosen to record in every medium what
was to eventually happen and to propagandize the subdued
survivors of that happening, waited.

They constituted the complete human material for restor-
ing civilization and for ruling a planet, in whatever great part
mere ruins. And they were occupied with myriad tasks, in
their gigantic catacombs, built, in the main, under the Ural
Mountains, the Caucasus, and the highlands around Lake
Baikal. They knew where stores of nuclear bombs were
safe-hidden against the day when all probable enemy bombs
had been expended and when the men who could have employed any leftover weapons had been destroyed. And yet
other Soviet groups with other storage facilities waited in two
areas hundreds of feet beneath the sea, in myriad caissons,
built for that purpose.

Some of the thousands of such refugees had inhabited their
regions for months, some even for years. But no one in the
free world—no one anywhere outside the U.S.S.R.—even
knew of that program, or of its completion, or of the timing
of the first strike, on that day of Armageddon, to match
infinitely-complex arrangements for the survival of these

selected "fittest," and for their subsequent overmastering of the undestroyed peoples.

To the personnel of the still-effective American redoubts and to those on ships and submarines (where sickened but valorous men steadfastly waited to learn if a second, massive, retaliatory strike would be ordered), the very fact that, when night came, all the United States was lighted by fire and nothing human that could find cover even moved in a nation that seemingly had turned to lava—even *such* devastation of their homeland was not a sufficient warrant to cause sickened but alert and waiting commanders to expend America's remaining weapons. No orders to do so had arrived by any of the many emergency means they still believed to be feasible.

They, far better than still-living, agonized tangles of panicked citizens, of remote families, of solitaries, knew what the American strike had done to the enemy.

So they waited—in most instances at long-ago-devised positions which would enable them, on land or at sea, to continue holding their fire—for the weeks they were capable of surviving. A very secret, few naval vessels, indeed, had intended no immediate attack. In one instance a vessel had speedily learned its potential for assault was plainly unneeded and, like the other few, that unit obeyed standing directions which sent them hurtling beyond probable enemy range.

By midnight, then, after the surge and countersurge of missiles, rockets, and planes, scattered commanders of deep, land-based rocket batteries and the captains of naval remnants were certain the enemy had been saturated. They knew that every important mile of the U.S.S.R. lay under a cloak of radiation at the level of three thousand roentgens or more, that the enemy's cities were in firestorm, and that the rest of Europe, like much of China, had been drowned in solar temperatures and coated with deadly isotopes. These military men assumed the war was finished and the victory, however Pyrrhic, America's.

To the Soviets, however, what had occurred was merely the completion of Phase One of a long-range plan.

6

THE MIND OF A mathematical physicist is not the same in every fashion as the mind of any other man. It is a mind that has come to understand the special language of mathematics well enough so that its possessor also understands certain logical concepts concerning time, space, and the nature and behavior of matter that cannot be intuitively comprehended even by the best brain that is ignorant of the special language.

In the case of scientists with Ben's special attainments, men who have had experience in the observation and measurement of explosions (an inadequate term!) of some of the mightier examples of nuclear weapons, another, uncommon dimension may have been added. And that mental increment had occurred in Ben. He was able to conceive of magnitudes of ruin, annihilation, super-light, and all violence with a clarity that common unfamiliarity (and its constant companion, fear) neither blurred nor disturbed. And he was capable of making lucid observations under conditions which would prevent most men from all willed thought.

As the elevator slowed, Ben held tightly to Faith's hand but remained almost unaware of that, for he was thinking of the enormous mountain of tailing, the "slide" of huge, blast-riven boulders outside the cliff-face on Sachem's Watch. Their significance was now plain: they had been removed to make this rectangular shaft . . . and whatever lay beyond. In a swift but very rough calculation he appreciated that, whatever the depth and size of the shaft, "what lay beyond" must still be of awesome extent.

Before their conveyance stood still Vance Farr confirmed that conjecture by addressing the other seven and, especially, two people: Ben, and the stranger with the open blue shirt who stood in a sagging way that suggested he might soon faint.

"We're only eight," the red-haired magnate said in a quiet, deep voice. "Nine, if George is on the job——"

The beautiful colored girl, Connie, interrupted: "He went

47

down . . . *came* down . . . a little while ago. We were playing tennis. Then he said he had to check something, and quit."

"Great!" There was relief in the deliberately-assumed tone of command and confidence. "*Fine!* All right. In seconds a door will let us into the main chamber of an air-raid shelter that I've had crews working on for years. The one tragedy of the moment is simply that we're so *few*. I have accommodations for fifteen people—for ample time."

Ben looked at Farr with surprise and unaware that he was licking his lips nervously. He finally ventured a question: "Air?"

"Plenty! Of all we need. You'll see. And I'm glad you're one of our number, Ben. This is a mighty complex establishment. We can use your skills, here." He hesitated. The elevator bumped to an almost imperceptible stop. Farr said, *"Now."*

A wall opened.

As the women stepped through the sliding doorway and the men, unthinkingly obeying custom, followed them, Ben found himself standing on one side of a prodigious, man-made cavern. Seventy-five feet long, he thought, about fifty feet in width and almost that high. A cavern carved from naked limestone, lighted by a half-dozen hanging fixtures of the sort used to throw a strong but not glaring radiance on department-store counters, and furnished with a long, bare table and a dozen plain chairs. Five dim-lit tunnels led from the chamber, like the passages connecting buildings with subways.

It held a single occupant beside themselves, a muscular, young Japanese who stood nearby, frozen-faced save for black eyes that attached themselves to the arrivals in swift recognition, or, once, with surprise that was brief as the blink of a flash bulb.

"I think," Farr said, and in saying it, for the first time showed signs of his measureless perturbation, "everybody knows George Hyama except you, Ben." Farr had overlooked the stranger in the blue shirt.

George Hyama came forward lithely. He was wearing tennis shoes, gray slacks, a collarless shirt. He shook Ben's hand and said, "I've read your papers, Dr. Bernman. This is an honor."

Ben felt baffled.

Farr laughed, shortly but pleasantly. "George Hyama," he

explained to Ben, "is the son of a very fine gardener who's been with us for many years. George was a math whizz at Fenwich High and went on to graduate from M.I.T. At the moment—and for some three years, as a matter of fact —he's been my full-time, stand-by technical man. Ready, I mean, to be here if the balloon ever went up, and run the place."

Ben said, "I see." He looked interestedly at George Hyama and felt he could not say any more than "I see" at the moment.

Farr went on, rather mechanically and as if he had rehearsed the lines many times until he had them letter perfect —which was almost correct, as he had endlessly gone over this scene in his mind. "Valerie, Faith—you and Connie can show Miss Li a room—let her pick from those you haven't already chosen. I'll take Ben. I suppose that when it starts we'll more or less want to be here. Together, anyhow. That could be any moment now. Meantime, Ben——?"

He got no further.

"It" started. . . .

The day just past, Ben Bernman reflected, had surely been the most catastrophic any human being had ever endured, and, for himself and those with him, probably the most bizarre of any human experience.

At midnight and as a new morning was to be born on the boiling world above, Ben sat in the communications chamber of Vance Farr's magnificent stronghold. Headphones were clamped to his ears. Off and on, that afternoon and evening, he had tried with his consummate skill to reach through the ionized air above, and, from the chaos of static, catch some signal. Now, Ben gently turned one of the scores of dials on the "black boxes" that lined walls around him, and after listening a bit, disgustedly threw down his headphones. Wearily, he slumped in a chair long-occupied and often, in that time span.

Somebody opened the door. Ben didn't notice. His eyes were fixed on the high walls above the batteries of electronic equipment—stone walls, naked, gray, showing clearly the marks of jackhammer drills, used to make holes for dynamite. Identical gray limestone walls formed the four sides of every chamber and corridor in the complex he inhabited, including the lofty central room, and the small, individual rooms for sleeping, as well as vast chambers that contained diesels, generators, fuel, endless ranks of storage cabinets, stand-by apparatus, prodigious "tanks" of oxygen, lakes of water and of other liquid supplies, the vast air-regeneration and air-filtration systems, a complete machine shop, and other unknown devices for life maintenance five hundred feet below the earth in the hewn-out midst of a limestone mountain.

The person at the door spoke. "Hi! Coffee?"

It was George Hyama, grinning. Ben grunted, "Sure," and added, "What's going on?"

"Not much." George put down two coffee cups, offered sugar and powdered cream. "Lemme see. There's a bridge game still, in the main hall. Miss Farr and Miss Li against the boss and his wife. Mrs. Farr is—well—she'll soon be going to bed."

"I see. How about Pete?"

The name of the stranger who had been taken into the shelter along with his heavy satchel was by then known to be Peter Williams. An examination of his wallet had disclosed that much. It had also revealed he was an electric company's meter reader and that (again, by inference) the young man (his driver's license had put his age at twenty-eight) had a hobby: collecting rocks and minerals. His satchel, at any rate, contained many pounds of rock samples, of some rarity but no real value. Presumably he had been on the point of knocking on the door of the Davey's cottage, when Paulus' daughter, "Connie," bursting out with the siren sound, encountered him.

No one after that had had an opportunity to question him. He had been *there*. The whistle had blown. There was ample room in Farr's shelter for more than the available people. So the young man had been summarily rushed underground.

When the elevator's passengers lingered in the central room, the naked rock walls began intermittently to shake, as did the surrounding mountain. Stone chips spattered about. They'd stood in silent panic, merely looking. The persons who at least knew the identity of one another remained too preoccupied with inner upheaval, with spoken prayers, tears, terror, and crushing thoughts of others dear to them, to pay attention to Mr. Williams.

After a few shocked moments—perhaps five minutes—when a near hit, possibly on Bridgeport, brought a quite large chunk of rock crashing from the ceiling, narrowly missing Kit and Faith, Mr. Williams fainted. Ben, having noticed a kitchen only rods down the nearest corridor, at once went for water. When he returned, Vance Farr already had procured smelling salts from the first-aid cabinet and Mr. Williams was choking.

After that, with the rest watching, he recovered his sensibilities briefly. At least, he asked, "Where's this? What happened?"

A relatively close explosion brought down an even larger fragment of the roof. Vance said, "Get into the passageways, everybody! They'll be safer!"

People started toward the various corridors leading from the main chamber. Ben assisted Farr in trying to lift the stranger to his feet. And Lodi Li attempted to explain:

"The *atomic war happened*," she said, stepping in front of the rising, wobbling man. "But you're all right. This is a very deep shelter."

"Atomic war!" the man bellowed that, then screamed, "I've got to get to Hartford at once! My mom's there—*alone!*"

Farr said, quietly, "You can't get anywhere, fellow."

The distraught man had by then focused his eyes on Lodi Li. Fantastically, he yelled, pointing a finger. "You're *Chinese!*

She snapped, "I can't help it!"

He continued to scream. "I've been *captured!* You want to *torture* me!" And he began to struggle so violently that it took both men, with Kit and George helping, to convey him by force to one of the bedrooms. There, nothing sufficed to diminish his frenzy. After half an hour of cold showering, of wrestling, of frantic efforts to reach his raving mind with calm words, they decided that a hypodermic shot, from the dispensary stocks, was necessary. That had put him to sleep for some hours, although later more sedation had been necessary to halt his screams.

Recollection of that facet of the day's experiences made the Japanese youth grin. "Pete's still out cold. Funny, how it hit him!"

"Yes. And sad." Ben picked up the headphones. "The rest okay?"

George nodded. "Asleep—or reading in bed, I think. Mr. Farr issued sleeping pills—you heard him say he would when we ate dinner."

Ben nodded. "Good thing." He felt in a pocket of his shirt. He still wore just that, and slacks, and loafers—his own clothing. George had changed to one of the coveralls stored in the shelter. "Hardly ever took a sleeping pill." Ben smiled. "Think I will, by-and-by."

"Still nothing?"

Ben shook his head. "Now and again a phrase comes through, on some frequency or other. Nothing intelligible. No wonder, either, with the radioactive disturbances up there."

"Like me to try awhile?"

"If you want." Ben knew by then that George Hyama understood the use of every item in the communications chamber. "Motors okay?"

George smiled. "Purring." He took the scientist's place. They exchanged an unselfconscious gaze, each reflecting on the change in the other—the hollow-eyed look, the paleness, the tendency to perspire, though the average, interior temperature of the chambers was, at the moment, seventy-three degrees. George asked, "Tried *every possible* frequency?"

"Everything, but for satellites."

"Why not *that?*" The inky, oriental eyes gleamed. "I think the weather-station people might be sending, still."

Ben said, "Damn! Never thought!"

Instead of leaving, he took a chair beside George and assisted in a complex tuning. "Wish," Ben muttered, "we had more aerial than the pair of antennas we could extrude."

"Get more pushed out, later," George replied. *"Hey!"*

They both heard the voice, faintly. They both turned dials, delicately. Words came in more clearly, though still with a far-away sound that at times faded to near-inaudibility.

What they heard was a very tired, male voice with a noticeably Yankee accent saying:

"Repeat. This is Station Three, Project Icarus, United States of America. Commander Clyde speaking. We are still in our original, experimental position, over the equator, at longitude seventy-five degrees west of Greenwich, altitude seven hundred eighteen miles. Arrived on station as scheduled, midnight, day before yesterday, Thursday." The monotonous words faded and came again—"gather that there has been an all-out nuclear attack. Entire mid-section of North America, under generally fair weather as of earlier report which was sent from this station and acknowledged, is now completely covered with dust and smoke, through which can be observed some hundreds of separate fires. From this position, they appear as glowing dots. Assume these to be firestorms in American cities—United States and Southern

Canada, only. No fires, Mexico; but Mexico overcast by edge of the dust envelope covering the United States. Initial bursts, individually or closely-grouped, visible here, eleven thirty-four, Washington time, and thereafter. Continental obscurity became total during ensuing hour. Brilliant flaring, and subsequent occlusion, direction of China and on British Isles and France, indicated thermonuclear strikes, those areas. Nocturnal glow now visible, in evident massive haze, to east, covering all visible portion of Soviet Union, indicated retaliatory weapons have had massively destructive effect there. Clyde reporting. Smoller, Dale, and self, okay. Request orders! What further details are desired? Shall we move station? Shall we return to earth? If so, what landing place? No answer, these signals, past twelve hours. Will repeat updated message in one hour. This is Commander Clyde. Weather Station Three." The space vehicle's location was restated, also its receiving frequencies. The sign-off words were brief and spoken plaintively, "All A-okay and go, here. But *please reply! Repeat. Urgent. Reply—anybody!"*

From the moment Ben had realized this message would be more than a baffling (or appallingly suggestive) fragment, he had sat at the table, under the banked black boxes, as motionless as a mummy. His imagination visualized with shock the state of mind of the crew of the high-altitude weather satellite: their stunned feelings, their likely predicament. For a while, as happened often with Ben, a fraction of his brain contemplated the electronic circumstances which permitted receiving that distant, short-wave message, on their present, usable antennas, in the midst of chaos of ions. After the sign-off Ben stirred and saw with surprise that George Hyama had been writing steadily during the broadcast.

Shorthand. Taking down the words. A singularly cool and very capable young man, Ben thought.

George perceived he was watched and looked up, grinning. "Box seat, eh?"

The weather vehicle was that: a "box seat." But at what a cost! For where would the meteorologists be able to descend, now? Ben gave a somber smile.

George levered up a typewriter in a covered well and began to copy the message.

Ben then left the communications room and looked into the smaller chamber beside it, where recording seismographs inked a record of the day's shocks. They were setting forth, at the

moment, in wavery, small, saw-toothed lines, proof of a
complicated mass of new tremors, some as heavy as the
violent quakes made by the uncountable enemy H-bombs.
Ben, at first startled, soon began, with steely concentration, to
"read" the record of oscillation in the earth and to
study the dials of associated instruments. These foresighted
installations of Vance Farr's were both sensitive and rugged.
They could register fine and faraway shocks yet still "take"
near, mighty quakes; they could also indicate the distance
and the intensity through the assist of computer-scanned data
from a second set of seismographs located at the end of the
most remote tunnel in the subterranean complex. This furnished an approximation of impact points.

As Ben studied the coded data, he realized that what appeared to be happening was a continuous series of multimeg-
aton explosions along the East Coast, offshore, and though
additional "information" was somewhat scrambled by the
nearer blasts, it seemed a similar series of much heavier
chain-bursts was occurring at sea off the West Coast. For
half an hour Ben concentrated perplexedly on the incoming data. Finally he left the seismographic chamber and
walked slowly over to and down the long hall, off which,
behind closed doors and in separate "rooms"—stone vaults,
he told himself—most of the refugees lay sleeping . . . or,
George had said, reading. Or weeping. Or in prayer.

He found Vance Farr—now alone but still at the bridge
table, the cards not put away—sitting back with half-closed
eyes. Hearing the scientist, Farr straightened up and smiled.
"What's happening?"

Briefly, Ben told of the message from the space vehicle.
Then he discussed his newer findings.

"What's your guess?" Farr asked calmly.

"It's just a guess. I'd say the enemy mined the offshore
waters with hundreds of medium-yield devices this side, and
monsters in the Pacific, which they are exploding in a rapid
sequence."

"Why?"

"I could guess on that, too. If the blast-yield is low on our
coasts, these ocean bursts won't rise so high. Much of the hot
material, in consequence, will be captured in the tropo-
sphere."

"I get you! If those devices are rigged to make appropriate masses of hot material for each coast! I read, years
back, that sodium would be 'ideal.' "

The scientist's mouth tightened. His eyes burned. "Sodium has a half-life of fifteen hours. It's just a guess. If we watch the counters outdoors—the few that still send readings—we can be pretty sure in a couple of hours. You see, the metropolitan areas—forests, too, along both coasts and inland— are in firestorm, or in its red-hot aftermath, so rising heat will be pulling billions of tons of air inland from such coastal areas."

"I'd anticipated something of the sort."

Again the scientist was astonished by Farr's foresight. Said as much.

"Anybody who could read, for the last fifteen years, could have known it possible." Farr drew a breath, expelled it in a slow sigh. "All hands here have turned in at my suggestion. Barlow wanted to sit out a night watch. I appointed him instead to hit the sack early and set his alarm for 4 A.M. Just to make him feel useful. Valerie went earlier. The three girls turned in without a murmur. Stunned. Everybody is. Do you realize, for instance, it was five in the afternoon and we'd been milling and sitting and babbling and praying around here for *five hours* before anybody even remembered we'd *missed lunch?*"

This time Ben smiled a little. "And Davoy and that gorgeous daughter of his jumped to the kitchen like shots!"

"And *that*," Farr replied, "is a thing we've got to change, at once."

"I wondered"—the scientist's blue eyes held a look of warmth—"if you were going to say that."

Farr's face relaxed in a grin. "Of course! There can't be any servant-master setup down here! We're all going to have to stand shifts. Cooking. Public-room cleaning. Laundry. Dishwashing. All other chores. Tomorrow we'll have a meeting and I'll prepare schedules of duties for everybody, with change-off times." He sighed deeply. "My wife won't like it."

Ben started to speak, and refrained.

Vance read his repressed thought: "How did she get liquor down here? Poor soul! I'm afraid she's lost in it. Remember —or *do* you?—when she hurried to the elevator, she was carrying a miniature trunk, covered with purple plush?"

"I remember a big, purple box."

"Her jewel case, and a collection of knick-knacks, she *said*. Kept it ready, on the outside chance that the thing she believed unlikely might happen and she'd be rushed down here. She perhaps *did* just that. The box actually held her most valuable jewelry—she was throwing it in when I passed her room. But it was extremely heavy. And so futile! What did she plan to do after she'd made those few bottles of—of, I'd bet, straight grain alcohol, last as long as possible?"

Ben merely shook his head.

"Even a gallon of grain alcohol would be gone soon."

"How long, with the number of people here, could the place hold out?" It was a question Ben had put to Farr without success during their tour of the underground establishment, though he had realized that Farr had planned everything for many, many times the period that civil-defense people had continued to stress as the probable maximum.

Even now he got no definite reply. "Long enough for the bunch of us," Farr answered. *"Long enough."* Then he leaned so his head rested on the chair back and his eyes fixed on the distant stone ceiling. "Perhaps, Ben, you'll help me make out the work sheets?"

"Of course, if you like."

"I do. I prefer it. I don't want this group to feel it is being run as a dictatorship. Today I had to make 'suggestions'—orders, in effect—because the place was unfamiliar to some of them. And they were in shock; so they responded only to pretty sharp authority. Except that Pete Williams! Funny, to get *him* in the grab! Do you suppose we're going to have a maniac on our hands?"

Ben replied slowly, quietly, "I can't even guess. I've been wishing all evening—since George Hyama seems able to cope with every machine and electronic gadget in the place —that instead of a physics doctorate I had an M.D. Be a lot more valuable to all of you, as a medical doctor."

Farr did not dispute that. He yawned gustily before replying at all. "I know. It was the only thing I was unable to arrange. A way to be sure, if the whistle blew, that an M.D. would be included in whatever group made it here fast enough. Couldn't hire an M.D. to merely wait. I wouldn't have anyhow. Three local men I talked to, promised to *try* for it, if circumstances allowed. I knew that was meaningless. They'd have maybe twenty minutes to get from their offices, housecalls, the little hospital in Fenwich. Did what I could, though." His casual speech came to a sudden stop. His gaze was now intently directed upward. He pointed. "Say!"

Ben followed the finger and saw only the gray limestone

ceiling, irregular, pale, with many linear drill marks its only variation.

Farr said, "Isn't it *lighter* than it has been?"

"Lighter?" Ben stared. "You mean, starting to glow?"

"Lord no, man! That wouldn't be possible! But it was a few shades darker, earlier, I'm certain. *Damp*. Down here from time to time you have to reset the air-conditioning machinery to take the moisture out of the place. From human breathing. Cooking. And when you do, the ceilings get paler. Lose the moisture they soak up. I haven't dried the joint for a month. And yet it *looks* drier than when we came in. I'll have a climb up and see. Why *should* it dry out?"

Ben had a one-word answer but Vance had already leaped from the uncomfortable chair, rushed across the great chamber, and was unlocking a door in one of its numerous passageways. "Gimme a hand!"

The scientist helped Farr take from a deep closet a lightweight extension ladder. They set it against a near wall and Farr began to pull a nylon rope which serially raised four, interlocking sections. Ben steadied the base of the now-long ladder.

"Magnesium," Vance grinned, as he pulled rope. "Got several of these ladders. Lighter than aluminum, and strong enough." He had, by then, started climbing. Halfway up the fifty-foot reach he called quietly, "Getting warmer!" He descended. "Take up a thermometer. What does it read yonder?" He pointed.

Ben hurried to a thermometer set in the wall near the place where the elevator, now closed off by a steel door, had brought them down. "Seventy-four."

Farr emerged from a big closet with another thermometer and began climbing again. From the summit of the ladder he called to Ben, who was bracing its feet, "Rising fast! Real hot up here!"

He descended, leaving the thermometer hooked on the top rung of the ladder. "We'll have to do some checking," he said quietly.

"How can we?"

"Elevator."

Ben pictured the "psi doors"—the three double portals, thick as battleship armor and designed to withstand blast forces of five thousand psi. These had closed and intermeshed, mechanically and in sequence, as they had descended. He

thought of other factors. "They may be jammed, now, Vance!
They may have broached. In that case—*radiation*."

"We'll carry counters!"

7

MINUTES LATER Ben and Vance, loaded with instruments,
stood at the closed face of the elevator. After the shortest of
consultations they had agreed not to trouble any of the
others unless they encountered circumstances that required
help. Vance opened a concealed, locked panel. Threw a
switch. The steel door of the elevator slid aside and its dim-
lit, empty floor appeared. They stepped onto it cautiously,
holding out metal rods attached to boxes. The earphones
they wore showed, to the unspoken relief of both men, no
increase in the clicks of the normal "background count,"
which was low. For the sake of safety, they closed the portal.

Farr manipulated controls set into the floor. The elevator
rose. Soon they could hear overhead a rumble-jangle as the
first mighty baffles rolled apart. The radiation-counting clicks
did not increase, even though, as the elevator ascended at a
slow tempo, the air became hotter. There was no smell of
smoke, or glow of fire.

Farr halted the lift above the level of the first psi door
and gazed up, in the dark, toward the second set of doors,
some two hundred feet above them. Shrugging, he started
the elevator again and the air became torrid. But the radiation counters clicked little faster.

Under the middle set of portals blocking the shaft they
stopped again. Farr went over to one of the U-shaped sidings
of the elevator and climbed it, blowing on his metal-burned
hands. He was about to reach up to test the temperature of
the four-foot-thick armor plate when Ben yelled, "Don't!"

Farr drew his hand back. "Why not, Ben?"

"Come back down! I'll show you!"

Farr joined him and Ben pointed. Farr then said, "I
don't——? Oh!" He ran to the controls and switched off the
dim bulbs. Then Ben's reason for warning was plain. In
the center of the shaft, where the two halves of the overhead "door" locked together, the metal glowed dimly.

They stared at that in a brief silence which Farr broke.

"Top doors must have been bashed in! That being so, it'll be radioactive as hell above this set!"

Ben answered, slowly, "Not necessarily. I mean—the top door could still be holding. Our—your—pressure gauges showed no blast wave, in this area, forceful enough to burst your uppermost door."

"Then, how the devil——?"

Ben walked to the nearest wall of stone. Touched it delicately. Farr followed suit, and whistled. "Hot as a smelter!"

"Yeah. Remember, around four this afternoon, we felt a *different* sort of crash? Didn't register as much, on the seismographs? But shook the place?"

"Vaguely. Yes."

"At the time it occurred to me something big and heavy had landed upstairs. Fallen out of the mushroom clouds, maybe. Like a whole building. I suspect—no way to be sure, of course—it may have been something very big—the lumber of fifty houses, say, picked up, anywhere within miles, tossed high, supported for hours by secondary explosions and rising heat in the icy stratosphere, where it *didn't* burn, and finally dropped above us, here. Been burning, along with your house, the woods below your place, the big planting of trees in your lawn, ever since. I'd assume the underlying structure of rock, even this deep down, was now heating up, from *some* such multiple addition of fuel to whatever was available."

Farr thought that over. "How good a heat conductor is limestone?"

Ben almost grinned. He said, amusedly, "A question that takes me back to undergraduate physics! I don't *know*. Offhand, I'd say, fairly good. But if we've got some accidentally added heat source, in a matter of, oh, say twelve more hours, the situation could be about like this: coals, piled deep at the entrance of your shelter, could make everything below ground very hot—even *this* far down. Some hot charcoal—tons—*might* have been shoved around the housing of the first door and be resting on this one now. Even *so*, I'd guess—but *merely* guess—the heat up top would be diminishing. Such heat might increase, perhaps, for hours in the deep rock. But not significantly, down where we are, I feel pretty sure."

"God, I *hope* not!" Farr switched the lights on. "We can come back and check. In a hour, say?" He saw the slight nod. "We could—if we *had* to—open a tunnel I had cut around the door up there." He looked at the dark steel ceiling with its faint, central bloom of heated metal. "It's plugged, but openable, so we could get fire-foam into the shaft above this upper door."

"Why a tunnel up there?"

Farr grinned faintly. "In the event that people did get down below in time, but lived in the old caves, say, till it got safe to leave. Or in case we found the two top psi doors jammed. We could still cut through with torches to that tunnel. Make an escape hatch. It's only about six feet in diameter. Has carved stairs and landings."

Ben said, "Oh." He felt the building of bypasses of the massive, upper doors had surely weakened the whole structure. But he did not say so. He was too appreciative of the ingenuity and foresight shown by the industrialist to criticize what he considered an inessential addition to the deep, so-far-effective maze.

They returned to the main chamber, which the group was already calling "The Hall." No one was there. Farr shot up the ladder again and reported, as he reached the top, "Ninety-one degrees. Not too bad."

From his level Ben answered, "Up three degrees. Not bad, either!"

The other man resumed his chair, glanced at his wrist watch, and then, remembering a nightly habit, wound it. "Funny. It was always cool down here, even in the hottest part of summers. In winter, though, it never got icy; but it would become pretty chilly. So I installed heating equipment. But I never thought of extra *cooling* machinery. Hope we don't *cook!*"

Ben took a chair facing Farr. "Hope not! In a few hours we ought to find out."

They sat thus, silent, for a very long time. Once in a while one or the other slightly shifted his position. That was all. But at last Vance Farr said, "Thinking about *everybody?*"

"Yes."

"Me, too." The redheaded man sighed softly. "I had moments of hoping some friends, a few relations—oh, people on ranches, or abroad, or visiting South America—were all right. *Some* may even be. But"—he did something Ben had not before witnessed: swore at length and vividly—"if those so-and-so's hadn't poured that *secondary* crop-dusting from the sea into the American air, quite a *few* might have come through!"

Ben raised a long, thin hand and lowered it, in assent. He had been thinking of his father, in Newark, New Jersey, his sister in Chicago, of her husband and kids, and of his other sister, in Detroit. Of his friends at Brookhaven, in Cambridge, at M.I.T., in California, at Caltech, at the Livermore Lab, at Los Alamos, and a dozen other places where they worked or had their homes.

Another stretched-out silence. Again, Farr ended it. "I'm mighty glad, as I've been meaning to say, that you're among us! Believe me! Not because of the help your knowledge brings. But because you're a *steady* man. Decent. Controlled. And we're going to need a *lot* of that!"

Ben's furrowed brow showed a question and his eyes, raised under those horizontal ridges, were puzzled. "I thought everybody was—terrific!—except that meter reader."

"Don't mean that. But we may not be able to leave here in any three weeks, as you must be aware, Ben. Or even three months. Maybe much, *much* longer. Depending."

"Three *months* ought to do it. If we're careful when we do get outside."

"As things are, yes. Suppose they attack again in a month? And again in three?"

Ben shivered, but replied, thoughtfully, "It would be preposterous, Vance, to assume—here, now—that my Q-clearance is still important. Right? Or that the facts I know about our defenses must still be kept secret. I'm too darned tired to go into them all. But let me say this: from what I know of our retaliatory power, its nature, dispersal, and so on, the Reds won't attack anybody, even a month from now."

Farr seemed surprised. "Could you *guarantee* it?"

"Almost. Not *absolutely*, maybe. One or two things that everybody in the United States who wanted to learn could have known as possible, *might* make a difference. But I'm pretty sure—after—after two weeks"—he blurted the words —"the enemy will be dead."

"You mean," Vance almost whispered, "there won't be *anybody left anywhere on earth?*"

"Lord, no! People below the equator should come through in good shape! The air doesn't exchange across the equator fast enough to endanger them. What I mean is merely, the U.S.S.R. will be a graveyard. Europe, too, undoubtedly. The North Temperate Zone pretty much clear around the globe. Except where people can hold out in shelters comparable to this, or in certain military bases underground. And so on. Submarines. They will be safe."

Farr made no reply. His expression showed his effort to visualize a circumstance he had, in fact, foreseen and prepared against. Yet even he, Ben decided, as he watched that taut face grimace, even this man, who had so imaginatively constructed a suitable refuge in his own home area, had not really been able to conceive of the northern half of his planet, from near its pole to its tropic seas, girdled with radioactive air and spread with universal death, on hot-dusted plains, valleys, mountains, seas, deserts, and tundra—all of it blotched, too, with the stratosphere-touching pyres of cities and by raging, uncountable forest fires. Half a world turned hell, and nearly everybody dead in that infernal belt. Or so vilely burned, so savagely injured, that death would come, finally, and be welcome.

Who *could* conceive of it?

Could he, really, Ben thought? Not clearly.

By-and-by, Farr spoke. "Hour's up."

Ben realized he had been dozing in his chair.

Together they re-entered the elevator and repeated their inspection. This time they thought—though they were not certain—that the faint blush on the underside of the mighty doors was less extensive. They returned and Farr climbed the Hall ladder. He found, to his joy, the air temperature at its top rung was still exactly ninety-one degrees. No change. A good omen.

Again they resumed their vigil, this time with more hope. Farr remembered something he had started to say to the scientist and forgotten, as their thoughts shifted to the world outside.

Starting to say things, and forgetting them in mid-statement, characterized their behavior for many days. But now Farr took up the matter.

"About the reason, aside from your science, I'm so glad you're with us."

"Oh," Ben responded. "That. Yes?"

"Assume we may spend months here. We'll have some sticky trouble."

"Trouble?"

"*Kit*. Possibly that Williams person, if he recovers. Even you. Or myself! George—absolutely!"

Ben was frowning. "The *men?*"

Farr smiled ironically. "Not *just* them. But, think it over!

We have five men in their prime—only Paulus is in his sixties. And three exceedingly attractive, young females."

Ben said, "Oh!"

Farr went on, calmly, "You, I am assuming, are what is idiotically called a man of the world."

Ben demurred. "I've led a fairly monkish life, if that's what you mean."

"*Fairly*, you said. It implies——?"

Ben felt a flush. "I've had a few casual love affairs. In college. And when I was in Europe, taking graduate courses. Or working, afterward, in labs in England and France. There were . . . *unashamed* girls. It was the way they lived. And physicists aren't prudes. At Brookhaven, for the last years, I have hardly even thought of women seriously or importantly. Till I met your daughter. And that thought, Mr. Farr—!" Ben grinned at the other's gesture and emended: "Vance—won't be of the slightest embarrassment to her. Ever."

The older man laughed. "I know. Ben, for mercy's sake! I could have guessed almost exactly that history for you. But see here! You're mature. You don't belong to the set—sets—Kit Barlow grew up with. Or my daughter. They're different from my generation. And even your more annual background was, I am sure, a bit nearer to mine in attitudes, than to that of my daughter! Even though you're only some few years older—thirty-five? six? Thought so! I also happen to know that George Hyama, who went to high school in Fenwich, before Tech, was the most audacious and successful wooer of girls—and of ladies older than he!—ever to attend Fenwich High without being tossed out in disgrace. Without, so far as I ever learned, even doing his many girl friends permanent harm, emotional or other. Seemed as if they all were excited by his Japanese novelty and his good looks, but never 'serious,' in the sense any Miss A was brokenhearted when he left her for Miss B, and Miss B for Miss C, or, village gossip said, even some *Mrs. C.* I have no reason to imagine George Hyama has changed a bit."

Ben chuckled. "I see. We'll have to watch him. Didn't know the Japanese, after a standard American upbringing, could turn out to be Lotharios."

"I'm trying to say just that: you don't really appreciate what we are up against! Kit, by the time he reached eighteen and after he decided Faith wouldn't soon settle down with him, had an intercollegiate reputation—and now has a café-society carbon copy. Woman's dream come true, though briefly for each 'lucky' woman. I know nothing whatever about Lotus Li's life. Born in Hawaii, went to the university there, came to what the Islanders call the 'mainland' two years ago to finish at Radcliffe. I seem to recall her father sent one daughter, for part of her education, to the Sorbonne. But he had several children and I'm not certain that one was Lotus. As for Paulus' Connie—real name's Heliconia——" He stopped. "Have you talked to her?"

"Not really. Not yet."

"*Looked* at her?"

"She's very beautiful."

"Beautiful!" Vance exploded the word. "You should see Connie in a bathing suit! From the time she was sixteen, I often thought—*even I*, a married man——" He broke off and laughed at himself with a sound that lacked complete integrity. It was the first falseness Ben had detected in him.

Farr presently continued. Needlessly, Ben thought. "I'm trying to be honest with you, and clear. I'm assuming you've got self-control the rest may not have. Anyhow. Heliconia—Connie—went to Fenwich High when George did. Now, about that 'bathing-suit' thing. I daresay Faith may have told you my wife's background?"

Ben shook his head, smiled slightly. "I've only seen your daughter a few times outside the hospital. For lunch. Usually, with others. She said very little about her mother. She realized, of course, I knew about you. As everyone does."

Farr ignored that. "Valerie's mother and father were old-school liberals—the Nineteen Twenties variety. The mother had inherited money—mines in the West—and gone to Smith. Val's dad was a professor in a super-permissive school for girls who are rich, reckless, vivid, and imagine they are—or are imagined by doting parents to be—brainy. So there was money, social position, academic status—and liberalism of the most enthusiastic, not to say, extremist, sort—all about Valerie, as a child, girl, and young woman. She first attended an advanced, *moderne,* or *cuckoo* kid's school up in Massachusetts, where they did things—were allowed to—that I still don't believe. Like, if you felt in the mood, during geometry, taking off all your clothes and singing songs that sailors usually keep to themselves. If you——?"

"—get it? Yes. Some of my colleagues still submit their

youngsters to that species of educational torment. Torment
. . . owing to the absence of all discipline."

"Exactly! Well, a lot of the ideas still adhere to Valerie.
Some, I've benefited from greatly. *My* people were ultra-
conservative. The complete opposite of hers. I suppose that
was what first so attracted me. Anyhow, when Heliconia
Davey reached high-school age, she went on for a summer
or two doing things she'd always taken for granted—including
one my wife insisted on. That is, mixing with other kids, like
Faith—" he hesitated an instant before going on—"along
with George Hyama. Even swimming together in our indoor
pool in the old place. But a time came when Connie quit.
She had the body of a leopard, golden-brown, and just that
taut, that alive. She wanted to be a dancer. Ballet. But she
had to work her way, in Vassar—earn whatever her folks
couldn't furnish from earnings and savings, which meant hard
work for Connie. Connie learned a trade. Pride and effort
—or *something*—changed her to a more intellectual person.

"But, as a *high-school* girl, past adolescence, she became
the most-chased young woman in this part of Connecticut—
and many pursuers were older men, also—white, rich, and
very respectable, except when they saw Connie. I'm not
sure what caused her to change her ways. I know her parents
went through agonies, certain their one child would end up a
grade-A bum. But almost overnight, in her senior year at
high, Connie stopped even talking to all white men and most
white women—Valerie and Faith and me, excepted. So far
as I know she's never dated—seriously or frivolously—any
white man, since. She never again showed up for a swim.
Till her graduation from Vassar she lived, I think, like a
nun. Since then, I can't say. On a glance, she makes ninety-
five per cent of all men of all sorts and ages forget she is a
Negress and concentrate on the fact she's a woman."

Ben said nothing.

That discomfited Farr. "Perhaps I should be a bit more
explicit, Ben." The scientist thought not, but said nothing.
"I myself am a broad-minded man. I'd have to be, married
these near-thirty years to Valerie. Understand, I love my
wife. I'd give—have given—all I possess, to have been able
to prevent her from—from—from putting a booze barricade
between her and life." Ben reflected that even without "all
he possessed," Vance Farr would have been comfortable
with his wife's inheritance; he decided it was an unworthy
thought. After all, people like the Farrs had never known what

it is to wait table and do odd jobs to get an education. Or
to be born in a family where the daily fluctuation in the
price of hamburger was important. Or to grow up thinking,
always, whether to spend or not spend a dime, as Ben had
done for the first twenty years of life. Vance Farr did love
his wife genuinely, although in a way Ben hardly regarded
as ideal. A way Farr now made even plainer and even less
ideal-seeming:

"It is destroying Valerie. Drink. A wonderful woman, too."

Ben said, quietly, "She'll get a chance, *here*. I mean——!"

Vance Farr shook his head. "No. You mean, there's nothing to drink in this labyrinth?" He laughed mirthlessly. "For
one thing, though I never told Valerie and didn't bother to
show you, this place connects, through steel doors up the
shaft, with a wine cellar Granddad built. I kept it stocked, in
the family tradition. You'll see! But the real thing is, I hoped,
if this dungeon had to be used, Valerie would most likely get
here in time. And I didn't want her to suffer the misery of
being an immolated-alcoholic, without a drink to assuage
that craving. There's plenty of liquor!" He eyed the scientist.
"Oh. That! I did wonder for a while how come Val managed
to get tight right off, without asking me, or somebody, to get
her a drink. *No*. If she ever 'finds herself,' she'll have to
do it *by* herself, and in the midst of people who go on
drinking. I'd hate myself for trying a forcible reform. You'll
get to realize, Ben, when you've come to know her sober—
which she is, nearly all day—what an extraordinary person
Valerie is."

"Couldn't she," Ben asked, rather vaguely, and not quite
sure just what he meant, "I mean—won't she—more or
less naturally act as chaperone for the young women you're
worried about?"

Vance stared. "Val? *Chaperone!* But I told you of her upbringing! You don't understand! To Val's parents free love
wasn't just one of four freedoms—it was all four! Why in
the world Val has remained faithful to me through all our
marriage, I'll never figure out! I don't deserve it!" He rose,
paced, sat again. "After all, a man in my business—a merchant—spends a lot of his life in other cities, other lands,
far from his home. I haven't been exactly a saint. Val never
expected me to be! Quite the contrary! Not a jealous bone
in her body! Of course, as we've grown older, and as I've become, I suppose, monotonous and over-familiar, less desired and desiring—and as Val, poor girl, has become more

and more alienated by drink—she's developed a certain shrewishness about purely imaginary 'other women.' Her mind is warping, I fear. For I've never to *her* knowledge been 'indiscreet,' Bernman. Never to her certain knowledge!"

The scientist caught again an overtone of sanctimoniousness, or a false undertone of self-righteous defensiveness. He wished the other man were not thus revealing a flaw in his personality. It wasn't necessary, and Ben had found Farr, otherwise, a sincere, very brilliant, imaginative person. He again said nothing.

Farr waited, drumming uncertain fingers on the bridge table. Finally, with a shrug, he said, "That's about it! I merely meant to explain that if we're entombed here for month after month, there are inevitably going to be some romances. When they begin, the inevitable result will be some pretty violent jealousies. In close quarters that emotion can be dangerous. I went into all this because I knew you'd be on the side of keeping order, preventing quarrels—fights, even—and demanding decency, or grace, anyway, from all hands."

"But," Ben said perplexedly, "naturally! What else?"

"Good man!" Farr seemed to have been relieved of a burden. He rose and clasped Ben's limp, surprised hand. "Knew you'd understand."

Startled, Ben thought for a second, returned the handshake mildly, and decided he had to be absolutely sure. "Vance," he asked solemnly, "do you, by chance, mean, in all that talk, that *you* are warning *me* to—to——"

"To what?"

"To leave Faith alone?" He blurted it.

"Good Lord!" Farr was chuckling. Fantastically, Ben felt. "*Faith* decides who leaves her alone—or doesn't!"

"Then"—Ben was still puzzled—"do you plan to give a similar talk to all the other men? As a general precaution?"

Farr shook his head, almost aggrievedly. "No. I simply gave you the background of those here, as I know it, for the reason I said. You're a solid-seeming type, emotionally. You have standards. And guts. Don't stop me." He raised his short-fingered hand. "I know what it cost you to face the fact, just after you came here, that you cared about my daughter, and wouldn't ever let it show. Proud of you for it! In a way, anyhow. But I feared you assumed others have as much self-command as you. They haven't! You'll see, I think. And I'm glad I know now that you'll help, if, or when, I need help, to keep things sane."

"I'm sure," Ben answered, "you're needlessly worried."

"I hope so. Anyhow, I'll worry less, since we've talked." Once again he looked at his watch. "Time, nearly, to check the heat situation. Shall we go?"

Halfway up the shaft they saw that the area of luminosity on the underside of the middle doors had grown dimmer and, they both thought, slightly smaller. Relieved, they came back.

Ben said, as the elevator portal shut and Farr started toward the ladder, "I think I might take the outside radiation-level readings after this." He held the metal rungs till Farr shouted from the highest: "Dropped back to eighty-nine!" He climbed down.

Ben was absent for fifteen minutes. When he returned Farr was lounging and smoking a cigar. Ben had wanted a cigarette all day, all this night, like the others who smoked and yearned to do so here—achingly, nervously, tensely. But since Farr had not smoked, Ben had assumed, like the rest, that their air supply wouldn't permit it. Now, seeing the thick, spiral-issuing cigar in Farr's fingers, Ben snatched a pack of cigarettes from a pocket and greedily lighted up.

Farr watched him, almost without awareness. Looked at his cigar. "Funny. I smoke a dozen of these a day, or even more. And hadn't thought to—till just now."

Ben explained that everybody else had assumed smoking was "out."

Farr's head shook. "Lord, no! The air's filtered constantly. We clean it, dry it, take out the carbon dioxide, add oxygen as required, and reuse it. Like a submarine."

Ben smiled. "About everybody will sure be glad to know that! But how come, with a cigar habit, you *didn't* smoke all these hours?"

Farr's smile was wide and yet his eyes were unamused. "Dunno. Just didn't notice the urge. What were the readings?"

Ben hesitated. "It must have been sodium," he said. "Not serious for us—short half-life—but——"

Farr clamped down on the cigar. "You're not making sense."

Ben still hesitated. "First gauge I read made me think— one George says came up on signal from behind a cave door, at the far rim of the quarry."

"I know. Go on!"

"I thought the system had blown! Reading was so high. Second one, in your north property, in a special well, confirmed the first. I still can hardly believe it! But *all* the gauges

radioing us any information—half of those you fixed up—
agree, more or less."

"Man, out with it! High, I take it?"

"The level outside, around your property—or what used
to be yours—seems close to one *million* roentgens."

"A million! No!" Farr blanched, sagged, muttered. "A million! Impossible!"

"Not if the enemy set off enough devices rigged to spill
maximum amounts of radioactive sodium over the American
landscape. It's what you'd expect."

"But, a *million roentgens!* When *six hundred* is fatal, if you
take it over your whole body for minutes!"

"Sure. And if you stepped into a million roentgens, you'd—
I don't exactly know! Sort of wilt, crumple, start to go black
and die, standing—at a guess."

"How far inland would it——?"

"Can't say. Clear across the United States in the next few
days. Some big fraction of that level anyhow, if they used
enough sea mines on both coasts. We've known such things
would be possible, as you said, since mid-1950. But we never
officially presumed any enemy would try it."

"Crazy!"

"The whole thing is! So's this place, for that matter!"

Farr sat rooted. "Nonsense! This place is the only fragment
of common sense *left* in—the whole world, maybe! But a
million roentgens! Even half a million! A quarter! And even
if half of the amount fades in—what?"

"Fifteen hours, if it's sodium."

"Will anybody survive it? Short of having——?" Farr
looked at the vast oblong chamber carved from stone.

"I'd imagine not," Ben answered listlessly. "Unless they're
airtight, like us, and heavily barricaded, like this place.
Small leaks of air, that hot, would be enough to do the job.
In the best of standard civilian shelters."

Farr rose like a man aged by some instant curse. "Incredible! Nevertheless, Ben, I'm going to lie down. I'm whipped.
I may not sleep. I may never be able to sleep again! But I've
got to rest. And I advise you to do the same." He started to
depart, raggedly.

"Yeah. I will."

On the comfortable bunk in the blank-walled room assigned
to him, Ben lay quietly, trying to think. To think about what,
he could not have said. So many things! And one above all—
the end of his world!—except this little pocket. Or maybe a

few like it. The end, actually, of half the world. His brain
spun, blurred, and made pictures that tensed his muscles, but
eventually that horrid process ceased and he dozed.

At four o'clock, which was not much after Ben drowsed
off, Kit Barlow's alarm watch woke him. It took him seconds
to remember where he was. Then, slowly and as if in pain,
the tall, rugged, handsome playboy dressed, in the already-
standard shelter outfit: coveralls, socks, shirt, and loafers. He
went to the kitchen and turned on lights. Their gleam on so
much stainless steel hurt his eyes for a moment. He blinked,
moved, filled a kettle, turned a switch, and minutes later
carried a thermos of coffee, a cup, a saucer, and a handful of
lumps of sugar into the vast main chamber. There he smelled
smoke and thought something was on fire, a thought that
brought him close to panic. Then he realized it was tobacco
smoke.

He rushed to the bridge table. One neat set of tipped-off
cigar ashes. Numerous crushed-out cigarettes. He raced back
to his room for his own package and returned with a cigarette
already going, to sit and merely smoke, with immense satisfaction.

By-and-by he made such rounds as he was capable of at
that time. All doors to private rooms were shut. Nobody was
about. In the remote chambers where diesels throbbed, and in
those where generators spun, the machinery seemed, to Kit's
inexpert eye, purring smoothly, under rows of brilliant electric lights.

He went into the communications room and read the message George had typed out. It chilled him but he shrugged
away the icy feeling. What the devil could he do about three
guys stuck in some weather satellite, a thousand miles high,
over—he looked at the nearby globe—over the southern edge
of Colombia, in South America? His eyes moved around the
walls and touched on the electronic devices, lining them. They
meant nothing to Kit. He glanced into the seismological
chamber, but merely glanced. The earth wasn't shaking or
rocking now, and no deadly hunks of stone were falling from
their ceilings, or likely to fall, so long as no more bombs
made near hits.

He returned to the Hall and poured another cup of coffee.
Soon he began to feel sheepish about accepting the suggestion
that he take this early morning "watch." Kit grinned faintly as
he realized that he'd been given that duty so he'd turn in, like
a good little boy. Old man Farr, he mused, is sure a smart

operator! Wanted people to go to bed, to sleep, and so steady up! And tricked 'em into it, in his case. He should have been brighter at the time, he thought. Bright enough to know there was nothing he could "watch," simply because everything ran automatically and if there was a breakdown of any sort, he could only wake somebody—George Hyama, specifically—providing he had sense enough to notice the breakdown. Doubtless there were breakdown warning bells, or some such gadgets.

In fact, he now reasoned correctly, failure of any apparatus on which their survival depended would certainly set off alarms in George's room. Farr's, too.

He sat there, smoking and feeling a fool.

Once in a while pain coursed through him as the thought of his parents, and other people he cared for, came burning into his mind. Like everybody in his group during the first day—a half day and an evening, actually—he shoved away as best he could such miserable reflections. He took to mere sitting and smoking, almost vacant of mind. Everybody had been—was—probably would be, for days—stunned as hell. Shock. And why not?

He had about decided to get a book or a magazine from the unopened room he'd been told was a library, to pass time till somebody else finally appeared, when he noticed, or thought he noticed, a change in the even, very faint humming that was the background sound of the Hall—and of the whole place, so far as he'd seen it. He listened, and decided his ears had tricked him.

Then it came again.

Three far-off, nearly inaudible taps, a pause, three more, and so on, till a series ended. A considerable interval followed. Then the sounds were repeated. This time Kit went into one of the exits and listened. He heard nothing there. Though if the noise had been made by machinery, he'd have heard it better.

Something, or maybe somebody, apparently outside, was making that distant, repetitive noise. It could not be true, but there it was.

Kit Barlow then went into several more of the passageways that opened off the main chamber. In each he listened. In none could he hear the faint, tap-tap-tap, pause, tap-tap-tap that was occasionally audible in the big room. He returned to it.

For perhaps two minutes he simply stood in the center of the lofty, oblong place. His forehead was wrinkled. He thrust a hand now and again through his short, tight-curled, dust-hued hair. His broad shoulders boxed up. He tried hard to think what nonhuman circumstance might cause the seeming signals. In that effort he clamped his big fists and his eyes grayed; the tenseness produced no idea. He scowled, though the normal furrows on his brow were not etched by hard study or meditation; they were the lines carved into the foreheads of men who, since prep-school days, have strained in athletic effort—becoming taut, in Kit's case, every time signals were called on a gridiron and he had knelt, usually at tackle, gazing up balefully at his opponent and preparing to charge, his forehead corrugated with the intent.

Now, he felt fear. Thoughts of the long-disputed problem of how people sheltered in nuclear war ought to react, if outsiders tried to force their way in, raced through his brain. Was it possible that anyone had survived up above? That they were, even now, signaling an entreaty for rescue? Or—and it startled him!—pounding drill holes with the intention of dynamiting down to this luxury and security?

He said to himself, aloud, but not aware of that detail: "Take it easy, Kitsie-boy!"

He had an idea and rushed across the chamber, pressing an ear to its naked, stone wall. When the chinking came again, it seemed nearer. It had the ring of metal hitting stone. And now the rhythm of the signaling changed. He heard one tap, then two, then three:

Tink, it went. *Tink-tink*. *Tink-tink-tink*. *Tink-tink-tink-tink*. And it ran on, up to six "tinks." Then a pause. Then the count began again.

He stepped back, afraid. Again unknowingly, he spoke aloud:

"Christopher! Don't let the little mushroom clouds get you down!"

Another sound made him whirl, almost as if to attack.

A tall man was shuffling into the room. He had on pajamas, much wrinkled but clean and new. Shoes—brown, low, laced. His face was greenish-gray. His pale-gray eyes squinted. His mousy hair was mussed. One thin hand kept patting his smudge of mustache.

Peter Williams—the meter reader.

Kit made ready to grab the man and hold him again.

But the twirp was no longer batty. Seeing Kit, he stopped, smiled—or tried to—and said, in an uneven but not unpleasant voice, "Then it's all true! I didn't dream it?"

"Dream what?"

"That somebody started an atom-bomb war? That some people dragged me into a mine shaft? That they were Red Chinese, and going to torture me? Then—that they were insane. Telling me I was safe in a deep shelter. *I* felt sane. But believed I was a prisoner of screwballs. It's not so—is it?"

Kit said, "No." He added, "Just wake up?"

The other man shook his head, his eyes slowly taking in the immense and bare stone walls, the scattered chairs, the bridge table. "No, sir! I've been awake for some time now. Thinking about it all. When I got up and found a light switch, then a door that wasn't locked, I decided I'd gone nuts myself, for a while. I'm sorry."

Kit nodded. "Whole world's gone nuts. My name's Barlow. Kit." He held out his hand.

"Williams. Pete." The tall, thin man's eyes were on the wall again. "Limestone," he said. "Noticed that when I came through the corridor back there—same formation. How long——?"

Kit gave the fellow a relieved grin. "It started just before noon, yesterday. Now, it's about 6 A.M., day after. Can you cook?"

Peter Williams gulped. "Matter of fact, yes. But why?"

"You must be hungry."

"Guess I am. But——?"

The distant tinking was again noticeable to Kit. Peter Williams did not hear it. Kit pointed. "First door down that passage, on your left—our kitchen. Freezers. Refrigerators. Stoves. The works. Make yourself something to eat. Others'll be getting up, in time. I gotta go on an errand—if——?"

Pete understood. He seemed, in fact, pretty sharp, now that he had recovered. "Go ahead!" Pete started toward the kitchen. "I'll be okay, now."

At Vance Farr's door Kit hesitated. From beyond it he could hear a loud and rhythmic sound. "Old boy," Kit told himself, "snores like a ram-jet." He started to knock anyway, and changed his mind. "Maybe the Brain would do as well. Pop needs his shut-eye." He proceeded down the lighted corridor to Ben's door, where he did knock lightly.

Ben had been asleep for some while. Myriads of horrible imaginings of the world above had raced through his dreaming head. And he had also puzzled, intermittently and as he briefly wakened, over Vance Farr's picture of anticipated trouble.

To Ben, even on such spotty reflection, it seemed that Farr was overly concerned about the likelihood of romantic liaisons and subsequent jealousies, even if their immuration did last for months. The people here were young, mostly. The three young women were very attractive—in three different ways. And this was an age in which all remnants of Victorianism had finally vanished.

But those in the group were intelligent, and all shared a terrible uncertainty about their common future. Certainly, Ben thought, relative trifles like lust or jealousy could not prevail here. Farr must be one of those oversexed middle-agers. The idea relieved Ben, and irritated him, also. Besides, he somewhat resented Farr's inclusion of him as one of the stable, hence elder, members of the shelter group. The whole affair had an off-key sound, a *motivated* seeming.

8

BEN HEARD A faint rapping on his door some while after his broken sleep.

"Yes?" he called softly, though the stone walls between the personal rooms would drown anything but a shout.

"Kit! Got a problem!" The knocking went on, more loudly.

Ben's light snapped on. He leaped into coveralls and went, barefooted, to the door. Opened it. Listened to Kit. His eyes widened over the information and his brows leaped at the final question. "Dunno," he said. "We should probably wake Vance. Wait up! Let's try George Hyama, first. He'll know if that tapping is a drippy drain, or a gadget, or something."

With sleepy-eyed George they rushed to the Hall. A faint scent of frying bacon pervaded it and lights threw a harsh rectangle into the passageway outside the kitchen. Ben noticed that and Kit explained. George by then had his ear to a wall. He stepped back presently, and eyed them with an expression Ben found as unfathomable as oriental expressions were supposed to be . . . and never, he'd thought till then, really were.

"*Somebody*," the Japanese youth stated. "Up, maybe, in the long side passage." A different light shone in his brown stare, and vanished. "This is a passage I am not supposed to know even exists."

"Where *to?*" Ben asked sharply.

"We better get Mr. Farr," George answered.

It took a minute to stop his snoring, arouse Farr to complete sensibility, and get him into the Hall. He, in turn, listened to the "tinking" wall. Kit, also listening, said, "Sounds *fainter* than it was."

Farr had grown white; his hands shook. He looked numbly from Kit to George to Ben. He said, in a semiwhisper and as if to himself, "I suppose it's *possible!*" He seemed, as they waited, to be weighing very desperate alternatives. At last he spoke. "When we started cutting the main shaft to this place, we ran into another, old, horizontal tunnel, running north. Entered, we found later, from a hidden, vertical hole cut into the floor of the wine cellar. The tunnel, which we explored immediately, led clear under the summit of Sachem's Watch. It was pretty old—decades—and full of dust, cobwebs, fallen rubble. It emerged at a place across the gravel road that then led through to our estate. There's a big ledge, at one point, where a very cleverly concealed door led out into daylight."

Ben asked, "The slaves?"

Farr shook his head. "It was more recent. But I realized, almost at once, what it meant." His eyes met the scientist's with evanescent amusement. "I told you my old man was a strict conservative. So was Mother. Dad, though, had loved travel—been everywhere, for pleasure as much as because of the business. His lifelong hobby was wines. He'd spend days— and whole nights—in his wine cellars. Even had a room in them furnished, so he could read, sleep, eat snacks, keep accounts, work. Mother beefed about that 'wasted time' to her dying day. On finding the tunnel I realized that Dad—probably even before I was born, when the old house, not Uxmal, stood above us—had cut the tunnel so, when he felt like it, he could get out. I mean, away from home. On what errands, I couldn't say. But I can guess."

He looked at their faces. They did not smile. Just waited.

When Farr continued, he spoke unevenly, but more rapidly. "I—well, a time came when I felt I, too, might want some private—well—call it, sanctuary. We were mining galleries down here then, and Valerie's house was just blueprints. So I reconditioned the tunnel. When I sold off our land to the developers of Candlewood Manor Apartments, I blocked the remote exit of the tunnel. Made another, after those big buildings were completed. In time I contrived a secret connection with one of the apartment houses." His voice dropped almost to a whisper and, though another man might have blushed, Vance Farr remained pale. "Well, frankly, only one person in the buildings—I believe—ever knew about that entry. Her name is Angelica Rosa and she has lived in a Candlewood cooperative—the one the tunnel reaches—since we moved into Uxmal. It is possible——!" He pondered. "We've got to try!"

Ben asked, "Where does the thing end, this side? Wine cellars, still?"

Farr shook his head. "It was easier to reach it by the elevator shaft. The tunnel ends up where I said there was a passage around the middle psi door."

All four went together.

It took them half an hour, in the furnace heat, to loosen toggles that held the first of three small steel portals. The second responded readily to its motorized controls and opened like a bank vault. The third had to be cut free with oxyacetylene torches operated in turns by the heat-blanched, frantic men. When at last a chunk of steel large enough to admit a man fell, red-hot, into the darkness beyond, a great blast of superheated air poured upon them. They raced for the elevator and sent it downward at full speed to keep from being baked alive.

But even as the jagged metal had crushed in, they had heard a far-off sound of pounding, clearer, now, than the rock-carried tinking audible below. On the way down Farr gasped, "Have to hose it."

Ben said, swiftly, "And fill it with superheated steam? That tunnel's like a volcano throat!"

"Somebody"—George muttered when they reached the Hall, carrying into it a wave of heated air—"is trying to bust through at the far end. You hear the sound? No signals now, though. Guess they heard us!"

"How long is it?" Kit asked.

"Thousand yards—give or take fifty." Vance wiped sweat and grime from his naked chest.

Ben spoke. "What's at the far end?"

"False door—steel this side, brick the far side—to match the cellar wall. It's in a subcellar below a trunk room, off a furnace room. If it's Angelica, and if she's trying to smash through, that means the motorized gear isn't working. Be a job, but a person with a sledge and muscles could batter through—given time."

"We gotta try," Kit said fiercely. "Suppose, though, it's a whole lot of people that got through what's happened *there*, and that your girl friend"—he did not notice the term he had used—"told 'em about this place?"

"Possible," Farr admitted. "In which case——!"

None of the others—stripped like Farr, as sweat-drenched and grime-smeared—said a word. Pete Williams then joined the group and was told the main facts.

Farr realized it was up to him to deal with Kit's question. He drew a shaky breath. "In other words, if, by some wild luck, a *mob* is still alive out there, we can't let them in because our *own* chances depend on keeping the group down to fifteen, or sixteen, maximum."

"That means," George said quietly, "up to six more or so we *could* take 'em——"

"—providing, always, we can get to them. And get them back."

"I say," George went on calmly, "we try. If there's a crowd, we take the youngest five or six. Assuming we can figure a way. If there's too many people—well!—somebody can be all set at this end. We've got machine guns enough for a small army."

Ben felt his body tremble. Pete murmured, "God!"

Kit said, "Somebody's got to see how far they can make it down that shaft." He turned to Farr. "Got any flameproof gear?"

The tycoon nodded. "Of course. For fires, down here. Gear for exploration outside, too. We've got an assortment of things. Asbestos suits. Radiation-resistant suits. Combinations, with interior oxygen supply. But before a man got a quarter of the way down that hell——!"

"I'll take a shot," Kit said.

Thirty minutes later Kit, in a cumbersome, Martianlike costume, tottered back toward a narrow landing on the stairway that bypassed the middle psi doors. The four men had been waiting there in air that was tolerable because it then came in a gush through a thick hose attached by George to distant pumps. They saw the figure vaguely as it neared, flashlight still gripped by a massively-gloved hand. Kit staggered and, as he reached the others, collapsed. Ben and George dragged him out of the tunnel. Took off the quartz face plate. Kit was panting mightily and managed, as the air hose hit his face, to say a few words. "They got their end open, I guess. Heard 'em. *Yelling.* One word. 'Help!' maybe. But no man'll ever make it that far."

Ben had been thinking. He turned to George. "You produce Dry Ice here, for storage lockers, right? Got any dollies? Trucks?"

"Yeah. To move stuff. Electric."

"Okay." He helped remove Kit's finger-searing cover of asbestos and synthetic fiber and went on: "Then we'll load a truck with Dry Ice. Build a sheet-asbestos face for it. That way it'll fill the place with vapor, but also more or less bathe a guy, running behind it, with cold CO_2. Give him a chance."

They carried Kit to the steel floor of the elevator and went down with him.

Farr said to Ben as they re-emerged. "That's nuts! Dry Ice'd steam away before a man had run five hundred yards behind it. His sides and back would still probably be roasted by hot air sucked in behind him."

Kit, his naked body red, his face and arms burned badly, looked up from the floor where Farr was already salving the worst of his agonizing scalds. "Don't even go in there, Ben! It's hot as the center of hell!"

"I'm a half-miler," Ben said. It wasn't true.

What was true was that Ben had perceived himself at last faced with a kind of challenge about which he had always wondered: a test of physical courage that relied, not on scientific skill for protection, but on plain guts. The test from which no fellow scientist or navy chief or anyone would save you if you flunked. And he knew that, panicky as he felt, queasy of belly and shaky of muscle, he was going to try. He had hitherto often speculated on how he would react to such peril as other men held to be the supreme test. The peril of combat, of death by means unknown or not possible to anticipate. Grimly, he now thought he would soon have the answer.

When George Hyama said, "Better I do it," Ben merely shook his head. "I'll get into another asbestos job, and you get me all the Dry Ice you can load in crates on a truck. I'll tie a rope—no, it'd burn through—some kind of wire around my waist. If I flop, I'll flop on the truck and you can haul me back."

"Frozen solid on your belly side?" Farr asked.

"Okay. We'll put some kind of insulation over the Dry Ice. Steel wool, say."

With much fast labor they put that scheme into effect. The

door was wracked open. At the head of the stairs where the melted-steel-hot tunnel opened up, with pumped air pressing back its temperatures, Ben, in the fire-fighter's suit, aimed the contraption he'd suggested at the blackness ahead. The Dry Ice had already started to fill the narrow landing with steam. Ben said, before Farr screwed on the face plate of the suit, "If I make it, I'll yank the wire three times. Any series of yanks—or any single, weak yank—will mean, pull me back. If I find anybody I——! Anyone here know Morse?"

"Me," George said.

"Sure!" Ben smiled feebly. "I guess I can remember it well enough. I'll use it, on the line, to give further data." Then he went.

They stood amid the hosed-in air, peering down the tunnel. Carbon-dioxide "steam" now swirled upward, toward heavy baffles in this bypass, so they could see Ben's light for a while and hear the wheels of his impromptu conveyance as they clattered on the smooth floor of the tunnel. Vapor erupted from the great, white lumps of Dry Ice loaded on the cart under a mat of steel wool. Erupted and enfolded him. Aluminum wire was paid out in shining loops as the scientist moved away, going as fast as his clumsy clothing, his power-driven cart, and the light wire permitted.

In the hole—a foot higher than his head, level, and perfectly smooth—Ben faintly felt icy touches of the vaporized CO_2. He also felt, in other, random places, fingers of superheated air. He flinched from both extremes and tried, against his will at times, to run, so as to keep his flesh clear of places in his suit that grew unendurably hot and then, occasionally, almost as balefully cold. He was gasping. His lungs seemed to be burning. He knew he was getting a rich mixture of oxygen from his helmet but even so he felt he'd soon have to stop.

This was like certain nightmare moments he'd experienced in underwater demolition training, when the instructor had ordered some "simulated" accident that obliged the deep-down swimmer to hold his breath till his head seemed about to explode and his vision grew crimson, while, meticulously, he went through, one by one, the intricate procedures that, if he could hold out, would finally restore air to his lungs.

This was worse, however. Because then, a Navy Chief would grab a man who passed out cold.

He'd gone the distance, surely, he told himself; but vapor

obscured the view through a thick glass window in the shield
set up on the truck-front.

He was in torment. It would feel like this if you were
burned at the stake, he thought, panically! The Dry Ice was
about spent. His light wobbled on the endless stone path as
he ran on, on, on. Then, appallingly, the improvised vehicle
hit some irregularity in the floor, bucked, and he lost his
flashlight. It hit the stone, smashed, went out. Ben shut his
eyes in sheer horror. Stopped. Felt the added heat caused by
stopping. Realized he would never be hauled that long way
back, alive. Realized he would begin to be deeply burned in
many places, and, soon, from head to foot—in a matter of
ten or fifteen seconds. Opened his eyes. Felt his heart leap.

Straight ahead through the last cool wisps and not far
away, light glowed dully. His brilliant flashlight had pre-
vented him from seeing it sooner. He raced forward again.

He could make out, in twenty strides, an irregular, large
hole at the tunnel end, its broken edges framing a feeble
gleam. He stopped the cart there, leaped it, and dove through
the hole, barely catching his balance beyond it.

The place was large and shapeless—a cave. A ladder led to
an evidently closed trap door overhead and a lantern hung
from a rung. On the floor, apparently insensible, lay a man,
a woman, and two children. With feverish but awkward effort he unscrewed the face plate. Pulled off a great glove. Felt,
with his bared hand, the intense hotness of this vast chamber. Touched the motionless figures. Their hearts beat.
Threadily.

Now he looked swiftly up at the irregular roof. It seemed
to have buckled downward in places. A few broken stalactites
had fallen from it. Next he grasped at the radiation counter
tied to his asbestos suit. He could, he knew, already have
received, in this cavern, a lethal dose of radiation. He carried the gadget to the wan light. Stared with unbelief at its
dial: nine roentgens. Then guessed that the ten-story? twelve?
fifteen?, anyhow, the entire apartment house might lie, as
protective rubble, above this spot.

The air could barely be breathed. He put his face plate on
again. He reefed in the aluminum line till it came tight
enough so he could signal his success. Then, knowing George
held the far end, he began a series of short and longer yanks
to represent dots and dashes. He could not be sure he remembered the correct dot-dash symbol for every letter. He
merely hoped that if any letters were wrong he could send

enough correctly so the gaps would be filled by guesses.

What he "telegraphed" back was:

"Two children. Woman. Man. Unconscious. Alive. Air here hot and exhausted. Radiation level okay. Can you fix hose on my line that I can haul through and get some fresh air here?"

Back came tuggings he had trouble deciphering:

"Wilco. Had already brought up and rigged air conduit. Start hauling. More wire on hose, for sending next message."

Ben thought by the time he'd hauled the ever-more-resistant hose three-quarters of the distance, he couldn't make the last stretch. He was soaked now with sweat. His breath came raw into his lungs and went out in sobs. He gained another hundred yards. Then he couldn't budge the line an inch. Desperately, gasping, he looked about. Under the hole broken through stonework, near a pushed-back door, were tools they'd used. Including a crowbar. Ben grabbed it, twisted the aluminum wire around its lower end, braced the point of the bar against the wall, and began levering the line. Foot by foot, with relative ease now, his lever brought it toward him until, at last, he grabbed the end: copper tubing! But almost anything else, he realized, would have melted. He took off his face plate and thrust the air-pouring end of tubing into his suit. Coolness coursed over his body.

A minute later he arranged the hissing tube on the floor and pulled the heads of the four unconscious people near it. He could see them breathing the air, slowly, but breathing it. He signaled back a second time, to report those acts. He added, "They seem okay. Heat rather than exhaustion of oxygen probably cause of their passing out. No bad burns, I think. How can we get them your side?"

That problem required time for its solution.

But Farr and George Hyama finally hit upon a method.

In two hours they had readied another battery-propelled cart, one that could tow forward, and push backward, an enclosed "cabin" in which oxygen bottles furnished an atmosphere and around which Dry Ice-cooled and double-walled top, sides, end, and bottom made possible the transit of the long tunnel, even though the rock it penetrated still remained so hot that the air in its middle stood at a temperature above that of boiling water.

By the time that conveyance, and information as to its operation, reached Ben, the two children were crying, the woman was sitting up, being sick, and the man—a dark-eyed, swarthy, piratical-looking person—was fully conscious and trying to help. Ben, by then, knew the man was named Al; the two children—ten or twelve, he believed—Dorothy and Dick; and the woman, Angelica. And that was all he knew: it hurt their throats to talk.

He sent the two youngsters, screaming with fear, in the first load. The second carried Angelica. The man went next.

When Ben finally opened the improvised heat lock of the automative vehicle, and ripped off his heavy, ruined fire suit, he lay down and fainted. He did not remember anything of the fairly fast trip back. He was dimly aware of being heaved out of something by somebody and vaguely conscious of surprise as the elevator sank. He could see, and he was breathing fairly well, when they carried him tenderly into the Hall. Everybody was there except the rescued people.

Valerie rushed up and kissed him, then drew away in shame because her kiss fell upon a raw cheek. Ben tried to grin, murmured "Thanks," and passed out again.

Next time he came to, he was in his own bunk and Faith was sitting at his side in a chair, reading. She looked up when she heard him stir. Her eyes widened a little when she saw his eyes, open, above bandages.

"How are they?" Ben asked.

She stood, came near. He realized she wore perfume. In a coverall, but perfumed! Nutty! But pleasant. She seemed to be baffled, then, quickly, to realize what he had meant.

"They're fine, considering."

"Good." He moved arms, legs.

"You take it easy!" she admonished.

"How about me?"

She laughed softly and took hold of the exposed finger tips of his right hand. "You—you wonderful, homely, tough, *hero!* You'll *be* all right. You've got a few bad burns—face, hands, legs, arms—but nothing that won't heal. Lucky, because we couldn't treat third-degree ones; bad second-degree, even. You'll live. You'll be up and around, Dad thinks, in mere days. You may have a few minor scars."

"Thanks." He tried to squeeze her fingers to emphasize his appreciation. It hurt cruelly to flex his hand.

"Water?"

"Please, Nurse."

He took it through a glass straw—great draughts of water. He had never been so thirsty. It gave him a little more strength.

"Who are they?"

"It's a long story."

"Shoot."

She looked at him dubiously, made her mind up, sat down, and began: "They had pretty good shelters over at Candlewood Manor—Connecticut law required them for all recent buildings. But when the sirens went, most tenants were anywhere but in the buildings. The men were mostly in New York. Whole families were away on summer vacations. Men were playing golf. People were weekending on the Sound. Angelica says, too, that the tenants, when the alarm began, in the main didn't even consider the shelters. They got in cars and rushed *away*. To get kids—or just get clear. Crazy, she said. She was asleep when the sirens started. Her brother, Alberto Rizzo—she *says* he's a brother, anyhow—was staying in her apartment. He woke her. She dressed fast. They went to the apartment-house shelter. About fifty people had reached it, *he* says, when the bombs began to go. The shelter in each building adjoined the cellar. The building over their heads began to come apart—with blast waves. Most of the people in the basement shelter got panicky and decided they'd be better off, out from under the building. Raced out some back exit. Somebody left those two kids!

"Alberto, brother or not—and incidentally, he's a handsome guy!—was afraid to leave with that wild mob. Angelica told him there was a furnace room, deeper down, and a trunk room, and, maybe, that she knew where and how to reach an even better shelter from there. So they went. Angelica grabbing the two kids, who would otherwise have been left all alone. They got to the trunk room, and moved one of her trunks over a trap door into a tunnel that led to the cave. Where you——" Faith paused, collected herself, and went on. "They stayed there for a long time but they couldn't make anybody hear their hammering at the other end of the tunnel, which Angelica located and Al battered open. It had been jammed, probably by earth shocks. Too much noise for us to hear—buildings afire and falling. Then, after hours, the cave began to heat up. The tunnel finally became so hot they shut the door. The whole building, they think, had by then caved in on top of them. We think it burned but that they were insulated enough not to be cooked. Finally the air began to get unbearably hot. They tried to get back to the trunk room and couldn't, because of a cave-in. So they started smashing the tunnel open again, and did, and what-

ever air-motion there was went from them into it, or they'd
have been cremated. They then began trying to signal with a
hammer, and passed out, one by one, doing that. End of their
story."

Faith thought Ben had drifted off, when his voice came,
"Sounds possible. In fact, only some such events *would* explain their being alive."

"Yes."

"I'm very glad."

"So is everybody." Before she thought, Faith had added,
"Except——"

He whispered, "I know. Your mother. And father."

She was silent for a while. "Yes. I suppose Dad told you,
when he explained about the tunnel? Dad's pretty humiliated."

"Oughta be." She thought he chuckled a little.

"You see," Faith said, after considering, "Mother knew
about Angelica, from the very night, years ago, when
Dad saw her in the chorus line of *Show Me the Way*. A
musical."

"Saw it, myself. Nice show!"

Faith looked at the bandaged man on the bunk with faint
surprise. "Did you? Anyhow, Mother guessed, from Dad's
very effort to hide his interest. And she knew there had been
other Angelicas before, whom Dad had thought were safely
kept secret. That hypocrisy of Dad's was why Mother got to
drinking so much. Dad never knew the *real* cause. Doesn't,
now. Funny. Except for Mother, I think no one ever guessed
that Dad had a——"

"Mistress?"

"Mistresses. Even I didn't, till recently. But it means nothing to you——"

Ben sighed, "Except, I helped save the lady."

"Helped? You *did* it! And her chi-chi Latin boy friend,
who—I bet anything—is not a brother. Which, I think, Dad
also realizes. With what emotions, I can't imagine!" She
laughed rather sadly. "The fool! I'm sure if Dad hadn't
gone to such infinite pains to hide affairs Mother knew about
anyhow—wives *do!*—that Mother would never have been so
—so—upset about it all!"

"Too bad." He said that, shut his eyes, slept again.

9

LOTUS LI WROTE, "August," and "Saturday," in her small hand, each letter engraving-clear. Then she stopped to count on her fingers—an uncommon habit for a math whizz, which the Chinese girl was. After that she wrote the date, left a blank line, and continued, rapidly, to fill pages of a thick, ruled notebook. . . .

"It is hard to believe we have been here two whole weeks! Time seems to drag, often; but there are no days or nights except what clocks show. So, I think, monotony makes the passage of days seem fast, on looking *back* at them.

"Everybody tries with all their might to seem not exactly cheerful, but not *stricken*. I suppose they really feel as I do. All day I keep as busy as possible, and smile, and read, and do things. But in this room, at night, I look in my heart and it is one great swamp of sorrow. Everything—everybody—*gone!* Poor Dad! Mother! My brothers and sisters and their children! Eleven people, in just my family, in Hong Kong, on the Mainland and in the Islands. And it is almost certain not one of them is still alive! I can only hope (and pray!) whatever happened to each one happened quickly and they did not—as so many must have—die in agony, over days, in conditions we are only now just starting to get some news of.

"Doctor Bernman—it is still difficult to call him 'Ben,' though we all are told to use first names and nicknames— has worked almost without rest, since he was able to leave his bed, a week ago. How strange I should find myself living here with the one scientist my favorite Radcliffe and Harvard professors almost worshiped! And am told to call him 'Ben'! *Odd*. But *thrilling!*

"And what a terrific person he is! Mr. Farr—'*Vance*'— told us, one day when Ben was working with George (as usual), that Doctor Bernman's volunteering to run the gantlet in that oven-hot tunnel was the bravest act he's ever seen or heard of. I'm sure it was. Besides, I often shake to think how scared the men must have been about the crowd Ben

might have found, alive, on the other side. They actually had
set up machine guns and got out grenades before Ben
'telegraphed' there were only four people. I remember
how, years back, arguments flared up over whether or not
people in shelters should let outsiders in, even if they overcrowded the shelters. And now the answer is plain: anyone,
apparently, would kill, if it required killing to save those he
had arranged for and held dear! Though, of course, Mr. Farr
had no idea it would be *us* who landed down here.

"We're still in a kind of stupor. Each day's news from outside, skimpy as it is, keeps us that way. We know, now, the
Soviets had always planned to wipe us out, shelters or not,
open cities and all. Of course, some people—scientists and
military people and any laymen (like me!) who wished to
keep abreast—have known for years, maybe almost twenty
in the case of my elders, that an enemy could, even that far
back, do what the Reds have done. The *information* was
there. The weapons could be made. The possibility was even
discussed in books and in magazines twenty years old. But
always the official viewpoint prevailed that no enemy would
dream of eradicating all of us and would, at most, try to
knock us out enough, militarily, so we'd surrender.

"All that sort of 'thinking' seems so unrealistic now! After
all, earlier in this country, in two so-called 'world' wars, both
sides did the very worst they knew how, to each other. And
military leaders were trying, even before Hiroshima, to find
some kind of gas or germs that would wipe out populations.
Father used to say germs and nerve gas would have been
used in the Second War, except that fire bombs, high ex-
plosives, buzz bombs, and rockets proved more deadly than
anything else people had, back then. Till A-bombs and H-
bombs and all.

"That being the case, why, why, *why* didn't our leaders realize that, in an atomic war, our enemy (anyhow) would again
do the worst he could with nuclear devices and weapons, not
some modified thing that wouldn't really represent their 'all-
out' effort? There were also lots of prophetic books and
movies about total war in the atomic age, and all of them
were practically as mistaken as plain people and politicians
and the Pentagon planners. In all of them that I recall,
except for one, we Americans took dreadful punishment
and then rose from the ground like those Greek-legend
soldiers—Jason's men—and defeated the Soviets and set
the world free. That one, which came closer to reality so far

as the Northern Hemisphere is concerned, showed how *everybody on earth* died. But from what George and Doctor Bernman are hearing, although things below the equator are in turmoil, it's not owing to radioactivity. Just to uprisings caused by panic at what's happened up here.

"Soon we should get a better concept of exactly what that is. There has been such a torrent of ionization in the atmosphere that, even now, only freaky scraps of radio broadcasting can be received—though the men have managed to get two of the (several) big antennas, buried deep in 'wells,' hoisted (by remote control, of course) up into the air, after the war ended. Mr. Farr had six such antennas planted deep to resist blast and to penetrate junk landing on them as they were raised by hydraulic pressure. Only the two worked. But it is at least a comfort to know that below the equator everybody is alive—except people killed in mob action and revolutions and panics—and that the scientists down there believe they'll remain safe. That information is not definite but has been inferred from such bits of broadcasting as George and—okay, *Ben*—have managed to receive.

"It's hard to tell exactly how our group really feels. Certainly the arrival of Angelica Rosa, and Alberto, and, from my point of view, the two children, especially, has made many great differences. The children are darling—and so sad! Big, light-brown eyes and curly chestnut hair and terribly nice manners. Dorothy Walker is 'going on ten' and Richard is twelve. They keep forgetting constantly that their parents, playmates, and all are . . . gone. They start talking, at meals or anytime, about someone as if that person, child, or grownup were alive; and then they remember and get very quiet and turn their heads down and grow tense and try not to let anybody see their tears. It's heartbreaking!

"Still, the adults also say thoughtless, even, sometimes, unintentionally hurtful things.

"The other day, at supper . . . it was Faith's and my turn to do the cooking and sweet Paulus Davey's turn, with me, to do the kitchen policing afterward . . . Kit made a *faux pas*. We'd put the meal on the Hall table and all of us were eating. The Hall, I ought to note here, contains more furniture now, and there are even big, deep-piled scatter rugs on the flooring—the only flooring in this whole labyrinth that isn't bare, smooth stone. It's covered with some new sort of neutral-colored plastic blocks.

"But—the *faux pas*. We were all at table. Vance Farr had

said grace: sincere thanks, mostly, for our continuing safety. Afterward, since nobody talked, but just began eating—we have long stretches of such silence—Kit made an attempt to break it up. He said something like, 'You were so right, Vance! I mean in being grateful to God that you and Valerie and Faith—even me!—made it down here. Because it's been a hoary old gag around the clubs and golf courses and in New York City offices that the only people who could build adequate shelters would be the well-heeled. And the well-heeled would have servants. And when the whistle blew—so the gag ran—the well-heeled heads of families would be shopping for mink or playing bridge or engaged in some other activity of upper-class *femmes*. So, *servants* alone would reach the only decent shelters.'

"He said that, and began to grow red when nobody laughed. Kit's a nice person, though. Because he stood up, right off, and said, 'I'm terribly sorry, people! Paulus, I apologize!' He turned toward George and then shook his head. 'Nope,' Kit said and he put on a dandy, *meant* grin. 'Not you, George! With the chips down, *I'm* better fitted to be a servant than you, and you're better equipped to be a boss!'

"Valerie tried to smooth over Kit's crack about servants being saved. 'I think,' she said, 'it's perfectly miraculous, this group! A real League of Nations, yet *everyone* an *American*.'

"Pete Williams, as he often does (to everybody's surprise, at first) actually got us past that embarrassing moment. 'A meter reader,' he said quickly, "is about three stages below a butler. Besides which, I never went to college.' He sort of bowed at George Hyama, Connie Davey, and me. 'But I always was crazy about collecting minerals. That's how come I'm down here. When I got to the side drive at Sachem's Watch, I stood looking at that quarried stone. That mountain of new-removed rock had always fascinated me. Of course, I'd heard why it was being taken out and left there. Down I went. But when I was sure it was all just cubic miles of blasted limestone and nothing really interesting, I climbed back and started in on my job, at the Davey house. Out came Connie all dressed up in a summer frock and looking like a Bowl Queen. She gave me that stare and nod people always give meter readers—and the sirens went. She grabbed me and yanked me up the hill, me not knowing *what* was happening. Startled me. But, folks, I had with me some rocks I'd gathered on my last vacation. If you like, I'll give you a knockout demonstration of how geology is taught in night school in Hartford.'

"We all laughed. And took him up. And, after supper, Pete got out mineral samples. He gave a very funny burlesque of a teacher trying to instruct a dumb pupil. For the pupil, he used Connie. She acted her part very amusingly, though Connie's anything but dumb! Pete calls her his 'Savior Angel' and other kidding names like 'Nubian Nike' (she doesn't mind a bit!). It furnished the best laugh we've had so far. He's a shy person, in some ways, is Peter Williams, but a wonderful clown.

"*Still!* And not just because of things like Kit's recollection of the upper-class joking idea their shelters would save merely servants! And not just because Valerie keeps calling the group our 'League of Nations'! But for some other reason I cannot put my finger on, for the first time in my life I *feel Chinese!*

"I'm not sure if I like it or don't.

"As a child, in Hawaii, being Chinese meant nothing very special to me. The kids in my class were all sorts of racial mixtures. Daddy always took a scathing attitude toward the pride my grandfather used to have in the fact that our family was still *pure* Chinese. I didn't care. I was *American*, like all the other kids, of whatever 'tint'—and I remember the absolute heaven we felt when the Territory became a state. My class—the fifth grade—marched in the Statehood Day parade. All of us girls wore grass skirts made of paper and all the boys, imitations of the feather cloaks the Polynesian nobles wore: chicken feathers, colored with Easter-egg dye. Very gaudy. After the parade I was one of twenty girls picked to do a hula for a group of important men from Washington. And the cord supporting my skirt broke so I had to go through the whole dance with only one free hand! I was so embarrassed! But U. S. Senator Willet picked me out after we finished and lifted me and kissed me and presented me with a tiny American flag that already had fifty stars. I never felt prouder, or more American.

"At the University of Hawaii, of course, nobody even noticed whether you were part Hawaiian and part Portuguese, part-Swedish and part New England Yankee—or what. One boy in one of my classes—statistical analysis and computer programming—told me, near the end of the first semester, it had only just then dawned on *him* that, among twenty-seven undergraduates in the class, he was the only—

he had to struggle to get the word I'd understand—
'Caucasian.' And that boy was six-two, an ex-Marine, with
tow-colored hair and blue eyes—as 'white' an American as
exists. With that sort of awareness by *anybody* of our
differentnesses, I never even kept in mind, in my first university years, that I'm Chinese. And in New York, if it
made a difference, the difference was fun: I was exotic and oriental and a sought-after young woman! At Radcliffe there
didn't seem to be any race prejudice. Certainly more Harvard men *dated me* or tried to, anyhow!—while I was there,
than dated most American white girls.

"Now, though I *do* feel Chinese. Why? It's from something
the others feel. But what? I must ask George Hyama if he feels
Japanese. Perhaps it's this: that the others expect me to be
more stable, less flighty, less spontaneous, more imperturbable than they are! Orientals—in cheap fiction—are supposed
to be that. And I find myself *trying* to be. Trying *not* to show
how sad I feel. Trying to look inscrutable and imperturbable.
Don't they know the Chinese are far *more* expressive of their
real inner feelings than white, mainland Americans ever dream
of letting themselves be? I think *not!* And if *that's* why I have
often felt my Chineseness down here, far more than anywhere
else, I'm going to bust right out some day and bawl, or have
hysterics, so they can see that being oriental doesn't mean
you're a different kind of human person!

"We're all edgy, though.

"It shows in unexpected ways. A week ago I asked Mr.
Farr—Vance—if he had stocked any diaries. I did it quite
thoughtlessly, since, after a week down here, we'd all begun
to think Vance Farr was a wizard. There seemed to be
nothing—absolutely nothing—you could dream of needing
that he couldn't produce from one of the stockrooms that open
off dozens of different corridors. The man has a simply
enormous amount of foresight—something businessmen aren't
supposed to have, except about their special enterprise.
(But *I* always knew differently, owing to knowing how far-
seeing and imaginative *Daddy* is!) *Was.*

"Anyway. I asked if there were diaries. And Vance Farr
had a fit about it. Pure remorse! Humiliation! You'd have
thought I'd asked if there was anything to eat and he had
forgotten to store food here! It was so amazing it was almost
scary.

"I hurriedly said I didn't mean a regular diary—just any
sort of notebook in which to write impressions, as time

passed and I felt in the mood. He said, of course, there were notebooks. Then, leading me through a maze—I still haven't seen a tenth of the rooms of this place!—he opened up a veritable stationery store. And kept on apologizing for forgetting *diaries!* And even added—which made me feel pretty somber—that he should have had diaries printed up for *next* year *too,* and stocked *them!*

"Later, at lunch, he told everybody, almost angrily, about forgetting to stock diaries. It was the first 'necessity,' as he called it, that he'd been 'caught without.' And, naturally, we all tried to calm down his self-rebuke. But he ate very little lunch and left the table first, muttering he hoped to God he hadn't overlooked any *other* 'vital need'! That may give some notion of our state of nerves.

"But, of course, Vance Farr has had an additional mental burden to carry, since Angelica and the others were saved.

"Even before she was on her feet again—and days before her alleged brother, Al, was up and about—all of us were told, by one or another person, that Angelica had been Mr. Farr's girl friend and had lived in a nearby apartment he rented for her: Candlewick Manor, or whatever it was. We were told that, I suppose, because those who didn't know were astonished at the sudden way Mr. Farr changed after Angelica's rescue. Changed from a vehement, active, very capable leader to a sort of quiet, hangdog man who forever asks somebody—Valerie, mostly—whether this or that should or should not be done. I mean, instead of just giving orders, though he had always framed them as mere suggestions, he grew *dependent.*

"Guilt, of course. Hard to imagine him using a long tunnel through a high, rock hill, to get away from a wife at night. Hard? *Impossible!*—to see a man as worldly, as sophisticated, as Vance Farr, rebuilding that old tunnel, so he, like his father, could sneak out, the father pretending to be turning wine bottles, Vance Farr, to be working on this subterranean wonderland. Mrs. Farr takes it calmly. But she goes on drinking.

"As for our eleventh-hour quartet, the children are the biggest blessing. Everybody's crazy about them, loves playing with them—and there's a nightly debate, after they're tucked in bed, about who will tell their daily story. Also, about who'll teach Dot and Dick what subjects, come September, and time for school to start again! Evidently we'll be here that long, anyhow.

"Al—the Italian-looking man—still limps around and wears bandages on his face and seems full of self-pity. Connie told me—she and I gossip a good deal together; she's a dream!—that Al actually doesn't need the bandages but is merely so vain he won't let us see his face till it's healed perfectly. And we're all sure he's not Angelica's brother—or even half-brother, which they both later told us. They don't talk like people from one family. Or look alike in any way. Al's slight, about—five-nine, with those dark, seeking, liquid eyes Italians have—Puerto Ricans, too, and other Latins. Black hair, slicked back from a middle part. Apparently, under the bandages, is a beaky nose—though nothing to match Dr. Bernman's. Al's mouth is womanish, too shapely, a bit pretty-looking, given to the droops at its corners—though he seems wiry and healthy and moves like some sort of athlete. So far he hasn't done much talking to anybody, I'm sure. Judging from what I saw of what was left of the clothes he'd had on when they brought him here, he's one of those 'chiffon-type dressers'—the Broadway hanger-on sort: mauve suede shoes and matching silk trousers and the remnants of a turquoise sports shirt piped in cloth-of-gold, no less! A gigolo costume! We are sure he was Angelica's boy friend—I mean her *real* one. Mr. Farr was merely the man who paid the bills, and saw her only now and then.

"As for Angelica, I personally like her very much. For one thing, it was she who virtually forced Al to take along the two, abandoned children, when they went to that cave. For another, she's dazzlingly attractive. Half Spanish—South American, maybe—and half Irish. She has that blue-black hair that some Italian women possess, but it's wavy and light, not heavy like most such hair. The largest, bluest eyes I ever saw, with that *Irishness*, that look of I dare you, and also of curiosity, which some Irish girls have. I can understand how it drives men nutty! She's beautifully built—with a doll's waist, actually (we measured) smaller even than mine, and with absolutely lush bosoms and legs anybody would go mad to have for a front row in a chorus. She's more than just a chorine, too—which she was when Mr. Farr plucked her, and 'plucked' would be the word. She had run away from home—some nasty-sounding coal town in Pennsylvania—in her third year at high school. To New York, of course! Worked as a waitress in divey-sounding joints and used her earnings to take dancing lessons. Then she got work in a theatrical road company and went on trying very hard to learn to be a great dancer, for three years. Traveled all over the world with two shows—I haven't seen either, but one was *Space Ship Stowaway*, the musical that the censors kept out of many cities, and the other was *How about Her?*, just as censorable!

"However, though Angelica has dancing ability and talent as an actress—and sings in one of those lowdown, belt-it-out voices, too!—her real lifework is, plainly, *Man*. Down here, I can see, she is making a tremendous effort to stop doing things almost instinctive with such girls. Girl?—she's about twenty-seven! Things, I mean, that make men go crazy, like the way she switches her head and makes that wonderful dark hair flash around. She doesn't seem the least bit embarrassed about her liaison with Mr. Vance Farr—in fact, she almost ignores him, and concentrates on the other men. Even gray-headed, reserved, sweet old Paulus Davey likes to watch her move about! And she gives George Hyama fits. Furthermore, she acts almost as if she had never even *met* Alberto Rizzo! I've seen him try, several times, to catch Angelica's eye. It never works. He just sighs—not aloud, but you can see his shoulders drop as air goes out of him— and I'm beginning to believe Mr. Rizzo is considering aiming those romantic, Venice-canal-gondola-glances at some other woman. *Me, even, maybe!* What a disappointment for him, if he does!

"Once, when I woke up thirsty at night and found I'd forgotten to fill the thermos on my bedside—really *bunkside*— table, I put on a housecoat and slippers and opened my door to go down the hall with the thermos to the showers and toilets, the women's, and fill it. I was just in time to see Al knocking furtively on Angelica's door, which he'd opened a little ways. She must have answered because he muttered his name and something about 'having to see her' and 'not being able to stand the loneliness.' Then I heard her say, so loudly it came through the door, '*Beat it!*' He pushed the door farther in after that, but it was on a chain. He slunk back to his place, farther down the hall—which is only dimly lighted at night, so he didn't glimpse me.

"After that I've put the chain on *my* door, though I feel it's rather silly of me. Only Mr. Rizzo, of all the men here, would annoy any woman. Of course, if a woman *asked* the man to call—*well!*—nobody has posted any house rules! But the *feeling* we have is that we must behave like monks and nuns. Partly because our world is dead. And partly because, if people started visiting, it could make all sorts of problems. I told no one of catching Al at Angelica's door, but I was sure he was not making a *brotherly* call. Even a *half*-brotherly one! And perhaps it is the discovery by Mr. Farr that his 'little lady friend' has her own 'boy friend'— or *had* one—that further causes Mr. Farr to act so morose and ashamed. He *should!*

"In spite of it all, though, as I said, I like Angelica very much. She is vivacious, full of fun, and not in any way ashamed of herself or her life, so I feel sure she has nothing to be *truly* ashamed of. Last night she danced a number for us all, with the record player in the Hall making it ring with music from one of her shows. Mr. Farr walked out, on some pretext. Al said his burns hurt, and retired. The rest of us, though, enjoyed it greatly—including Valerie, who was already 'gauzy' but seemed truly delighted by Angelica's attempt to lift our morale. Angelica's kind. Affectionate. And, no doubt, *very* passionate. So what? Should women continue *denying they are that, forever?*

"It is men I feel sorry for, sometimes, when I see them look at Angelica. It always makes me think of a Chinese proverb my mother used to repeat, in Chinese. In English, it might sound rather dull:

To men, lovely women are flowers;
They would pick every sort;
Only women know that the picked flower withers . . .
As does the one left untouched.

"Not that *philosophy*, but the attitude it shows, in men, is what I refer to. They watch Angelica laugh, or sing, or dance—even, load the dishwasher—and they are seeing a flower of a sort they must pick. They cannot help trying. It is so tragic! Or is it funny?"

That was the third entry in Lodi Li's irregularly-kept diary.

Other written records were also made. Some, like Ben Bernman's, were full of scientific terms and contained little about human doings within the shelter. Thus, while the Chinese girl was noting her impressions of people and moods, Ben, in the communications chamber, wrote, under the same day and date and year, the following:

"This afternoon the amateur radio sender who signs himself 'Buckie' and whose call letters are W2HL6V, sent the following message, with a steadily-more-uneven 'key':

" 'Seems we were mistaken about the air-filtration capacity of this dump. We have no means of determining outside radiation levels but they must be high. Far higher, at least in the first few days, than our system could cope with. As stated yesterday, radiation sickness first appeared among us four days ago. Dr. Stannar, Mrs. Jeffry L. Teal, Mary Teal, Evelyn Bishop, and Reverend Thomas C. Bullen have died, since my previous message was sent. Am ill myself. All those remaining alive in this shelter are ill and plainly dying. List of living, now: Mr. Charles Tobin, Mrs. Perry Wigman, Genevieve Phelps, Collin M. Wetmore, and an unidentified man rescued from street before this deep shelter was sealed, who has not regained consciousness and is now near the end. Plus self. Have raised no other ham operator anywhere. Static still unbelievable. Nearby Des Moines apparently still burning, as our air remains smoky. This will probably be my last trick. Buckie.'

"At Sachem's Watch Center," Ben wrote on, in his scrawling hand, "we have now received parts or the whole of some fifteen messages similar to the above. One by one those amateur radio operators, so often of great value in past disasters, have apparently met the same fate. All, in any case, seem to have gone off the air. Today the first word of conditions in the Soviet reached us, as we intercepted—and Connie Davey translated from French—part of a government message sent from a powerful station located in Africa. In the midst of a long description of political and social turmoil in various African nations (and an accompanying request for aid in 'pacifying hysterical native tribes') the message merely noted that 'information' now reaching them 'indicated' all of European and Asian Russia, Siberia included, was 'dead and motionless, mere cinders, without signs of life.'

"George and I speculate this report may have come through messages from space-station personnel or even some plane making a very dangerous reconnaissance over the U.S.S.R. It confirms my own estimate of the effect of the successful American penetration of enemy defenses by the anticipated one-third to one-half or better of our various bombers, besides sea-borne planes, missiles, and submarine-fired weapons. The U.S.S.R. lies dead!

"The ground levels of radiation here have now dropped to an average of about 150 roentgens—far higher, after a two week period, than had been anticipated by the federal officials and military. But this may be due to some special accumulation of hot isotopes in our particular area. The incredible (but not quite!) million-roentgen levels produced (plainly) by deep, oceanic mines surrounded by sodium oxide and set off along our coasts, has, of course, halved its level every fifteen hours and is not now a major factor in the residual readings.

"I have recommended, however, that any attempt at surface reconnoitering be deferred for some weeks. In such a lapse of time, I estimate, the radiation in this immediate environment will have sunk to perhaps ten roentgens, or less. However, we must be conservative about emergence, as it may require blasting to open an exit, not then readily closed off. Also, wind and rain may abruptly raise local levels of radioactivity. We must not, I feel, open any hole from this amazingly-efficient shelter until we are sure it is safe to do so. We can, after all, probably subsist here, in comfort, for a period of time Farr privately mentioned to me which I still am unable to contemplate: *two years*.

"We have twice reoxygenated the recycled air in the vast caverns Farr excavated. We shall do so weekly. No outside air has been drawn upon and the system now in use works better even, I think, than that of the latest-type nuclear submarines. With our presently-used capacity for dehumidification, the removal of CO_2, smoke, and other noxious substances, and the recycling of oxygen-enriched air, together with the near-incredible *extent* of the shelter and its accessory tunnels and chambers, it will not be necessary to draw upon external atmosphere for several months, for human use. Even then, after a careful examination of the outer-air-filtration equipment I am satisfied we could, for a long period, bring atmosphere of a much higher radioactive level than now exists into the system and remove almost one hundred per cent of all hot atoms. Fortunate, indeed, Farr had the private resources to build such systems! And ironic that an adaptation of the gaseous-diffusion plant at Oak Ridge, which made possible the first two uranium-isotope bombs, has enabled at least this group to anticipate such long-period survival.

"I might add a note about water supplies and waste-disposal facilities, only just now inspected by me. These are as ingenious and costly as the long-range means for maintaining a breathable atmosphere. In tanks only slightly less deep than the main Hall (515 feet under the summit of Sachem's Watch) enough pure water is in storage to supply all the possible wants of our fifteen persons for well over one year. In addition, as this water is used, pumps bring into other tanks, from very deep, semiartesian wells, fresh stores of water.

"Farr states some artesian wells in Connecticut have been found by drilling to a depth of as much as seven thousand feet! His own drilling struck, at 3670 feet, fresh water with pressure, or 'head,' enough, to rise to within 670 feet of drilling-site. It is cold, pure, hard water. When drawn into holding tanks it is first measured for radioactive contamination. (To date, there has been no trace of increase in the carefully-established 'background' level of this source—a very low level for deep-rock water—.007 microcuries.) Radiation contamination of any measurable degree in that water source should not be expected, Farr says, until next spring, as Farr (fantastic man!) had geologists determine the origin of his well water and check their theories with *tracers!* The water was shown to come from a wide area of the Berkshires. Tracers showed that autumnal rain falling there did not appear in the deep water table penetrated by Farr's drilling till the ensuing April or May.

"Hence our air and water seem virtually inexhaustible.

"We can see why other short-term survivors in deep, otherwise safe shelters (who had spark-gap radio or other forms of communications gear) have already perished: they perished owing to slight interchanges of their air with the briefly, immensely radio-contaminated air over the United States.

"As to sewage. This is carried through ordinary piping to a central vent where the water accompanying it, from sinks, flush toilets, etc., takes it down on a slanting course, through a three-foot-wide shaft, to a point almost nine hundred feet beneath this elevation. There (as was the case at many levels) more natural caverns were found. Through one, an underground river made its way. Initially, Farr planned to use it as his sewer-disposal outlet.

"Subsequently it occurred to him that, granting all-out war, the soils hereabouts might be too 'hot' for successful farming, for some years and to a depth of many inches: a depth making the task of clearing away the layer of radiation-contaminated soil virtually impossible on any scale practical for agriculture.

"He therefore diverted the subterranean stream and recut certain of the deep caverns for sewage-holding. In them the wastes are treated automatically, by bacteria and chemicals, and stored, by natural flow and by layering through valving of the water source. This uncontaminated and very fertile material will then be available, through a stand-by but heavily-plugged access tunnel, as fertilizer, if needed—just as the treated end-product of many big-city sewage-disposal plants is now sterilized, bagged, and sold, at a profit, by such municipalities."

(On rereading that day's entry Ben struck out the word "is," and replaced it with "used to be.")

"The technically most difficult problem Farr faced," he wrote on, "was air supply and exhaust disposal for his powerful diesel motors, on which we depend for all our electrical power. Farr says he first considered installing a pair of nuclear reactors. But he decided their operation, even though they required no air, as do internal combustion machines, was too 'tricky' for whomever might manage to make it down here in the event of nuclear onslaught. He also feared some nearby enemy bomb hit might crack any feasible reactor shielding and so make his great subterranean 'city' uninhabitable. Hence he settled for diesels of the greatest obtainable efficiency. Their fuel is in 'tanks' like those that hold our supplies of water: enlarged caves and, also, gigantic chambers cut into the naked rock, all lined to prevent seepage. The air system now in use will adequately supply the diesels for months, as well as the people here.

"The diesel exhausts with their load of toxic substances are drawn off and expelled under great pressure, into a vent that was cut to the base of this hill, or, as they call it, mountain. There, after passing numerous baffles, it is extruded into the open atmosphere. However, in the early days of our stay here exhaust gasses were stored (under ever-increasing pressure) in certain caverns. Only when the exterior radiation reached a preselected level were the openings of the vent—immense steel blocking-doors—automatically moved away. If they'd been fused, or if the vent had been rubble-blocked, it could have been opened by detonating preset charges! Positive pressure now expels all exhaust fumes at the foot of the cliff in a valley now half-filled with the rock Farr removed and dumped below us.

"Of course, if the exterior radioactivity should remain high for so long that the reoxygenation and recirculation of our present, reconditioned air should begin to threaten to use up our oxygen stores (owing to high air consumption of the diesels), our gaseous-diffusion system could be set going at a rate that would furnish safe air for the diesels only, while the people here continued to breathe, for a long additional time, the preassault, reworked and wholly safe air we now use. What *ingenuity* and what *determination* Farr has shown!"

His final entry that day read:

"It begins to appear that, save for expectable human chaos, the subequatorial half of the planet is safe. The few broadcasts we have intercepted through the still-highly-ionized static, which have included monitor readings, show these to be, at Lima, Accra, in Colombia, and at Rio de Janeiro, of about the order they reached following the 1966 tests of massive H-devices by the U.S.S.R.: i.e., from 1.5 roentgens down to a (commoner) reading of a few score microcuries.

"Morale in this group remains high."

That same evening, while Lodi wrote in her diary and while Ben brought up-to-date his report of the status of the outside world, various other now routine events occurred. A bridge game was being played by Valerie, Connie, Al—who played shrewdly—and Peter Williams—who, though a beginner, was an eager and quick learner. Some others kibitzed or read one of the thousands of books available in the shelter library chamber. George Hyama stubbornly struggled to find a means to damp out the ion-uproar over the continent and receive some picture and sound he could tune in on TV— either from a space relay or from any station still operating and in his range. Kit, toward the standard bedtime hour, saw Faith come into the Hall alone, carrying a book, and with a nod he succeeded, much to his surprise, in making her turn around and walk back quietly into the passage.

He overtook her as she opened the library door. He followed her inside. No one else happened to be in the large, book-lined room. He waited for the door to shut, automatically. She replaced the book and turned to him, her face flushed a little, its expression resigned. Kit seized her vehemently, kissed her, and after that lifted and carried her to one of the lamp-lit divans. He set her down and turned to retrieve one of her slippers, which had dropped off as she had been unexpectedly lifted clear off the floor.

He replaced the shoe, started to kiss her again, and halted, stiffly, at her first word: "Don't."

"But, damn it, Faith, we're engaged! We've been in this hole for two weeks! And I haven't had even ten minutes alone with you." He could see the beginning of anger in her eyes, and retreated a little. "Okay! I understand! Up to a *point,* I do. But it isn't only *your* friends and *your* family's friends and *your* relatives who are gone. *My* mother and dad. *Sis.* Everybody else I care for, too! I mean to say, we're all even, in that way. So we're all in shock, call it, and we're all in mourning. The good old U.S.A. is gone, and the enemy, too, and everybody else who wasn't lucky enough to be somewhere below the old equator at the time. Still, life has to go on!"

He stopped, realized he'd begun to flounder, and made a more careful effort, raking his crew-cut, pale hair and letting a faint smile show. A smile he was aware of, one which, he hoped, had a look of empathy about it and was—again, hopefully—a bit cryptic, too. A brave and somewhat unreadable smile; the look of a man tried, torn, compassionate, courageous, and yet one who had an undecipherable question in his good-tempered expression, too.

Kit had been reared to think of himself in dramatic and romantic terms, being an only son of unwise and indulgent parents. The fact that his self-appraisals were such somewhat hid from him the deeper fact that they were unconscious, fundamentally very selfish, very self-centered, and, under any great stress, at best, immature.

To Faith, in this moment, foreseen since their entombment, postponed with a rising anxiety, Kit's simper was asinine.

"Don't make speeches," she said. "And don't bother to get out the old false faces of chivalry, or whatever you think they are."

"I could be angry at that!"

She nodded, her face almost without expression, her eyes averted, their arching brows knit slightly. "I know. And I don't really want to make you mad."

"Fine. Then all you need to do is move over a bit. Better still, give your thus-far-noble fiancé an appointment for a little tête-à-tête in some secret corner of this catacomb—preferably, your own boudoir——"

Her head was shaking. She saw him grow pale.

"Why not?" His words were two slaps.

Faith stared at him as if he were not human, but some unpleasant living thing—a spider, perhaps, come upon unexpectedly and when she'd assumed all American spiders, like all known Americans, were gone: a harmless but ugly-looking stowaway. But, slowly, her eyes crinkled, she smiled, and she reached out to ruffle his bristly hair. "Kit, you dope!" She said it affectionately. The instant of surprise and repugnance was gone; she remembered him as she'd always known him, and always felt about him: familiar, rather superficial, very handsome, spoiled, amiable Christopher Barlow, her neighbor.

"More like it," he said.

Her eyes now did meet his and their gaze was warm, tender even. But it was an evanescent look and a sigh erased its last trace. "I think I know exactly how you feel, Kit. Or think you feel." She shrugged a little and smiled again, but owing to some inner need for smiling as a way to conceal unease. "Let's face it. I know what you want. Me, in short."

"You— in short. And always and forever. And also, right now!"

Faith nodded and that made the gleam of the floor lamp play on her hair. "I know. Well, look, Kit. You can skip any planned peroration about our being engaged. And you can also skip any hortative discussion of my past life and its abandoned ways. I know we are engaged and I have no intention of trying to change that. But, for a whole lot of reasons, I've lost the incentive to be my old, dissolute, gay, loving self. And I strongly suspect it'll be a long, long time before I even feel female, let alone amorous female—if I ever do, again. Oh, don't get mad at *that!* I will, *sure,* someday! But right now—under these circumstances—being engaged, in love, or even caring for love, that *sort* of love, seems——"

"Not to me, it doesn't!"

"I know." Her smile became almost supplicatory. "But it takes two, remember?"

"If you'll——?" He touched her. She pulled away. His face turned red. "Look here, Faith. I——!"

"Look here, nothing! You don't own me. Yet, anyhow. And plenty of people still think—thought—that mere engagement isn't a license to practice being married. I'm feeling, say, something like them."

"Sure is out of character!"

"Not really. Not when you consider the terrible things that happened to a billion people—" she pointed upward— "around the earth. Or when you consider what it must look like, in all the many places we knew. The *silence.* The *smell,* for that matter. Don't you ever realize things . . . like that? And doesn't realizing, sort of . . . deplete your libido?"

"I don't dwell on it," he answered, reprovingly. "Or else it might start *me* into a funk. Like your's."

She ignored it. Her voice went on, softly, "And then, the utter preposterousness, of us."

"What's so damned *preposterous* about us?"

"Fourteen people," she answered, but as if answering to herself and not to his interrupting and sarcastic query. "Just fourteen people—and they are probably all those left alive for miles and miles and hundreds of miles, except, maybe, Ben says, military people, who won't last so very much longer, likely. *Us,* though. We *will* go on. Alive. Day after day. Month after month!"

"Maybe," Kit said quietly, "I ought to slap you. Shake you. You sound half nuts. That isn't preposterous. It's real. Nothing funny about it. I've been trying to say just that. We are here. *Ergo,* we have to carry on as before, till the pop-out moment arrives. And believe me, *that* can't be soon enough for our Christopher! I'm *suffering* in this hole, Faith! Always had a touch of the old claustrophobia. Down here, no matter how many miles of stone rooms and halls your Dad dug, it gets you! Know what I mean? You feel, day after day—and every night, especially—the old stone hill sitting on top of you, every cubic mile and every ton of it. Sometimes till you get perspiring, shaky, want to yell!"

She heard but answered only as to half-assimilated words: "No use trying to work on my sympathies, Kit. I never heard you speak about claustrophobia before, and even if you work up one, now, it would be futile. Nobody would be especially sympathetic for anybody who developed a phobia about the very thing that saved his life. But I meant something else. If you want to see *how* crazy, *how* preposterous I feel it all is, then think how many steps could have been taken to prevent what happened! How many millions of Americans could have gotten together to take measures to avoid this. That didn't. How many Presidents had how many opportunities to save us all? Starting with—who was it?—Truman. When only our side had the bomb! And on and on, right to Conner, with the cold war the only sane chance either side had for settling anything. And the cold war always being neglected, evaded, compromised, not fought—by us—till things got *this* crazy! If . . . no! . . . *since* the people of the United States and their leaders had no better sense than to let things happen that ended with perhaps exactly fourteen survivors in the whole nation, then that's *eminently* preposterous! It's *cuckoo!* We *ought* to be hysterical with mirth at it. We ought to chortle night and day! All the Christianity, technology, education, freedom, democracy, wealth—and whammo! Gone. With fourteen remainders! A time to bellow and roar with glee. A time to churn with laughter. A farce, Kit—*farce.* See?"

"All I see is, you're losing your grip."

"My *point,* Kit. There never *was* any grip."

He had been standing in front of her, watching with the narrow-eyed care of an expectant psychiatrist. But she had said what she had said without much emotion and with no concurrent or subsequent hysteria. Just said it, smiled a little, and stopped. Looked up at him, quite calmly, a little questioningly. Her mind, he decided, was going glassy. What she needed was a bit of shock. A touch of the old realism.

He applied a calculated measure:

"You leave your door unlocked tonight, and lock the one that connects with your mama, even though she'll be out cold, as per usual, dear. I'll come by about midnight. And we'll take up this engagement as it ought to be conducted."

"Oh?" Faith said.

"Yes 'Oh!' That, or I'll speak to your father about how do we get married in a joint like this. And *get* married."

She held out her hand and opened it. The ring with the great diamond blazed on her palm. "Want it back?"

"No." He said that instantly.

She slipped the ring on again. Looked at it, at him.

He said quietly, "It's this Bernman?"

"No." She thought a moment. "It's everything."

"He's a good Joe," Kit said, rather surprisingly. "Might even be interesting from a gal's standpoint. I mean as an experiment. Well. I'm broad-minded. You know that. But you'll also remember, I expect a certain *quid pro quo,* and you're not the only alluring female in this dungeon."

"I know," she said in a gentle way, a sad-seeming way.

"So *okay,* dear." He went.

Faith sat in the large room alone, tears sliding down her cheeks. Once or twice she laughed, shortly; and once or twice she sobbed, slightly. Finally she rose and just before she went into the passageway, but after she'd repaired her careful, light makeup, she said, aloud:

"It *is* preposterous, though! *Everything here!*"

10

BEN BERNMAN emerged from the communications room and rather worriedly sought out Vance Farr, whom he found, finally, in the chamber housing an elaborate machine shop, turning out on a lathe what Ben assumed were candlesticks. Farr at once explained:

"Valerie's been beefing about the absence of footstools in the joint. She always likes her feet up, when she reads, and so on. Making legs for one. We'll make most of the furniture we'll need. Help pass time."

"I didn't know," Ben smiled, "you were a master carpenter."

"No master. But I always enjoyed it—lathe work, especially. Never had time to do much." He now perceived the tension in the other man. "Hey! Something wrong?"

"It's just this, Vance. I thought you ought to help make a decision. As you know, for several evenings George and I have tuned in bits and pieces of TV programs, broadcast from below the equator and dispersed world-wide, on the international repeaters."

"A plain wonder," Farr muttered, "they weren't blown out of their orbits! Or to smithereens! Like everything else."

Ben smiled fleetingly. "They're still in orbit. Well. We now know that we can get a good picture and clear sound from various stations. And tonight, beginning at eight, there's going to be a program of film and photos and other material, showing the devastation in the United States."

"Who's transmitting that?"

"San José, Costa Rica."

"That's *above* the equator!"

"Sure. A few degrees. But they're all right. City's surrounded with mountains that shielded them from most of the fallout that reached that far south. Not very hot stuff. They also took precautions—and still are taking 'em. But, the thing is, do you feel we should tune in whatever they project, for everybody?"

"Yeah."

Ben said, "Okay. But it could be pretty hideous."

"Bet it will be! Let's get a set hooked up—if you can do it—in the big Hall. Eight o'clock, our time? Right! Then I'll have the dinner shift feed us at seven sharp, and no alibis for delays. We maybe need to see some of the reasons for being glad we are here."

After that meal the two youngsters were told they would have to stay in their rooms—together, if they liked—as a "film for grownups only" was going to be shown in the Hall. Obediently, they accepted those orders.

Dot and Dick were biddable, and besides, they had not yet completely recovered from the numbing knowledge of their abandonment as their crumbling air-raid shelter was deserted by their own mother, or from the dreads that came afterward, even though all such alarms were kept as unfearful as the people who'd saved them or had been saved with them could manage. These shocks had made slow-healing wounds in ten- and twelve-year old children. As a result they were still abnormally docile.

The adults arranged themselves, just before eight o'clock, in two rows of chairs facing, at some distance, the white, curved surface of a TV set, a surface the size of screens made for the exhibition of home movies.

George and Ben manipulated the dials of this most modern TV set, and soon a color picture appeared—the head and shoulders of a handsome, somber man, who was talking rapidly. Headphones on a trailing wire were given to the group's linguist, Connie Davey, who had a place in the center of the front row. There was no need of turning on the loudspeaker, inasmuch as the beautiful colored girl alone knew much Spanish.

She immediately began to translate what was being said by the Costa Rican announcer:

"You are about to be shown what this station has been able to gather together of photographic and taped records of the American holocaust. The first sequence you will see was taken by an American photo"—Connie hesitated—"photoreconnaissance plane. This plane was dispatched from Homestead Air Base, in Florida, United States, on the mission of photographing effects of the United States attack on the Soviet Union. When some way out over the Atlantic, one of the plane's six jet engines failed, and then another lost power.

"The commander was therefore forced to turn back. Information had reached him by radio that his home base in Florida was nonexistent, and also many other air bases in the United States. Hence he flew his plane to the middle American coast, which he reached north of Charleston, South Carolina. The plane arrived at that point some three hours after the start of the first Soviet strike. By then the plane's flight engineer had restored power in one of the two crippled engines.

"The men in the plane were shielded against radiation because its mission was expected to involve flights through enormously-contaminated enemy air. The film and cameras were specially designed and protected to operate safely and to prevent film from damage by radiation, up to tremendous intensities. The crew had been trained to regard their planned mission as militarily essential even if their own radiation dosage passed the lethal level and insured their ultimate deaths.

Now, on the TV set, came a still photograph of eight young men in the uniforms of the Air Force of the United States. They looked familiar, and yet, somehow, a little less vital and less military in bearing than most such crews.

The announcer apparently began talking over the "still" picture, for Connie went on:

"These are the eight officers and enlisted men on board that plane. After reaching the eastern coast of the United States they headed north, hoping to locate some field, military or civilian, where they could land. They had fuel for many more hours of swift flight. It did not at once occur to them that, since their mission had been—" Connie again seemed to have missed the Spanish word, then found it— "aborted, they might usefully employ their special aircraft and its equipment to make a record of enemy damage to their homeland. That opportunity was realized only as they approached Norfolk, Virginia. You will now see Norfolk, a great naval base, as their cameras filmed it."

Connie fell silent.

On the screen came a distant horizon and, along it, a stretch of land, in the middle of which rose a rosy-orange cloud of smoke that intermittently broke into what seemed mile-high surges of flame. The picture faded. The screen went blank.

Connie spoke: "The next views are of Richmond, Virginia."

The city was on fire from scattered suburbs to its center, but not yet in the single pyre of firestorm. From high up it looked like an endless city dump spread over many square miles. The jumbled mass of unidentifiable objects that had once been homes, apartments, stores, skyscrapers, hospitals, police stations, movie theaters, and so on now lay in shambles, eaten by ten thousand fires and marked by as many smokes.

The camera, after panning across that immensity of leveled city in conflagration, focused on a special area, and the stunned viewers realized that either the plane had descended or a telephoto lens was used. For what was displayed seemed close: a hole. A hole, in farmland, near the vastness of the burning ruins. As flattened farmhouses and roads became discernible, they realized the hole must have been a mile in diameter and hundreds of feet deep. Nothing moved in the hole except, here and there, a thin rise of vapor. A yet closer view revealed the pit was gouged from rock and its cliff-like sides had melted down into the bottom. The material lay there still, glowing faintly and steaming, a liquid like hot tar. That grim vista vanished.

Connie next said, shakily, "Washington, D.C., the national capital."

There was not much to see. The plane tried to obtain views of the ground near Washington, but towering walls of fire intervened everywhere. A new angle of the camera caused Farr to gasp, "Good God! That's twenty miles *up* the Potomac! And *look!* Not a house standing even *there!* Not a bridge over the river, even that far away!"

While many aspects of this holocaust were shown, Connie translated more comment:

"The plane is now skirting the firestorm. From some few, last-minute radio messages it is known that approximately eighteen bombs, of some five megatons each, hit the Washington-Baltimore area. It has been obliterated and we see here the beginning of the absolute end. In a moment a longer shot will show you the wall of fire, rising two miles wide or more, over Baltimore, and the continuous reach of fire and smoke between the two cities, where small towns, isolated farmhouses, all other buildings, stalled traffic, and all woodlands blaze."

They saw that: a reach of sky-licking and continuous combustion some fifty miles in length.

Now, huskily, Connie said, "Philadelphia."

Again, from an altitude of, George audibly suggested, about five miles, they beheld another city-and-suburb-thick pillar of flame and smoke that continuously surged to a far greater altitude than that of the plane. The pilot had taken his craft close to this Cyclopean blast furnace. They could therefore even see *objects* hurled up in the incredible skyward thrust of the superheated flame. In some glimpses the things shooting aloft were momentarily recognizable: a heavy sedan, turning end-over-end; a farm tractor, its wheels ripped off; a locomotive; some connected bars that Angelica suggested, in a gasping voice, were "part of a jail" and that George stated, flatly, afterward—and probably rightly—were animal cages from a zoo.

That incredible portion of the "tour" ended and the announcer prepared his viewers, wherever they might be, for another:

"New York," Connie moaned, ignoring all else the announcer said.

New York existed as a far-vaster firestorm than Philadelphia's, on a screen that showed, in the distance, a mountain-range of moving fire stretching from edge to edge.

That titanic—actually incomprehensible—sea of flame faded out. The face of the announcer reappeared.

"We will now interrupt that awesome picture of New York —the five boroughs and all adjacent suburbs and towns and cities—just seen in a single measureless blaze. For we have, by chance, some film of New York and its environs, taken only last week by special cameras operated from remote-controlled, or 'drone,' planes, which were flown over the region from an aircraft carrier, the USS *Conner*, lately commissioned and, on the day of assault, cruising in the South Atlantic, hence unharmed."

What appeared was worse than the firestorms.

Manhattan, Brooklyn, the Bronx, Queens, and King's County and Staten Island were no longer easily recognizable. The firestorm had burned out, although individual fires still flickered here and there and smoke still rose from myriad unguessable objects on an endless landscape of devastation. In the merely murky air, each bomb hit that was close enough to the earth to leave its print could be discerned. Like pockmarks, often a mile across and more, these craters—some many hundreds of feet deep but others shallow—lay on the land amid mile upon mile of surrounding debris.

Manhattan itself had been sliced in half at about the southern edge of Central Park, which contained two more, quarry-like depressions. It was not recognizable as a park at all, inasmuch as rubble, heaped in uneven mounds that rose to heights of many stories, had erased lawns, lakes, and all else.

Downtown Manhattan was no longer a needle-pack of sky-scrapers but a wilderness of melted, shredded, and blackened stone, concrete, brick, and steel—a domed-up slag heap. Long Island, out as far as Mineola, was the same. Newark and other New Jersey cities were simmering reaches of carbonized nothing, as desolate, cratered, and empty of movement as the surface of the moon.

Somebody was sobbing. Ben did not look, but soon he recognized the person from the very intensity of the effort summoned to try to stifle the sound. It was Lotus Li, moaning for her father, surely, since he had died somewhere in the blasted shambles that had been Manhattan. No building, identifiable as such, could be discerned. Streets had disappeared under moraines of rubble, created, not slowly, as by glaciers, but in seconds. One feature, shown in one sweep from south to north, *alone* could be explained and exactly located—a great, straight streak of shimmering material which Ben was first to identify:

"Melted glass," he said slowly. "The earliest hit must have smashed all the windows on Park Avenue. That would make a few miles of broken glass a couple of stories deep. A following burst evidently threw the buildings *away* from the thoroughfare, in both directions. And that bomb, or some other—mere firestorm even—melted the deep, smashed glass that had choked the avenue."

Nobody debated his analysis of the shining spear of congealed material that evidently ran from where the New York Central Building had once straddled Park Avenue, north, to about Ninetieth Street.

The camera now quit looking at titanic potholes, down-bashed bridges, titanic rubble heaps, and the belt of water that, in mid-Manhattan, connected the East and Hudson rivers.

The drone plane circled north, and soon, east.

They were given a long-range glimpse of the Connecticut shore line and its nonextant cities, their grave pits, their spattered buildings, and their blackness from burning. At one point, however, as the plane turned back on a westward course, Kit said what all the straining, dazed viewers were thinking, "In the distance, where you can see a high mound bare of trees, is where *we* are, right now!"

The announcer reappeared on the screen and Connie re-commenced her translating, in a strained, dry voice:

"You thus have seen the present, or, more exactly, recent state, of New York City, first photographed in firestorm by the reconnaissance plane. We will now resume a display of that first plane's pictures as it flew west, encountering nothing but cities blazing and towns and villages flattened and burned, or, as you will notice, unruined but without life—a strange phenomenon exhibited by one town the plane descended to circle, a town we have not yet surely identified but believe to be Zanesville, Ohio. It represents the state of many towns, villages, and small cities that escaped blast and fire."

When sights of more metropolitan areas in firestorm—Pittsburgh, among others—had become almost familiar to the appalled audience, there came swiftly into camera range a distant, good-sized town which had suffered no visible damage.

It stood, intact, with surrounding farmhouses and barns untouched. Streets of red-brick houses, a downtown area, shopping centers on the town edges, manufacturing plants, schools, hospitals, and all the other structures and appurte-nances of an ordinary American town or small city now were shown from low-level, slowed flight. It made a vista so well known to all persons who had traveled by air in the United States that, at first, these viewers felt like cheering at the sight: a big town, undamaged and, they would have thought, full of thousands of nice, ordinary folks, still pre-sumably going about their business at the hour when the picture was taken.

But though the plane flew around the center of the town at an altitude at which the camera would have shown even a small dog, had a small dog been there, what they saw was a town empty of life. Not a car moved. Not a single person walked across the streets. No one appeared in the myriad yards and lawns. No truck budged. The town—or city, as its inhabitants probably had proudly insisted—seemed to have been abandoned. Even beyond its streets and highways, on the farms they viewed, no people were seen, no cows, pigs, or chickens stirred.

The announcer evidently began explaining, for Connie gave a little gasp before she undertook a tremulous transla-tion:

"This area, like numberless others photographed in that flight, made so soon after the first strike, apparently received warning enough of what was happening or imminent else-where, and apparently had a well-enough-organized civil-defense program, so that the inhabitants shut off electric plants, turned off gas, took cover, and so on. It may be that in the scenes being shown, some persons were still under cover, even still alive. Along with their sheltered farm animals and pets. However, the fact that subsequent photographs taken of similarly intact areas *still* show no evidence of life anywhere, suggests two things. First, towns like the one here being reconnoitered must have been enveloped, very soon after the strike began, with extraordinarily radioactive fallout, coming perhaps on a freak wind current so that right after the inhabitants had taken cover, intense radiation swept through the area and destroyed all life in it.

"We also know that in the night following the rocket-and-plane attack, a great mass of immensely radioactive material was created by submarine mines of a special sort detonated along both coasts of the United States. And we know that a continent-wide juggernaut of short-lived, but incredibly radioactive material spread some distance inland on the East Coast and was carried by the dominant weather pattern eastward, as in normal, from the Pacific clear across the United States and over much of Canada and part of Mexico.

"That marching 'rain' deposited on all that immense area—some three and one-half million square miles—a layer of invisible radioactive sodium. It had a radiation level of, initially, upwards of one million roentgens, and before moving off the land and out over the Atlantic, even in the last-coated regions, some tens of thousands of roentgens.

"Here in Zanesville, if we have named the place correctly, a very efficient civil-defense preparation must have led to the swift taking of shelter by all persons and even, in the farmland beyond, to the gathering and sheltering of domestic animals in barns and so forth, where presumably what was thought to be adequate fallout protection had been installed on roofs and walls. Then the freakish wash of extra-high radioactive gases and dusts fell, and so great and swift was the penetration of the radiation that here—as everywhere with the sodium assault that night—all civilian life was exterminated. For the people of North America had not, anywhere, prepared shelters against fallout of such high levels. It was known that weapons could be easily made to deliver that radiation. But, alas, it was also known that even the United

States lacked the technology, wealth, and even the political means to create equal defenses."

The screen momentarily went blank, then was overspread with another horizon-to-horizon wall of smoke beneath which miles-high flames wavered, shot upward, and swirled spirally. The scene was different from others shown, in one way, however. In its foreground lay a stretch of water, churned by mighty waves so that it dizzily reflected its background of flame and infinite smoke. Connie translated: "Cleveland."

The face of the announcer now reappeared, a long sad-seeming face with all the tragedy Latin eyes can express in its steady, dark-eyed gaze. The man had very curly, gray hair, and a thin hand that touched a trembling mouth, tremulously. He seemed to gather his courage in order to go on talking.

"The plane," he said, and Connie's hushed translation obviously echoed his tone, "next flew to Chicago. Here the city was not yet in firestorm, though it lay in ruins, and among the ruins many hundreds of big fires and thousands of small ones, as you will see, showed that firestorm would soon cremate what was not already wrecked and dead.

"The reason for this delay in the combining of Chicago's multitudes of fires into the usual, single, city-storm of flame, was deduced by our scientists, who have viewed all the film we are now telecasting. Evidently, though either six or seven hits were made on Chicago and its suburbs, destroying the whole region, a bomb, or more than one, of large caliber and probably dropped from a Soviet plane either missed Chicago and exploded in or above Lake Michigan, or did so owing to some deliberate plan, the reason for which cannot be determined by us. For it is apparent that one or more tremendous explosions in or over Lake Michigan, shortly after the initial strikes on Chicago, literally lifted up the water in the southern end of that huge lake and hurled it onto shore.

"The paths of the ensuing, unimaginable tidal wave over the already-ruined city, as it surged inland and, later, when it withdrew, can be discerned. That inundation undoubtedly extinguished the uncountable fires set by the land hits. Only later, as the film you will see clearly shows, did new fires arise and the soaked hundreds of square miles begin to burn again, and to dry out in new heats, and so, to meet the final fate of all hit cities that follows blast, heat, and raying: the firestorm fate."

Now they looked down at the self-illuminated, fire-patched residue of the great Chicago urban area. And they could see, from the high-altitude photography, linear streaks that indicated the coming and going of the unimaginable tidal wave. Someone else in the group was now sobbing softly, for the orientation of Chicago was plainer than that of any other of the devastated cities save only for the second views of New York. Chicago could more or less be recognized, Ben mused, by the visible still bluish shape of the lake edge. You could guess from that the specific location of any part of its flame-spattered, flood-strewn remains you had known.

It was old Paulus Davey, the butler, who now sobbed, almost without sound: just a little, sad rasp in his throat.

Ben began to wish that the broadcast would end.

And in consequence he felt gratefulness when the scene changed back to the studio in San José and showed the composed but tormented narrator. An *alive* man, Ben said to himself, with a relief like joy.

The Costa Rican now stood in front of a large map of North America. He held a pointer:

"The officers and men who took these remarkable pictures had found no base useable in the area thus far surveyed. They had heard some signals from what they thought to be a military base in Texas, so they headed that way." He traced the plane's course. "All the way south they found the same conditions prevailed in all major cities. St. Louis and Dallas were burning. The base they had expected might be safe was a great compound hole, like a volcano crater, such as the mile-wide one in my country's famous active volcano, Poas.

"By then, too, fuel was becoming a matter of concern. The commander realized that the only possible method of escape left, was to fly on south. He hoped at first to reach Panama. However, the crew feared that in spite of the United States agreement with the Panamanian government and the subsequent dismantling of all military emplacements there, the Canal and airfields might have been attacked. They were not, as a matter of fact. Russian visitors had, apparently, informed Moscow that Panama had been stripped of all weapons, and the U.S. agreement thus carried out to the letter. Panama is therefore unharmed.

"However, after consultation they finally determined that they would pass up nearer fields sufficiently large for landing, even providing such fields, in Mexico and Central American countries to the south, were still useable. They elected our largest field, on the outskirts of San José, the capital of Costa Rica, as their last but best hope, and they began radio requests for permission to land, explaining with great candor that their plane would be far too radioactive even to approach safely.

"With characteristic Tico courage, we bid them descend." Connie explained, "Costa Ricans call themselves 'Ticos.' "

Now they saw the plane come hurtling onto the great field that lies some twenty miles from the heart of San José, on undulant upland, between two mountain ranges. It made a perfect landing on the edge of the field, not using the recently-extended main airstrip. The plane bumped to a floppy-winged stop. Fire apparatus and trucks rushed toward it. Men in uniform began to emerge from it and to climb down a ladder they swiftly lowered from what had been a bomb bay and was converted to a shielded photo-reconnaissance chamber. They carried with them only some very heavy boxes which they dragged clear of the plane as the Costa Rican equipment approached. This approach the flight crew evidently feared, for they made waving motions to the vehicles to stop.

The scene changed to the portrait of the eight men and their airplane, in a weedy, end corner of the landing field. The announcer spoke again, and again Connie's voice manifestly echoed his in mournfulness:

"These are the men, then, who made that flight. This picture was taken from a long distance by a camera with a telephoto lens. The reason for that was very simple. The plane itself, having flown so far through such immensely radioactive atmosphere, could not be approached at all safely by an unprotected human being. The men, themselves, in spite of their effort to assume a look of"—Connie questioned her translation—"jauntiness?" she said, and then repeated it with conviction—"in spite of their jaunty look, and in spite of the shielding protecting them within the aircraft, knew well—indeed, knew almost to the roentgen—that they had received far more than fatal doses of radiation. They asked for nothing except that their film be recovered and developed and their plane buried by shielded bulldozers. They gave instructions about all that to an English-speaking airport official, who relayed them to our scientists, including the proper way to remove the film from its lead containers safely.

"Within an hour after the landing of their ship, one of the

eight men collapsed. Our brave medical people—doctors and nurses and others—insisted on trying to care for the victims. The still-able seven were asked to strip their clothes off. They were washed at a distance by hoses, and then taken to an improvised hospital, in spite of their protests of futility and of the danger even of touching them. All of them died within thirty-six hours. They were very brave men, those *Norteamericanos!*"

The announcer came again, and now he stood before a different map of North America, one where, from southern Canada into Mexico, the entire continent had been shaded, and in that shaded region, which included all of the United States, were some thousand or more black crosses.

"This map," Connie translated, "shows, in the shaded portion, where the very high sodium fallout had an intensity of at least ten thousand roentgens for at least a six-hour period. The crosses show where, to the best of our information, bombs of five to one hundred megatons struck. There were perhaps more hits than we here indicate. Much of the data on which this is based was given us by a United States aircraft carrier, gathered from monitoring gear in operation during the missile-fall and bomb-drop and from its own reconnaissance flights by unmanned planes, made some ten days to two weeks later. As you see, the United States of America was obliterated as a nation of cities, and burned to death after that in all main urban areas, then smothered the same night in a death blanket which could be escaped only in the most elaborately-prepared shelters. Doubtless some few missile and other military sites survived. In chance canyons, mines, and so on, some may also still be alive.

"But there *is* no United States, as this map discloses.

"Next," the sensitive man continued, "we shall show some extraordinary pictures of people in a Southwestern city of the United States, taken in the hours after the Soviet first strike began but before this city was purged of life by the sodium blanket." He looked off, questioningly, toward what obviously were the control-room people and, as plainly, he was signaled to continue talking, owing to some technical delay in the running of the next film.

"For those who have recently tuned in," he said firmly, let me repeat:

"This telecast is give in the interests of the future. It has been determined by the federal authorities of the Republic of Costa Rica that the films shown and those to follow, although they came by chance into our hands, should become the property of the surviving world. They represent, so far as we now are aware, the most complete and perhaps even the only record of the fate of the United States. Other such films may exist and may have been conveyed safely to other areas by unknown persons, but if so, they apparently have not been displayed on a world-wide relay satellite.

"Our purpose in the display and in displaying any future film we may receive, is simple. The surviving world needs to know—must know—what happened to the world that is dead. That knowledge is essential if, in the years and the generations to come, men are ever again tempted to employ as a military means such instruments as have eradicated most of half of our planet. And it is our solemn belief that no better way exists than this for instilling into all men and women and children who will look, the truth about such otherwise indescribable war and its victims, their helplessness, the pity of that . . . and so, the *total* folly of the men on both 'sides' whose decades of arming and whose concomitant failure to resolve—even, to lessen—that ever-more-appalling situation, resulted in suicidal madness."

He looked off again; this time he nodded.

The camera moved closer to the nameless Costa Rican. People in the audience stirred uneasily.

His face, Ben reflected, showed not just the empathy of an actor and an intense emotional expression, but it also suggested trained intelligence. The man was, perhaps, a scientist; almost certainly, a professor or teacher; although, on further reflection, Ben acknowledged it was possible he was a politician.

After all, he mused, Costa Rica had spent half of its total budget, for decades, on education and public health. Meantime, three-quarters of all the federal funds of the United States had gone for armaments, for what had been called "defense," which had now wholly failed, and for debts incurred by older wars, along with bonuses and special bounties to the veterans of those old wars.

Thus, by comparison, Costa Rica was many times more "civilized," in any realistic sense, than the now nonextant United States. Were the differences expressed in familiar terms, Ben thought, Costa Rica would long have been—what? A small mansion in a manicured estate, and by comparison the United States would have ranked as—what? A colossal pigsty!

To argue that the intransigence of the U.S.S.R. and Red China had caused that was not, actually, correct—even though such intransigence had obliged the United States to maintain and augment its status, although lesser than Costa Rica in real and human terms. For the United States had paid out most of its income owing to war, all Ben's life and even before the U.S.S.R. had been dangerous, while all that time half Costa Rica's funds had gone actually to education and to public health and not even to a token army, for the little country had none. Of course, the Monroe Doctrine had protected the people of Costa Rica. . . .

While Ben had acidly made that perhaps not precise but somewhat justified comparison, the screen had gone blank, then briefly showed the skyline of a city, gone blank again, and so, sent George Hyama hastening to the controls. After checking them, he said, "Okay, here. We'll just have to wait for them."

"They" presently recommenced telecasting. The same city skyline showed, rising at some distance from a flat plain that looked dry and hot. Texas, Ben decided. He thought he could name the city and was about to do so when the announcer's voice came, a little too loudly, Connie said, which made George flash back to the controls again: "We will not name the city you see in the distance because what you will see of the behavior of its citizens was *universal* in the United States where similar conditions prevailed. To name this particular place would be a libel. Its citizens were no more bestial, or brave, than others elsewhere under comparable conditions."

The screen now displayed a series of stock shots of the city in ordinary times . . . and Ben knew its name, for certain. So, he realized, leaning to look, did Farr. But Farr caught Ben's eye and gave his head a minute shake that meant . . . let's accept the Tico's wish and keep the place nameless.

Over scenes of residential areas, manufacturing districts, superhighways, schools, churches, and a swarming downtown section where skyscrapers rose in a pointed package (senseless seeming, amid such spacious environs) the announcer went on:

"This city, as I stated, did not receive any direct strikes or near hits. Why, we do not know. Most likely, missiles aimed at it or bombers briefed to destroy it were themselves destroyed by United States defense systems or planes. But perhaps they were diverted by the attackers, while on course, to more vital targets. In any case, the public behavior was violent.

"This city, like those that were not destroyed in the first hour or so of onslaught, knew about the disintegration of the nation in which it stood. The people in this city, like people in others and in countless towns and villages, increasingly anticipated the skyfall of doomsday upon themselves. They had prepared, like most urban areas in the United States, shelters in large buildings and, to some extent, home shelters, for community and private refuge from fallout. Of course, word that other cities, in the state where this city stands and in the forty-nine sister states, were being devastated, were in ruins or even in firestorm, did negate presumptive value of shelters in the minds of those few who remained able to *think* coherently. But that number, within a very short while after facts about the initial strike began to be repeated on the then-still-workable TV and radio stations in the city, must have been a small fraction of the total populace.

"The record of happenings we will show, commences about an hour after the first news of the staggering onslaught elsewhere had reached the inhabitants. The film was made by a motion-picture news photographer who was a plane pilot, too. He had been assigned, by chance, to fly that afternoon to Panama to film the annual Panamanian 'Day of Liberty' fiesta celebrating the demilitarization of the former Canal Zone and the turnover of the Zone and the Canal to the people of Panama.

"The news cameraman's name was Waldemar Schultz. Yes. Was. When he saw the rising panic of his fellow citizens, as details of annihilation elsewhere poured in, Schultz made every effort to get a record of the reaction. As his pictures show, it required enormous personal courage to achieve that goal. You will see, for instance, one scene that indicated not only the fact that Schultz armed himself, but that such a step saved his life, temporarily, along with the film he exposed.

"Only when the situation grew so perilous that further camera work was out of the question, did Schultz give up. By that time Schultz had realized that all streets and roads leading out of the city were impassible, owing to multiple collisions on such routes and even on country lanes—due, of course, to the crazed driving and the murderous speeds of people trying not only to escape but also to *get into* the city. In some instances that was done to try to succor friends or relatives, but far oftener the inbound rush was of people who merely wanted to see the 'sights' of a city reported in turmoil. In every disaster the morbidly curious pose just such needless and congesting problems to refugees.

"Schultz managed to reach the airfield he had expected to leave in midafternoon, much later and on foot, carrying his film but not his camera. The air terminal was in chaos as tens of thousands of persons tried to get passage south, from their dying nation and murderous city. No planes were arriving and few were leaving; the operating personnel had, by and large, fled the ticket booths, control tower, hangars, maintenance shops, and so on. Schultz therefore simply reconnoitered the smaller planes standing, in some numbers and still unused. He managed to start one and flew to San Juan, after landing for gasoline in Mérida, Mexico.

"His film was contained in tight, metal cans which were further protected by the metal sides of the airplane luggage compartment. Schultz himself, however, had no such protection. He flew with the cockpit windows open and at only modest altitude. In consequence he passed through some areas of invisible and therefore unsuspected radio contamination —the drift of hot, isotopic debris from hits on other cities than the one where he began his flight. He saw distant evidence of those strikes, including at least three firestorms, but he did not consider himself to be in any danger. Four days ago, however, like the United States Air Force men, Waldermar Schultz died of radiation sickness.

"The first of his dramatic, and horrible, pictures follows. It was taken from a high window in a downtown office building and shows some of the events around a large, marked air-raid shelter designated by the federal government and reinforced by the state. The shelter is underground, beneath a skyscraper hotel."

What appeared was a wide street filled, building-to-building and for the two blocks visible each way, with people. They seemed to be compressing.

Next came a closer view of the thousand or so persons nearest to the entrance of the hotel. The camera panned, as if sardonically, to show a sign over the heads of the jam-packed mob. It read "Shelter Area," and an arrow under the words pointed to the hotel entrance.

Now the camera returned to the mob and it could be seen that there was a strangeness about its members. That strangeness was explained by a cut to a still-closer view.

The people nearest the entrance, which was barred and boarded, were being literally squeezed to death. Many, already limp and motionless, were being supported by the press of those around them. From the mouths and nostrils of some—both the dead and the living—blood trickled redly.

Soon, individual faces were picked out and the agony, where they were the faces of the still-living, was as sickeningly fascinating as hideous. They were cheek by jowl with the dead but could not get clear an inch from the upright cadavers. These living, too, were being tortured. Where an arm or leg of a man, woman, or child had been allowed to stay free among the mass in some less-compressed time, or where a limb had been pulled or pushed away from its owner into the melee—they were being broken, dislocated, even pulled out at their roots. It seemed, in the minute or so of camera search, that the pressure grew greater, the blood-flow swifter, the agony more terrible.

Rib cages cracked with suddenness, like crates under trip-hammers, and people thus slaughtered were lucky, for they died quickly, in gouting blood-vomits or a last explosive belch of red-frothed air.

The announcer spoke, gently, Connie suggested by her tone:

"This shelter was well known, of course, and also known to be commodious and strong. Across the street some hour and a half before this picture was taken, people had formed a crowd owing to the announcement that a bargain sale in the store beneath the photographer was to open that day. The bargain-hunting multitude made the nucleus of the self-killing crowd you see. The shelter they seek to enter, of course, was filled within minutes of the first word of the national attack. Realizing that the almost-instantly crammed shelter would be subject to further assault, the hotel management put in effect a scheme readied for that possibility.

"Planks, backed by steel bars that fitted into prepared holes in the terrazzo entrance and overhead girders, were hastily emplaced. To no avail. For you will soon see the human ram break down planks, steel bars, and all, just as now you can see the tide of humanity pour, bleeding, against and through the great plateglass windows of the hotel."

They saw that.

Next they saw another, similar mob trying to force impossible entrance into a different shelter that, lucklessly, had lost its portal, or, perhaps, never got it closed. A ramp-like street led to an opening big enough to admit a truck. Now, however, the pressure of the mob on the ramp, against those in the shelter (fortunately, Ben felt, only dimly-visible) was so immense it was reasonable to assume (and the announcer did) that all those who had gained entrance to the shelter were lost. It had been built to accommodate nine hundred persons but now contained, the announcer said, five to six thousand or even more. These were already dead of suffocation, de-limbing, crushing, trampling, smashed chests, and blood-loss.

"To get beyond such often repeated scenes in the city's center," the evidently quiet voice went on, "scenes of stampede wilder and more deadly than any eruption of cattle herds, Schultz said that at several points he climbed out of second-floor windows, dropped on solid human masses and, in his own words, 'walked on shoulders and heads, being careful to try to pick dead stepping-stones where I could, as the live ones sometimes bit.' Fortunately for Schultz, he wore Western boots. These, however, plainly were badly torn by human teeth when he landed outside San José."

A series of not-dissimilar scenes followed.

Then the camera and its apparently nerveless (or un-human) operator had reached the suburbs. A shot of a clock on a church spire established the local time: three-five, and afternoon.

Next came a private-shelter version of the awfulness just witnessed in the downtown area.

First, they beheld a horde of persons—women in slacks, men in sports shirts, children in light clothing, the boys often shirtless—a typical hot-summer-day suburban group, of some hundreds. The crowd had gathered on the extensive front and side lawns of a large, handsome, modernistic mansion that immediately suggested Uxmal to the beholders. This mass of persons was motionless, or nearly so; it looked forward, as if waiting intently for some unguessable event. Then the camera moved and showed a face-on view of the stagnant, slack-jawed, irresolute, but strangely grim people. A third angle revealed the cause of their hesitation:

It disclosed a smooth, high rise of lawn and planted shrubs that covered with greenery and some feet of earth what plainly was a back-yard shelter of considerable size. Its access door was battened tight, and looked formidable. In front of that was a kind of earthwork and, peeping over its grassy verge, the muzzle of a machine gun. Now and again the face of a man, tense, middle-aged, and sweating popped up for a brief look at the crowd that coveted the safe, or presumedly safer, refuge of whomever this man was ready to defend, behind him in the shelter. At intervals a younger man, resembling the elder, also bobbed up for a look and to call out what evidently were warnings to the crowd.

The camera, as before, now examined individuals along the front edge of that ominous multitude. They were, by dress and general look, ordinary, middle-class suburbanites and, in some cases and by the same tokens, quite well-to-do people. People no doubt like the owners of the mansion and its commodious-looking, earth-and-grass-shielded, semi buried shelter. But there was nothing ordinary either in their silence and watchfulness or in the emotions on their faces. Some women fell to their knees and folded their hands to entreat, pointing afterward at children beside them.

Schultz had no sound-recording equipment but this tableau was self-describing.

Rightly or wrongly, these gathered neighbors and neighborhood people felt the builder and owner of the shelter—who now stood ready to defend it—could, or should, give admittance to a larger number of persons than those now behind its steel portal. As rightly, or as wrongly, the two defenders were adamant.

"Schultz," came the announcer's words by way of Connie, "says he was told by a number of people who weren't actually part of the crowd gathered on the lawn, that the owner was not liked, a 'mean type,' and that only his wife, two daughters, and three servants were behind that door . . . in a shelter large enough, the bystanders insisted, 'to hold a hundred people, standing, anyhow.' Whatever the fact, as you will see, the crowd decided, like others, to take matter into its own hands."

The ensuing shots showed a slow advance, perhaps owing, mainly, to pressure from behind but, somewhat, to hateful and visible belligerence. It moved perhaps twenty feet before the camera switched to the redoubt. From it, with no further warning, the machine gun commenced to fire. In a dizzy blurr the camera swung back and showed men and women and two or three small children as bullets hit them and sent them pitching backward, dancing in pain, bleeding, with baffled looks on their faces, or collapsing in weakening-jointed death.

The mob retreated some ways. As it did, men went

back and snatched up prone or writhing infants and young-sters.

Then, however, gunfire came from the crowd, as some few of the householders drew pistols and tried to hit the two defenders. After a time, since the machine gun remained silent and the youth did not appear above the green-grass parapet, the mob once more edged forward.

Although it reached nearer to the defense position—which looked like a golf-course bunker—the reaction there was sudden and formidable. The machine gun's jumpy bursts be-gan, and went on. And the camera tilted up to catch a series of objects hurtling through the air, then tilted back to watch them explode: grenades. They left, with the machine gun, a gory havoc that set the unhurt attackers running in all directions: a wriggling, tottering, yowling scrabble of people, of women without clothes, of a child crawling as its knees pulled out its own intestines, of a mother hugging a headless baby to a shot-off breast. . . .

Then it was later, and without comment from the narrator in Costa Rica they saw a lovely girl running down an empty suburban street, with an occasional backward glance of sheer horror. Three plainly drunken white men rose in her path and grabbed her. They commenced to strip off her clothes as she screamed and fought. But before she was quite naked, a Negro of great size, with the name of a Moving and Storage firm on his clean, white coveralls, ran into the scene carrying a heavy wrench. He began a quick, grim skull-splitting.

He then helped the girl to her feet and she ran on, nearly nude, blonde, fawnlike. But that was not the end.

The end was, perhaps, predictable.

The Negro, smiling a little, giving a kick of disgust at one of the downed assailants, suddenly sagged and a rose of scarlet opened on his coveralls. A slug had hit him from be-hind and expanded as it went through heart and rib cage, chest muscles, ebony skin, and his white garment. He fell.

A young man with a revolver in each hand tore into the scene, leaped the heap of dead drunks and the Negro savior, and stopped. He looked directly into the camera, his longish, curly hair falling back in place, his eyes narrowing as he raised a weapon. There was an instant in which his expres-sion, incredibly ferocious and yet, more incredibly, smiling, looked off in the direction taken by the girl. Then, his smile gone, the weapon steadied and bucked, with the result that the camera shimmied from a hit. Then the handsome, quite-young pursuer regained his unholy look of glee and recommenced his chase. But he did not get far.

Quite suddenly, he grabbed his abdomen and his body could be seen, as it toppled, to flinch from well-aimed bullets.

"Our cameraman, Schultz," Connie translated.

The photographer and his equipment had not, evidently, been seriously injured. For the lens swung up the street and showed that the running girl was not running any more. She lay, stripped, on a lawn near a flagged sidewalk and hardly had breath or strength left to fight the two men, then three, who had emerged from somewhere and caught her. Others were running up, grins on their faces . . . such grins as no one in the Sachem's Watch shelter had ever before seen.

At that point Farr shouted, "For the love of God, Ben! George! Cut it off!"

Ben did so.

Somebody switched on lights.

The stricken viewers looked, slowly, at each other.

They said nothing.

By-and-by, in ones and twos, they rose and left the Hall for their own rooms, still wordlessly.

Finally, only Farr, George Hyama, and Ben remained.

They looked at each other.

Nothing to say.

All questions answered.

They had overwhelming cause to believe, now, that they were practically alone, among the living, in all their once-fair, utterly-desolate nation.

They knew the answer, even to what "good citizens" would do if ever "the whistle blew."

And it was nothing to discuss at all.

Something to forget, as much as a man could.

Ben shrugged, realized his cheeks were wet with unnoticed tears, uttered one violent oath, and started away.

Farr said, *"Right."*

George Hyama, usually so buoyant, made the only complete comment that night, a single sentence: "I feel less bad, now, about the outrages my fellow Japanese committed in wars in years past."

He bowed then, ceremoniously; both men, without any sense of novelty or any self-consciousness, returned the bow.

Ben switched the lights off, leaving only a few dim nightbulbs to illumine what otherwise would be the total blackness of a hole, five hundred feet down, in a rock mountain.

11

FOR THE NEXT several days, the deep-dwelling survivors went about their tasks of housekeeping, cooking, furniture-making, machine maintenance, and the complex rest in a withdrawn manner. Laughter, which had become superficial but frequent, and had occurred over trifles, was not heard. Even Faith and Kit lost the unexplained coolness they had shown earlier in each other's presence. Not the mere abstract knowledge that the world—their half of it, anyway—was dead, but the dramatic display of how horribly and on what a colossal scale it had perished, left them stunned.

One afternoon—for the group still meticulously kept track of the outside time, although it would have been impossible, lacking clocks and chronometers, to tell one hour from another in the labyrinth—Vance Farr walked into the machine shop where Ben and George were hard at work, assisted by a very grease blackened and very concentrated Lodi Li, operating an automatic drill press.

Seeing Vance, the three workers shut off power. For Vance obviously had something on his mind. He slumped tiredly against a workbench and looked from face to face, his usually expressive eyes now showing only worry, his square, mobile face set with new lines of stress, and his mop of red hair rumpled and streaked, Ben then noticed, with a few strands of white. "How's it coming?"

Ben shrugged. "We're still trying to figure out how to use one of the two aerials that came through in reasonable shape, for outside sending."

Farr nodded. "I had six antennas installed in 'hard' bases. It's a little sad to think we could only get two of 'em to rise above their silos after it was over."

"Two out of six is dandy," George said sturdily, "when you consider the forces and temperatures they survived. And besides, six out of twelve self-reading, automatic-signaling radiation monitors! That is a near miracle!"

Vance shook his head slightly. "I was the one who supposed he could foresee everything, and arrange to come through anything. Except, possibly, a direct hit." He turned to Ben. "I gather you offered to show anybody how to tune the TV in the Hall, on any of the relay stations using them?"

"I did. Why not? After all, not everything eventually to be broadcast from South America, Africa, Australia will necessarily be like that Costa Rican stuff."

"I know. But nobody accepted your offer?"

Ben's head shook. "Afraid they'll tune in some more pictures of what happened here. Or what's happening still, in Japan, in the northern Philippines. One night, alone, I did. Got some shots of firestorm refugees." He shuddered.

Vance stared. "You've heard anything new?"

"More of the same stuff. On the small TV in the communications room. They're all dead out there, pretty much. And the rest dying. They've had a dusting every time the weather took a circuit of the earth, and now everybody, pretty much, has had it. Japan—Europe, too—what the Soviets didn't destroy in order to be sure nobody—England *or* France—had a nuclear weapon left."

"Something," Vance then said, "has got to be done to stop this blue funk. Whole gang of us acting like pallbearers."

"We sort of are," Lotus Li said in her small, precise voice. "Pallbearers for half the earth. The last to weep——"

"Not quite!" Ben spoke sharply, perhaps unintentionally. They stared at him, so he went ahead: "I haven't said anything, and I'm not sure I should now. But the seismographs have shown, for the last ten days, some individual missile hits, bomb bursts, here and there over the United States, and lots more in the U.S.S.R. Plus some very heavy strikes that I deduce to have been the hits of groups of missiles hitting the Reds—Russia *and* China."

Vance's eyes widened. He then scowled. His mouth made a flat line. He stared at the scientist as if angry. "How do you explain it, supposing it's not just—oh—nuclear arms that blow up, when fire finally reaches them? That *sort* of thing?"

Ben answered quietly, "I picked up, on radio receivers, some of the starts of our own stuff. *Account* for it? Easy, isn't it? Here in the United States—and to some extent, over there —they must have had quite a few very hard missile bases that were under orders not to reply to any early strikes, and to wait for word later, in the event our retaliation, and the Reds' double assault, left any targets whatever.

"I'd suppose those bases held out, waiting for orders, until their margin of security ran out—then they just shot. Wasn't it always obvious—it was to me!—that if you ever started a war like this, any people surviving who could do it, by *any* means, *would* keep on shooting at the enemy? Even run H-bombs from England up the Baltic in motorboats and explode them by hand, to recreate or crop-dust Leningrad? Fly bombs over the enemy even in commercial planes, and nose-dive? *Anything?* The fury of any survivors, taken with the fact they know they are probably doomed by radiation anyhow, will lead men on both sides to pointless acts of vengeance. It's *been* that way in war before. So, I used to say, it would be if we got in this. Only *more so.* And no central government or command remains to order a halt to men in charge of isolated posts or civilians with a weapon and a soldier to show how to explode it plus a way to get it across the sea. I think *that's* what's happening."

Vance brooded on that, after saying, "Horrible! But I suppose human nature!" Soon he added a fierce declaration: "By all that's holy! If *I* knew where to reach even *one* still-workable H-bomb, and if *I* could find a plane that would go the distance—so help me! *I'd* blast my way out of here, and go to that bomb—hot as the ground *still* is—and *take it over to 'em!*"

Ben's head bent in a sort of rueful agreement. Since Vance's eyes rested on him, still, hotly, and as if seeking blame, Ben said, "I'd be with you, because I could figure how to rig the fuse."

"Me, too," George said in an icy tone.

And pretty, soft-looking Lotus, giving a toss to her hair, now held with a silver hoop in a dark river that coursed down her back, said, so softly it was that much more shocking, "And I would also go, to see it hit them!"

For a moment the four people shared the blazing rage that by inference had been driving some fellow Americans and some Soviet people, soldiers or civilians, to acts of wanton wrath. Just seeing, in one another's eyes, and in drawn-back lips, the intensity of that mutual fury seemed to act as an emotional catharsis.

It was as if they'd said, "All right, I admit I'm insane with a wrath that is utterly pointless," and having said it, challengingly, having heard it echoed by all, they felt *relieved* in not being alone with an unendurable burden of tamped hate.

Vance finally grinned. "Good!" His eyes now shrewdly appraised the other three pairs of eyes. "I think, then, as a first step, we ought to conspire to get the whole gang admitting that not just shock, and not just anguish, not mere loss and grief, but *fury*, also, is eating us up. Because, after that maybe we can start the thing I came to discuss."

Ben lighted a cigarette, Vance accepted a light for a cigar and hopped onto a draftsman's stool. George held a match for Lodi's cigarette and his fingers shook a little; but he laughed at her delicate first puff. Lodi had not smoked before the entombment of the group. She was learning—for something to do, she said.

Vance waited till they found places to sit or perch. "It is recreation, I was talking about."

Ben said perplexedly, "But don't we have plenty? George and Lodi and I are busy all the time we have to spare—here, or in communications. You, your wife, and her gang, are doing wonders with furniture-making. It was an inspiration to stock all that lumber, carpet, water-base paint—what-not —so we could get the joint looking like palace halls and jewel boxes *after* landing down here! Valerie is a near-genius with colors, fabrics, everything of the sort!"

"Sure," Vance grinned again. "Val has taste, and imagination." He sighed with quiet regret. "And everything else that makes a woman a real damn wonder of a woman! By day." He shrugged. "But you guys are talking about *work. Hobbies*, or very valuable enterprises, all that is still *work*. We've got to start *playing*. Having fun."

Ben nodded. "See what you mean. Games—besides just bridge. Maybe——"

"Maybe what?"

"Well, Angelica is a dancer and Connie wanted to be one, and they've given some exhibitions. What about a *class?*"

Vance chuckled. "Exactly! Moreover, I've got a real stack of junk we can start to break out. Though I think we should do it a caper at a time, to stretch the novelty as far as we're able. For instance. Did you notice the kind of synthetic floor tile I had put in the Hall?"

George spoke when the other two were silent. "It's Owensite. Practically indestructible. And smooth as glass, if you wax it. Perfect dance floor. Yet a tank couldn't scar it."

"Right!" Vance responded.

That talk explained why, after dinner—and after a strange sort of confessional in which everyone present was led, casually, to express the rage that went locked with their separate sorrows—the mood of the group was deflected and reshaped, deliberately, by the four who had conferred.

All the furniture in the main chamber was swept to its walls. The rugs were rolled up. A stereophonic recording began to boom from a loudspeaker—a waltz. And Vance, accompanied by Ben and George, produced the evening's awaited "surprise." When little Dorothy saw it, she gave her first whoop of delight in that long time. *"Roller* skates!" she shouted, and ran toward the men, followed by her equally-elated brother. People rushed away to change shoes, or tried on shoes bounteously dumped from boxes by Vance, till they found a pair that fitted.

The music became the "Missouri Waltz."

George, among the first on the floor, swung expertly in reversing circles. Dot and Dick went tearing after each other with the sidewalk competence of kids.

"Haven't skated," Angelica yelled, "since I was sixteen! But here I come!" She immediately tried so difficult an evolution she fell down, hard. Laughing. Kit rescued her, set her back on her feet, and began experimentally to see if he remembered how to skate backward.

Vance and Valerie, who was not yet rubbery from drink, crossed hands and were soon skate-waltzing so expertly that Ben, arms pinwheeling to maintain balance, shouted, "You've done this before! *Cheats!"*

"Only on ice," Valerie called back. "When we were first married." And she said, so only her partner could hear, "Vance, darling, I'm beginning to be almost glad, in a hideously selfish way, that this happened. I mean, glad for me. *Us."*

"I know what you mean," he replied, and spun her into a twisting turn which he led with his finger tips.

She laughed. Her eyes shone now with something of actual luminosity. And her long, curly, dark hair streamed. It had been cut expertly. For the women in the group had soon learned, with delight, that Heliconia Davey had worked in a beauty parlor, to earn part of the cost of her college years—a beauty parlor that stayed open evenings, for students. And Valerie had decided—though Lotus Li had not—that long hair, in style at the time, was too much trouble under the existing circumstances.

Looking at her, feeling the rhythm of their singing skates, hearing the fond, familiar music, Vance thought, then said,

"Honestly, Val, there was never a lovelier female, anywhere, than you!"

She pulled close to him. "That brings up another matter."

"So?"

"We are, after all, married, Vance."

"Thank the Lord!"

"So, do we *have* to go on living in two bedrooms?"

The red-haired tycoon almost fell, in his surprise. "I have longed to suggest, dear, without having the nerve—too ashamed of myself—the very same idea I think you've just been *brazen* enough to——?"

She turned a skate sideways, stopped them both, kissed him. "I never cared a damn for another man. *Why*—who can say? Maybe it's your red hair. Shape of ears. That square, ugly-cute face. You're sure it won't give *others* ideas? Maybe we better just *sneak* together." She paled. "I'll—I'll *try*, Vance, to drink less, if you and I——"

Vance grinned. "Do that! But *sneak?* Didn't you mention we are married? Why be ashamed of its natural consequences and act like scared kids? As for giving people ideas, they already have 'em. *Look.*"

She looked, and chuckled.

George, the expert, was skating with Lodi Li, the beginner. He was giving her rather closer, stronger, and more constant support than the lesson required. And the Chinese girl's face was radiant. Her hair flew as George turned her. And she not only accepted his unnecessarily-close hold, but, while the Farr's watched, actually cuddled closer to the good-looking young nisei.

The skating went on for an hour. At its end Vance cut off the music. "Everybody!" he called gaily. "Tomorrow evening, from nine to ten, and every evening people want, we'll continue!" There were cheers, which he waved to silence. "Furthermore, for persons who wish to practice, I'll have a store-room on the 'A' Passage cleared entirely, and you'll find it's paved like this room. It'll be open to anybody, all day."

Dorothy shouted, "Even us *kids?*"

"Sure. Everybody. Now, it's bedtime for you and Dick. Some of you put back the rugs and furniture. It's my night to tell the youngsters their story."

A little later, with the bronze-headed children in pajamas (made, like all their now-handsome garments, from stocks of material, on sewing machines stored against such putative need), Vance Farr sat on the lower of the two bunks in the children's room. They had been far less miserable after they'd been given one room with a new-made, double bunk. The man said to his expectant audience:

"One upon a time, in a faraway island called Tasmania——"

"It's south of Australia!" Dick said proudly.

Dot said, "Shut up! Geography, fui!"

"—in Tasmania," Vance repeated, "there lived, in the rainy, cold forests, common there, a bear with a sad affliction. He was stone deaf. So, when he was little, he was often attacked, and sometimes quite badly hurt, by other animals, just because he couldn't hear them coming up, stalking. By the time he was—oh—half grown, his handicap had led him to develop other faculties, far more than is common in bears."

"What are 'faculties'?"

Vance thrust fingers in the little girl's chestnut curls. "Well, he learned to *smell* far better than any other, even fullgrown, Tasmanian bear. And *see* farther. And *run* faster. To make up as best he could for not being able to hear anything. So, in *some* ways, this youthful bear was a genius. His name, by the way, was Arbutus—which, his mother had heard, someplace, was a very rare and lovely flower that grew in a distant land. So she named her baby son Arbutus. And he became, as I said, in some ways a superbear. But he was still very sad. He never had heard the rain fall. Or birds sing. Or motorcars on the road that went through the forest. Or *music*—not a note!"

The story of how Arbutus, the Tasmanian bear, finally, owing to his heroism in saving two lost children, was rewarded, came in swiftly-contrived, expressive words from the ex-tycoon, who hadn't told stories to kids since Faith had been eight or perhaps younger. But these two didn't feel themselves overage for preslumber fables. No one had ever told them what they called "real stories" before: that function had been left by their parents to TV.

Now, with fascination, they listened to the man, who enjoyed his own invention as much as they, describe how Arbutus led two lost kids (just their sexes and ages) through the forest, fighting off most-unlikely tigers and lions, and delivered "Alice" and "Dewitt" at their own home.

"And their mother and father were so happy," Vance concluded, "after so many days and nights of dreadful worry, that, when they realized Arbutus was stone-deaf, they put him in their car and rushed him to Hobart, Tasmania's capital, and bought him—guess what?"

Dick did guess: "A hearing aid!"

Vance clapped the thin shoulders. "Right!"

And then he described the bear's ecstasy at hearing noises, and music, and whistling, and other things. Vance whistled to illustrate, whistled in a low and melodious way a lullaby that soon seemed to be having the desired effect, for he saw Dick's eyes shut the moment he had been lifted to the top bunk; and Dorothy stayed awake only long enough to blow Vance a kiss as he closed the door.

He went back to the Hall to see if Valerie was playing bridge, sewing, reading—or drunk.

She was merely waiting for him—smiling softly and trembling a little when, hand-in-hand, they said goodnight to the others.

Ben was hidden by a large volume concerned with electrolytic condensers, a part of the restudy of the mechanics of electric, radio, and electronic communicating devices, which his present work necessitated. From behind his book, however, Ben noticed the departure of Vance and Valerie and understood, with a surge of gladness for them, what it meant. A man and a wife, become that *anew,* and with renewed tenderness. A very extraordinary man, and a woman who, at fifty-odd, Ben thought, was more desirable to behold than most women at twenty. It was a plain miracle.

Covertly, he glanced toward Angelica, the latest of the many causes of Valerie's long distress. Angelica had, plainly, seen as much as Ben. And she watched with fascination as the older couple moved out of sight in the corridor. But it was, Ben thought, just that: interest, fascination; not wrath, disappointment, or scorn.

Now the voluptuous girl swung her head toward the back of sleek, suave Al Rizzo, playing bridge with Connie as his partner, against Lodi and George. The girl's eyes filled with contempt for Albert. They moved away from the Italian-American hanger-on of Broadway, who had not even tried for long to maintain their prerescue decision to pretend being brother and sister. . . .

Alberto had, instead, as Ben well knew, attempted to get Vance Farr to pay him money for maintaining that lie, and Vance had found himself in serious trouble. For if Ben hadn't interrupted the scene, Vance would surely have done his best to beat up the too-handsome boy friend of the young lady he had maintained at Candlewood Manor Apartments. And Vance might have been killed. Ben mused on that strange episode now. . . .

What happened had been embarrassing to all three men. "This lout," Vance said as Ben appeared, "was spending a lot of time with Angelica before the war. I didn't know it, of course, or I'd have done some stooging around till I caught him and, I suppose, beat the tar out of him."

Alberto, mean-eyed, white-faced, said, "You try!"

Ben came nearer the wrathful pair, who were alone in the library, the place where Alberto had found his chance to try to blackmail Vance.

"I think," Ben said quietly, "Mr. Rizzo has a switchblade. At least, he had one, when I sent him here through that tunnel."

Al whirled. "You wanna be stuck, too?"

"Nobody," Ben answered, "will be stuck, Al. Everything around here is on the level. Has to be. Nobody ever believed you were Angelica's brother. Or half-brother, as you said later. You ought to go down on your knees, every day, in front of Vance Farr, to thank him for saving your scrubby life."

"And a second time, flat prostrate, before *Bernman*, here, Al—for the same reason," Vance added, coldly.

"I'll take the knife," Ben said.

"Lemme see you!"

Underwater demolition training is among the most rugged of military drills. It includes training in hand-to-hand combat, both on land and, later, under water. What happened next was a small display of a skill learned by Ben in his years of voluntary service with the Navy.

He moved toward the slick-haired Rizzo on the balls of his feet, slowly. The man dug in a pocket and out came the knife, its long, silvery blade jutting from his hand with the click of a button. Ben edged some inches closer and feinted with his right. The knife flashed to cut the swift-extended right arm; instead the wrist that held the knife was caught by Ben's left hand. The grip was so much like that of a sprung steel trap that Al yelled. However, with the speed of his hoodlum *expertise*, Al snatched the knife in his still-free hand.

He was a little too slow, again.

Something—a hand-heel—took him under the jaw and almost broke his neck. Could have done so. Al saw stars and staggered back. The knife was then batted from his relaxing fingers. A face, inches from his own, with ice-blue eyes that bored into his swimming, black ones, said words. "Want more?"

Al barely managed to reply. "No. Okay. I'll play it on the level, now."

"What," Ben said sarcastically, rubbing his wrist, "would you have *done* with money, now?" He swept up the knife and turned his back on Rizzo. Then saw Faith, standing pale and horrified, at the library door. He froze, and could think of nothing to say.

Vance spoke. "Thanks again, Ben." He turned to his daughter. "Al was trying to blackmail me into his continued pretense he and Angelica are related. Damn gigolo! Ben wandered in. You saw the rest."

She said, "Yes. I saw it." Her eyes returned to Ben, in worry and wonder. "Where did you—oh! The Navy! I keep forgetting you left your labs and everything to——!"

Ben shrugged. Alberto slunk away.

Vance sat down in an upholstered chair and motioned Faith and Ben to do the same. The older man finally grinned. "Hell of a handy guy to have around, you are, Ben!" Then, almost to himself, he had said, "You know, I can't even remember *why* it was I found Angelica so irresistible."

"Because," Faith had responded quietly, "for one thing, she is. Is . . . what your generation called a doll or a dish. And very *nice*, as a woman, too, I'm beginning to learn. She was just brought up the hard way, is all."

Vance went on as if he hadn't listened, "Or the other pretty girls I cherished. Ever since we've been down here, I've been positively baffled by my reason for——" He shrugged. "I suppose it was the thing men did. Many like me. And after the first time—that was another show girl, Eloise. Then Valerie began drinking so much, it got to be a habit."

Faith said to her father, tartly, "It was the fact you thought you were fooling Mother that—that drove her nuts! If you'd admitted you had a playgirl complex, being Valerie, Mother would probably have cheered for you. She's that liberal—which, I must say, is carrying it beyond my notion of generosity or sense! But a sneaky husband! That she couldn't stand!"

"I know," Vance sighed. "Lord, I know! I wonder how many men as supposedly sane and even intelligent as myself get all balled up over a pretty face, tapering legs, batted eyes."

"Angelica," Faith had repeated, "is a lot more than that! Don't slander her! Or yourself! If I were a man and wanted a mistress I'd have picked one like her providing I was lucky enough to find one. Now, *stop* apologizing to all of us, for heaven's sake, Dad, and simply face the fact that your vanity took an uppercut, with Angelica's rescue! She won't make trouble! And I bet Al's through trying. So, can't you be a *man* about it all? Nobody ever thought you were perfect, and poor Mother only thought you'd always be more frank and candid than you've been till now."

Ben had left them then, the daughter still talking to the father as if he were a teen-ager caught in some off-base foolishness.

What he most remembered of that scene, which had occurred in the fourth week of their existence in the rockmaze, was the look in Faith's eyes when, having disarmed Al, he'd turned to discover her standing in the doorway: a look of such dazzling wonder, such sympathetic alarm, such shining approval, such—well, a look he could not name, really.

For Faith was Kit's fiancée.

Another strange association, besides the fast-growing and reciprocal interest of Lodi Li and George Hyama, was becoming manifest. Ben learned of it from those two, one afternoon while they started tests of the rotary spark-gap equipment they were building in the hope of being able to send, as well as receive radio messages from the surviving world. . . . .

Lodi and George were smoking together at the doorway of the communications room one day, while they watched as he started the rotor spinning and sent sparks flashing across the gap.

When he shut off the apparatus, satisfied with the progress, his two assistants were giggling.

"Joke?" Ben smiled.

George chuckled. "Connie. She just went by with Pete in tow. As per usual."

Ben's brows lifted. "Connie? And Pete? As usual?" He pictured the lithe, lovely colored girl, and the tall, shy, somewhat mousy meter reader. Lodi laughed musically and nodded. "They call it studying."

George said, heatedly, "They *study*, all right."

"Oh, sure! They hardly do anything else, when they both have the same time off!" Lodi chuckled again. "But imagine! A beautiful girl like Connie, and a sort of mama's boy, bean-pole type like Pete."

"Clarify." Ben grinned.

George said, incredulously, "Haven't you noticed?" And when Ben shook his head, he clarified: "For days now, Connie has given all her spare time to Pete. Nights, he does 'homework' she assigns him."

Ben said, *"Whaaaat?"*

"I mean *homework!* He's studying five freshman college courses. He only went through high, you know. And some geology at night school. Connie's the prof, for all five; though, when he needs to, and gets up the nerve, Pete'll ask questions of the rest of us. It's perfectly straight. She's trying to give him a start on a college education. They've got plenty of books for the quadrennium, as you know, and for virtually any graduate work a person could think of. But for the present, he's doing his first year at a speeded-up rate—in English, Latin, Spanish, college algebra, and geology. Geology— mineralogy, rather—was the poor oaf's hobby, anyhow. And Connie never took it. So *that* they're learning together. The other subjects *she teaches.* And he works like a dog! One day, recently, he asked me to look over his math lesson, before he dared let Connie grade it. It was about a week's work for the usual freshman."

"But," Lodi now took the subject a step further, "it's not *merely* that Pete wants to be educated and Connie has nothing better to do. They're *nuts* about each other!"

Ben said, "Be doggoned!"

"Why *not?*" The Chinese girl spoke defensively. "He's nice! And she's unbelievable! That shoe-polish-suave Alberto also is crazy for Connie. But she won't look at him! And why?" Lodi hesitated and then said it quietly: "I'm not a white person, either. Alberto *is.* And no matter how wild he got about Connie, he'd think, every second, she was colored. Pete—well, to Pete it doesn't matter. He's already forgotten he's white and she's black, at least mostly that, like most colored people. I'd say gold-brown, actually. So, naturally, Connie finds attentions from men like Al horrid. But when somebody doesn't remember color any more, that makes everything *different.* And Pete is so sweet and so very eager!"

Ben shook his head, his face showing some anxiety.

George had listened to Lodi with tense fascination. But

now, he laughed. "Don't worry about it, Doc! Everything is under control."

"Hope so."

George turned to Lotus Li. "Am I right?"

She nodded, eyes serious. *"Yes."*

After that Ben realized it was true and he had not "noticed" what he had just seen and, now, continuously saw. At mealtime Connie and Pete usually sat together. They had arranged the housekeeping schedule, which was shared by all, equally, so as to work together. And when the group was not at meals, asleep, or roller skating, at which they were gradually becoming proficient in various degrees, Connie, in slacks and blouse and slippers, black hair tied in a ponytail, could be seen in the library, or in some corner of a room furnishing at least partial privacy, quietly delivering a lecture to the tall youth with the smudge of mustache and the retiring glance.

Ben noted, too, that Paulus Davey, who was the least talkative and the most inconspicuous of them all (and who seemed, still, to be in partial shock over the loss of his wife and the rest of his family, and his world, too), would sometimes take furtive, anxious observations of his beautiful daughter's constant concern with Peter Williams.

Finally, on such an occasion, Ben had murmured to the gray-haired former butler, "Paulus! You mustn't worry. It's an *all right thing.*"

Brown eyes full of sadness were lifted. "I'm pleased to have you say that, Mr.—I mean—Ben. You see, Heliconia was a wild one, a few years ago. Then she settled down. I'd hate to have her change back. And I'd sure hate to have her shame herself with all these fine people."

"She won't, Paulus. I'm sure. We're all her chaperones, if that's needed."

Relieved, the old man had smiled, and gone away wordlessly to the kitchen. It was his shift on the dishwashing squad. . . .

And so the days passed.

Forty-two days, at last.

The random, intermittent bombing had stopped.

In the shelter Ben and his aides had their spark set almost ready for trial sending.

12

AND UNDER THE mountain ranges of the U.S.S.R., in certain caverns, and in two man-made, undersea living spaces, tens of thousand of the Soviet elite were readying Phase Three of the long-planned and ruthless program for dominion of the world—or, of its surviving half.

But though the first two phases had led to the near extermination of human and animal life in the North Temperate Zone and the same massive, horrible death everywhere in the U.S.S.R. (except in special places), their heinous program was not going to be carried out as they had expected: that is, with no further act of war by the once free, now blasted world.

Certain long-range American units, briefed before the war to meet any imaginable set of enemy depredations, were still operable. Not many. And even though an iron curtain, long kept more tightly closed than ever in the past, had not leaked a word of the Soviet's ultimate schemes, the Reds had been similarly unable, even by the most effective of all espionage systems, to uncover all of the American "Last Ditch" program and destroy its implementation entirely.

Thus, at the end of the agreed forty-two-day wait, and after reports were in, from very-high-altitude and heavily-shielded drone planes that, on clear days in late September, had photographed all of Europe and the United States (in their stricken and often still-smoldering ruins), the many thousand Red people stirred. They had maintained a discipline of quiet in two concrete dwelling places set on the bottom of northern bays—cells with intercommunicating tubes. Now they began preparations for emergence. The mountain caverns opened tentatively, too.

Such activities involved considerably more sound than the long but quiet purring of oxygen-supply machines and air converters and the soft hissing of air-filtration systems that went into use when the radiation outside made it needful—systems not unlike those in use where Vance Farr and his group lived.

138

When exit time approached in the submarine refuges—when the shielded boats were prepared for launching, when the pumps raised pressures in the flotation tanks, when the many motors to be used outside were given test runs; and even though the Soviet hydrophones, radiophones, and other detection equipment remained alert—a long, dark shape, deep beneath the Kara Sea, drifted to a stop. The United States nuclear submarine *Tiger Shark*, fifth of her (latest) class, and one of four still cruising the world's seas, had detected distant sounds of submarine origin but, plainly, of a mechanical, therefore human, causation.

Now, with "listening" devices far more sensitive than anything known to, or anticipated by, Soviet scientists, the *Tiger Shark* began to move again, gathering speed, but with engines and propulsion gear of such a sort that the most delicate Red instruments could not detect the deep, black approach of a hostile vessel still armed with mighty H-weapons and crewed by one hundred and eighty Americans dedicated to revenge and nothing else.

The skipper of the submarine *Tiger Shark*, like many men who take to the sea, had been born far from salt water, in Denver, Colorado. His name was Hugo Denton and his rank, commander. He was a fairly tall man, brown-haired, with piercing gray eyes; and his commonest expression was a disarming, attractive grin. An Annapolis graduate of the Class of 1962, he had distinguished himself in sports and scholarship, standing, when he received his diploma, seventeenth in his class and twice narrowly missing being chosen (because of the sheer superiority in height and weight of his opposite number on the Navy football squad) as an All-American end.

He had been given command of the new-class submarine two years before the appalling war that, in twenty-four hours, had left most of his countrymen dead and most survivors (save for those in some naval units) in mortal peril.

His selection for command of the enormous vessel, with her near-infinite range and her world-shaking arsenal, had been made only after the Navy brass had screened thousands of promising officers and picked this one for courage, brains, endurance, ingenuity, a natural aptitude for responsibility, for popularity with sailors and brother officers, and, above all, for the imagination he had displayed not only on gridirons in situations both emotionally and physically demanding, but in his Academy themes and essays. In many other ways, both before and after his graduation, Denton had proved himself. He had earned an M.A. in electronics at the California Institute of Technology, a salient point in his favor, considering the propulsion and weapons systems of the new, shark-class sub.

His officers and men called him "Dingo"—a nickname dating from Annapolis days, probably derived from Hugo and Denton, and referring, more or less, to "wild dog." He was actually not so much a wild dog as a shrewd, and now a very dangerous, *person*.

Turning this way and that in the conning tower, to read dials and receive messages relayed by a "talking Chief," Dingo Denton eased the *Tiger Shark* south beneath the Kara Sea. This, actually, is a deep gulf in the Arctic Ocean, north of Siberia, protected from the Scandinavian Peninsula by an island that is almost a peninsula and is called Novaya Zemlya. It was for many years the site of large, Soviet nuclear tests.

The *Tiger Shark* moved ahead in that region, kept above the shoaling bottom of this sea by her electronic Fathometer and by set, automatic controls. It moved until, fearing possible Soviet subsea scanning comparable to his own, Dingo signaled for the extrusion of specially designed sound-reflecting gear. Held in position ahead of the advancing *Tiger Shark,* this apparatus would show up, if at all, on enemy instruments as a school of large but not phenomenally-large fish, thus masking the boat.

The skipper found it difficult to believe what his outreaching wave-detectors were reporting: the existence, under waters some distance off the Siberian shore, of about two miles of installations, from behind which came, increasingly, evidence of people and machines in vigorous activity.

He called in a whisper—the order for total silence had long since been given—for the most recent Intelligence reports on this area.

These were supplied by an equally astounded communications officer.

Such intelligence, by that time, was everywhere fairly elaborate. The "open-skies" policy of free, international surveillance, first suggested by President Eisenhower, had been rejected by Russia's then-Premier, Khrushchev. It had been followed by the U2 espionage-plane fiasco. However, by the early 1960s both nations had orbited vehicles capable of photographing all the earth and of being recovered, as well as other vehicles with the capability of sending back television pictures of the scanned globe.

From such sources the *Tiger Shark's* skipper now refreshed his memory.

Railroads had been built to the vast nuclear testing grounds on Novaya Zemlya long ago. A port had been constructed in Kara Bay at the southeastern end of the similarly-named sea. Deep-covered iron ores had been discovered at the northern terminus of the Ural Mountains in the 1960s. A year later coal deposits, similar to those in Spitsbergen, were found on Northland Island, far to the east. These resources, together with the costly but dogged Soviet effort to develop its sub-arctic lands and waterways, had led to a swift build-up of docks, smelters, steel mills, and many fabricating plants around the port.

Vast movements of freighters, railroad freight cars, tank cars and, with the completion of a modern road linking the port with the industrial complex east of the Urals, an enormous amount of trucking had been noted for years. It was now obvious to the skipper that under the cover of such extensive operations, the Soviets had managed, probably by working at night, especially in the long polar nights, to create, offshore and well below the sea surface, a virtual city—a honeycomb of ferroconcrete caissons, probably, sunk and interconnected, manned and equipped for some sort of post-nuclear-war emergence. The data received made that conclusion almost certain.

He shared this thought, which was being constantly more clearly revealed by the *Tiger Shark's* far-probing "search" equipment, with his Exec, Lieutenant Commander "Bunch" Cunningham, of Atlanta, Georgia, and, also, Annapolis. The Exec, almost white-haired from birth, with a rubicund, long face and narrow, steely blue eyes, was stringy of build. His nickname thus reflected a commonplace choice of opposites, for familiar address. He gravely studied the data, both that being gathered and the details on file. His final, whispered suggestion, was, "Even if it's as broad as it is long, we could pop one Amanda-B rocket in its middle and bust the works!"

"Thought of that! But, *look*. All the dope we've gotten from our own people, so far, makes them sure almost every Soviet citizen, soldier, and sailor is kaput. *You* know! When our retaliatory stuff was launched and airborne, word went out that the Reds were hitting all our cities, and every dam' missile and plane of ours was redirected that needed to be. So—and *no wonder!*—the Pentagon assumed—the dispersed brass, I mean—the U.S.S.R. was a slag heap, like home. Only, here's a *colony* of the so-and-so's alive! Under this dam' ocean! Suppose there are *more?* In *other* seas? Under the mountains? Dug in deep, anyplace? Suppose we are absolutely right not only in the assumption they picked their ideal day and hour for starting the massacre, but that enough of them, and enough thermonuclear stuff, were by then snugly stowed, so that they could come out, by-and-by, and take over what's left? That, and only that, would explain perfectly why the Soviets deliberately knocked off everybody, including the entire nuclear-weapons cache that Red China was building up. Which the Soviets must have done, judging from *that* series of blasts. I merely mean, would they, in such a case, just have this *one* safe spot?"

"We can pop it, and go look for the others."

"And warn 'em—so, maybe, not locate them? And maybe get sunk *ourselves,* by a Red nuclear boat still cruising. Or by still-ready land-based rockets?"

Bunch Cunningham nodded. "Could be." His long face was crosshatched with wrinkles of concentration. "Wouldn't be a bad idea, yours, Dingo! With the United States and Europe totally out, with nobody else, anywhere, having even a few leftover H-weapons! And blast and damn the Aussies, incidentally, for finally refusing to let England test there any more, and for making the poor dam' British take their stuff back home! I mean, if a nation arranged to wipe out *all* nuclear danger, though it got rooked by doing it, and if it *then* poked out its pre-saved heads, even a few thousand Reds who still had some stashed H-stuff would be a cinch to take over. Take over all hands still on deck—all the folks below the equator, and a few more."

Dingo said, "Yeah."

"Maybe we better stick our nose out and break radio silence?"

"Maybe." The skipper turned to the Chief, who stood near, wearing headphones and a throat mike. "Tell 'em to back away, maintaining silence, maintaining the screen, and using the silent propulsion gear only."

"Aye aye, sir."

"You going to start talking?" Bunch Cunningham's eyes glittered with excitement. Great excitement, since the *Tiger Shark,* like certain other American nuclear subs, and one ship had maintained complete radio silence for six weeks now. At first they had waited orders to carry out "Operation Last Ditch," which involved errands of horrifying redestruction. But such orders had never come.

Commanding officers in the ultrahard, land-based missile silos had, however, finally fired, as their endurance-time grew short and as Soviet missiles continued to hit the United States in random patterns of, apparently, mere savage vengeance. Having hurled at the enemy such missiles as they still could, they left their deep-buried posts with their command and returned to the barren surface, of necessity.

Some aircraft carriers had done the same thing early in the war. They had paid for their independent plane-launches and assaults; they were located and destroyed by submarines or from remaining Soviet bases. But several shark-class subs, on standing secret orders, stayed silent and "alive" as did one aircraft carrier, which had been refused permission to berth, by Australia, some while after the holocaust and had since presumably cruised aimlessly in antarctic waters. Even these were unable to carry out the secret plans to the letter: receiving no orders, they had simply maintained their instructed silence and listened to such reports as they could intercept, from any and all stations in operation, in their movable places on vacant areas of open sea.

The Exec's enthusiastic hope that at last the *Tiger Shark,* one of the few undestroyed, long-silent, but still-deadly American units, might announce its continuing existence and its ready state (not to mention the cold and ruthless fury of its crew!) was understandable enough to the skipper: the announcement might get a reply—an American reply, or even replies. But after some thought he shook his head regretfully:

"Nope, Bunch! We're going to back out of here, going deeper as the Fathometer permits, till it's safe to turn around and whip due north. Then——"

Then, in a matter of many hours of at first slow, finally swift, northing, just before the fall of the now lengthening arctic night, the *Tiger Shark's* periscope emerged, between the ice cakes of a broken floe. After a careful, 360-degree search, her snorkel and then her conning tower rose, scattering ice chunks with a roar. At last her decks came clear. Men in radiation-shielding arctic clothing then charged on deck wearing masks and began the strange operation of wiping down the wet, somewhat rusted plates of the sub's "sail," or superstructure. That job completed, they applied themselves, in the dark and using dimmed hand-lamps, to a second, odd chore: all the upper works of the boat were painted white. Thus, when the sun again rose for its next brief curve across these wastes of polar ice, the visible part of the boat gleamed white, and near-unseeable, amid the ragged heaps of berg and pack ice around her.

Meantime, Kim Daley, the communications officer, had not slept.

Trying one frequency after another, one channel after another, now this communication band, now that, he had gathered in hundreds of messages—most, mere scraps of useless international talk from below the equator, but a few, of consummate interest.

In the morning, on orders, he wakened his skipper, after the latter had allowed himself a three-hour sleep. Seeing Daley, and as he put on those few garments he'd removed, the skipper said, "You got news for me, eh?"

"Plenty!"

"Okay. I'll grab some coffee. Come on! Anything from the U.S.S.R., though?"

"I'll say!"

When they were alone in the officers' mess with two mugs of coffee, the skipper's "black," Daley's "blonde and sweet" —in Navy parlance, sugared and with cream—Daley's report began.

"All the Soviet signals were in code. Brief. And fairly short-range. But *Russian alphabet.* Besides——!"

"You got *fixes?*"

Daley nodded. "The whole navigation gang stayed on it all night. The enemy is talking from what seems to be three spots down in the Caucasus area, under the mountains. From made caves, I'd think. Three more in the Urals. One in Baikal area. And one in the Sea of Okhotsk, inside Kamchatka. A job like the one we located yesterday, we assume. And just before the sun rose, our lads tuned in on *our* little Soviet submarine city, loud and clear. Millen, Davis, MacKaye, and Dunn are sweating to break the code."

"Even if they can't, we've got *nine* of the hide-outs staked! Boy!"

"We could handle up to a dozen. *Easy!*"

The skipper was annoyed. "Buried how deep, under mountains how high? With openings how small? And how well blocked up? We could hit, or hit near, all nine, but we gotta get *help,* if there is any to get, to make sure all of maybe

nine, or ten, or twenty—are given a dose that'll make it not
just red-hot in their holes but, if we can manage, not even
possible to walk away, for a long, long time! Besides, we
gotta try to make sure that the points of sending you located, aren't remote from the damned ratholes! Aren't
blinds. Again, if that can be done! So what we do first——"

"Break radio silence?"

Dingo ignored that. "—is, get on down below the equator—fast—checking at night, for new bearings on the ratholes, and *then* let out a peep, to see if anybody else can
join what, I hope before God, will be a really total massacre.
The ——s!"

Daley responded to the lurid names his skipper had called
the enemy with a smile devoid of amusement. "I'll buy that!
and raise it to the *n*th power! History's most treacherous,
murdering huns, vandals, barbarians, you-name-'em, were
amateurs, compared to those Soviet—hell! there's no word
in English that *fits* 'em!"

"Yeah," Dingo nodded. "Anything else?"

"Lot of miscellaneous stuff, giving a better idea, if we
needed one, that what we used to call the good, old U.S.A,
ain't! And——"

The captain was hurrying away when he heard the last
word. He halted. "And——?"

"—one, kind of odd thing." Daley shrugged and went on,
since the skipper waited. "We got a message, in plain Morse
code, sent rather well but by an amateur, the gang thought,
from *some* spot in the New England area, where a handful
of American *civilians* are still holed up."

Dingo said, almost disgustedly, "Hell! In spite of the shooting and the sodium bath the Reds gave the home folks, there
are probably thousands still alive! Temporarily."

"I know. But these folks are far better fixed even than
any military people in rock mountains. Against the worst.
Better off than those who've shot their wad, come out, and
died."

"*Yeah?*"

"Thought you'd like to know that. Twelve men and women.
Two kids. Asking 'anybody' to answer, and stating they
are set for an indefinite period. Their words. Giving their
exterior radiation level at sixty-three roentgens. And other
data. The poor-so-and-so's!"

The skipper smiled briefly. "Maybe a day will come when

we can answer 'em—even go *get 'em,* somehow! Though, more likely——"

No need to finish. More likely, in a final mission, the *Tiger Shark* would pay the price its officers and men knew other submarines had paid for striking Russia, however swiftly they'd submerged and however stealthily rushed away: convergence of Soviet subs and planes from unknown but still-secure regions, on the belated attacker; discovery; and extinction in subsea nuclear upheavals. Still, now, there seemed a thin chance. . . .

The "poor so-and-so's" for a time had been sending their dispatches over the radio set Ben had designed, to employ available antennas, and with on-hand materials. They ceased to flash forth their, for a time, regular announcement of the group's location, status, safety, long-range living capability, and so on, after some weeks. The reason for ceasing baffled them:

No one had replied.

They had listened to countless distant stations that seemed *able* to reply, if they wished. But nobody did.

What could be inferred from that silence?

After lunch, on the sixty-first day underground, Farr launched on one more repetitive discussion of that startling circumstance.

"Of course," he said, "the answer is, they are *scared* to reply to our signals. Ben is sure and so am I that we've been heard—in Africa, Latin America, Central America, probably even Australia. *Why* are they scared to respond, then?"

"There could only be the one reason we've already mulled over," Ben said slowly. "They won't respond because they still fear some sort of Soviet retaliation. On *them.* Which means they must know or at least suspect that the Reds still have, somewhere, the power to hurt, and hurt bad."

Faith spoke—Faith, who had proven to be very well informed about the Soviets and had steadily added to that unexpected knowledge by reading, since their immolation. "Perhaps nobody in the Safe Zone—" they'd come to call the nonradiated half-and-more of the planet by that term—" has the nerve, yet, to do anything but care for themselves and yell for help, for themselves. I mean, maybe they feel their internal troubles will continue——"

George interrupted, "There've been no H-shots for weeks."

"Do we know everything's over, for sure?" Faith smiled

apologetically at George. "After all. Does anybody? Was there any surrender? Are Commies in the Safe Zone raising hell? Has victory been proclaimed by a single soul?"

"I agree with Faith," Vance said. "She's argued, whenever this thing came up, that the Reds had the world so scared, even before they erased the Temperate Zone and got rubbed out for doing it, that no one will risk anything that sounds like a friendly act toward the United States, even if it concerns only a mere fourteen Americans."

"Oh, heck!" Peter "the Meek" (as they occasionally called him, in amiable, private talks) said that. "Surely, somebody has guts enough to radio something to us! I'd do it!"

Vance chuckled. "By golly, Pete, I believe you would! But remember, you haven't survived a world holocaust *outdoors!* It may make a lot of difference."

Valerie re-entered the Hall just then, saying, "Who's for roller-skating practice with me?"

She completed the cheery question, then staggered.

The seated people felt the Hall heave, the floor shake, the passages vibrate. An alarm bell rang in Passage C—a bell that meant something had stopped one of the diesels.

Dust and bits of stone fell from the now pale-rose ceiling, far overhead. The earthquake was repeated, less violently. Then, it seemed, the deep-buried labyrinth began to shudder under an interminable but diminishing series of temblors.

Ben leaped to his feet, got his balance, and rushed for the seismographs. George was on his heels. Lodi, just then entering the Hall, pale and questioning, turned to follow without a word.

The instruments soon let them compute, in general, what had happened—what was, in fact, still happening, in a wave of titanic explosions that moved westward from the Atlantic Coast to the Pacific: a great sweep of the United States by many hundreds of blasts.

While the group had been considering any possible further Soviet menace, the menace had materialized. But not really as a coincidence, inasmuch as they spent many hours over the question, once they had slowly, and dejectedly, realized their signals were not answered.

Ben began studying the zigzag lines drawn by the quake-measuring instruments, racing to those located at the far-thest-practicable distance and gathering more material there, making pencil calculations for which George and Lodi ran about gathering data from other recording devices. In half an hour they could report. By that time not even the faintest tremor could be detected.

A computer had spilled out a string of figures and letters, a message coded in its special language. Ben translated it to the entire group standing in the passageway:

"It looks," he said hoarsely, "like this: some three hundred or more bombs, of about one megaton each, exploded in about five bursts per cluster, near the ground, starting here. One, the biggest shock we felt, was very close to us. These shots moved east to west in a random but apparently pretty thorough plastering of all the United States. Some short while after each burst of five or six near-the-ground warheads, a real monster of a blast in the atmosphere far above went off. Say, about sixty-seventy of such high bursts of, maybe, fifty megatons each."

"It's insane!" Vance Farr cried from the passage.

Ben nodded. Then leaped to his feet. "The counters!" he shouted, and rushed toward another chamber.

There, again assisted by George and Lodi, he first listened with earphones to a roar of "clicks" far too fast for enumerating. Then, as his two assistants switched them on, he, Vance, Valerie, and the others looked numbly at dials that computed outside radiation levels at various distances around the top of Sachem's Watch.

Those dials had shown for weeks a steady drop in the outside count. But now they were quivering up and up until they reached a point at which Ben and George switched them over to other mechanisms designed to register not in hundreds but in thousands of roentgens. And those big-scale dials moved, shakily, up and up, past two thousand, three, four, five, and continued climbing.

Farr cursed softly.

His wife prayed, in a clear, quiet, steadying voice.

Nobody else spoke for a while. They kept watching Ben and his two helpers. George and Lodi merely gazed at their chief. He was reflecting, leaning against a naked stone wall in a room jammed with equipment and piled with electronic "black boxes," his body relaxed, his blue eyes blank, his fingers tugging at his scimitar-like nose. Presently, still oblivious, he lighted a cigarette. And at last he turned to speak:

"It can only be one thing, I believe. If I'm right, a mighty ingenious, a devilish, thing. A thing probably set up to go off at this late date automatically or, maybe, on command. A battery of specialized, invulnerably-hidden super-rockets—less than a hundred, if our computer's correct. This battery—or these batteries—have sent over the Atlantic huge rockets that in turn ejected toward the American earth five or six smaller rockets apiece, accelerated so as to strike the earth far ahead of the main vehicle. The comparatively small ones blew up on or just above ground. Then, after they'd exploded, but not long after—the timing had to be good! the big hydrogen warhead in each still-high-up main rocket went!"

Lotus, whose *expertise* in mathematics had already been applied in many practical fashions new to her but in which she had proven extremely able, said, softly, "I *think* I see! It was rigged so the big, high burst would blow *back toward the ground* some great part of the hot material from smaller H-blasts beneath, pressing it back, to spread out in the lower air, *instead* of rising to the stratosphere?" She looked inquiringly at Ben.

He nodded. "Must be."

"But *why*, at this late date, in the merciful name of heaven?" Farr asked.

Ben tried to speak in measured tones. "Well. First, we long ago had some piggyback rockets a lot like that, though without the big high bang, delayed feature. So it's a workable gambit, rocketwise. Second, because as the counters made plain, the one-megaton low-level bursts were very dirty. Very radioactive. H-bombs with cobalt jackets, maybe. Cesium. Strontium. Take time to tell, by measuring the radioactivity from its peak into the first phases of decrease. Time to calculate half-lives of the hot elements to be sure *what* they used. And Lodi's correct. The big bangs high up, pushed back the already-rising, very radioactive lower bursts, and so, spread the fallout. Very smart."

"But, man, *why?*" Vance's voice was tortured.

"I suppose," Ben said, and by then the entire company was pale with dismay, "because the enemy figured that around now, any remaining, safely-sheltered Americans— civilian or military—would have about used up their facilities for holding out in shelters or caves that maybe did spare a few mountain people this long, or people in mines, or in certain military 'hard' bases that I've heard about. Three weeks was the civil-defense idea of a time limit for safe coming-out. The military, I believe, figured on about sixty days for its 'hardest' installations."

"Wasn't it *enough*," Farr said hollowly, "to soak us with sodium?"

"Evidently not." Ben's head shook in a sort of angered stupefaction. "Plainly, they wanted to make *sure*, when enough time had passed, that the United States would get one more *general lathering of hot isotopes*. And it, I think, will be something that will *stay* hot for a long stretch. Not like the first, sodium shots from the seas, with their half-life of a mere fifteen hours."

"Like *how* long and *how* hot?" Vance asked almost in a whisper.

Ben shrugged. "If it's cobalt, cesium, or strontium, the half-life could be fifteen to twenty-five years. Oh, hell, Vance! I can't say! Could be sodium again, and soon gone. *Could* be, if my interpretation's in error. We'll simply have to wait and watch the radiation count."

Stoically, perhaps even with considerable hope, they waited out the initial hours that followed the delayed devastation caused by what certain Soviet war-planners had long termed Phase Four.

The count did not rise to the fantastic levels measured in the hours and first days after the sodium bath of the nation. But it reached some five thousand roentgens, plus or minus a thousand, depending upon the location of the counter radioing measurements from the bleak landscape above and around them.

As days passed, that new level fell very slowly. Ben concluded, tentatively, that the nation, this third time, had been "salted" with radioactive isotopes of cobalt. In that case, much of it would remain too "hot" even to step on, for a long, long while. Years . . . in most areas.

A few moments of exposure to any surface dusted with radioactive material of that intensity would result in certain death, even for a person plucked into some safe area afterward. Continued exposure at that level, as Ben and those who had begun reading up on the medical literature of radiation-poisoning and death knew, would cause sickness and sure dying, in less than an hour.

This third assault had still another effect upon the occupants of Farr's shelter. Fiendishly planned, mechanical, executed by Reds who were now dead or, at best, alive as a remnant not unlike their own, it added a new kind of anger to their depression: an infuriated feeling that a large and so-called scientific part of mankind—a Russian part—

had thought of humanity as if the species was a kind of bug. It was enraging because it was so *belittling*.

Ben kept to himself, in consequence, certain of the likely aftereffects of this toxic and massive new showering of the United States by a blasted Soviet Union. It was bad enough that his shelter companions knew the long-range physical effects to be expected. Such added biological and, especially, ecological effects as were bound to be caused by the new bombing, sure to be multiplied enormously by it, were not thoroughly understood and had, in prewar days, been largely ignored by engineers and military men.

Many biologists and radiobiologists had long tried to break through the curtain of disregard maintained by those physicists, soldiers, and politicians too, when they contemplated nuclear war; but the dire concepts of the biologists concerning the unlivability of continents after nuclear assault (owing to the strange effects of radioisotopes in and on living things) had seemed too unearthly, improbable, incomprehensible, insufficiently proven, and unresolvable for most experts in war and for their principal scientific advisers.

Even without the grewsome expectations Ben now envisioned (since he was one of the few physicists who had listened to the biologists), the mere fact that the United States had once again been lethally "crop-dusted" with hot material of a much longer half-life than that of sodium oxide, reduced people in the shelter to an unprecedentedly high level of frustration and so, in certain cases, to a new fury.

There had been quarrels in the past, of course.

But in the immediate aftermath of this thing, there were more quarrels. Tempers burned hot and broke out with slight cause. It was a situation bound to lead to explosion. . . .

One evening, at bridge, Pete the Meek scowled suddenly over some misplay he attributed to George Hyama, his partner. George, usually in control of a temper that was, however, mercurial, saw the scowl and said instantly and sneeringly, "If you didn't like that finesse, say so!"

"It was stupid," Pete responded, paling but continuing. "You ought to have known from the bidding that the king of clubs was in the other hand."

George's chair fell over as he stood. Valerie and Faith, playing opposite the two men, normally would have intervened then. But the prevailing mood was abnormal. Besides, Valerie was consuming a fifth or sixth highball and not herself.

Pete thereupon strode around the table and Valerie said, thickly but with a certain taunt, *"Fight?"*

Faith spoke bitterly to nobody in particular: "Oh, for God's sake!"

Her disgust and her mother's fuddled, approving cry launched Pete at George.

For half a minute the tall man and the wiry Japanese stood toe to toe, slugging each other. Valerie shouted hoarsely when either landed a hard blow. Faith ran from the room and found Ben. He raced back ahead of her, in time to see both combatants stagger apart and stand, panting, bleeding from cut faces, but gathering rage to go on. Ben lunged between them, face fixed. "Quit it, you idiots!" His voice was so high and so stressful that it astonished everybody. That tone had never been used by Ben before. Pete and George glared at each other. Ben shoved both apart with his long arms, sent both sprawling. They rose, after that, Pete daubing his cuts with a handkerchief and George wiping skinned knuckles on a just-pressed, clean jacket.

Nobody had heard Kit enter the Hall with Angelica in his wake. But they heard Kit's words, addressed to Faith: "So a fight started and you went for help from our Navy-trained, judo-Jew! Why not for me, *darling?* After all, I boxed in college!"

Faith said, "Oh, simmer down, Kit! I didn't know where to find you."

Kit was staring at the now embarrassed Ben. "I wonder," he said, nastily, "if you really are a better man than I? I've got fifty pounds on you, about. And I never did believe your dirty fighting tricks could stand up to a real man, even handicapped by only knowing how to fight *fair*."

The others looked from Kit to Ben.

In that next moment Ben nearly succumbed to the general stress and the sense of helpless anger. He almost invited Kit to "put 'em up," with an offer to stick to the Marquis of Queensberry rules. Ben felt he would like to find out for himself whether or not he could outbox Kit Barlow. But though his lips began to frame a challenge, his voice never sent the defiant words through them. Instead, he said, "Don't be childish. So things are worse outside. Is that a good reason to worsen things here? If we ever get away, it'll be by sticking together. Not"—he turned from the flushed Kit to the now humiliated George and Pete—"by acting like kids."

Valerie Farr poured half a tumbler of whisky into the remaining half of her highball. Her too-wet, too-bright eyes fixed on Ben. "You ruined," she said unevenly, "a peach of a fist fight!" She lifted the glass to take what they knew would probably be the evening's final self-dosing of alcohol that would send her weaving and swaying to her room and alcoholic unconsciousness.

But she did not drink. Instead, her eyes focused, imperfectly and by accident, on Angelica, who had simply stood watching the violences. Watching miserably. And Valerie Farr saw the misery. Very slowly, she sat down the whisky-laden highball. To nobody, she muttered, "I *encouraged* that fight!" The words were spoken in a sort of shamed wonder.

Faith said, "Forget it, Mother."

But Valerie was still eying Angelica. She said, "Come here."

The black-haired girl half closed her sapphire eyes and stood where she was, paling a little.

"Come here!" Mrs. Farr's tone was clearer and contained command.

So Angelica drew near, with reluctance, even fear.

Faith watched the highball, fearing her mother would use it, and her sudden-released but endlessly pent-up emotions, to hurl on the lovely ex-mistress of Vance Farr. Valerie did no such thing. When Angelica was almost within touching distance, Valerie said, quietly, "I want to apologize, dear, since all our emotions are being stripped naked tonight, for treating you as I have, ever since you came here."

Angelica's eyes widened. "But you've been perfectly wonderful to me. When you consider that before the war, I——"

"The hell I have! I've gone on getting half cockeyed, night after night, almost as I did all the years when Vance cheated me and pretended a sickly innocence. We've been in this stone trap over two months now, child, and I've kept on drinking. Without cause. But *you*. You never even gave my husband the eye. It's you who've been the——" Valerie said a word she had usually employed with scorn but now meant in its ancient sense—"*lady*."

This scene was watched in silence.

And it was swift-ended.

With a reach and swing Valerie Farr retrieved her drink and sent it, ice, glass, and all, spinning and spilling, over the floor lamps and the pretty, hand-made furniture to smash against the beige paint they'd applied to the once-grim walls. She then closed the little distance between herself and the lovely Irish-Italian girl, threw her arms around Angelica, and kissed her. "You're an angel, and I'm tired of being a bum. You *and* Vance deserve something better!"

Head high, she left the Hall.

Faith whispered, "Lord!" and ran to Angelica, who had started to weep.

George Hyama said to Ben, "Sorry I mixed it up." He turned to Pete, hand out. "Apologies!"

Pete said, humbly, "It was my fault," and took the hand.

Faith made the statement that ended the matter. "If this fracas has caused Mother to see what she's been doing to herself—to all of us—it'd be worth staging every day!" She smiled tentatively at Pete and George. Then Ben. Then Kit.

It would be weeks before they were certain—Farr, especially. But, in time, they were to know that Valerie Farr had meant it.

She never took another drink.

The ensuing days were marked by a phenomenon they had already experienced, the scrambling of TV and radio signals. For a time they were out of touch with the voice of surviving humanity. Gradually, however, the messages began to come in clearly.

They learned that the Costa Ricans and others to the north of them now had suffered. "The hideous and evil monstrosity perpetrated by automatic action in a dead U.S.S.R.," as San José put it, "caused new millions to take all precautions against poison-clouds that, thousands of miles in length and about twelve hundred miles wide (at first) are now repeatedly circling the globe, with ever-diminishing radioactivity, but with ever-widening menace."

When a frozen turkey was served with trimmings, in the Sachem's Watch caverns, for Thanksgiving, the survivors had less to be thankful for than they had expected, some weeks earlier. If it had not been for the enthusiasm with which Dorothy and Dick attacked the meal and enjoyed the festivities, that day would have been drearier than any. As it was, every adult felt privately grateful for the presence of two youngsters, to whom the facts of life, or of death, inherent in radioactivity meant little. Youngsters for whom, moreover, every grownup felt he or she must keep up an appearance of calm, however fearful and depressed in fact.

It was Dick, in the middle of consuming a drumstick, his chin anointed with gravy, who suddenly heightened the festive pleasure shared only by his sister and himself. Hopefully he asked, "Isn't it now only a month . . . to *Christmas?*"

Valerie broke a dead silence. "Why, of *course!* What a perfectly *wonderful* thing to realize, Dick! And I bet Vance has even got a *Christmas tree!*" She sounded ecstatic, and looked hopefully, even merrily, though it took a strong will, at her husband. He beamed back, with a matching effort to assume the right expression. *"Naturally!"*

Valerie chortled. "Didn't I *tell* you!"

In truth, she had guessed her husband would figure a way to make an artificial Christmas tree. She did not know—and he did not disclose for some time—that the storage chambers contained an immense tree of aluminum—a Christmas-tree substitute for dangerously-flammable evergreens that had become popular in the early 1960s. . . .

As time passed, all the adults busied themselves with secret endeavors—the making of small gifts, the writing of verses, the painting of funny pictures that would be exchanged as gifts once the tree was brought out and decorated. Both youngsters had volunteered the information that they had not believed in Santa Claus "since we were babies." But both, and Dorothy especially, seemed very reassured to be told by Valerie again, and in a most confiding manner, that, "There *may* be no Santa Claus, children. But if by any chance there *is,* I know this: not even atomic bombs can bother the North Pole, where he would have been living, and he can come down an air-raid-shelter tunnel easy as a chimney!"

A week before Christmas, since the suspense had grown unbearable for the youngsters (and since Vance realized many of the adults were showing signs of dangerous depression beneath tight-controlled exteriors), the great aluminum tree was set up. It turned out to be the kind the children's parents had provided. Abundant ornaments were produced in their boxes; a tall stepladder was placed beside the tree; electric bulbs in long strings were unpacked; and everybody, at one time or another, then had a hand in helping the two young people to decorate what Ben one afternoon mournfully reflected was surely the only such tree in the United States.

A few days before Christmas, Farr came into the shop where Ben and his busy assistants were fabricating parts for a newly-designed transmitter. Farr motioned Ben outside. His face was troubled, and Ben went out nervously.

Farr spoke in a low tone, "I've just been checking over the oxygen tanks and so on. I'd say we'll have to start feeding the diesels outside air in—oh—two months, at a minimum, if we even want *six* months of comfort *beyond* that."

Ben felt somewhat relieved. "I know."

Vance gazed at him. *"You* do? I didn't realize you'd even familiarized yourself with that plant!"

"Sure. Spare time. Nights. Our 'sleep time,' as they all call it. When I couldn't sleep, I mean. I've been pondering the thing myself. We can take air, as full of hot material as the monitors show to be lying on the ground, and filter out so *much* that it would be a year, in my opinion, before the diesels actually suffered. Be nasty to *service* them, though, after a time."

"Brother!"

"But I'm not sure exactly what the actual, atmospheric radiation level is now. After all, your outside gauges had to take one hell of a beating before they poked out of what were virtual bank vaults. Hot junk could be thicker, near them, than in the air above them. Besides, I believe it has rained like hell, all through October and November."

"Why?"

Ben grinned. "You ever climb down the shaft, to the caverns where our sewage is treated?"

"Lord, no! Man'd almost suffocate!"

"Not with the masks and oxygen packs we have here."

"Okay! But it'd take a mountain climber!"

"We did some pretty rough cliff-work in the Navy. And there are cliffs under the sea, too, you know." Ben was grinning. "I made a trip—steep slope but there are plenty of old steel pitons, some steel ladders, on the way down. So you only need a few good lengths of nylon rope. It took three trips, hauling down line, before I reached the bottom. Been there several different nights."

"Man! But why?"

"Curiosity, the first trip," Ben smiled. "After that, oh, less than a couple of months ago, to see if the radiation outside was appearing in the underground river you diverted for sewage-layering down there."

"Was it?"

"Not then. Not noticeably. Today that water course is pretty hot—maybe two hundred roentgens. Your automatic safety system has cut it out. The sewage now settles without being washed into place. That part works perfectly though, so no worry. Point is, on my latest trip the flow of water in that subterranean stream was about triple the rate up until then. So I rigged a gadget on a thousand-yard, synthetic line—fishline? right!—to keep me informed of the subterranean water flow and level, without necessitating that damned, long, rope-rock-piton-and-ladder crawl. Especially since the untreated sewage now remains exposed till the treatment gunk mixes in it, and it has a—a less——"

"Less intoxicating?"

"Call it less overpowering, state. I deduce it's been raining beyond any past records, if my geology's not too rusty and if I correctly read the underground signs on the sides of the chute through which that river runs."

Vance nodded. Frowned. Finally said, "Maybe I'm dumb, but——?"

"The matter of air intake." Ben pulled Vance farther down that particular passageway, into a fork that led to a small chamber, unnamed, but marked L-17. Inside were racks that contained enormous, bound sets of mechanical and geological maps and drawings. Ben picked one volume without hesitation and opened it to a marked page. He pointed as he talked: "This shows, as you'll realize, the five potential air intakes you drilled. Then blocked, mighty thoroughly! All five near the summit at Sachem's Watch. Now. I expect that rounded summit is burned bare, maybe even sliced off or melted slightly, and somewhat fissured. However, bare. With the rains I believe we've had, these three possible openings—" Ben pointed to each—"would likely have been washed pretty clean, even if the rain was hot itself. Say, comparatively clean. Cleaner by far than the cavities from which we extruded the counters. They'll be chock-full of debris: hot material, water from hot rain, and so on." Then he winced, for his back had been mightily pounded.

"Meaning, we might get fairly low-level air from one of those tunnels?"

"Yeah."

"*Brother!* Never occurred to me! When do you think we ought to start a mining-and-blasting act?"

"Tomorrow." Ben smiled.

"Great!" Vance whacked Ben again. "I'll rally a crew!"

That night Ben inadvertently witnessed a scene that was moving, but not, he felt, threatening. In due course, however, it led to a not unexpected but new difficulty. Lotus Li and George Hyama were involved.

The circumstance that led him to witness it was accidental and Ben's act of eavesdropping, very uncharacteristic.

After dinner that evening Vance told the assembled group about the need of an outside, filtered air supply for the diesels and the plan to open up one of the long, concrete-plugged ducts, and others if the first proved a source of too-radioactive atmosphere.

Some of his listeners were plainly exultant at the mere prospect of a hole (even if it would be, initially, only six inches in diameter) bored, at last, to the outside world.

Vance acknowledged their reactions and went on explaining: "Ben and I have also decided that miniaturized instruments can be extruded from the orifice with a protective umbrella for some of them, so that we'll from then on know, providing the effort comes off, when it's raining outdoors, and what the temperature is, and how much snow falls, in addition to how radioactive the air is above ground. And even more, if Ben, Lodi, George, and company can achieve more."

All but two of his hearers understood perfectly what Vance had said, the women included. . . .

Women, in the past decade, had increasingly demanded and increasingly received a considerable education in technology. Their homes and the myriad ease-making and labor-saving devices on which they depended were, mostly, electrical or electronic.

Women—and nearly all men, too—had grown increasingly frustrated by the constant need to get quick repairs and swift service for their ever-multiplying gadgets. An electric stove burner would go out—or the entire stove—and the then paralyzed housewife would be obliged to wait for hours, even days, until overworked repair-and-maintenance people answered her summonses.

When they did arrive, the cause of trouble would often merely be a blown fuse, a loose wire, the need to take out an old burner (or electronic tube or the like) and replace it with a new element. Each such call entailed a high basic charge. So women, at first in small numbers, but soon in their majority, began to demand knowledge that would enable them to diagnose at least the simplest breakdowns of domestic equipment and to make repairs, adjustments, or replacements.

An average girl graduating from high school at the time of the Third War could competently handle more such problems than the man she would marry, unless he happened to be specially trained. A woman college graduate who had majored in home economics would be so able a gadget-tender that she would rarely need to phone imploringly for aid when the dishwasher, spin-drier, electric eyes, motors, or even the TV set failed.

Angelica Rosa had not, however, enjoyed such an education and the technical facts she had encountered had not "rubbed off." So now she raised her hand, gazing at Ben. He nodded. She said:

"We know it's still terribly radioactive outside. So won't the hole you bore let it leak down here and hurt us?" Her ebony curls glittered and her sapphire eyes dilated in dread.

Ben gestured at Farr, who grinned at her, his expression paternal and without any sign of awareness of what Angelica had once been to him. "Nope! We'll enter the pre-bored shaft from a room made airtight. In it, and so up the working shaft, we'll maintain a positive air pressure. That is, Angelica, when we finally hole through to the outdoors, air will blow from us to the outside, until we determine it's safe to bring it in and run it through our filtration-diffusion plant to supply the motors."

"Oh." She seemed abashed.

Vance went on. "The job will take time, gentlemen, and hard labor. Three sets of thick, metal doors can presumably be swung back, after their bracing is removed, and lowered into the workroom. But above that there's a steep-sloping stretch—the shaft's not much bigger than a manhole— that's empty for a long ways. *Then* we encounter one hundred feet of solid concrete.

"We can blast through a lot of that—say, half. But, for safety's sake, Ben and I agree we'll then merely drill a six-inch test hole, the last fifty feet. Miniaturized gauges— which Ben has sketched and George will design in detail, and all our three engineers will then make—will be put through that, after we're sure it's wise. If it then proves equally practicable, we'll draw air. For so big a job, I need volunteers. It'll be hazardous, scary, dirty labor, in a confined place."

To Ben's surprise, the first hand up was Alberto's. "My old man," he said, "was a coal miner. I tried it when I was a young punk, and decided it wasn't for me! But I've done it! And I'm getting as flabby"—his glance went briefly and with near-admiration to Ben—"as a custard pie around here! So count me in!"

Vance was as delighted as surprised. "Great!" He saw Pete's hand up. "Fine!"

"And me," Kit nodded. "Heavy work, that's *my* meat!"

Davey's hand was up too. "I'm not any feeble old cane-needing man, Mr. Farr. Vance, I mean."

"Right. Thanks, Paulus. Well, the five of us will start at 9 A.M., tomorrow. That leaves the housework to the ladies."

"We'll manage," Valerie said, dryly. "Haven't we, for maybe a million years?" They laughed and she went on, musingly, *"Funny!* I remember—oh, long ago—when that man, the 'father of the H-bomb'—what *was* his name?—Edward Teller—said all people in any shelters suitable for nuclear survival *should have mining machinery*. I half thought it was ridiculous—and half, got a chill. It *implied* so much! That an adequate shelter would be deep in rocks, or have skyscrapers fall on it, or something! But that was way back in the *1950's*, I think."

Her husband smiled at her fondly. "Yes, dear. It was. And how right Teller was that one way! But we have the machinery! If there was coal within a mile or two, we could mine it. Oil, we could drill a mile or two for *that*. We're set—and thanks only in a small part to such dim prophets as Dr. Teller!" . . .

The usual evening's recreation began. But soon there were few participants; the men who intended to start their hard task next morning went to bed early.

Ben roller-skated—proficiently now—with various lady partners, and alone, also. But he soon retired, too. However, his mind was busy with the many problems that would certainly or possibly, be encountered, once a hole had been driven from the cement-plugged, sloping shaft they had selected to try first. That set of problems was his assignment.

By-and-by, in moccasins, chosen from the stores, for bedroom slippers, wearing a dressing gown, Ben left his room and headed for the drawing boards in the big "shop." He had sketched out rough designs for miniature gauges and other instruments to be thrust through the proposed six-inch bore; but now he had hit upon some ideas, as he had lain awake, derived from the varied instrumentation of the many satellites put in earth orbits or used as space probes. It would be possible, he thought, as one adaptation, to put together TV Iconoscopes which would slide through a six-inch hole; once outdoors, they could scan the surroundings steadily and send back the view, at various distances.

When he reached the passage entry of the shop, he heard voices and stopped. He then found himself eavesdropping, not out of curiosity, but in reluctance to interrupt. George Hyama and Lotus Li had evidently not retired either, but gone to the shop in their dinner clothing. For the women, that now meant dresses they had made of the bright fabrics; for the men, flannel slacks and sports jackets over sports shirts. By this date the nightly group was not just well-clad, but handsomely clad.

Ben glanced in and then stepped back unseen: to interrupt what was happening might prevent its occurrence, for good.

Lodi Li was standing in front of a desk where she had been making mathematical calculations for George Hyama, until he'd left his drawing board and taken the lovely Chinese girl in his arms. She was saying, "You know, George, the Chinese have always detested you Japanese." Ben was transfixed by that calm recognition of a horror he well understood. Race prejudice.

"Yes, I do, Lodi." George sounded shy.

"I suppose we felt very superior with our thousands-of-years-older civilization. Which the Japanese stole."

"Probably you Chinese *were* superior!"

"Do you think, George, *any* race of people are *that?*"

"Not really. No. And remember how quickly we Japanese borrowed Western technology, given the chance?"

"I don't like it put that way! Everybody's borrowed ideas from everybody. The Chinese and the Japanese, though, have *both* produced countless original ideas. Think how many Japanese have won Nobel Prizes! And Fermi Prizes, like Ben's!"

George laughed huskily and held her, still loosely, arms around her waist. "Very well. We are all geniuses, in some minute percentage."

Her laughter was soft. "In Hawaii even, many Chinese people used to loathe Japanese."

"The rape of China by Japan and all that?"

"Oh, it went back much further! On the other hand——!"

Since she fell silent, George repeated, softly, "On the other hand, Lodi?"

"Many—anyhow, quite a few—Japanese boys and girls, and young men and women, even before my day, *fell in love.*"

"And did they marry and live happily ever after? And

were their kids glad to be half-and-half of two sorts of orientals?"

"I knew a Japanese boy who lived a few doors from us,"
she answered, obliquely. "When I was very little, I used to
call him what the other kids did: 'Monkey face.' 'Monkey
man.' One day, after we'd all screeched that at him, I happened to find him in his family back yard, behind a big,
stone garden lantern. Crying! So I kissed him. And never
called him names any more."

"Quite a lotta us Japs do look like monkeys," George said.

"Some," she murmured, "are very, very handsome, though."

"Look, Lodi——!"

"Yes, George?"

There was a long, long silence. Ben, moved deeply by this
effort to bridge an ancient prejudice, a thing he compassion-
ately felt, peered shamelessly around the entry. They were
kissing, kissing ardently, the lovely Lotus on her toes, head
back, dark hair showering over the slightly taller George's
pressure-whitened hands. They broke apart suddenly, yet reluctantly. Ben ducked back into the dim passage, ashamed of
himself, yet held magnetically and unable to slip away.

"Lodi—I—" George hardly made words, for a moment—
"*Lodi,* I've never been a guy to fall in love. I mean, the real
thing. So much that you want the girl day and night, and no
one else ever, and forever—and you're sure, and that's it!
Not me, Lodi! I was somebody who always liked girls—sexy
girls, for sexy me! I never cared about what kind—white,
brown, colored, Chinese, Japs, Filipinos—just as long as they
were full of passion, and very pretty, and wanted me. And
me, them. I was that way, Lodi. I think it used to make me
feel a little less like—like a monkey man—to know that, almost always, if I could get a first gleam from a pretty gal, I
could get the gal. But now——!"

"I know all that, George." There was laughter in the voice.

"You do! But how——?"

"Women talk! Faith has told me all about you. *George!*
I have long wondered this: why haven't you made a pass at
Angelica? She's gorgeous! And dying for almost any man
here, except two. Three, counting Paulus. Some man to offer
to take her on a good-night stroll. I mean——"

George chuckled. "You needn't say! Angelica's one of
those girls who isn't living unless some guy's wild for her, and
they are being wild together. *Sure.* She made it plain enough.
Is that, Lotus-baby, very sinful, in your book?"

The Chinese girl replied, doubtfully, "Well—it is—kind of—unchoosy."

Ben heard a cigarette lighter snap, papers rustle. They would be sitting on her desk then, smoking. And he knew he ought to go. But he couldn't. If he tried, he rationalized, they might hear him: he was probably shaken enough to be that clumsy. If he came in now, he'd break up something . . . some relationship as near to what Ben would call "sacred" as any act of which people are capable. And to shatter that would be, for Ben, "sin," in truth. So he stayed.

"*Unchoosy?*" George now repeated her word, questioningly. "I think not. I think—and I guess I've seen more of the seamier side of life than most people here, because, after all, I worked on freighters, summers, to help with the college tuition, and I spent two high-school summers with a road gang out West, and besides I also spent a couple of my early years with Dad and Mom, in an internment camp for nisei. Not pretty! We were there, even though two of Dad's younger brothers joined an American Japanese regiment that won a ton of medals and was all but wiped out. Both my uncles were, in Italy. Wiped out, I mean."

"I never knew that!"

He laughed gently, disarmingly, "Why should you? The Hyama family was big." He was silent. Spoke again. "I'm glad my mother didn't live to see this! And I hope my father got it quick, with Mrs. Davey, down in Fenwich!" He again paused. "Why talk about them? Thinking is bad enough!"

"Did they come here from Japan?"

"My father and his brothers? Heck *no!* Their grandfathers did. To help build railroads across the United States. They sent to Nippon for 'picture wives.' I mean——"

"I know what you mean. Girls picked out, in their home towns, by relatives who mailed pictures."

"Sure. That. But my granddads—and Dad, and my uncles—all married American-born, Japanese girls!" He said it with such pride that she laughed. His retort was heated: "What's wrong with that, for goodness sake?"

"Nothing," Lodi replied, very gently. "It's just that I always felt, till we got down here, so American, *too!* I know exactly why you spoke that way! My father and his father were merchants in Honolulu. But *their* parents came to Hawaii to do field labor. I found that out in old records, in Territorial files. But I never let on. Because Dad had always told us a myth about our being descended from a long string of mandarins, very powerful, rich, and wise. Only lie he ever told. I suppose he did it, partly anyway, to make us kids live up to his hopes."

"*Golly!*"

"Is that *all* you have to say about such silly pride?"

A pause. George answered. "Yup! '*Golly*.' No further comment."

Her laughter was like sleigh bells, sweet, high, and beautiful. "*George!*"

"Yo!"

"You were trying to tell me, you *love* me!"

"Was I?"

"*Weren't* you?"

Another pause. George spoke, then, in his flattest and most measured voice, the one he used only under great stress. "I was trying, Lodi, to ask if you could believe that it is true, I love you. My past doesn't make it look very likely."

She said then, with a sultry, taunting voice that reached Ben almost as a shock after her laughter: "It must be mighty difficult for all you men here—except Vance, of course, and maybe Kit, who is at least *engaged* to Faith—to go around being so *noble!*"

"What you call 'nobility,'" he responded carefully, "seems, for one thing, to be a sort of unspoken house rule. For another, Lodi, though I love you, I never even tried, before, to know what a woman's really like. Except for Mom and my sisters, maybe. But you I've watched in all the scares here! And doing math—I never could! Talking with Ben, almost as an equal! And learning, so quickly!, to be damned near a master machinist! Yet remaining a lady, even when you were grease-smeared and running a lathe, with hot steel curling all over your little mitts! If you had ever started to help some guy here to be 'not noble'—well, I'd have been mighty depressed!"

"Suppose the guy was you?"

"Why me?"

"Suppose, George, I felt the way you do?"

"About me?" George let a long moment pass. Then he whistled softly. Next, judging from the silence, he kissed her again. And afterward said, "What do we do now, child?"

"*Child?* I'm twenty-two."

"But you're no female confection like Angelica! A woman used to men being at least enough in love to answer some desire of the moment! You're no hungry lady wolf! You——"

"I grew up, remember," she said softly, "in *Hawaii*. It is not the most blue-nose region on earth! By Polynesian standards—and all of us Hawaiians sort of inherited them—I'm middle-aged and ought to have six kids already. Even by American standards, as they've been adapted to Hawaiian customs, I'm not exactly——"

"Say nothing!" It was a sharp order. "To me, you are as pure as your name. A flower. A *lotus!*"

"And so are you, George, to me."

He clearly tried to divert their rising emotion. He said, "Now, with Angelica, I think I understand. But you may not. Any man, just about, that's presentable, if nobody more glamorous is around, is for her. Even though, inside, that little brain has one different, but very determined, aim."

"What?"

George thought over that question. "Ever watch Angelica with Dottie and Dick?"

"She's wonderful with them! She adores them! And they do, her!"

"They adore you too, Lodi," George said, almost as if it were long since noted and even taken for granted. "What I'm getting at is, Angelica's main motive, in all she is and does, is to catch some one man she likes enough to love, who can give her all the pretty things she never had till she got them the one way she knew, and to marry that man. If she had ever managed to do that, I'd bet a world she'd have been the most faithful wife you ever heard of! She's really a good person, born to a not-so-good way of life."

Lodi mused on that. "I guess you're right. Anyhow, there's something very lovable about her, in spite of her obvious, perpetual—well—hunger, for a man. Any man."

"That's what I mean."

"You don't believe all girls can yearn that way—at least, for some *one* man?"

"Not yearn like guys, they don't! Guys——!"

"I know," she said, and went on, not unkindly, but with satire in her tone: "Men just are different *biologically*, and they simply cannot 'stand around forever, chaste but content,' as women are supposed to be able to do! A lot of rot!"

"Is it, Lodi?"

"Yes, it is! Every time I look at you——"

"Me, too." Ben heard him drop lightly from the desk, pace

a few steps away, and back. "Look, Lodi. *I* didn't start this!"

"No. *I* had to! Because I wished you would for so long—and you never did—that I was simply forced to! If *that* confession sounds like a female taking over one of your touchy 'male roles,' why, go be—upset!—by this one, loving, but modern, woman!"

"I'm not upset." There was a final pause. "I guess you know that I had to learn something new, for me: you're the only woman I ever said I loved, that I meant it for." He laughed. "Or *have I* said it, yet?"

"I've believed, before now—" her voice was reflective, but unsteady—"two or three times, that I really was in love! It always turned out though, George, I was mistaken. And glad to learn the error, even though I'd tried hard to make each such crush the real thing. You deserve to know *that* about my past. It helps me, though, to understand you really love me. And that you finally gather I truly love you. So there is only one more thing. Do I have to bring *it* up, *too?*"

George said huskily, "That's okay. I can bear it easy, darling, till the day we get out of this dungeon!"

"But that's not what I meant!" She said it nervously. "Just the opposite! We can't get married down here, of course! I'd be crazy to have a child here! But there's no need of that, and hasn't been, for years! I *meant*——" She hesitated. "Well, suppose the radiation levels outside keep dropping only at the apparent rate? Will we ever get outside? If we do, how long will we last? *That's* what I meant! Sort of."

The longest silence yet, followed Lodi's words. George finally murmured, "I see." Then, in a high, taut voice, he continued, "Such being the case, what the hell are we sitting around a *machine shop* for?"

They didn't kiss again, but came toward the passage, hand in hand, flushed—almost transfigured, Ben thought, as they saw him in the doorway.

Ben said, "Sorry, kids! I eavesdropped. Couldn't help it! Maybe if you think *why* I did it, you can forgive me."

Lotus Li was unabashed. It was George who flushed and stood speechless for a moment. But he presently smiled a little.

"It was none of your business, Ben," he said coldly.

"No, George, it wasn't. *Isn't!* You kids *beat it!* I want to make a few sketches."

They started. George turned. "You don't hold me to be——?"

Ben half shouted over a shoulder, "*No!*" And Lodi pulled George away along the passage, saying, "Don't you understand, ape? Ben is Jewish. He feels our feelings!"

Ben found his hands shook too much then to use the drawing implements. He lighted a cigarette. He reflected that mankind, long ago, ought to have realized—as Lodi and George just had, for each other—that the "differences" made by race and religion are superficial. *Environment, and the attitudes of other people to anyone, or to any minority group, regarded as "different"—and, of course, in consequence, as inferior—make the only important differences that exist. And all of that . . . illusion.*

A dozen branches of science, in thousands of unanswerable tests, had shown no special quality or superiority in black man or white, red, brown, or yellow; Jew or gentile or Moslem or Hindu. But most human beings, and the arrogant white man in particular, had refused to examine the evidence and accept the truth; and in that rejection of known reality, they now had lost . . . everything.

For their sins?

Ben considered.

The white man had colonized, subjugated, and exploited all the others, ruthlessly, for centuries, calling them "lesser breeds," in Kipling's irredeemable phrase. They'd enslaved Africa. Spain's Cross and sword had decimated the natives of Latin America. New Englanders and other European-derived pioneers had swept away the North American Indian as if red men were animals. Asia had been the grab bag of the white world, till India won independence for itself, and China, by merciless Communist force, had been "liberated" —for a more bitter slavery.

The same "white men" of Europe, Ben mused, had kept his forebears in ghettos for a thousand years, because of a different belief, and without even noting there was no such thing as the alleged "Jewish race."

Attitude—mere arrogant, wrongheaded belief—had inflated the white peoples with their mercilessness and their "righteousness." The very words they revered in their Christian faith and the words they wrote into their "free-world" constitutions, they honored by besmirching: freedom, equality, brotherhood, mercy.

And now, save for a subequatorial remnant, the white man was gone . . . the world-conquering Europeans, the Americans, the world-aspiring, once-Greek-Orthodox-Christian (or Catholic) Slavs—gone.

Ben smiled sadly as he recalled how the Old Testament Jehovah would have spared Sodom or Gomorrah had either contained even one virtuous person. Now, the white man's world, along with the helpless islands of the Japanese people and their world-conquering aspirations, had committed suicide. The millions who were innocent of prejudice, along with the bigoted billion!

Christmas came . . . and passed.

The adults, for the sake of the generally-ecstatic Dorothy and Richard, played at the game of Christmas with enough artifice to convince the children. But both of them, more than once, had fits of silence and even tears, as this Christmas recalled all their others, spent with their beloved, vanished "Mommy" and "Pop."

On the day after that heart-heavy festival the mining squad gratefully resumed work.

Steel baffles on the lower end of the manhole-sized tunnel had been removed and lowered into the air lock. The rest now waited while, in turns, one would creep up the endless, slanting tube to the face of the concrete "plug" at its end. There, braced against driven steel steps, the lone man, sweating, dust-strangled, half-crazed by claustrophobia and the fear of some fatal crash of a loosened chunk of the ragged concrete above, would operate a chattering drill, a jackhammer. A bare electric bulb, metal-shaded, would be his only light—till his utmost will and strength gave out. Then he would clamber and slide the long way back to the air lock, where the next-in-order would shrug and climb a ladder and vanish into a dim-lit, infinite-seeming hole that led upward on a steep, sloping angle.

Alberto, to everybody's surprise, had been able to endure such shifts three and four times longer than any of the others. And Kit was not able even to try the drilling job: far up the tunnel there was a place where some freakish effect of the blast of bombs outdoors had narrowed the shaft just enough so the athlete's shoulders would not pass. So he had said. Ben was skeptical. He felt sure it was claustrophobia, not breadth, that made Kit state he could not get through. And Ben felt no criticism of that. He merely wished that Kit— that Faith's fiancé—had admitted his true condition, not blamed the tunnel. Claustrophobia is not a weakness.

However, Kit did take as his chore the moving and piling of huge and lesser fragments of concrete as the men drilled deep enough and dynamite was capped, thrust in the drill holes, abandoned, and detonated from below. Then a vast spew of cement fragments, which often weighed hundreds of pounds each, came thundering down the tube and burst uproariously into the chamber. Kit rolled and levered away each such cascade.

The man to go up after every blast was most threatened by loosened chunks of the concrete plug, which, if they fell, could catch him climbing toward, or standing at, the work-face. Alberto usually insisted on that trick. And in the dynamiting, as well as in the final effort of drilling a six-inch hole through the last, estimated fifty feet of the plug, Alberto won the respect—even the affection—of all the people in the group, including the women. Guts, they would say —*but guts!*

Meantime, in the machine shop, on power tools and at drawing boards, Lodi, George, and Ben developed and built what they, not surprisingly, began to call the "package," which would be extruded from the final bore, if radiation levels in the outside air allowed.

They were checking the perfected device—a tubular, man-high assembly of glassware, circuits, transistors, aluminum, and electronic gadgets—when, one afternoon, Vance Farr burst in, dust-caked. He shouted, for his ears were ringing like the ears of everybody in the mining gang, and even a shout sounded faint to him: "Hey! *Everybody!* We're coming through! Got the monitors set to run out and measure?"

13

IT TOOK TIME, a long time, for the emerging Soviets to do much. Even they, who had planned, prepared for, and launched the cataclysm of World War III, had not anticipated everything. In particular, the American retaliation had been greater, longer-lasting, and more destructive than expected.

Thus, for one thing, though they had launched, from "ready" caverns, drone planes, to make a search of all possible hostile territory, their expectation of keeping a constant watch on the globe was wrecked. American pilots had found and annihilated the caverns from which satellites were supposed to have been orbited—vehicles with TV scanning apparatus. Also, the vast antennas designed before the evil day of the Red strike, to "see" what the satellites saw, were simply gone. Neither the rockets, with their TV space vehicles, nor the receivers could be replaced with on-hand materials after the war ceased to be even a random shooting by dying rocket men in the free world's last remaining silo centers.

However, early search drones had brought back mile upon mile of film showing utter desolation. No seagoing warship could be detected on that film by the experts. The seas were empty of such craft. No enemy submarines had been heard during the long confinement in the hidden Red bases. None showed on the film. None was reported by the solitary Red nuclear sub to survive.

Those naval officers who had managed to reach, later, via that single submarine, the arctic base (where, as planned, they were admitted under the sea to the vast, submerged "city") reported "absolute and total" destruction of all European, American, and other, even potential, enemy craft, surface or subsurface. Their certainty was, doubtless, based in part on their well-founded fear of what would be done to them if they reported anything less than complete elimination of all enemy naval craft. They were sent out to make sure, anyway.

Listening attentively from their wait-areas under two seas and three mountainous regions, the Reds heard the world, both below and near the equator, talk—but never a sound or signal that could be attributed to an enemy vessel, and, in time, none from any enemy land base, however deep-driven in rock; no hostile sound in the United States, or Europe, Canada, or Japan.

The ingenious apparatus that had been extended forward of the silently probing *Tiger Shark* had not even been indicated by Red equipment as a "school of fish."

Therefore, in time, the first Soviet men emerged from the mighty portals of their tremendous forts—emerged through a series of huge "locks," wearing radiation-shielding garments, and later in radiation-shielded vehicles: especially bulldozers. No plane ever flew within range of their now circling radars, either of enemy origin or any military sort. A few forays were noted by unarmed planes—no bombs were dropped—and these planes were apparently shielded. All were civilian in type and of non-enemy origin. Hurriedly, they shot across the U.S.S.R. at high altitudes—plainly, to observe. Some were shot down. Those that were not, never came within optical or radar view of the emerged and moving men and machines, so far as could be ascertained. And if they did—and if they got back to base (Africa, probably, and only Africa, and only south of the Sahara)—their reports would certainly show a U.S.S.R. in ruins and without menacing life.

Little by little, then, as better radar facilities were set up, the work parties grew more bold. In time they had made ready some three-quarters of the rockets set, before the war, in remote, unlikely spots, deep-buried, and uncovered now at great cost in labor and life. These rockets carried heavy-megaton H-bombs as warheads, and were so designed that with the rise anywhere on earth of any rocket aimed at the U.S.S.R., they would track such a rocket or rockets, lock in on their source or, serially, their sources, and destroy with absolute certainty the point-of-launch of such an unanticipated weapon or weapons.

The satellite system which operated those defense weapons had been put in orbit years before the war, and checked out to the mile and millisecond. Unfortunately, those orbiting vehicles had not been equipped for any other type of TV scanning and reporting.

Moreover (and in this the Reds were again luckless, though measurelessly less so than any of the nations they had attacked), a secondary system, by which the "reports" from the orbiting vehicles could be used to intercept and destroy any missiles or rockets on course toward the U.S.S.R., proved useless. The very violence and extent of the British, French, and (multiplied by a factor of thousands) American assault had wrecked irreparably the delicate mechanisms of the rocket-destruct apparatus. Thus the Soviets, on emerging, found they could still destroy—after a very large theoretical salvo, or perhaps two—any five-mile-square area, anywhere on earth. But they could not, as they had planned, intercept incoming missiles. There was no evidence, however, that men with such weapons, or even such weapons unmanned, existed any longer in all the world except for the Soviet Union.

It was not a grave matter, the Reds were certain. And, consequently, they went ahead with their next phase.

They were mistaken, as are all men at times, both individually and in groups the size of the greatest nations.

For now, at a point remote from the cratered nothing that had been Moscow—and the similar, lunar leavings of Tiflis, too, and Vladivostok, and all the rest—a plan, made by the United States Navy and never ferreted out by Red espionage agents, was put into effect by at least one unit of those designated to take part in "Operation Last Ditch." The unit was a submarine, the *Tiger Shark*.

The point where she commenced that operation was not far from eighty degrees east longitude and fairly close to twenty-five degrees south latitude—the exact position determined long before the war. Therefore, it lay in the emptiest and least-cruised reaches of the warm Indian Ocean, between Africa and distant Australia, and more than a thousand miles below Ceylon.

One night the *Tiger Shark* surfaced, after a cautious survey by radar and periscope of sea and remotest sky. A tall spar then was raised, briefly, above the sub's mast. At exactly twenty-three minutes past midnight, that first time, a powerful radio transmitted from that height, three short dashes. At once the *Tiger Shark* dove and cruised rapidly away.

The next night, at another, predetermined position, and at a different, prearranged time, she sent, from the reaches of the Indian Ocean, one dash. On a third night the position and signals were again different. But always, both signals and new position would be of a sort already known to a few American commanders of various, specific vessels—if any such still existed.

And this went on for days, a week, then more days.

No sea-bursting enemy weapon ever followed the signals. No enemy, or other, plane or vessel appeared in the ever-shifted area. It was therefore evident that the surviving Soviets lacked the equipment for detecting the boat, or the signals—or else, and even likelier, the brief radio signals at their seemingly random times, if heard, had no meaning in a world full of scrambled radio chatter.

Ten nights of taut effort and then all-day hiding. *Twelve.*

Hope ebbed. The officers and men on the *Tiger Shark* had been intensely optimistic at first. Though she could set up, at will, on sixteen places of choice, anywhere, a volcano, followed by a splash as from a gob of the sun, with an aftermath of wide death in fallout, the *Tiger Shark* was hardly capable of exterminating the number of bases, at their distances from each other, now known to exist. And in two days more it would be time, by the plan, to remove to the central Pacific and try again. With less hope.

The men were in perfect shape; the boat was hardly less immaculate than when she'd left Norfolk, long ago. More than six months of provisions remained in her lockers. It wasn't that diminishing future which lowered morale, but only the failure of any friend to show up and the consequent lessening of any chance of demolishing so evil a foe that men in all times had probably never hated other men with as much ferocity as blazed aboard that submarine.

The long trek of the *Tiger Shark* above the mid-Atlantic deep-sunken mountain range (where convection currents and even volcanic noise furnish some concealment) and round the Horn, submerged, then across the vast Pacific and south of Australia to the present position—all that had merely whetted vengeful hopes. Daily, now, they dwindled.

But on the night of their twelfth vigil, before they surfaced, Dingo, trotting in a circle as he swung the periscope, suddenly went stone-rigid. For a while, he fiddled with the handles that focused the scope. In the moonlit, warm night he'd seen an object. Cautiously, he ordered the *Tiger Shark* to close, and finally his tenseness changed so suddenly, the Exec and Chief nearby almost panicked.

Dingo straightened and let out a yell which the wincing auditors below decks first thought meant someone gone nuts.

"Yoweeeee! One of us!" Dingo bellowed. Then: "Take her up!"

It was the *White Shark*.

In darkness, with muffled flashlights, the skipper of the *White Shark*, his Exec, and three submarine chiefs rowed across the starlit sea to the *Tiger Shark*. They were welcomed aboard with whoops of joy. But those whoops faded when the arrivals went below and could be seen clearly. They were gaunt and sick-looking. Their captain, Randy Bleek, known well to Dingo Denton, told the story in one word: *"Starving."*

"Lord!" Dingo was amazed. *"We're* not even halfway *through."*

The other skipper sat down on a handy bench, below the mast and conning tower, in the control room. "We ran across a carrier—oh—long ago. Out of grub. The *Conner*. Nuclear."

"Know her!" Dingo grinned. "Skippered by the toughest admiral in the seven seas!" His men were already bringing coffee and sandwiches, with mountains of food on the way.

The *White Shark's* captain talked as he ate: "The *Conner* hardly got in the war. Afterward, some days, she put in at Puerto Limón, Costa Rica. Those people got scared of her presence, finally, and shooed her away. Her captain—your admiral—thought Australia would be safer, anyhow. But the Aussies i ised to let the *Conner* even approach. When *we* met the carrier, we gave her two-thirds of our grub. Over a thousand guys aboard her, after all. And that's about it." He grabbed another sandwich.

"Where have you been since?"

"Around." Commander Bleek chuckled weakly. Then he fainted.

Ten days later the officers and crew of the *White Shark* were rapidly gaining weight and strength, as both boats followed the twenty-four-hour pattern of assembly, signaling, and hurried departure—along with new night work: fishing. They also maintained constant radar, and other search efforts. And a third, identical "mast" hove into dim view, at the pre-established point of reconnaissance, that tenth night.

The *Leopard Shark* had arrived, all hands in good shape, ample stores, weapons in A-one condition, her delay explained by the fact that she had been near-missed by a nuclear depth charge in the first hours of combat, and had been forced to spend weary months in hiding, on a remote Antarctic island, while repairs were made by hand, to ready her for this return to service.

The three skippers decided to give it another week, inasmuch as they were now signaling a coded word of their rally. By then they also had a very good concept of the location and even of the numbers of the enemy, now alive and hard at work—preparing for some sort of military operation, they agreed.

When, in a week, no other vessel met them, they chanced an additional week. No air or sea patrols of enemy origin had come that way, after all.

The *Whale Shark* nosed up on the next-to-last night of that stretch of waiting. Her crew was woefully shorthanded and those aboard still living were barely able to operate the submarine. The reason was as simple as appalling: while surfacing, in a routine "war watch" off the eastern coast of the United States, near Long Island, during the night after the attack, mines of great power had exploded inshore. Before the *Whale Shark* could slam all ports and dive, enough radioactive sodium had been hurled aboard to sicken all hands, with fatal results for most.

Running clear of the contamination, ventilating the whole boat repeatedly, and washing down with uncontaminated water—all done as swiftly as circumstances allowed—had not been enough to save the officers and men from death, or, at best, weeks of terrible illness. Great blotches of subdermal hemorrhage had appeared on their bodies, faces, and limbs. Every man had lost his hair. Internal bleeding and nausea had caused the first of many to go, in agony.

For months thereafter, the sub had merely cruised at random in the South Atlantic, South Pacific, the Indian Ocean, and back to the Atlantic, while the men aboard barely had strength enough, among them, to hold a course and to prepare occasional food.

Her skipper said, "There was a time, I can't say when, but it lasted for weeks, during which no one could stand up even for half an hour. Some of us, after that, started getting better. Some more died. A few—you'll see when you board us. Radiationwise we're a 'clean' ship now, and have been, a long while. But a *few* are sure as hell still *going* to knock off! We heard your signal—oh—three weeks back. We don't even know the date! We thought we'd never get the *Whale Shark* to the rendezvous. But we did." The pallid, drawn, ruin of what had been an Olympic athlete, bared yellowed teeth, in what was thought a smile.

The three able crews were swiftly "raided" of manpower. The ill were given improved care. And all four submarine skippers decided that they might profitably wait yet a little longer, though they grew daily more anxious about the possibility of an enemy fix on their changing signals or their shifting rendezvous, with ensuing possible annihilation, by plane, ship or, perhaps, rocket.

The anxious delay paid off.

One night, toward the now very jittery end of that vigil the stupendous silhouette of the United States aircraft carrier *Conner* hove into murky view. Another major unit in the small surviving "Last Ditch" forces!

With eleven hundred and fifty-seven men, with only three planes sent into action and lost, with all other weapons systems intact, this great ship was the answer prayed for by the submariners.

After she had been ordered away from Costa Rica and then Australia, she had "vanished," encountering only the

Whale Shark. In actual fact she had taken a position near the continent of Antarctica.

On that grim, polar ice mass the aircraft carrier had soon, however, located American scientific bases and found that, immediately after the undeclared outburst of war, the Americans had flown in their specialized nonmilitary planes to the three Soviet outposts, where some four hundred men and seventy women had been taken prisoner. The Soviet group had not been forewarned of their government's attack plan and had not sufficiently recovered from shock to resist the smaller number of civilian Americans, mostly scientists, who shared the wastes of ice.

Soviet radio stations and other Antarctic communication equipment had been destroyed and the enemy personnel were marched or flown to the American camps. There, guarded but fairly free, the Soviet party had lived ever since, grim, humiliated, and helpless.

Admiral Sydnor, the captain of the *Conner,* a man of fifty-one, tall, broad, erect, black-haired and beetle-browed, described the events that had followed:

"We thought we and the *White Shark,* if she lived, alone of all the U.S. Navy had come through. No special orders for us were received *ever,* although for weeks we expected such orders." His listeners well understood that circumstance. "With summer coming down there, I decided the best move would be to take the *Conner* into the Pacific to an island I know where very deep water intrudes the land. It's uninhabited and densely jungle-covered. We did so, after the Antarctic people swore to keep our existence secret. They're okay by the way. In that natural "slip" we managed to camouflage the whole carrier, at first with cut material and, as soon as possible, with growing, *potted,* living stuff—whole palms, tree ferns. Meantime, divers kept the ship's hull clean and all hands maintained ship and weapons. We were still there, aware, as you are, of the —— Red's emergence, when we got your first signal. But we greatly feared it merely meant some *Shark*-class sub, or other craft in the 'Last Ditch' plan, had been captured, and some poor so-and-so, after enough torture, had turned us in. Our *plan,* I mean. So the signals could be the enemy, trying to lure together any U.S. Navy units left, so as to dispose of them. Meantime, we'd orbited a satellite." Seeing the submariners' amazement, the captain chuckled. "Yes, we can do it! And from it we've figured exactly where the enemy is, what he's doing, and about what he intends to do. We have been trying to decide lately how, with the carrier alone, we could get in close enough to end all that. Various weapons system can be altered, and fabricated, on board. And *have* been, to fit our solo-attack plan. But with *four* Sharks to take aboard their quotas of the things we've prepared—*well!*" He dropped his deep voice to a mere growl. "I think, gentlemen, we're on the winning side. Merely *think*. For what that's worth *now!*"

The moment when their first monitor was extruded through a six-inch bore (from which air instantly flowed outward) arrived about two hours after Vance had summoned Ben and his aides to the pressure chamber.

As telescoped aluminum rods elevated a gauge above surface ground that, the bore-length showed, had been blasted away for six feet, all eyes watched the dials recording the level of atmospheric radiation.

They read above a thousand roentgens, until Vance pressed a button that would, electrically, remove a metal covering of the gauge and cast it aside. Then, the reading dropped to four hundred and eighteen roentgens. The gauge was elevated ten feet. Down went the reading to ninety-six roentgens. With another ten-foot elevation, it dropped to forty-one r's.

Vance then said, quietly, "I suspect, if we shove the dingus as high as we can—fifty feet—we'll reach air the filters can make breathable, safely, for *people*, not just, *motors!*"

In the next whelming moment, when the guess proved correct, Ben felt an unprecedented, strange urge. An inward voice rendered it aloud: *"Thank God!"* he whispered.

He had never used that phrase and meant it before.

Why, now? he wondered. Why am I not amused at myself for "thanking" some "Being" in which, or whom, I don't believe?

Another question erased the first:

How could the rapid drop in radiation in so short a rise be explained?

He pondered that, but it remained baffling.

Meantime, he was vaguely aware of people shouting with joy. Of Kit taking Vance Farr in his lion-strong arms and whirling him in a circle. Of George raptly kissing Lodi. Later on he also remembered that kiss had lasted beyond any time to express mere relief, and that he had seen Kit let Vance down gently to stare with a gathering frown at the Chinese girl kissing the Japanese boy and the possessive return of the kiss.

At the time Ben's mind didn't even register Kit's ensuing scowl of anger, jealousy, or whatever it was—an emotion not directed at the two lovers exactly, just an emotion Kit had felt and for an instant displayed, clear as night fire. Ben saw and ignored seeing. He joined briefly in the celebration held in the Hall, right after that, with everybody present, champagne flowing and people doing extempore dances and swapping kisses in pure jubilation.

For cause.

Now they knew, or at least could expect, that fifty feet above the scarred dome of Sachem's Watch there was air sufficiently free of contamination so their diesels could run and so that they themselves could be sure of going on breathing, for a long time.

By-and-by, however, Ben went back to the machine shop. The "package" would have to be fitted with a longer extrusion-pole than they'd figured. To make that addition of aluminum tubing wouldn't take long. He set to work. Soon, Lodi and George appeared, and helped.

However, it was late afternoon in what they were coming to call by a name Lodi had long ago given it, "Outdoor Time," when they had finally hauled the "package" and its telescoping base up to the bore, fastened it to the long extruding rod, and gently begun to raise the whole above the rock-surface and slowly into the air above the surface.

While Ben and Alberto had sweated in turns to set up that gear, George had brought the latest-model, giant-screen TV set back into the Hall. Ben checked the elevated instruments. Its hollow, telescopic support was also serving as a pipe, to draw air from fifty feet above ground through the resealed bore, for a test run of the elaborate "atomic filter."

All people in the shelter were at last gathered, nervous but silent, as the screen showed what the TV set "saw" while, slowly, it turned around and around, scanning the landscape both near and afar.

This first sight of the world outside was not recognizable to anyone, from its past appearance. No sign remained of the many-level buildings that, connected by walks and steps, had been the Farr mansion. Just bare, cracked, shattered and, in some spots, sheared rock ledges. No garden. A few heaps of unidentifiable rubble. Toward what had been Candlewood Manor, no trees, evergreen or other, remained. No lawn. Again, just naked rock and blank earth patches in a lowering sunshine, where the apartment buildings had stood. These were vast jumbles of brick and steel girders that had been melted, bent, twisted like hairpins in a child's idle fingers. The bricks showed a little red, much black: red where rain-washed, black where the soot of holocaust still clung. There was no forest beyond, to the north.

To the east, south, and west, little could at first be seen, as a ground-fog was driving along in the valley, a fog that eddied up almost to the TV camera outside. That, Ben mused, did explain the swift changes in levels of radiation: the first monitor had been poked into—and only at last, above —this wind-hustled thick, very radioactive fog!

But before the sun set, Connecticut's seaward slopes could be seen, as George altered the focus of the iconoscope outside. There was not much to look at. Just a somber-hued rubble, once Fenwich, and other ruined towns, on a great, rolling ash-tinted slope that gradually flattened out and ended at the edge of Long Island Sound. No trees. No motion. Nothing but desolation, leveled ruins, rock, earth, air, dissipating fog, and the blue, empty Sound beyond.

For the next four days Ben was occupied, almost without sleep, in analyzing the air sampled at the upraised intake. After that, by lowering the telescopic support ten feet at a time to collect more samples, then blowing clean air through the intake before sucking back more dust samples, Ben finally could present an anxious but patient audience with a reasonable picture (from the radiation standpoint) of the situation prevailing near the top, and above the top, of Sachem's Watch.

Ben summed up his findings while the others sat about the Hall in chairs and lounges they had made and upholstered to speed time's passing and divert melancholy.

"You'll want to know first, I'm sure, how long it will be before it's safe for a person to go out there and just walk around. Well, for an *unprotected* person, it will be *several years*. The ground is loaded with radioactive cobalt, and other, less important elements with long half-lives." He saw their dismay.

"But that's not utterly discouraging!"

The shocked and bitterly disappointed faces brightened.

"Right now, *properly protected*, a person on stilts, so to speak, or on a platform raised, say, fifty feet, could get along for hours, if he or she were careful to wash thoroughly afterward.

"In a year the levels up there—if the rains grow cleaner at the rate I'd expect, and, you know, it did rain, *hard*, two nights ago, so we already have our first rain sample!—*such* rains, in a year, ought to make it safe, say, to stroll around the bare *summit* of Sachem's Watch—oh, for an hour— without getting radiation enough to be worrisome. And that's very conservative. The time lapse would be half, with cleaner rains, cleaner snow melts, spring, and so on.

"But what then?" he asked rhetorically. And answered:

"Downslope, in all valleys and on all lower-level lands, the count will be very high still even in ten years, and even with phenomenal rains and snows of a less-contaminated sort than we can reasonably expect.

"It may well be *twenty* years before a man could sensibly plow and plant out there—even much longer.

"When spring comes, we can see whether or not the heat, radiation, and fallout around here have literally killed every living thing, vegetation and seeds included. Till then, I believe —even if the U.S.S.R. has no further missiles to launch, assuming there are people in the U.S.S.R. to launch them, which we now think, as you know, there *are*—some two decades must pass by, while all, or all but a random and tiny fraction, of the United States remains useless, uninhabitable, not crossable, even for a *few miles* by an unprotected person. And that, from what we now know and infer, about says it. Any questions?"

Hands went up. Ben said, "Angelica?"

She stood, like a schoolgirl. "Then *we* can't survive?"

Ben smiled. "As Vance has hinted, and it's now time to say clearly, we can survive all right, since we can get usable air."

"*Then* what?" she asked, and sat down as if her knees had buckled.

"Then—*before* then; in a year, eighteen months, I'd *hope* —we'd have made contact with people below the equator who could, and might well, come up north in a ship with, say, a helicopter on board, and take us away. To some place below the equator, where it is still safe, and will be. Of course, it would be tricky for them. Their ship would move in waters probably quite 'hot.' They might have to stay mostly inside the ship, shielded. And their helicopter—suppos- ing all this happens—might possibly have to be shielded too, and using its own air system. Probably not that bad, though. But that's all conceivable, and, really, it's not too difficult a situation to lick technically."

A groan came from Kit. "Lord! A *year!* Eighteen months!" He was staring hungrily at Faith.

She stretched her long legs and pretended to yawn. "But a chance! that's all that matters!"

Ben nodded. "In a pinch maybe we could rig some sort of lead-shielded conveyance and build a boat in, say, a specially erected, decontaminated, outdoor structure, air-supplied from here. Tow the boat to sea. Sail it south to safety."

"Some job!" Alberto muttered.

Ben acknowledged that and looked at Vance. "Possible?"

Farr shrugged. "Maybe. Have to consider." He shook his head pensively. "Be very hard to do. Best hope is *rescue.*"

Pete had a hand up, and was acknowledged. "We still can't figure, can we, why the devil *nobody,* though we receive them, ever *answers* us? Right?"

Ben said, "You field that, Vance."

Farr took Ben's place, standing before the others. Ben dropped into a straight-backed chair near an ash stand and lighted a cigarette.

Vance then began, uncertain about the right tone. "Well, our three communications specialists have been pretty nearly constantly working on that 'package' out there." He nodded at the TV screen, pictureless, as it was now dark outdoors. "But such radio listening and monitoring as they've had time to manage makes it sure there are people alive, and sending plenty of chatter to each other. The whole Southern Hemisphere. And a little sending in the Soviet Union. What *that* means, we can't say.

"Connie, here, who has been studying Russian since before we arrived last July, is going to try, with Lodi's help, to see if they can translate the Soviet messages, which they already know are in code. Be hard to decode, even if somebody knew Russian like a native. I'm adding my wits to that project. Volunteers are welcome.

"But even uncoded, Russian's a tough language. As for the meaning of some evidently safe people in the U.S.S.R., your guess is as good as mine. I'd say some had managed, before they touched off their attack, to hide away safely, much like us. But the messages are few, the sets weak, and, I suspect from that, such Reds as still live are worse off than we."

Kit spoke without rising. "But they may have stashed away enough H-weapons to be sure nobody left could or would even *argue* with 'em, whatever they plan to do?"

Vance's nod was a single, grim head-jerk. "Could be."

"Wherefore," Kit's voice throbbed with frustration and anger, "even rescued, we'd probably ultimately become slaves of the Reds!"

Vance smiled at the powerful younger man with sympathy but spoke firmly. "The first step, Kit, would be to get rescued, or find a way to rescue ourselves. Once that was done, Red danger to us *could* be real. However, the southern half of the world is pretty big. It would take time—years and years —for small bunches of Red survivors to search it, let alone subdue all its people. In those years possibly enough skills and materials and energy sources could be gotten together— say, in South America, or Africa, or Australia, *somewhere*— to enable the anti-Commies to give the Reds an argument. Even a nuclear one, if they want that." He turned to Ben. "Given the technical resources, could you make H-bombs?"

Ben was startled. He became silent and thoughtful for a time. Then answered in a cautious tone, "Given the technical resources that would enable me, with a lot of helpers, to separate the radioactive isotope of uranium and build the gadgetry to make heavy and heavy-heavy hydrogen, I guess I could! I know *how*, so to speak—as most physicists did, everywhere in the world, pretty clearly, by—oh—1957, say. *Yes.*"

Valerie entered this bizarre discussion. "I wouldn't be a bit surprised if Vance *had*—down here—that uranium, and heavy water, and *all!*"

Ben stared at the tycoon. He was grinning. "I do have a good many things you'd be amazed at!" Vance broke off. Frowned. "But not *that*. Lord! Never considered any such necessity. All I had in mind was getting *away* from the consequences of the worst the enemy could do with those damnable weapons!" His frown deepened. "I'm sorry. My disastrous lack of *foresight*, again!"

Ben said, "Nuts! How'd you have gotten such materials? And even if you had 'em, would you want anybody experimenting with making an A-bomb, let alone an H-bomb, down here? *My* guess is, we've had the works—the general rocket assault, the hot sodium clouds from the seas, and a long-delayed plastering with radiocobalt! That, *I'd* think, has used up the Soviet and world arsenal, in attack and retaliation."

He stopped, feeling sure, yet not wholly. His eyes caught Kit's stare at Faith. Kit was gazing at her with a kind of repressed amusement, as if her capture by Reds would have a funny aspect. Then he looked at Angelica, and paled. Swung around:

"Why encourage us to kid ourselves, Vance?" Kit stood angrily. "You know perfectly well that if the Reds *planned* on *surviving*—and some plainly *did*—they'll have the nuclear stuff to get an absolute surrender from each and every nation, or continent, or jungle tribe still existing. Why not admit it? We're *through! Whatever* we do or try!"

Vance said, quietly, *"Maybe* we are."

"No maybe about it!" Kit yelled.

Vance spoke sharply. "Easy, there, son! Have it your way, for you. For me, while I'm alive and free, I'm not finished."

There was, at that, some scattered applause and murmurs of a loud, unintelligible sort. Ben joined the hand-clapping.

Kit sat down, flushed and silent for a moment. Then he whispered something to Faith, at his side on a divan. Her head shook. Kit's face became more stony and enraged.

The talk around them was now general.

But Ben saw, before returning to his computations, what the rest missed, saw it because he was worried by Kit's unexpected defeatism and rage.

He had been about to speak to Kit, before leaving, when he noticed that Kit was staring at Angelica; she was gazing back with bold, excited eyes and a strange, small smile that showed her even teeth. Ben then glanced back at Kit and saw him nod slightly and grin covertly at Angelica.

Faith, though she was pretending to be listening to the talk of others, also had noticed the exchange. She was embarrassed. Ben had wanted to help, to interrupt, to try to jolly Kit out of his rage and out of his apparent, and to Ben intolerable, responsiveness to Angelica.

But at that moment, and before Ben could think of a suitable way of breaking up the tableau, Faith leaned back and whispered something to Kit. He then looked at Faith with astonishment. Looked away. Looked back, still dazed. Shrugged. Smiled oddly, at last.

"Who's for skating?" he loudly asked.

Some were for skating, and said so.

Furniture was being moved when Ben departed, somberly. He did not see that Faith went to her room soon after that. . . .

From his desk in the communications chamber he could hear the waltz music, every recording very familiar by now.

With all his will Ben tried to resume the endless calculations that were necessary to keep up with the flow of new information from the "package" outdoors. There could be, he kept thinking, violently and against all wish, only one way for a woman—even as composed and fine a woman as Faith— to stop such flagrant efforts by Angelica to flirt with the men, and, especially, with Kit.

Ben thought that Faith had been forced, just to save part of her pride, into telling Kit he need not continue the obviously chaste form of engagement. If Faith had done that, it seemed to Ben she had sacrificed something he'd believed to be innate and untouchable in her—a sincerity and an authentic self-regard. For he had believed she would have acted under duress, not from choice—defeated, by another woman.

Maybe he, Ben thought wildly, could become the male upon whom Angelica's wayward, incessant yearning finally fixed. She'd always been nice to him; and he was, actually, quite fond of Angelica. He pondered.

In her own fashion Angelica, too, had "authenticity." During many monotonous days and nights she and Ben had had long conversations. Monologues by Angelica, mostly, to which Ben had listened gravely, or amusedly, and at first with shock. For Angelica had talked about a way of life he knew only vaguely and mainly by reading—about Broadway, the theater, motion pictures, TV, and night clubs; and about actresses, actors, directors, chorus girls; and boys; and many other people in the so-called entertainment world.

Ben had grown used to Angelica's habit of coming out with names and facts that had initially embarrassed him. She would say, hearing a "tut-tut" note in his response, or seeing him flush with embarrassment, "But, Ben! Why *shouldn't* I tell you John Bakerly was my lover when he won his first Oscar? After all, it was in every gossip column!"

And it was not just the invitational shape of Angelica's body, the even-more-inviting way she moved, her taunting eyes and voluptuous lips, her pert nose, or the witchy way she flicked her inky hair that summed up Angelica's charm. There was more.

Born and brought up in an age where any woman had been enabled by science to love as lightly and as often and with as little physical consequence as she chose, Angelica, in her sordid childhood, had been given no basis for restraining what she, in consequence, felt was natural. Women reared with "all the advantages," Ben realized, were, nowadays (*had been, till they perished!*), often as confused as Angelica concerning what was right and wrong in "love," lacking even an aesthetic standard for choosing whom to love and whom not. Angelica was generous, bright, cheerful—and no worse than numberless women her age who, like her, had lost old values and replaced them with no new standard.

That, he had long ago learned, was a sign of the age. People had shed their sex morals in millions, as fast as science had enabled them to escape consequences . . . just as people, in tens of millions, in hundreds of millions, had lost all sense of international morality when science had handed to various nations what appeared to be atomic means to world dominion.

He was fond, then, of Angelica. And she liked him.

He was fond, he now thought, of every single person in the group. Very fond. Each, in his or her own way, had shown great bravery, persistence, patience, and love for another, in that best and greatest sense of love, which involves a sacrifice of selfish ends for the needs of others. He had even become fond of Alberto Rizzo! Amazing. A thing Ben would once have thought impossible.

But the stuff that sleek young man was made of had finally appeared when, turn by turn, the mining crew drilled and blasted, heaved and bored the long way up, beyond the slanted crawl-hole. It was Alberto who toiled double and triple the time of the rest, though equally afraid of cave-in or of a head mashed by some down-shooting, dynamite-loosened boulder, and suffering, in the tight stone tube, the identical agony of heat and thick-flying dust, the intolerable jack-hammer sound, and the ache of muscles under unnatural stress. Alberto had taken his extra-long shifts with a pretense of cold insolence toward the risks. In consequence there was no man in the group who did not feel the original, velvety "gigolo" they had known Al to be, now measured up to all the rest, and surpassed them, in certain fashions.

Alberto was no longer merely accepted but his acceptance had led to a change in everybody: a certain new relaxation, new amity, and the discovery of Alberto as a wit, a man full of fun, a great entertainer of the children, and of the adults too, merry and clever. He'd won his stripes, and thereby the worth of everybody had been augmented.

Still—Ben went back to his problem—there was no chance

that Alberto would prevent an always avid Kit from courting Angelica. For Angelica treated Al as she had Vance Farr, with casual friendliness and absolute disinterest in his sex. That, perhaps, showed Angelica, in her way, did have a kind of morality, or code, though it was different from any Ben had encountered.

How could Faith be saved, then, from——? A sad loss of face, call it. He cogitated. . . .

Ben had been yawning over a game of solitaire one day, when Angelica had brightly asked him if he would take her on a "tour of the machines and stuff." He now thought of what followed.

He had assented and, for the whole afternoon, he'd led the alluring young woman through the passages and chambers of the Farr redoubt. These, fanning out like the galleries of some long-worked, vast mine, with their intricate machines, had fascinated Angelica. But in the end she'd seized his arm, when they were alone with the silent vastness of one of the "stacks" which contained gaseous-diffusion elements.

She had murmured, "Gee! I didn't realize you could get so *far away* in this joint! I bet nobody looks in here even, for weeks on end."

He'd nodded. "That's right, Angelica! Nobody needs to, till a day comes when we blast to outside air, and perhaps find we can use it."

She then sat down on a long wide bench. Lay back and sighed, feet dangling, relaxed and smiling a little. He'd said he was sorry she was so tired. And she'd sat up, almost angrily. "Let's *beat* it, Ben!" She looked up at the near, enormous installation. "Gives me the creeps!"

Now, remembering, Ben chuckled a bit ruefully. Angelica had made that tour, not from any curiosity about their maintenance engines and equipment, but to see, instead, how she would feel when she had him alone and far from the others. And she'd found she felt zero interest. So, anyhow, he'd inferred. It hadn't entered his head that his lack of any reaction had caused the briefly-inviting beauty to rise and alibi her behavior to spare him from distress.

No wonder. He was ugly. Not hideous. But no bargain in the good-looks department.

He'd never needed a mirror to affirm his opinion of why the world's Angelicas (and Faiths, too! and all the lovely rest) rarely even looked twice at him and his freakish features.

As well as a mirror, he'd had in addition, and for years

now, a very vivid recollection of an afternoon at Brook-haven. . . .

Needing a special piece of equipment, he had left his lab and walked down a hall to a stockroom. There, as he hunted for the thing he required, he heard three men approach. They were talking in German, which most scientists learn and Ben knew perfectly. Two of the men, indeed, were Germans — visitors from the Munich Radiation Laboratory for Experimental Study. One visitor asked, as they came within earshot, "Who's that kike we met who looks like a cross be-tween your American eagle and a turkey buzzard? The doc-tor with the bat-wing ears?"

The answer, in German, was made by their escort, Dr. John Hazelwirt, Assistant Director of the wonderland of Brookhaven. It was an answer spoken with some hurt, but with a partly-amused chuckle, and, at its end, with pride. "That must be Dr. Ben Bernman, the fellow who has just won a Fermi Prize for his theoretical equations showing a rela-tionship between quanta and relativistic mathematics."

The other German said, "Ach! *So!* A Jew—and *that* prize! I wonder from what Anglo-Saxon he *stole* his theory? Which, I admit, is brilliant."

"I am sure," Hazelwirt said aggrievedly, "Ben never stole anything, let alone that theory!"

"He is a *Jew!* Whatever he did, he *therefore* stole it, from some non-Jew! The myth that Jews can produce original thought is a Jewish deceit! They rob other brains; they then bribe or blackmail their plundered victims to silence! From whom did Einstein steal relativity? We cannot say. But he surely stole it and perhaps did away with the real creator! Yes? So! We *Germans* know the Jew mind!"

Then they passed out of earshot.

Ben had stood a moment, raging, the wanted apparatus in his shaking hands. He found himself thinking: For almost a generation the bones of Hitler have rotted in their unfound grave, yet the Nazi lie endures, like an endemic disease, ready to burst out in plague!

He had considered pursuing the trio down the hall and confronting the VIP guest from Munich.

It would have been a pleasure to take them apart.

And Ben Bernman was a man who could do just that, however gymnastic or soldierly the two Nazis might have deemed themselves to be. Which act would disgrace Brook-haven, himself, and Doc Hazelwirt, who, as the three retreated, by his tone was bitterly repudiating the black libel.

Ben had returned to his job.

But he never forgot the incident. The phrase "American eagle crossed with a turkey buzzard," had made him avoid looking at his face as a whole even to shave. It became Ben's measure of his ungainliness. Added to that were childhood recollections of the days when his Newark schoolmates had called him "Bat," because of his outflung ears. . . .

Now, realizing how long he'd sat musing, he also realized how ridiculous had been his fantasy—the dream of saving Faith from the humiliation of accepting her fiancé as a lover, simply to prevent the fool from taking up Angelica's invitation. And it would be humiliation, Ben knew. For Faith had been very proud of Kit, and of their propriety, since their immolation here. *So* proud!

That pride would now be diminished. For it was not likely any man and woman in this place, despite its vastness, could keep private any intimate relationship.

Thus, in spite of all their circumspection, George and Lodi were known to be having a love affair. However (Ben smiled), everybody had uncritically and without comment accepted that relationship of his two assistants. Then he remembered one exception to that—remembered how Kit, at the emotional instant they had reached usable, outside air, had first hugged and spun Vance Farr, and afterward glared hatefully at the special rapture in the embrace of the Chinese girl and the young Japanese man.

In that now recollected look, unexamined at the time, Ben had been given a clue to the menacing sensations rising in Kit Barlow.

And done what? *Nothing*.

With a tremendous sigh, a glance at his wrist watch, a shrug at the lateness of the hour, Ben at last bent again to his work. . . .

He would have done so in a very different, though still-pained mood, had he known what Faith actually had whispered to her avid fiancé that evening.

For Faith, noticing Kit's flagrant stare at Angelica, hitherto considered by her as a mere "Kit-like" fascination with what Valerie called "dolls," had suddenly faced the truth. For months she had considered her fiancé's patent and reciprocated passion for Angelica in exactly the manner Ben had imagined. Faith had finally, and scornfully (but without quite knowing why), determined she would never break her original and proud decision to keep Kit at a distance, especially just to halt mere playboy urges toward herself.

So, that evening, she had actually whispered to Kit: "Look, dear! I had presumed you might cheat on me if we married. I was going to ignore it when you did! So, if you can't resist that rich dish of Irish-Italian, why, I'll ignore it *before* the fact of our marriage. Seems only fair."

To that, Kit had given his startled, double look, the first of shock, the second of greedy joy.

The look Ben had wholly misinterpreted and, after some foolish plotting, thought of as evidence of a different surrender he could not prevent. A different sort of face-loss for Faith. And a potential trouble source.

Blind spots in the minds and hearts of brilliant, versatile men are often as strangely extensive as their perceptions.

Nocturnal assemblies in the vast, void midst of the Indian Ocean were made as few and as "secure" as possible. They took place on one or another of the submarines, the boat used thus being crowded with skippers and other experts in sundry techniques. One sub was used for each conference, because while the carrier tarried in the area, she presented a far more likely object for detection. So the men gathered nightly while the three other submarines dove and scattered and the *Conner* zigzagged till near dawn and "pickup time."

First, it was decided—from the accurate data furnished by the evidently unsuspected satellite the carrier had launched —that the Soviets, in their many emergence points, did not constitute an immediate threat to anybody.

Time after time, as immensities of poisoned air—so largely of their making and entirely their fault—circled the globe and returned to them, the Reds were forced back into their underground and subsea retreats. When they were able to work outside, they were at first, and for weeks, busy with the decontamination of the near environment. For that, they used hydraulic-mining hoses that drew, plainly, upon stores of uncontaminated water.

Much of two flat regions near two bases had been covered with some unidentifiable material before Phase One. The stuff was removed, obviously to make airfields. But the fields, it seemed, had not been sufficiently protected by the material. So, in cumbersome, shielded bulldozers, crews of men were currently trying to scrape those surfaces clear, to a usable depth. The job was not only taking time, but, after some weeks, the observable fact that the bulldozers were being operated by men unfamiliar with them and learning on the job, indicated that the dozer crews spared for such work as this airstrip-clearing had succumbed, and almost certainly to radiation sickness.

The exact location of the now barn-sized openings to the land bases was known. Behind those maws there would be baffles, but parades of heavy-duty equipment in and out of the caverns revealed that all such radiation-screens still in place were not very numerous or heavy; they were opened and closed too readily to be very ponderous.

Land bases now under construction near the "cities" under the two seas, it could be seen, had accomplished their initial objective, which was, to open deep silos where they had placed missiles, of high yield, suitable for fusing and aiming by computer—obviously, as a protection for the surviving thousands in the U.S.S.R., against attack from precisely such American vessels as now had gathered. There were twelve such "ready" missiles, in two locations, and presumably many more lay ready at the bottoms of concrete wells, or silos, elsewhere.

The Americans were certain, too, that somewhere—in the known caves and subsea cities or in other caverns unlocatable —the Soviets would have stocks of hundreds more nuclear weapons for the purpose of subjugating surviving nations and peoples when they were ready to undertake that act.

Two recent drone-plane launchings—doubtless for round-the-world reconnaissance—had been observed. However, one such plane had crashed at take-off and the other had plunged into the Pacific. No further planes were brought out, indicating the enemy had to be sparing with that resource.

In general, the Americans also gathered, order was being established by many subequatorial peoples and surviving nations, some of which had been in pandemonium. Persons, in millions, who had fallen ill of radiation sickness in North Africa, much of India, Central America and, spottily, elsewhere, had now either more or less recovered, or died. Radiation levels were growing lower steadily, south of the equator; they had not been widely dangerous there at any time. Some nations were intercommunicating now, in the tacit belief that the United States, the U.S.S.R., most of China, Japan, and other North Temperate Zone regions had been depopulated, or virtually so.

The only peculiar circumstance in this round-the-Southern-

Hemisphere reporting of the widespread rerise of man, society, law, and of uncivilized activity, too, was the silence of Australia and New Zealand. Satellite information showed that subcontinent and island complex to be physically unharmed. Its people were going about their usual affairs with seeming vigor and purpose and in excellent order. There was not much traffic, as no shipping was accepted and gasoline was probably very short in supply.

The puzzled Americans wondered if perhaps the Australians had suffered some freak radiation damage, or feared they might—although their scientists by now would certainly know they were not threatened. It was finally decided that Australia, having long ago refused the *Conner* permission even to dock, was sedulously keeping itself to itself. And New Zealand was following suit. Merchant ships were sometimes seen being turned back by Australian naval craft. And it made sense.

For the Aussies had been stripped, at their own request, of all nuclear weapons. So, the attentive Americans finally decided, they were afraid of being overwhelmed by the peoples of one of the surviving, overpopulated states. In that fear, they refused to communicate, turned back alien vessels, and were keeping to themselves, while they still, certainly, listened to the now-chattering part of the world that had endured.

"They are probably," Dingo Denton said, at one of the last conferences, "getting set in case of invasion later on, by *anybody* in the Southern Hemisphere. We know their industries are going full blast. They are moving daily back and forth, in what the photo experts say are wood-burning buses, tens of thousands of factory workers. Making, I bet, the best possible conventional weapons, to be able to meet any extant weapons which might be used in such an attack. If they hadn't been so bloody peace-minded, they could now get up a sky-spy like ours and learn the Reds are still after them, and the world. Be a shock, if the Reds land one day— in Melbourne, say—and demand that Australia turn Commie at once. And that's what the Reds will do. Maybe."

It seemed the likeliest summation of Australia's rejection of the world outside and its internal, immense activity. And evidently Australia could not hear the infrequent, brief directional radio broadcasting in the U.S.S.R. Or else it regarded what was heard as an interchange by forlorn, scattered survivors.

Code experts of the Navy, meantime, had finally broken the Soviet cipher and now could read the rare messages sent back and forth within that area. These messages meant nothing on their face; they evidently had been prearranged to have special import but to look and sound like the wan, frightened, occasional talk of little groups of Soviet citizens who had survived and still lived and possessed, or had rigged, radio sending and receiving sets with barely power enough to communicate with each other.

Indeed, with the passing of months each group even radioed to the rest the alleged names of its asserted "total of survivors"—in no case more than fifty per group, whereas the observant but undetected United States Navy satellite had disclosed about a hundred thousand people, minimally, and perhaps twice that number, as still living and urgently at work.

In a final conference Vice-Admiral Sydnor, the carrier's skipper, summed up the American plan for a truly "last-ditch" effort:

"We've agreed, then, gentlemen, that as soon as I return to my ship, she will head due south under full power and, skirting Antarctica, return to the natural "slip" where we originally hid her, there to be quickly camouflaged." His brilliant eyes looked from face to face beneath black, beetling brows. "You sub skippers will join me, at the intervals arranged, by following courses you know, one at a time, first rendezvous to occur ninety days hence. It will be hard on your men. You will have to depend more and more"—he grinned—"on our night work. Thank God, the *Conner's* deep-freezes are again full of *something*, even if it's only tuna! Albacore. *Whatever.* Night fishing here, by all hands, Denton, was a *hell* of a *bright* idea!"

"Thank you, sir."

The carrier captain's tornadic personality was renowned. A Virginian, Lee Warington Sydnor seldom was lavish with praise. "My men," he said unthunderously now, "went crazy over that first meal of fresh meat you anglers supplied! They are still fish-crazy."

Dingo's Exec smiled without joy. "Our gang doesn't care what it eats, just so it eats something *long enough!*"

Vice-Admiral Sydnor bellowed, *"Right!* And let's get on with it! In ninety days, on the carrier, we will have done our job. New warheads will be ready for the missiles on your four Sharks. You will enter our hidden slip in the manner described. The rearming of your missiles will be done as planned. We shall then conduct the mission as per orders you know. I think that's about all. I daresay you gentlemen would like to have one more final and general conference with me before we make our effort. It will not be necessary, I believe. If it is, I shall inform you at rendezvous, as you, in turn, come alongside. But I would prefer to avoid any maneuver that might result in your four boats and my carrier being even within a thousand miles of the same spot at any one time. *As you know.*

"My carrier may well be located by the enemy and destroyed before your arrival at the Pacific hiding place, in sequence and separated, as you will be, by great distances. The carrier also may be found and vaporized *after* any one of you reaches her and while that boat is being rearmed. She may be destroyed later on. Any of *you* may be found en route and destroyed by some Soviet nuclear hunter-killer sub we don't know of. Or from the air. Even from space. If the carrier *is* lost before we rearm you, then you, at least, can attempt what is essential. If any of *you* are lost, those who remain can try at the set instant, carrier or not, new warheads or not. That, I believe, is all. I'm damned anxious to get my ship away from this area. It's too dangerous for my liking, in several ways." He shook twenty hands.

"Good luck!" echoed as he was taken from the *Tiger Shark* toward his distant, uneasy carrier.

Immediately after he was piped aboard the *Conner* headed south, and in minutes, it seemed to the men on the bridge of the *Tiger Shark*, she had vanished at tremendous speed, vanished under the lush, tropical stars, her bows throwing a briefly visible, phosphorescent wave as she'd gathered speed and knifed into the slow, easy swells of the Indian Ocean.

The Shark-class submarines took back the officers and specialists who had attended that final conference. Then they too vanished, and even more rapidly than the carrier. Its immense bulk had settled beyond a star-marked horizon, but the four boats submerged and at maximum cruising depth scattered in four directions. When dawn seeped across the indigo immensity of the region, no sign remained of the strange, long vigils held there.

The *Tiger Shark,* like the rest, was shorthanded, owing to the men transferred to her stricken sister sub, the *Whale Shark.* She headed west. In the next ninety days she was expected to make a cautious, slow voyage up the Atlantic after rounding Africa at a distance. On, from there, beneath the north polar ice, into the Pacific, and south, standing off the Alaskan, Canadian, and American coasts. South, still, off

Central America, and at last, timing the turn to allow the *White Shark* to precede her by a specified interval, west beneath the Pacific for her remeeting with the carrier.

The *Tiger Shark's* skipper had drawn the shortest of four matches, held by Vice-Admiral Sydnor. He would, consequently, be last rearmed, and last away for attack, saving only the carrier herself.

The voyage, even though made shorthanded, could have been accomplished far more quickly, had that been desired. Dingo Denton had at first worried that his crew, spending all their days and many nights submerged, would grow restive —for the *Tiger Shark,* being last in line, would not reach the carrier, providing she would be there to reach, until the ninety days had passed for weapons refabrication and twenty more had been allowed for the scheduled rearming of the other three submarines.

Dingo had worried for nothing. His crew, to a man, was single-mindedly devoted to the now-hopeful chance of action against an incredibly ruthless foe—a satanic foe, they felt. So they bore the long watches without complaint.

On the second of the major legs of the vast journey, however, there came a period of great strain and fear, then near-panic, shattering all plans.

The *Tiger Shark* was some hundreds of miles clear of the Aleutian Islands when a Chief came to her skipper's cabin, knocked and stated, "We've made a distant contact that could be an enemy sub."

Dingo hit the deck and, shoeless, shot up the ladders to the conning tower. The *Tiger Shark* already had shifted to its slow but far more silent propulsion system, moving a hundred fathoms down and sliding deeper, with every man on board tense and speechless, save for whispering, and every man at his battle station, straining to collect information or carry out soundlessly signaled commands.

Even the first problem was great:

Was it a whale they could now dimly sense? Or a mere unusual echo from a convection current? Some unknown shape and sound of sea-life that merely suggested another sub?

When they finally knew a submarine lay ahead, at about their depth, the problem changed: *enemy?* Or some American submarine, not part of the "Last Ditch" program, but still in service?

During the next hours of chase and retreat, of loss and recovery, those questions were resolved, one by one, through the patient analysis of incoming data. The answer was as appalling as it was challenging: they had come upon a Soviet nuclear submarine. But by the time that was certain, other data made Dingo whisper, from sweat-bordered lips, to his sweat-drenched Exec. "She's stalking us, *too!*"

Then, blindman's buff in the depths became a game in which the fastest-reasoning skipper of the more-maneuverable (or the luckier) boat had, at best, a minutely better chance to survive.

Only that.

For if either ship fired, the other would reply. Both carried torpedoes with multi-kiloton warheads that would home on the enemy vessel, however she twisted, plunged upward, dived. With such weapons loosed by the vessels, neither could expect to escape sudden destruction amid a sea-compressed, nuclear fireball.

The Soviet boat suddenly went dead.

Bunch Cunningham whispered in horror, "They're going to shoot!" Sweat then dripped from his forehead to the chart beneath his eyes.

The skipper unconsciously watched its falling drop as he answered, "Looks like it."

Then his eyes fixed on the sweat-pinked chart. Far below them the irregular sea floor rose in hummocks with sharp cliffs. At the moment the *Tiger Shark* lay above a deep vale in that subsea cordillera. Dingo perceived as much, and acted. His orders were whispered to the death-pale Chief "talker" and went, electrically, to men in the control room and in both the forward and aft torpedo compartments.

The *Tiger Shark* burst into life, heedless, then, of noise, her men aware of an appalling fact: the enemy had fired.

From the *Tiger's* bow tubes, two homing nuclear torpedoes surged toward the soundless, motionless foe, miles away. From her stern tubes a torpedo-shaped object was ejected. Upon clearing the boat it expanded, as mechanical arms swiftly opened a vast, tight-packed bundle of steel wiring that became a submarine-shaped, sub-sized framework of wire. Self-propelled, it at once began to back slowly away from the diving *Tiger Shark*. By then, hydrophones and computers had reported the course and speed of the torpedoes fired from the enemy boat. But by then the *Tiger Shark,* decks sloping beyond any regulation-allowed level, was plunging under full thrust of all power, toward the walled valley below.

What then happened was reconstructed later. The cliff-like sides of the submarine mountains did, in time, shield the *Tiger Shark* from the homing enemy torpedoes so that their pursuit devices, momentarily losing track of their metal target, in the next instant received informative pulses from the great, wire, shadow sub. The torpedoes made an error, "built" into them by engineers who had anticipated that the enemy might try to dodge behind a rock mass on bottom, but not that an enemy sub could or would produce, so swiftly, so large-sized a moving steel "dummy" in its stead. The pair of torpedoes therefore veered on a course that would strike the heart of the wire mock-up, and, as American engineers had hopefully foreseen, one grim weapon ran slightly ahead of the other. The wire sides were encountered; they gave upon impact of the leading weapon; but the framework lacked rigidity enough to set off its detonating mechanism. However, the torpedo running parallel, but a length behind, now cut in to hit the most massive metal it could "discern," its own fellow weapon. This second torpedo exploded.

But by that time the tremendous shocks of the *Tiger Shark's* two hits were felt. In spite of the protection of the cliff, they hammered the deep-running submarine as a maul might bash a steel pipe. The *Tiger's* lights went out. One nuclear reactor ceased supplying power. And before any command could be given by the shaken skipper, a second blow, from the single Soviet torpedo to detonate, wrenched the *Tiger Shark* anew, and from a nearer region.

In the chaotic dark, shouted reports poured in to Dingo. His boat was leaking in a hundred places. There was a rise of radiation in the chambers nearest one reactor. The helm gave only sluggish response. His command to bring the boat up was answered with volleys of, "Aye aye, sir!" But the *Tiger Shark* did not soon surface. . . .

In a late, clear afternoon, after forty minutes of ponderous surge, of valiant human struggle and violent brain-and-hand work done in the gleam of flashlights, she finally wallowed into daylight.

On the surface, pumps began pouring out water that by then had the lowest decks awash. Taking a risk of exposure that was now essential, the officers studied the damage. One reactor was out of commission and leaking; they had no immediate knowledge of the reason. Many plates had been sprung. The other reactors, and three still-operable motors, should still keep the boat moving, but only on the surface.

Lead-brick walls soon were raised. They blocked the radiation so the men not at once affected were safe. Other men, in suitable gear, could enter the nuclear engine room, learn, and perhaps repair, the damage—or at least stop the leak providing, always, the core hadn't been smashed up in such a manner that it would "run away" before they could act, and drown them in radioactive death. There was nothing to do but remain surfaced and try.

A week later, with two dead and three still critically ill from radiation sickness, the *Tiger Shark* had dumped overboard the ultrahot (but shielded and unrepairable) core of plutonium that had done the radiation harm. The boat, although one reactor short, was still adequately powered. Her plates were being repaired by men in diving suits and men above the water line.

Day and night the undersea and atmospheric glow of welding torches winked on and off in blue dazzle around the submarine. Had a ship or plane come that way, the *Tiger Shark* would have been easily sighted from far off—a vessel smoke-shrouded by day, and at night set about, above and below, with electric sparklers. So it would seem, even to a distant plane or vessel.

But none came that way.

As more time passed, the surviving officers and men became certain the Soviet submarine they had destroyed, at such cost and with such appalling risk, had not dared to signal her contact with the enemy to the active Red bases, the nearest of which, behind Kamchatka, was not distant, considering a submarine's signal range.

It had not occurred to Dingo, either, to make any attempt in that deep-sea hide-and-seek eternity, or during repairs, to send a message to the presumably-hidden *Conner*. Signaling the carrier or a sister sub would be tantamount to announcing to the U.S.S.R. the existence not only of the *Tiger Shark*, but of some other vessel. Even if you were to be atomized, moments later, in this final dueling, you said nothing.

The cold, foggy seas—when good visibility did sometimes occur—were empty. Time passed. In due course Dingo determined his boat was fit for the rest of its voyage and for the planned effort after that. He ordered the sub down, still with comfortable time to complete the cruise to the lonely Pacific isle where, it was fervently hoped, the hidden aircraft carrier would be found, safe and ready.

14

VANCE FARR came into the communications room and watched George and Ben, who were trying, on various frequencies, to send word of their situation to somebody, or anybody, who might reply.

Ben's now practiced hand worked at complicated controls after George set humming a new and far-more-powerful transmitter, one that hurled the human voice from a tall antenna above the air intake, with power enough to carry around the globe.

Idly, Farr leaned over Ben's shoulder to read the typed words being dispatched:

"This message is coming from fourteen persons, alive and well, in an air-raid shelter built before the war five hundred feet down in a limestone mountain in Connecticut, U.S.A." Exact latitude and longitude followed. Then came details of the "shelter" and its equipment, a description of the outdoor radiation levels, and a listing of the people in the shelter with their ages, sexes, and where it was appropriate, "Japanese," "Chinese," or (twice) "Negro."

It continued: "We appeal to the people of the world for help. We cannot, with our on-hand resources, hopefully cross the contaminated land area around us and transport a vessel that, hopefully, might carry us to safety in or near your hemisphere. So far as we are aware, no other citizens of the United States of America survive on this continent. We are without significant arms, without nuclear weapons or resources to make them, so we are not to be feared. Our future survival time in this area is uncertain. Any person or group listening in—even if said person or group lacks the means or the intent for our rescue—please reply. Please reply. Reply, please. We hear you loud and clear, up here. We hear Rio de Janeiro. Capetown. Colombo." A long list of cities, nations, single sending stations, followed. Then:

"Hello, Australia and New Zealand! Hello! Why don't you transmit? Repeat. Why do you never transmit signals of any

198

sort, Australia, New Zealand? Are you alive and okay? Please communicate, our station. Somebody. Anybody."

Farr's brow furrowed as his mind went back to a similar message from another, cut-off group: the men they'd heard in a weather satellite reporting the aspect of the Earth in the first stages of nuclear war. They, too, had begged for word from "anybody"—and, perhaps, received none, like themselves.

Vance wondered what had happened to them . . . and found himself slightly astounded by the fact that he had not, previously, ever wondered about their fate. Why not? The reason was simple.

In the hours, then the days and weeks, after that eerie plaint had come through the chaos of ions to Sachem's Watch and the people it sheltered, he—like all the rest there—had been too concerned with the death of the entire North Temperate Zone and all its fringes, to give further thought to men stranded in a satellite with no orders about returning to America and, soon, no America worth returning to. That Vance had forgotten them was a measure of what he did remember.

Ben talked steadily. At the end of his message he gave some speculative information about the sea around the region: "It is our assumption, based on nearby monitoring, that the Atlantic could be cruised, with due caution and by shielded parties on ships, in safety. Anyone considering our rescue may communicate intent and we shall then endeavor, if possible, to make long-range measurements of radiation levels in Long Island Sound or open sea so that said rescuers would have information on that matter prior to sailing, flying, or steaming to our area. A helicopter would be needed to transfer our people from here to sea, in whatever series of short trips were required by its passenger capacity, from Sachem's Watch to rescue craft. Seaplane landing may be feasible in Sound. Please reply. We will gladly transmit all requested and gatherable data to any respondent.

"Also please note. We realize the mission to rescue fourteen survivors out of a whole population would be hazardous and expensive. Also realize United States currency without value. However, we can amply repay any rescuer with certain stocks of rare and highly refined metals on hand here for that or other purposes."

There followed a list of rare metals and their quantities that Vance had stocked in the shelter, partly for a post-war exchange medium and partly for just such a purpose as reward to any rescuers after an all-out war, since, as Vance had assumed, such rescue might entail some risk, much work, and so, considerable expense. Other stocked metals were on hand for use in electronic assemblies.

Ben ticked them off: germanium, titanium, molybdenum, tungsten. . . .

At last he ended the sending and, with a sigh, recommenced:

"Mayday. Mayday. SOS. SOS. Mayday. This message is coming from fourteen persons, alive and well, in an air-raid shelter. . . ."

He stopped. Put down the tensely held mike. Massaged weary fingers. Said, "The hell with it!" and looked up at Vance. "Every so often, George or I get a notion to try again. And do. But never a single reply! Never!"

Vance eased into a chair. The look of weariness which he'd worn in the first months of their immolation had now left his square features. They'd softened, and seemed, in a way, younger. The reason for that, everyone knew: Valerie. The new Valerie had not only recovered the marital love of her husband but, at last, had decided to drink no more. Decided in an instant, and with the obliquity of so many female motives, to forgive and forget and to include Angelica in her always-broad affections.

Valerie, sober, had become a round-the-clock tower of strength and sustainer of morale where she had been that hitherto only until evening brought her habitual fuzziness, fatuity, false coquetries, maudlin repetitiveness, and in the end her staggering retreat to alcoholic oblivion.

Valerie had changed and that change had changed Vance.

Ben said, "Anything on your mind?"

"You psychic?" Farr smiled.

"Absolutely." Ben, after grinning, frowned at the telegraph key. "I can pick up all sorts of thoughts. It's just radio signals to us I never detect."

"Forget it. Keep at it. Someday, maybe, you'll be surprised."

"Maybe."

"What I wondered——" Vance carefully lighted a cigar and Ben realized by that the import of this visit to the communications chamber. Farr's cigar supplies were not low, precisely; but he had smoked more in the initial months than he'd anticipated, so he was rationing himself. A cigar lighted by him at such a time as this, a time not on his familiar schedule, meant self-indulgence which, in turn, meant tension. "What I wondered was, should we do anything about our anniversary."

Ben's gray-blue gaze was steady. He even smiled a little. Exhaled breath with some force, afterward. "Wondered if any of you realized." He turned. "Hey, George! Cut off the set, huh? Come on over. Conference."

"Just four more days to the date of that fatal Friday at the end of last July," Farr said above the hum. He waited till the glow died in a multitude of electronic tubes as George cut their signaling apparatus.

The Japanese dragged up a third chair. "About a birthday party?" He smiled.

Vance Farr looked at him and he, too, smiled, eventually. "Yeah."

"The question being," George went on, "what form? A religious ceremony of Thanksgiving? With a feast? Like the Pilgrims? Who'd want it?"

Farr nodded. "Exactly. Paulus will do his praying by himself, of course. But who else? No—not religious."

Ben suggested, "We could entertain everybody on TV with outside fireworks. I daresay George and I could whip some up, with the chemicals you've stocked. Still, fireworks seem sort of shabby. Been enough 'fireworks' for all eternity."

George started to make a suggestion, fell silent, and went on with it only when Farr said, "What were you saying?"

"Just that, since the gang's more than normally low, with the outdoors really messed up by that cobalt dose, it would be dandy if we could break out some new . . . diversion."

Farr nodded. "Thought of that. I've got some reserve games. Oh, croquet. Half a dozen others. Tennis. Badminton. Bikes."

His two listeners showed animation. Ben exclaimed, "Great! Be fun to bike around the passageways, instead of using those electric carts."

Then George said, "What about *swimming?*"

Farr turned. "Swimming?"

"Thinking of it for weeks. Water supply's still adequate. Cold, as it comes in. Warmer, when it's been cleaned. Plenty of hot water, besides."

"But . . . where?"

"Storeroom-'K' is almost empty. Lined, too. Suppose you blocked up the lower-level door. Then filled it. Used the second-floor gallery as a pool rim. We could put in a springboard. Wouldn't take long to clear out the room and move the stuff out. Wash it down with chlorine. Run the pipe. Fill it up, without explaining the idea. After all, somebody's always running pipe, laying cable, cementing up this or that. Then, come the anniversary, we could all *swim*."

Vance grinned, when months earlier he would have expressed chagrin. "Never thought of a swimming pool down here. Lot of things I never thought of. Great idea! Let's say, on our anniversary day, the ceremony consists in opening up a pool. It'll be, roughly, ten feet deep, fifty long, forty wide— the balconies, then, at water level, nearly. Right? Great!"

The talk turned to other matters.

How, for example, to make good on their promise to supply any potential rescuer with the radiation levels of the waters of Long Island Sound, and elsewhere. This was a subject they'd touched on before.

The best method suggested that night was to construct balloons which could be inflated beyond the airway. On a favorable wind they would carry radiation monitors with radio-telemetric gear over any ocean waters to be measured. Arrived there, they would, on command, vent their hydrogen and so lower the monitors into the sea. There, floating, they would signal levels of radio-activity. Ben's idea. It was tentatively accepted even though it involved a good deal of work on balloons and new instrumentation.

The trio was about to break up when footsteps approached. Halted. Came on, determinedly. A woman's footsteps.

Connie stood in the doorway. She was wearing a nightdress of gauzy, crimson stuff. The outline of her body could be seen as she entered—a feline, dark body, a black panther body. Her face was intense and her dark hair disarrayed, as if she'd been asleep. Her lips were without lipstick. She looked at Vance, then the other two, shrugged, and said, "May I come in a minute?"

The three men had risen. Vance said, "Sure." George brought another chair. The nubile woman sat down, languidly, looked from face to face, cleared her throat but not of all its huskiness, and said, "What are the chances of our ever getting out of here?"

Vance said, "Good." He always did.

Ben looked at Connie and then, over a shoulder, at the vast assembly of communicating devices that had sent out so much and received nothing whatever that was intended for them. He said, *"Why,* Connie?"

She didn't answer immediately. Instead, she regarded the men one by one, weighing an answer. Finally she asked a question. "You think I've been useful to Pete Williams?"

Vance took it. "If it hadn't been for you, daughter, he probably wouldn't have made it. As it is, he's a man. Grade A."

"He's white," she said. That seemed cryptic to Vance.

But Ben understood. "You gave up white men long ago."

She nodded. "It was too easy. And too wrong. And too tempting."

Farr blushed, Ben noticed. Just . . . blushed. Decent of him. Not that he'd ever been a lover of this calm, intelligent, highly-educated, yet feral woman Merely that he'd seen and desired.

Ben said, "So? You're thinking of changing your vow?"

Connie shrugged. "Not yet. I mean. If I knew we'd be here for good. Die here. Even if that was the likely thing, I would. Pete wants me. I want him. Only human. But I know more than Pete about things. Down here we could be fine. I think—" she looked at Vance—"he may even ask you, if I go on saying 'no,' to marry us. Or, as near as can be done. And I'd be for that, too, if I was even pretty sure the end would come here."

"But if you felt we had a decent chance of rescue, or escape?"

She smiled at Farr, wistfully. "Down here with all of you, I can be Pete's friend. I could also be his girl friend. It wouldn't matter. Being the people you are, you'd probably even be pleased. And I could even become his wife, or as near to that as you might agree on. After a marriage service of some sort and papers signed. But I also know Pete. And myself. And what that tells me is, if we ever get back to humanity, it wouldn't go on working—for Pete. Or me. I'd feel the way I got feeling before the world blew up. I mean: I'm colored and I'll always be; and a white man too close always feels he's too close—to a colored girl. I hate that. And that would smash up Pete, outside among strangers, worse than he was broken before I helped put him together here with you. If that's lucid."

"It's lucid," Farr said. "But is it necessary?"

"I came to ask."

Farr shook his head in quandary.

Ben said, "Can't Pete accept that situation as stated?"

"No."

"Why?" Ben was perplexed.

"Because Pete's an everything-forever or nothing-ever kind of man, Ben. And so are you. And so is George. And so *you've* become, Vance, lately!" She rose, smiling. "Then *that's* my answer, isn't it? So I'll have to start weaning Pete of wanting me." Her smile vanished. "And vice versa. I'll need help, right?" She started out. Stopped as a thought struck her. "I might get some . . . from Angelica."

"Angelica?" Farr repeated, not comprehending.

"She's mighty bored with Kit," Connie answered. "Haven't you noticed?" His head shook and she said, "What girl wouldn't be?" Her "Good night, all" came from the passage-way.

Reluctantly, Farr put the butt of his cigar, a minimal stump that threatened to burn his lips, in an ash tray. "Some woman, Connie!"

Both men nodded. Ben yawned. "Bed?" he suggested. . . .

Time continued to pass and apprehension to grow.

The swimming pool changed August into a month of new interest, fun, and partial forgetfulness.

In September "school" started for Dick and Dorothy. The youngsters attended what was probably the best-taught and most strenuous seventh- and ninth-grade classes in the world. Their teachers were devoted women, of whom one, Connie, was a language scholar and another, Lodi, a mathematics major, and equally-devoted men, among whom were a Ph.D. from the Massachusetts Institute of Technology and the holder of a Fermi Prize who'd been certain of a Nobel, too, had Nobel laureates still been chosen.

Then it was October and the rains began outside.

Still no answer to the irregular but detailed and impassioned appeals sent world-wide from bleak, radioactive Sachem's Watch.

November 11. . . .

That day the caverns, passages, rooms, and chambers under the Connecticut hill trembled for more than an hour. Seismographs showed incredible explosions at nine different sites in the U.S.S.R., and many beyond it.

No one knew what to make of it.

The Russian-studying would-be code-breakers had not managed to interpret the few, faint messages received from the devastated areas where, apparently, some Soviet survivors had now either been blown to atoms or exhausted their resources for survival and so destroyed themselves.

During the days after those remote but repeated earthquakes the living world flickered with radioed questions: what was it!—where?—who did it?—why?

Answers did not come quickly.

In subsequent weeks, as the world's weather brought the atmospheric debris from the U.S.S.R. across the Pacific and also across an almost lifeless continent in the middle of which stretched what had been the United States, Ben and his two assistants shut down, for a period, even the air intake that had supplied the diesels. They switched over to filtered air, highly compressed, stored lately in the emptied oxygen tanks.

It was lucky they'd had the foresight—or that *Ben* had—to refill those "tanks" to capacity, against any subsequent radiation rise, however unexpected. On account of that foresight the fourteen people went on living comfortably while very radioactive air swept over them, left its fallout, rounded the northern hemisphere, repeated the dosage at a lowered level, and moved on around the earth again. Without the refilled air tanks, relying only on the remaining oxygen together with the original recirculation air-cleaning-and-conditioning system, they would have been forced to reduce their activities, as well as to contaminate their filtration plant to a hazardous degree, thus shortening their expectable time of staying alive.

Faith kissed Ben for the act, when all were told of the new cloud of hot isotopes above.

And she went on studying.

Ben set himself to ascertain, from the circling clouds, what had happened in and around faraway Russia. His ultimate determination left him perplexed. The cloud had contained, for one thing, an almost fantastic amount of unfissioned plutonium, considering the blast forces. The surviving Russians, he decided tentatively, must have blown up all the fissile stuff they had, with most of it not fissioning. Inefficient, but who would care about that, he reasoned.

Who, in destroying himself because living had become impossible, *could* care? And would not a self-exterminating people also, in a sort of general effort to shrive their measureless guilt, make sure that every ton of residual atomic explosive remaining was blown to atoms, with their deaths, in widely separated fireballs? And would not such deliberate holocaust include the random flight and burst of many still-operable missiles?

It seemed understandable—even, likely.

It was not the fact.

In the timeless dark of Arctic night, as the November fringe of pack ice crept steadily southward sending ahead thin-formed, transparent ice windowpanes wherever the sea was calm, a new event had occurred. Where snow-deep floes were hilled up by the hulks of growlers and sometimes split on ink-dark waterways created with a roaring, continuous crash, the again-white mast of the *Tiger Shark* heaved, cold and dripping, into an open place. As thick-clad men rushed onto the decks, stars shone above, steady, brilliant, and sharp. Among them, vague-tinted light played like waved gauze—the aurora borealis.

Looking at its curtains of faint red and green, Dingo wondered if the Northern Lights would bollix up Soviet radar or radio, or both. He hoped so. He knew they would have no effect on the guidance systems of the missiles he would, God willing, begin to launch at an exact instant chosen long before.

Already men on deck had begun to inspect the tubes which, opened mechanically, contained sixteen missiles, preset, their fuel systems triple-checked in the past twenty-four hours, their warheads ready—the monstrous products of special labor on the *Conner*.

Time dragged. Long-confined men paced outdoors in the icy air without their usual appreciation of release. It would be soon now, or never, and for them soon could not be soon enough.

During the next slow passing hours, infinitely precise checks were made of the location and drift of the boat. With the drift, small, exact, and constant alterations were made in the "brains" of the missiles. Half of the tubes, after inspection, were reclosed for diving. Half the missiles remained ready, their sinister noses aimed at the stars, their silhouettes vague, huge, portentous, in the tubes, star-lit, silent, but somehow seeming alive.

The time neared finally and men took stations. Last checks were made. The last stage of countdown began. Dingo spoke, precisely and with no emotion, the words these men had lived so long, under such appalling conditions, to hear:

". . . Four, three, two, one, fire!"

From the *Tiger Shark* four mighty rockets lifted, burying hull, open water, and the floes around in golden fire. They came out of their cylinders slowly, slowly heaved higher, gathered a little speed, pulled their thundering fire-tails clear of the red-hot decks, accelerated triflingly, and at length rushed with violence into the black, star-pricked sky. Thirty seconds passed. Then, four more rockets, pre-aimed and meticulously guided in flight, went the same way, toward the identical four targets: three east of the Urals, and one nearer by, in part under a freezing sea and in part on the land around that water.

After the second launch the *Tiger Shark* submerged, cruised fifty miles on a prearranged course, surfaced, and prepared to launch another four rockets, then four more.

The first four found their targets, or a point near enough so it did not matter. The mouths of three vast warrens east of the Urals were invaded by sections of the gigantic fireballs of twenty-megaton H-bombs. Within those labyrinthian workshops, storage places, and habitation areas, all that was alive died, and all that was fusable melted, including metal. Outside, on the extensive work areas, by then cleared of radio active contamination and in multiple use by many people, the same fireball, its radiation and follow-up of blast, ended all life and shattered all equipment.

Retaliation rockets, zeroed in by radar warning and by computer calculation of the trajectory of the incoming missiles, had already lifted off, however. So, well before the H-blasts knocked the region to hot gas and flinders, they were beyond damage.

The second set of American missiles behaved, at detonation point, very differently. Their fireballs were comparatively less brilliant and certainly longer-lasting. Each created a shallower crater than those in the first salvo and from each there fell to earth a seething eruptive ball of light, too brilliant for any near eyes, had there been any. This nuclear fire, spreading, lake-like, boiling and erupting, threw out for a distance of many miles both superhot liquid and gases, overwhelming the region. The molten glare faded out; and yet, lying there, it emitted such an intensity of radiation that, for a century, were a man to approach the area, he would die.

The same fate overtook the undersea city and the port structures rising around its shore. A first missile burst underwater, imploded the ceilings of thousands of caissons on the people and things inside, let in the frigid sea, and also swept the near land bare of life and all objects, with blast and a following tidal wave. Thirty seconds later this region too was lighted by the sullen, slow-cooling nuclear reactions that would deny it, for a hundred years, to living beings. But additional retaliatory rockets had risen in revenge.

The *Tiger Shark's* second, double salvo was unnecessary, but had been ordered. As she re-emerged, officers and men could plainly see, fifty miles away, the glowing sky-fudge of the first enemy reply. Grimly, perhaps daunted, but no less determined than before, they later discharged their second salvo, in the same timing and numbers. This but smeared and spread wider the awesome havoc at the target areas. Heat had jammed certain launch tubes and some minutes were required to close them.

The Tiger Shark then submerged a second time.

But her luck had run out.

From distant Soviet areas electronic instruments had tracked this new, second volley to its point of origin. So, as the *Tiger Shark* slid down beneath the ink-black Arctic, a great light burst above still-spreading ripples she had left, and a fist, with cosmic force, heated to many thousands of degrees, rammed into and through the water. The submarine, along with its officers, men, and their every trace, vanished, even before the mushroom carried their minute fragments skyward.

The *White Shark* met the identical fate, in the Gulf of Alaska, after she had erased the colonies of Red people and their machines the same way: both those in the Sea of Okhotsk and those near Lake Baikal. The *Leopard Shark,* in an effort to run the Bosporus, submerged, struck a Soviet nuclear mine long in place, and so, vanished, failing to fire at all. Her sister ship, the *Whale Shark,* on duty as stand-by in the Persian Gulf, swiftly detected the evidence of that disaster. The *Whale* then launched her double series and destroyed the unhit targets, the last vestige of the enemy and their possessions, before that submarine, too, died in a fire-ball.

Shortly afterward, planes that had long since left the *Conner's* decks appeared in those areas of recent enemy activity nearest the Mediterranean. There the carrier lay, after a bold decision to race past Gibraltar. The pilots of some of those high-altitude, heavily-armed bombers saw the *Leopard Shark* die. No pilot saw the mother ship as she launched swarms of missiles, directed at all targets. Then the carrier also disappeared, in a nuclear fireball five times her length.

The planes flew on to assigned destinations without interference, as had been expected. Upon the red-hot, smoking, dust-occluded, cratered hells their Navy comrades had already made, some dropped added loads of blast and of widespreading, enduring, radioactivity. Others annihilated the deep pits from which the defense rockets had soared. The store of these was exhausted but the bomber commanders did not know that.

Some planes then turned about and started, hopefully, for the Mediterranean and, with luck, a safe landing on the *Conner*.

Of them, most found the place where their carrier had been. And knew she was no more. They turned inland and, in certain instances, found fields where they landed safely— fields near which they soon died of the lingering radioactivity that covered France and Italy and Spain.

Other planes, after redemolishing and repoisoning the distant enemy bases in Siberia, tried neither to return (they lacked the fuel) nor to go on, there being no place to go. They solemnly shook hands and dove their planes the long way to earth. It was a quicker end than any other. And jubilant. For these Americans alone knew the mission had been accomplished. Operation "Last Ditch" was a triumph.

So, within hours, the last effective adherent of communism and its last effective instrument of force vanished.

The doctrines of Marx, Engels, Lenin, Stalin, Khrushchev, Merov, and Grovsky were finally undone . . . at the cost of half a world and of the vast majority of people who once called themselves free and civilized.

15

UNDER a notation of the year, day, and date Lotus Li wrote in her journal:

"April, already! Or should I say 'at last!' *Another* April! Twenty-one months underground without a glimpse of sky (except by our color TV) and not one breath of true, fresh air, for me!

"And not—the fact brings tears—*any* answer to our endlessly repeated requests for help!

"Some of the men, dressed in weird-looking suits that cover them completely (and weigh, they say, a hundred and ten pounds), *have* been outside, though. For more than a month they slaved to get the machinery working in the middle and top 'doors'—great, double-jawed steel things a yard thick. The lowest 'psi door' (antiblast portals) always did work. They got the middle pair to open, fairly easily. (These are in the very big shaft where we came down, on a huge, flat elevator that had already brought down everything which has made our survival possible.) Finally, they decided the top pair of doors would never be operable, so they carefully blasted the rock away all around them, and then, in their radiation-shielding suits, rigged up winches and a derrick that removed the beat-up, fused mess of those enormous, outermost barriers. Afterward, they shoved them aside on the now-naked rock dome of Sachem's Watch.

"Then, they fixed the elevator so it would reach the surface again. After that, using the psi doors as radiation baffles, and with a lot of careful washing and decontamination of themselves in special shower chambers up the shaft, they *finally* built a steel-pipe stand on the elevator, with a platform raised fifty feet above its floor. On that perch, later moved to one side of the shaft, Ben and Vance, in fresh suits, were first to ride up and out.

"Day by day, monitoring every foot of the way for radiation levels, they then worked down the tower to the ground and gradually across the sloping summit of the big hill— or little mountain—toward the area where, by then, the last snows were melting and things like 'skunk cabbage' (whatever that is!) were shooting up green sprouts. Since that time (March) they have moved the tower off the elevator and carried their explorations to something like five hundred yards (in some directions). But it is always dangerous and the rountine they go through to decontaminate themselves before they rejoin us takes *hours!*

"What they've learned is *far* from encouraging!

"Where bare rock has been exposed to the rains, snow-melts, and winds, the level of radioactivity is not bad. A person could stand in such spots for some time and not get sick. But if you come to a crack in the rock that contains a little dirt, or charred humus, or what-not, look out! Hot isotopes will have collected in such spongy spots. The jumble that once was Candlewood Manor Apartments is still, radiationwise, 'hot' as a nuclear blast furnace. Down the slopes of the now skull-bare summit of Sachem's Watch, these pockets of radiation become increasingly numerous. And once you reach a place where vegetation has started up—though its a very greatly reduced number of species!—a place, say, that used to be covered with a tall, second-growth pine-and-hardwood forest and is now just ashes—*another* alarming thing occurs.

"The burnt earth, of course, has soaked up and concentrated a lot of hot material—cobalt, much strontium and a little cesium, plutonium, and a score of other scarcer, but 'hot' elements. So, walking on plain dirt and ash is dangerous and must be undertaken only with inch-by-inch radiation measurement! The men (we watch them on TV) creep along with the extended gadgets like soldiers in the Second War nervously hunting for land mines, buried somewhere ahead of them.

"But the really *horrible* thing is this:

"Assorted forms of life that cannot be predicted will pick up and concentrate various radioactive elements. We also, therefore, have a 'hot laboratory,' built on the rock, outdoors, and I think I'll be allowed to work there soon—though everybody is afraid to let us women be near much radiation. That doesn't make sense, if the men are near it! *Either* way, radiation can do damage to our reproductive organs, and so may harm the genes of any children we may bear—and theirs—for a *hundred generations!*

"However. Some kinds of trees, bushes, weeds, wild flowers, insects, and lower organisms concentrate various radioactive elements (in the slightly radioactive areas around them everywhere) to as much as *one hundred thousand* times its intensity in their environment! Even, *one million* times.

"Ben says that biologists had known that fact since the early 1950s! He says, even then, at Oak Ridge, in an only slightly radioactive pond (one you could swim in, every day, without harm of any measurable amount (certain *algae*—the green slime in ponds—were found long ago to concentrate radioactive elements to that degree: a hundred thousand times the radiation intensity of the water! So, though you could swim there all your life, if you had grabbed and carried home even a handful of that species of algae, you'd perhaps die!

"Outdoors it's that way *everywhere!* Some microorganisms and plants seem even to 'prefer' the hot to the stable form of elements they used to feed on. And others apparently 'pick up,' and thereby, of course, concentrate, radioactive isotopes of elements they *never* used in their natural state. No one knows why. But the result is simply appalling.

"For if you want to move through places where there's bare earth, and, far more so, green stuff (which seemed, even last summer, to be growing rankly everyplace, though always in fewer species than before the bombs fell), you have to measure every *inch* ahead, and every plant and leaf and bug and blade of grass, and the scum in every ditch, before you dare step toward it!

"Long Island Sound lies some forty miles away. The men at first thought that once outside they might hitch one of the tractors Vance Farr has down here to some sort of shielded, high-wheeled cart, and so, by easy (if rough) going, transport, first a boat, then *us,* to Long Island Sound. Such a boat *could* be built and provisioned, one that would carry us all, by sail and engines, to South America. Everything needed for that is on hand.

"But the plan is now regarded as hopeless.

"We *could* build the boat and get it to the sea. But safe passage of a cart would require it to be too heavily shielded by lead, for moving. Moreover, it would have to be airtight for such a slow trip. Dust and pollen stirred up by the wind can come in sudden, very 'hot' gusts! A littler cart, making many trips, involves merely a longer exposure for whoever runs the tractors. Besides that, the men are now pretty sure such largely landlocked waters as Long Island Sound would be found full of 'hot' areas where various microorganisms (as on land) and many algae, jellyfish, and other biota—living sea things—would occur in great, hot patches and be unsafe to cruise through!

"This has made us, with our unanswered pleas, pretty blue.

"For our food supplies, already rationed, will not last more than another six months at best. Soon after that, our systems for decontaminating air and water would become so loaded with radioactive debris they would not function, and then we'd have *no water or air!*

"If it weren't for dear George Hyama, I'd about die! But he is the most wonderful man that ever was! Every time I feel his black, black eyes fixed on me—and they move so fast you can't see them shift and you will think he's watching someone else, when with no warning you find him gazing at you!—every time he looks at me the way he does, I feel *warm* all over, and less miserable about our likely, sad end, and also *glad* I'm a woman, Chinese or whatever sort!

"I used, not so much to envy, but sort of wistfully wonder what it was like to be one of those graceful, tall, blonde women that nineteenth-century novelists used to call 'willowy.' Angelica is too shaped and too dark-haired to qualify, but Faith does. And I know what it is like to be like Faith.

"Not a bit different from being slant-eyed and Chinese! Or from being colored, like Connie!

"*Except* that Faith has had a dismal time since 'way back, when her fiancé started 'answering' Angelica's look. Not that I blame Kit too much, or Angelica *any*; I know myself how she felt, even if I only felt it about George. But Faith did not, plainly, feel toward Kit as Kit feels toward any pretty woman who reciprocates. Or maybe Faith was too proud to compete that way. Not 'maybe' I guess.

"Faith would have about perished of humiliation, if Ben —that total genius!—had not had the inspiration of getting her interested in science. Since that day, though she's remained sad about the Kit-Angelica *affaire,* she has devoted herself to studying, with an ability you'd never dream existed in any rich man's onetime debutante, almost playgirl, daughter, even if she did graduate from college!

"I've helped teach Faith and in doing it come to know her intimately. And she's a real *femme suprême,* as people said in the days before the war started. She's now learned all the math I know and all the physics George studies. Ben takes time, when he can, to run classes for the three of us, in relativity, in quantum math, and in his new concept that relates both, for which he received the Fermi Prize, and would surely have gotten a Nobel, too, if the world hadn't come to an end. Our world, anyhow.

"Poor old Paulus Davey now has completely white hair and he is calmly getting prepared to 'meet his Maker.'

"I said, though, that we are all depressed.

"But the most restless one is Kit. I've tried to talk privately with him. So have others. And he finally said to me that 'what ate him' was the fact he wouldn't get out of here *with Angelica!*

"I asked, 'What about Faith?'

"He virtually shrugged that off. 'Faith, too, of course,' he said, sounding uninterested. 'Because if Angelica and I made it out, Faith would; and doubtless we'd get married. But I wish Faith would understand that I can't even *face living* without Angelica!'

"What do you say to a man who says *that?*

"It's only *part* of how Kit feels, I believe. He is getting what was called, in slang, 'stir daffy.' It meant, 'crazed by confinement.' He roams around here like a caged tiger, day and night, unless Angelica is free. Then you don't see either one.

"I'd say Vance Farr and Ben Bernman are the men—with Pete Williams; as well, naturally, as my George—who are steadiest these days. But even Vance is jerky and abrupt and preoccupied. Peter became a quiet, strong, determined, affectionate, grown-up *man*, entirely because of all Connie's effort and affection. But something went wrong with them. They cooled off. They are friendly, but not loving any more. And so Peter's slowly getting to be another nervous, restive, low-spirited person—maybe, like Kit. Or the way Alberto used to be. At times cross and mean, the way the kids have become lately, catching it from the general melancholy and Connie's new aloofness.

"I have no idea—nobody has, I guess—whether or not that gold-brown, deep-voiced, orchid-handsome Heliconia and Pete were having an *affaire* that came to an end. I doubt it; probably people would have learned, sooner or later. Yet of all of us who might have fallen in love and lost their inhibitions (near impossible to keep one's inhibitions after twenty-one months jammed together down here!), Connie and Pete are the one pair who, perhaps, could have enjoyed a concealed love *affaire*. For everybody's so fond of Connie, and so proud of the way she is still educating Pete (not to mention, so immensely *glad* the utterly-crazed Pete who arrived here became a pillar of the community) that when Connie and Pete study, work, or talk together, no one bothers to spy or listen or hunt them up or gossip or anything. We all love both too much to risk embarrassing them! But if it was an *affaire*, it's over!

"George and I didn't really try very long to hide *our* love. We *couldn't!* It showed like a banner against a blue sky. What Pete and Connie feel, and may do, is another matter, though. Pete's naturally not communicative; a person who likes privacy. And Connie's the soul of discretion now, though she didn't used to be, as a younger woman.

"Valerie leads the females, in calm, in continued interest in everyday activities, in caring for the kids—in *character*, to state it with one word. She's actually a *titan* of a woman inside, as well as superior in beauty and intelligence! By just observing her I learn thousands of things, big and little, I can and should and try to improve in *me!*

"Someone ran past my door a moment ago, and then another, so there must be some excitement. I'll close for now. . . ."

In negligee and slippers Lodi soon ran down her passage to the Hall, where others, similarly clad, were gathering. The group was tensely staring at the elevator shaft. Emptiness behind its opened door showed that someone had gone up into the night.

"What's wrong?" Lodi asked.

Pete, who was nearest her, answered. "We don't know. The elevator went up an hour ago. Ben and your George, I think, to make some night observations, or work in the hot lab. Then someone sent it back here—I was in the kitchen, thought nothing of it. But soon it ascended again, and then I began to wonder. I looked at the schedules. Nobody but Ben and George were listed for night duty. I got worried. Tried to get the elevator back but they'd locked it up there. So I tried phoning. No answer. Then I got Connie, and together we started knocking on doors— she took the women, me—I—the men. Now, it seems, *Kit's* missing."

"Kit!" Two voices said it simultaneously, and with the sound of two differing sorts of alarm: Angelica's deep voice, Faith's level contralto.

Valerie rushed to the wall phone and pressed a button to ring the one above the shaft, in the night. She pressed and pressed. But no one answered.

No one could, at that instant. . . .

What had happened was an act of madness.

Ben and George, in lightweight shielding garb, were measuring radiation levels of a soft, southerly breeze, in moonlight, atop the steel tower, when they heard the elevator as it rumbled down. They exchanged baffled glances.

"Maybe," George said, "something's wrong below. And someone's coming up to tell us."

"They'd *phone!*" Ben answered.

"Suppose a big short circuit, lot of smoke, hard to reach the elevator phone?" But even as he spoke, the elevator rose, far below.

By then Ben had snatched up the outdoor instrument and was pressing its ring button. He tried repeatedly. At that time, however, Connie and Pete were hurrying through passageways, knocking on doors, counting heads. So the ringing was unheard in the Hall.

A short while later the elevator drew near.

When its flat, vast floor was level with the rock surface, George and Ben saw in the moonlight, with horror, a lone male figure, in sports clothes. By build and size, Kit. Kit, without a shielding garment, and bareheaded. As the elevator clicked to a stop, he walked over and locked it in place. No one, now, could push the Hall button and bring it down.

Ben yelled, "You idiot! Go back!"

Kit's voice came smoothly, almost amiably, but strangely, "Lovely night!" They could hear him inhale. Chuckle.

George was first to start down the ladder, muttering to Ben, "Off his rocker!" Ben swarmed down behind George.

But when they reached the steel floor, Kit was not there. They leaped up on the rock. Raced around the lead-lined, concrete block building constructed as a "shielded lab."

Saw Kit again.

He was moving, in loping strides, down the rocky ledges of Sachem's Watch.

Ben bellowed, "You fool! *Come back!* In a hundred yards, dressed the way you are, you'll get a serious dose of radiation!"

Kit heard, stopped, and turned. His mellow voice floated up across the nocturnal landscape, a stark scene softened by the moon's rays. It was loud enough to carry clearly. "I simply don't believe it! The other day, when I was helping you ——s haul gear to the lab in my little lead suit, I saw a flock of *birds* out yonder"—his arm gestured in the blue dusk— "and they were *alive* and peppy!"

"Damn it!" Ben bellowed. "*Sure!* Last spring, apparently, *some* migratory birds somehow realized their old flyway wasn't usable and *stayed far south! This* year a few species, in small numbers, are trying it again. Instinct! They've come up over the *Atlantic,* but they won't last a week here!"

Kit replied, "Phooie! Know what *I* think? I think you and your scientist pals have a conspiracy! To keep us buried till we die! Jew, Chinese woman, Jap kid. You're taking a revenge on the white race. I'm fed up with those caves and Angelica and I yearn to go on a moonlight stroll! So I'm going, as a test! When I get back, and when the gang sees how you've betrayed all of us, you'll be slaughtered, Mr. Jew Doctor Benvenuto Cellini Bernman and young George Hyama! Then we white people will all come out, and your crazy plot will be futile!" He laughed and began to move away, yelling over his shoulder "Foiled! . . . Foiled! . . . Foiled!" and running like a deer.

George lunged toward Kit. Ben grabbed George. "Keep your senses, fellow! Look at the speed he's making! Could you catch up? And suppose you did, a mile or two down the valley, your shielding clothes all ripped from falls and skids, leaking?"

"We gotta try for him, Ben!"

The scientist stared into the lucent murk where Kit's figure was merging with shadows below the pale-lit rocks. Ben stared, and held the struggling George tightly.

"You heard what Kit said," he murmured. "That was not the real Kit talking, but a man gone mad. For cause, too! Guilt. Frustration. Passion spent, or misspent. Rotten manners. Claustrophobia. You name it! If there was one chance in a million of getting him, I'd be gone, with you. But could we even lick him? Together, *maybe*. But catch him? Racing away like that, into that shambles of blasted rock, thornbush, creepers? And suppose he's armed? *No*, George! I can recognize insanity when it's that violent! And I won't allow a good man, or even, myself, to get killed on a hopeless try."

By then George, although tense, was calming down. "I know," he answered slowly. "You're right! But——!"

"Sometimes," Ben panted, his voice sympathetic in spite of that, "it takes more guts *not* to play Good Samaritan, when the effort's absolutely hopeless, than to make a damn-fool try! You learn that, learning to be Navy, I suppose."

George then said, "Thanks!"

"Okay." Ben loosed his hold on the young Japanese.

George, still breathing hard, suggested, "Shouldn't we switch on the searchlight—pointed up?"

"Won't hurt!"

They climbed the tower and sent a piercing beam of light vertically upward in stabbing opposition to the moonglow. With that sudden, thrusting finger of light, from very far in the distance they heard sounds of mocking laughter.

After calling repeatedly they at last descended, unlatched the elevator, went down to a decontamination chamber built above the middle set of psi doors, meticulously followed the wash-off drill, dressed, and took the elevator again to break the terrible news to the people below.

It was received in silence by all save Angelica, who ran, sobbing hysterically, toward her room. Presently, Valerie followed her. Neither returned. Faith merely sat quietly in a chair, pale, without expression, making no comment. Somebody served coffee.

Several fresh sets of lightweight shielding garments were brought out. A watch was posted on the tower—George first, then Vance, Pete next, and Ben for the daybreak period.

Just after the sun had risen above the bleak, flattened landscape and the far-off, blue Sound, Ben saw, in the powerful telescope mounted for a different purpose on the tower, the figure of a human being coming slowly, from a place about two miles distant, near the rubble acreage that had been Fenwich.

Kit was plainly exhausted. And doubtless, Ben surmised, pretty ill already. Once or twice Kit stumbled, almost fell.

Meantime, through the 'scope, Ben surveyed a path toward the reeling man that he had already monitored for some distance. He considered the resistance of the garment he was wearing, added up theoretical roentgens, multiplied assumed minutes, and presently rang the phone.

In the Hall, dozing, Vance answered.

"He's coming back!" Ben said rapidly. "Get two men in the heaviest suits we have, and bring them up! Prepare to flush off the elevator after we take him to decontamination. It's going to be nasty!"

Farr said, "Right," three times. Now he snapped, "And you *stay where you are!*"

Ben said, "Check!" making it sound sincere.

Then he went lithely down the ladder and started out over the sloping ledges, and on into the tangled greenery, until at last he came up to Kit.

The man's eyes were glazed. Tremors racked him. He recognized Ben, however, and grinned sheepishly. "Apologize, my friend," he said.

"Sure!" Ben wrapped a supporting arm around Kit. Waited, while Kit vomited. Half-carried the heavy man back toward the bare, less-radioactive rock where, presently, others emerged to help.

All that day, behind a lead-brick screen in his room, Kit lay unconscious, his fever rising. Paroxysms occasionally seized his muscles. His feet, then his lower legs, hands, and arms, slowly turned black. Purple blotches appeared on his torso as blood vessels burst there.

The women, in heavy shielding suits, took turns sitting outside the lead-block wall, against the chance Kit might become conscious enough to ask for a drink of water, or speak a name, or need some other attention.

That never happened.

Limp, barely breathing, shriveled-seeming, and black, he died before the outdoors darkened again.

Ben became sick three hours after his rash, if gallant, effort.

He, too, was feverish, weak, nauseated, and marked with the splotchy hemorrhages beneath his skin.

It had been possible, however, to wash from Ben such radioactive material as had entered the few rips in his shielding clothes. No protective wall was therefore needed, and no special costumes for the women, who, round the clock, then tried the best they could to care for the often-delirious man.

After some days his symptoms grew less severe. One morning, a week later, he opened his large, blue eyes and they met the anxious and immediate attention of other eyes—Faith's.

Ben smiled weakly. Was kissed.

"You wonderful, crazy person!" Faith said. It seemed insufficient. Even silly. "You——!"

Ben held up a hand, weakly. "Moron," he finished for her. "What's the diagnosis?"

"We've done everything we could manage. Typed everybody's blood. Given you six transfusions! You'll be okay."

Ben stared with feeble amazement. "How come?"

Faith laughed happily. "Dad played doctor. Did it from books. And also, as we only just learned, from *watching*. Half the nights Mother *thought* he spent with Angelica—maybe *more*—Dad was down at the Fenwich hospital learning all he could."

Ben frowned, "Didn't tell *me*——!"

"Nobody's been sick! Till now!"

"Oh?" He drifted off. Opened his eyes again. "Allowed—allowed—any water?"

She held the glass, put the sipper between his cracked lips, raised his body. He drank thirstily. . . .

In two weeks, insisting he was "good as new," Ben was able to resume his work, though on short shifts, as he still tired easily. He had a few, less-dramatic relapses. But such studies as they could make of his blood and general condition indicated no permanent damage had been done to him by his considerable dose of radiation.

When June came, he was entirely well.

With the first day of June, however, the long sense of doom that had overshadowed the adults noticeably increased. In less than two months they could "celebrate" the second anniversary of their immolation. Because the labyrinths had been prepared by Vance Farr for two years and fifteen people, and they were now thirteen, and because that preparation had been lavish, they could and would continue to exist for an uncertain number of months after the second year below ground.

But their hopeful reliance upon rescue had become pessimism. Nobody had ever replied to their continuing signals.

At night now, quite often, when all the rest had retired with no more than sad, silent nods, Vance and Ben would sit till late, turning over in their minds, chiefly, the reason for the refusal of the world unharmed, or relatively unharmed, even to send them messages.

On one such mid-June evening, reviewing the possibilities, Ben's summary gave him a new idea. He said, that night:

"There's a reason we're ignored. *Hatred.* I'd imagine the remaining world despises every human being whose nation participated in this thing. It may also be that in the surviving nations, the Communists known to be there at the war's start have taken over."

"The world?" Vance objected. "Even *Australia?* South Africa, where the 'white-supremacy' and 'far-right' folly prevailed? Every Latin nation?" Vance shrugged. "Hard to agree, and I'm sure, from all the radio messages we've intercepted, the Commies outside the U.S.S.R. had no notion of what was coming. Still, with the inevitable chaos following the razing of a hemisphere, it's *possible.* The Reds everywhere were always well organized, secretly armed, ready to step in when public uproar gave their all-set and willing minority a chance. Remember Castro, and Cuba? Or were you too busy studying——?"

"I remember. And other countries, since. There's just one objection to that theory. All else fits—the silence in places like Australia, where a lot of game guys live. But which was socialist, anyway, and had a lot of Red citizens. A point. Even the refusal of white, far-right Capetown and the Union of South Africa to recognize us. *There,* I suspect, from the mixed-up months of yells for help, something pretty serious happened. Though Capetown comes in loud, clear, and sensible nowadays. But suppose——?"

He ceased his repetitive words.

Farr said, gently, "Suppose *what*, Ben?"

"Remember last fall—November 11, it was—when the Soviet survivors apparently committed united suicide?"

"Naturally." Vance's voice was dry.

"Suppose, since all that went up in nuclear blast, and in several areas, widely separated—Urals, Caucasus, Baikal, Arctic Sea, Okhotsk—suppose it *wasn't* suicide? Suppose the U.S.S.R. big shots had decided on this thesis: that in any all-out war with the United States, the Soviet homeland, Siberia included, would be wiped out. Suppose they *then* decided there was only a *single way* to make Marxism become the world religion—or tyranny. You name it! Actually, there *was* only one way!" Ben stopped, gazed pensively at the brightly-painted and handsomely-decorated interior of the immense Hall.

"And that way would be?"

"This kind of place," Ben replied. *"Only* on a *tremendous* scale. And with thousands of people—specialists of all essential sorts—hidden ahead of the first strike in places like this, Vance, but hundreds or thousands of times larger. With nuclear weapons stocks. And with the intent of remaining, like ourselves, till exodus was possible. Then even a few hundred nuclear-armed Reds, let alone thousands, could easily dominate the remainder of the world."

"How? Oh! I get you! Nuclear blackmail of the remaining nations, not one having an atomic weapon, or the means of making 'em, short of spending three-four years, maybe more, on the task. All right! Go on with that 'supposing.' Though it's hard to believe even the Russian Politbureau would sacrifice the entire population of the U.S.S.R. to gain the residual half of mankind. Still, a man like Grovsky——!"

"Exactly! A *truly* 'believing' Soviet group, a group actually all-out Marxist-Leninist, does take the theoretical viewpoint that the world *has* to become all-Red, in order to complete the Red dream of earthly heaven. Nothing that advanced communism, anywhere, was deemed 'wrong' or 'evil.' Anything that hindered the spread of Marxist tyranny was 'sin.' Ethics and morals, in short, turned upside down. Perverted, totally! A people believing *that* could do anything! Hitler killed his millions. Stalin, his tens of millions. Grovsky might easily decide to destroy a *billion and more* people, including *all* but a *few thousand or tens of thousands of his own*, to gain the real and basic Red goal: *world dominion!* After all, the Soviets thought in terms of generations, even centuries. While we——" Ben shrugged. "And, after a few generations, you could safely repopulate the Temperate Zone."

Vance said bitterly, "Whereas we thought in terms of *next year's* balance sheets."

"More or less. Even as physicists we thought only as far ahead as the end of the twentieth century. Establishing a permanent colony on Mars before A.D. 2000. Nothing further, in science. *American* science."

"But how could the Red scientists even have *gotten ready* for such a thing without our knowing—intelligence agents, spy satellites, all that?"

"Not easy." Ben pondered. "But making great supershelters under mountains—Urals, Caucasus, near Lake Baikal—could pass as 'mining.' And if the immense amount of gear they'd need was hauled into such giant strongholds *at night* and the heat dispersion of the hauling vehicles was kept low, or maybe if they used inside winches to pull gear into their initial diggings, our infrared satellites wouldn't have recorded that as anything special. The oceanside places are harder to account for." He paused and then said, startled, "Hey! Suppose they were *under water!*"

Vance had stared, astonished. "I'm no engineer——"

"The hell you aren't!"

"—but how could that be done, successfully?"

Ben had then risen. He paced the chamber, meditated, and finally said, "Caissons! In units. Sunk deep. Linked up. The work all done at night, and they have months of night up where they were! A submarine city—two, apparently—so far under the sea that land blasts, even nearby, wouldn't damage 'em!"

"Tremendous enterprise!"

"Sure! And haven't the 'tremendous enterprises' of the Soviets *always* happened? And *always* stupefied our free-world experts who, nearly always anyhow, said the Reds couldn't do it?" Ben's pacing had stopped and his eyes widened. "In that case, Vance, what we thought of as accidentally-fired, random H-blasts, picked up in the arctic, and north of Japan, and in the Mediterranean, and at this end of the Black Sea, *may not have been accidental!*"

"Don't get it!"

"Look! There used to be rumors, among physicists like

myself, though we weren't then working on weapons, that the U. S. Government had some sort of supersecret 'ultimate-weapon' program. I'd always thought of it as one of those 'doomsday machines,' like those sodium-jacketed H-bomb mines we knew *could* be made as far back as the late 1950s. That Pentagon plan had a super-supersecret name I heard a few times. 'Operation Last Stand.' No! 'Operation Last Ditch!' If it wasn't some 'doomsday machine' that we didn't touch off, it *could* have been a program for special units—of the U. S. Navy, say. In which case, the hits outside the U.S.S.R. were *counterfire* on a long-delayed *American attack* that destroyed all the bases in the U.S.S.R. we've here hypothecated. But suppose *one* base even, was *not* found and destroyed. Suppose, from *that* presumed base in the U.S.S.R. the world has been forced, under threat of H-bomb attack, to become Red. And forbidden to contact *us*. You know, Vance, that idea seems plausible, however hideous it would seem as a war plan to genuinely civilized people! And we can *check* it!"

"*Check* it? How?"

"By studying the seismographic and other records we kept in that period. Come on!"

Neither man slept that night.

And their scrutiny of their abundant and varied information at long last told them the truth: there *had* been aimed, rocket assaults—many, in fact, on each area they'd previously heard conferring by coded radio. And from those same bases, before they were annihilated, counterrockets had risen, and apparently gone home on their targets—evidently American nuclear submarines, or possibly aircraft carriers. That became plain when they made a minute study of the timing of the many, enormous explosions and the location of each, in relation to time. But if any Soviets had survived that horror, they had maintained radio silence since. . . .

On another night Vance and Ben had been discussing possible, last-minute methods of somehow getting safely away from the deep caverns and from Sachem's Watch above.

Ben had listed the ideas, in pencil, along with the relevant objections:

1. Build a helicopter. Range too short. Aerodynamic knowledge insufficient.

2. Build a plane in a lead-shielded hangar above. Probably could not build good enough plane in time left. Also: how to take off?

3. Clear low-radiation path to sea. Build boat, transfer it to Long Island Sound. Load personnel. Head for Costa Rica or other safe and relatively near place. Impossible to clear that much land of very hot debris and vegetation.

4. Radar recently installed aloft shows large lake formed, evidently when the H-bombing of Hartford threw massive wreckage into the Connecticut River. Lake might be reached, in shielded cart towed by shielded tractors. Lake might also be less radioactive than land. How to survive in lake? Build boat? Live on fish, if any there and safe to eat? Probably the best remaining chance, if all efforts to get outside help fail. We will start working on equipment for that in another month, if appeals are still unanswered.

It was at that point on that particular evening of moody converse between Vance and Ben, when George appeared. Both men said then, in unison and with smiles, "Where's Lodi?"

"Asleep. I couldn't. Sleep, I mean. Been looking at TV on the small-screen set in the communications room. Rio de Janeiro's about to broadcast that stuff you saw, Ben, long ago, from Montreal. Vance, you told me you'd like to see it."

"Not 'like,' George. But I did feel compelled to. But why now?"

George grinned ruefully. "Oh, those Latins love gory stuff. I suspect some even like to see what happened to us gringos and Yankees." He smiled again, at their nods of unconscious assent to his inclusion of himself with "gringos" and "Yankees," and went on. "The excuse for the broadcast is kind of ironic. Tonight's the anniversary of the Grovsky-Conner agreement to begin a final and effective disarmament discussion. Remember it? President Conner even thought the Reds *meant* it? And then, about six weeks later, the world came apart!"

Ben reluctantly, Vance face pale, followed George to the unpainted, black-box-crammed chamber cut in rock. They took chairs and listened to the incomprehensible Portuguese prologue. After it they saw the films Ben had watched, long before. Films taken by news photographers around Montreal in the early hours of the war and up until dusk. These films had been flown, by a Canadian jet, out over the Atlantic, to avoid the spreading atmospheric radiation, and south, to Rio and safety. The flight had been authorized by Canadian officials when they learned the film existed and realized it might be preserved by no less drastic means.

Montreal, Ben explained during some early shots of distant, horizon-to-horizon smoke, had not been hit. Apparently, of two or three weapons aimed at that city, only one had escaped interception and that one had fallen so far south and east of its target that, since the winds in the area were from the northwest, Montreal had remained unscathed until, that night, light fallout reached the city from the initial bombardment of the United States and from nearby Ottawa. Actually, till three and a half days later when the residual sodium clouds had arrived from the Pacific Coast, Montreal had remained alive though panicky.

The film now relayed from space and transmitted by Rio de Janeiro at first merely showed the shocking and violent efforts of the inhabitants of that city of well over a million to take cover, anywhere, or to escape in any sort of vehicle.

The onlookers had witnessed somewhat similar scenes, long ago, in films relayed the same way by Costa Rica.

But order was soon established in undamaged Montreal. The firestorm at Ottawa was visible as a mighty smoke cloud, but the winds bore the fallout away from Montreal. Quebec's disappearance, in solar temperatures and bloody agony, equally had no effect on her sister city. What followed that was appalling: an endless variety of scenes showing the arrival of refugees from the United States.

They came, at first, in a trickle—cars and trucks loaded with the blind, the burned, the savagely cut, the dead. They came from Manchester, Vermont, and from Lowell and Lynn and Worcester and Springfield and even Boston. From all of Massachusetts. And from Albany, and later from the Buffalo area in New York. The licenses of their vehicles made their origins partly clear; and words, spoken, groaned, or screamed, supplied the rest of the information.

These were citizens of the United States—men, women, children, teen-agers, babies—who somehow had escaped from one or another ruined perimeter of an H-burst—rocket warhead or plane-dropped, giant bomb. As the first of the arriving trucks, buses and, mainly, private cars grew to a flood that choked all roads leading to Montreal from the south, Canadian police, soon reinforced by soldiers, halted the columns at a distance from the city.

Filling all lanes of all highways, amid the roads through woods and farms, in hilly country and flat, the titanic, wailing exodus came everywhere to a stop.

In each vehicle was at least one man or woman—the

driver—who had not been blinded by seeing a fireball close enough—and in many cases forty miles was "close enough" —to lose his sight. But each load of refugees was in varied conditions that, even when shown one by one, beggared description.

Many were naked and of the naked, many were burned scarlet or, in places, black, from head to foot, or on arms and head.

The ears of thousands were gone. Their eyes had "melted" and lay on their cheeks in phlegm-like gobbets. Their noses were not there, and they breathed through holes in crisp, black faces. Their hair was gone. It was impossible to tell of thousands (unless they walked) which was the front, which the back of their horrible heads.

A sound rose from the stopped and backed-up caravan. It was like a dirge played on demonic, stringed instruments bloated in scale with the endless columns, a sound the ears even of the TV watchers could hardly believe, yet, on recognizing, recorded forever: the sound of thousands of people screaming and groaning and begging, often simply to be shot, by soldiers who tried, sick, nauseated, almost unable to carry out their orders, to give some sort of help to this interminable cavalcade of anguish.

But the soldiers did try! And they did not, could not, on orders, follow their often discernible desire to gratify some American, faceless, viscera in his own hands, burned to the rib bones, and still carrying a dead baby perhaps, who implored to be shot.

After a half hour of such horrendous viewing, came a series of pictures, all in color, in motion, of a great stadium. In this refugees were being assembled. It was half full when the cameraman had arrived. Nurses and doctors in white, or ordinary clothing, moved among boxes and reserved seats and in the bleachers and on the green, immense playing area.

They were constantly augmented, yet never enough for the ever faster accumulation of terribly burned or wounded refugees. The camera then showed the region outside the stadium. Ropes that seemed a mile long, fastened to stakes, were being followed by queues as long as the ropes, queues of bashed, smashed, burned, and sightless hordes who were able to move, on foot—or on what was left of feet—toward the stadium, by clinging to the guide-lines. Often, from that hideous queue, a man or woman or child would fall, and perhaps rise to grope again for the rope, perhaps crawl away to die, or, frequently, die where they had dropped.

In another sequence Canadians in white, heavy clothing that covered them from head to foot, with transparent plastic face masks for seeing, were walking along a highway clogged by four vehicles abreast, all of them motionless, unless ordered out of line. These men in hoods carried wand-like, metal objects which they passed over and around the standing vehicles. Quite often they would wave a car or bus or truck out of line and order it, backed up by armed soldiers when that was required for compliance, to leave the highway and drive to the farthest possible edge of vast grain-fields flanking the road. Already those grain fields, ripe but not harvested, had been flattened by passing vehicles which stood in motionless rows at their far sides.

These vehicles and their passengers were, plainly, too "hot" to be allowed to continue toward Montreal.

A close shot of one such inspection showed, on the hood of a family sedan, a radiation reading of 760 roentgens. The reading on top of the car was higher. Inside were two young people and their three little children, frightened but seemingly uninjured. At the wheel was an old man who argued with the Canadians until the rifles of the soldiers made him go, grumpily, unbelievingly, toward the quarantine area of too-radioactive vehicles. All five in that car were, at the time they had been photographed, unaware of any hurt. But all five were as surely dead as if they'd had their hearts removed. One by one, in minutes, or hours at most, they would sicken and die from the almost invisible dust of a Massachusetts fallout area which they had brought, unknowingly, to this place of apparent safety.

When the TV scene returned to a now overcrowded stadium, Vance muttered, "Let's shut it off!"

George obeyed.

"It's not we who need to see such examples of the hideousness that wiped out our world," Farr mused. "It was the people who were eradicated—that billion-plus. The facts were public that could have told them all that happened was possible—told them fifteen years ago or more. The one stark fact that when war starts the combatants may go all-out and the more terrible such fighting gets the more awesome and deadly the response on both sides—that, too, they could have applied to any picture of a war to come. I . . . *did.*"

Neither George nor Ben replied; but both nodded.

"All the fools—physicists and military men, politicians and congressmen—assumed that whatever happened the United States would win. The experts never fed their computers with information about human hatred and cunning, or the problem of what our enemy would find itself obliged to do, in an H-war, even to have a shot at even a *sort* of victory."

George objected: "Our Navy did, kind of."

Farr grunted and took out a cigar. Put it back. "Operation Suicide, it was. Mutual suicide. The Rand Corporation, Kahn, all the rest, chatted about 'doomsday machines' and how to make them and then ignored the likelihood they'd *be* made. Sodium-jacketed H-mines. Depressed radiocobalt dusting a continent. It was *all* known to be possible. Only, von Neumann's *Theory of Games* was used by ten thousand dullards wearing uniforms or plastered with academic degrees, to extrapolate such wars, in an atomic age, that like *games* the United States might win. To calculate the blotting out of the North Temperate Zone, a new kind of stalemate, a stalemate of annihilation of both sides and everybody in between in both directions—*that* wasn't 'military.' Because to be military you must imagine you can fight and win. They fought, God knows! but where's your winning side?"

George said, grimly, "The Southern Hemisphere. The non-white peoples and the Latin Americans that so many white citizens of the United States considered not quite white. *They* won. And the Anzacs, unless something went haywire down there we don't know of."

Farr shrugged but said nothing.

The second anniversary of the descent to the shelter of ten people, later increased by four, was not celebrated. Everybody knew the date of the first cataclysm; everybody, even including Dorothy and Dick. But they had become sensitive to the moods of their elders and so, whispering together in a passageway that morning, the growing boy and girl agreed not to mention the special day and its meaning, unless somebody older did so.

And no one spoke of it.

That day was spent, like its recent predecessors and many following days, in a careful inventory of remaining stocks.

There was fuel oil enough to run the diesels for six more months.

The water would last about that long, in a drinkable state.

But the air-cleaning plant, the filters and gaseous-diffusion elements, had been under the unexpected strain of handling, for a long period, an atmosphere contaminated by cobalt at a high level of radiation; it was now showing signs of unreliability. No "backwash" or purgative equipment had been included to refit the system for service after a cleansing. Ben had been trying all summer to figure how such a process might be contrived and equipment to perform it built. He had not been successful. The myriad "screens," through the minute pores of which air passed, molecule by molecule, were clogging up with hot material. In some ten weeks the efficiency of the plant would dwindle. Air let into the labyrinth would then begin to contain fractions of a roentgen of radioactive substance, minute at first, but constantly increasing.

Balloon-carried monitors with telemetric devices had shown, in the past months, that the new lake formed on the Connecticut River was, spottily, too "hot" for an outside refuge. Similar measurements had disclosed that the sea beyond Long Island could safely be entered and occupied, if constant caution were observed against long contact with masses of dead, floating plankton or "rafts" of radioactive seaweed.

But they had not yet built the tractor and boat that, presumably, might transport them over the rubble landscape and the tangled, new (and sometimes new-to-botany) vegetation lying between their refuge and the Sound. Such a trip, with the most shielding they had devised, would at best leave them sick from radiation poisoning. And there was no way to go on, safely, through the radioactive masses in the Sound and out to sea.

Food, also, was short. Some of it had spoiled and some had been mysteriously reached and ruined by what seemed to be a new species of beetle that was itself somewhat radioactive. Up above, then, certain life forms, animal and vegetable, were adapting, through a series of violent mutations, to the new conditions; these forms moreover, plant or insect, were exhibiting tendencies to overswarm such vines, bushes, annuals, and insects as still survived unchanged.

Water, air, and food. Those three necessities approached three different "terminal" points, none susceptible of absolute prediction, but all near at hand.

They might survive to about the thirtieth month beyond the commencement of troglodyte existence. *Might.* Not longer.

And it seemed certain they could not get away from their continent by any means.

Those facts, kept secret from no one, had led to a steady lowering of morale, to zombie-like behavior, to silences and to fits of tears, and to desires for solitude which, often, led one or another of the group to seek out, and stay for hours in, some remote part of the galleries. Persons who did that were no longer hunted for, found, and cheered up.

For though they could be found by search, they could not be made cheerful.

One September afternoon a desultory game of table tennis was being played by Ben and Faith.

It had been her suggestion, after she'd found him laboring, pale and drawn, over diagrams of a tractor-trailer. "You've been up all night, again," Faith had said.

"Sure. Why sleep? If I could only figure how to get us *out!*"

"You never will, if you work this way. Beat. Feeble. Tired to exhaustion. Come on and play table tennis. The exercise'll be good for you. Then supper, such as it will be. And some genuine, all-night shut-eye, afterward. You need it!"

They'd played two sets. And started a third. It was Faith's serve, but suddenly she didn't serve. Instead, she removed the engagement ring Kit Barlow had given her and tossed it on a chair as if it were a marble, not one of the vanished Tiffany's most spectacular and costly stones. "Hurts my finger," she explained.

Ben nodded and again prepared to return her serve.

It never came. Faith crossed to a divan made in the woodworking and upholstery shops long ago, and set in the Pingpong room for spectators when it had become frayed.

She dropped into it and beckoned to Ben.

For a time they sat side by side, silent, panting a little, Faith flushed, her hair disarrayed and shimmering . . . Ben pale, gaunt, tired.

"Mess," she said.

He nodded. "Shame, too. After all your father's effort. Ingenuity. Outlay." A queer thought struck Ben. He expressed it, the way people did nowadays, giving utterance to many things they'd have kept to themselves earlier. "Wonder how much this marvel cost him? Never asked."

Faith smiled slightly. "I did. Dad doesn't know exactly. But somewhere between a hundred and fifty million and two hundred."

Ben wasn't startled. Farr had a fortune large enough to permit that immense outlay . . . for a refuge that had now been proven inadequate, owing to conditions no man, however imaginative, could have predicted. No sane man, at least. Vance Farr had outguessed every one of his countrymen, experts included. Only the Reds had guessed beyond him.

Another thought, a whimsy almost, made Ben grin, or stretch his lips in something like a grin. "In other words, if the Pentagon, White House, Rand Corporation, civil-defense people and the rest ever *had* taken a realistic view of a third war, they'd have foreseen, at most, what your father did. With the result that they'd at have realized it would cost about ten million bucks a person to shelter any part or all of the U.S. population for the at-least-conceivable period of two years. And then *that* would have proven far too short a time. *Man!* Wouldn't such a situation have put our so-called and long-deceased leaders in a tizzie!"

Faith smiled. Then in a low, odd tone, she said, "Ben."

He turned abruptly. He'd never seen that expression on Faith's face. It electrified him, which in turn disconcerted him. He tried to shunt aside whatever emotion had kindled the look. "Right here, Faith. On Hand. What ho?"

"You always loved me."

His eyes shut. His head turned away. He said nothing, but Faith saw his nod. She spoke again. "And I always loved you."

"Don't be absurd." He kept his head turned.

"I'm not. I always have. From the first time you visited me at the hospital."

"Kit?"

She meditated and he dared look at her. "Kit," she repeated. "Why get engaged? Because mother wanted it? Long habit and ancient expectation? No. Because, Ben, I was afraid you *didn't* love me, then. Or maybe afraid that the society I'd lived in wouldn't take kindly and unanimously to a Faith Farr becoming a Mrs. Dr. Benjamin Benvenuto Cellini Bernman. Which you'd have hated." She laughed. "You thought we didn't know your middle names? You never used them, but they're noted in some book here in the library. What's wrong with them?"

Ben answered meekly, "It was Mother's idea. Very chi-chi, she felt. *Too* fancy, I felt. Cellini? Hell! I'm merely a sort of super-engineer!"

"What you are, is a darling."

"—is a scarecrow."

"With a grin on that ugly face, you're *pure* darling! The

rest of you is *more* man than most any man. And that's the thing we have to talk about."

"*What!*"

"I didn't throw Kit's ring away just now because it cut into my finger. I threw it aside because I realized you weren't ever going to take it off. That I'd have to do the telling. That you'd never acknowledge your own real feelings——"

Ben interrupted. "Quit it, Faith. I admit the feelings, wholly, and as of that first night when I brushed snow from the face of a lovely young woman. But we might still get out somehow."

"Might. Yes. And what?"

"Connie and Pete——"

She laughed. "Sure. It was wise and brave of Connie to stop everything between herself and Peter. He's hurt, but not wrecked by it. He's come to realize that outside, if we ever got outside, it perhaps wouldn't work. Not yet. Not for another generation or two. So, it better not be continued here. But there's nothing like that about us. You're Jewish—so what? Does it really mean *anything*? No. It never did, except to idiots who felt so inferior themselves they thought a whipping boy made them bigger. That's *all*. You're the bravest, brightest, ablest, kindest, most *attractive* man I ever met— or ever would have, even in a lifetime, and even if there never had been a war. I love you, Ben. Damn near worship you! And I want you to quit being noble and admit you feel the same."

He answered, dully, "All right. Admission made."

"Then kiss me." As he hesitated, but with a changing look, an upwelling of inward radiance she'd never seen before, she said, "Kiss me now, here, *immediately!* Then we'll go to my room." He hesitated at that, the kiss not quite commenced. So she went on. "Maybe you think it would be ghoully to begin our love-life in what may become our graves. *I don't.* And neither will you, after even one kiss."

That was how George Hyama found them.

George, in socks, unaware he'd kicked off his loafers during a just-interrupted vigil in the communications room. George, sweating, trembling, almost unable to speak, his face the pale, lemony hue Ben had noticed before under conditions of stress and terror.

For a long moment, George merely stared at the pair on the divan. For another, his tautness lessened and his eyes shown with an empathy and tenderness that Lotus Li had been first to discern. Then he made words come. "We need you, please!"

Ben moved away from Faith. Stood. "Trouble?"

The cropped, black head shook. "It's——!" His voice broke and he tried again. "Australia! At last."

Faith and Ben raced behind him.

All the others were gathered in or just outside the communications room. Farr sat beside a glittering, many-colored instrument panel. On the table before him, a mike. As the three approached they heard Farr's voice, shaken yet resolute, complete a question:

". . . and we wonder if there's any hope of rescuing us, here?"

Back through a loud-tuned speaker came the response, clipped, cheery, suspenseful without meaning to be. "We'll get to that matter in a sec. A few things to tell you first. Such as why we haven't responded to your signals sooner. Our apologies. I'm duty-bound to explain. We knew, from the beginning of—of it all—that the Russkis were denned up like snakes, ready to emerge eventually and take charge of the world. The residue of the world. So we blanked out all radio and television sending, down under. New Zealand joined in. The next thing to do, quite understandably, was to pick up where we'd left off. We'd stripped ourselves of rockets and H-weapons, you know."

Vance's hoarse voice filled a pause. "Yes. We know."

Ben muttered incredulously, "When did this——?"

George almost smiled. "Been talking with them for the last few minutes. Just out of the blue they came in, loud and clear."

Ben felt Faith's shoulder touch his and, unconsciously, put his arm around her. The Australian went on explaining:

"For all we knew, the other peoples in the Southern Hemisphere might attack us also. Overcrowded, this hemisphere, excepting Australia. Others might want to move in on us. Anyhow, our engineers, scientists, technical chaps, soon had us rearming. Then, almost a year ago, the Russkis did come out, and your people blasted them to bits. Nuclear submarines. Along, we thought, with a carrier we'd refused to allow to approach us. Evidently they were all blitzed in their effort. At least none returned to this area. None ever signaled again. But it took us most of the past year to be certain we dared show our hand. We had to be sure beyond all doubt that the Reds didn't have some alternative scheme for conquest set up—nuclear weapons and all, in South America, Africa, where-not. Once we were positive—and we are, now—once Australia and New Zealand knew that all the H-bombs in being belonged to us, which was a very recently determined fact, we could plan something for you people."

The man paused. Vance said, unevenly, "Thanks! We are——"

A chuckle answered him and the Australian continued his summary. "Took a bit of reconnaissance to be certain that we even could do anything about your group! Your North Temperate Zone's a tomb, from upper Canada to southern Mexico and, unevenly, around the globe, with Europe, the Mother Islands, Siberia, North Africa, the Near East, most of China, and so on, exterminated. Except for your people, of course, there's not a sign of human existence in the whole, ruddy belt!

"Our parliaments—Australia and New Zealand, too, incidentally—are creating a world outfit, as rapidly as we can. Everybody's coming in—the Latins, the African nations, Indonesia. International government, of course. In partial being, already. Has to happen. The H-weapons we made will be kept in our deserts till the world government's strong enough to take charge of them, and to keep them as a perpetual guarantee that nobody, ever, hereafter, will try to set up any new orders, soviet system, or tyranny of whatever sort. Meaning—men are to become free and equal, from now on in. Without race differences. Took the extermination of half a world to bring it about. Worth it, though, perhaps, eh?"

Vance was supposed to answer. He said, wryly, into the mike before him, "Some price!"

The voice agreed. "Righto. Northern part of the white race *in toto,* save for us cousins down under. Slavs. Japanese —gone. Most Chinese. *Quite* a high fee for perpetual liberty and individual equality. *Paid,* though. Your people ought to enjoy the world that's coming up. After all, you're thirteen United States citizens. But you're a rather mixed bunch yourselves."

Vance said, so softly Ben felt it might not be heard, "We're as near to being one as if we were all brothers and sisters."

"Don't we know! You Yanks aren't aware of it, but your broadcasts, the past two years, have been front-page headlines down under, from the first."

"What?"

"Why not? Without the telly, without radio, our people

have depended on newspapers. They followed your doings minutely. So did Parliament."

"Parliament?"

"Why not, Mr. Farr? There's been a constant debate in our Parliament as to whether we should take a chance before we knew how we were coming out in the world situation, and could come up to get you. People raised hob. But we waited." Another pause and the voice became reflective. "What has happened since the Third War began tends to create an extra bit of caution. And that's about the summary. You'll find a new spirit, around and below the equator. A whole world—that is to say, the residual half a world—is determined to establish peace forever and forever to stop war. And in our world the means to enforce that ideal are at hand . . . not just on order or in the making. You'll be entering a federation of racially, nationally free and equal people. Clear?"

"Magnificent!"

"Now. About your rescue."

Again a moment of silence. The people in the room walled with electronic gear, and the people gathered in the passageway, shifted positions. Farr, sweating, yet strangely relaxed, spoke into that silence. "We can hold out, sir, for many weeks."

The response came: *laughter!* "My name's Jenkins. Oliver. Sorry I'd not said. Bit excited myself. See here. No wait necessary, to speak of, Mr. Farr. You haven't taken a bearing on the point of origin of this station, I gather?"

Farr gasped. "We assumed Australia."

"I'm on the *Capricorn Queen,*" the suddenly-identified Oliver Jenkins responded. "We wanted you to have a general picture of things before we went into the rescue details. They may be a bit surprising and you may want to end this talk when you hear the rescue plan."

"I don't quite understand." Farr said what the rest felt.

"You will."

A second voice was briefly audible, though its words were not discernible. Oliver Jenkins soon went on. "A last detail I was to mention. If you do have those stocks of refined, rare metals, and if you don't mind our carting them back to Australia, we'll do it, gratefully. The material you spoke of is mighty precious down under at this time. But if you were just offering an imaginary booty to try to get help, no matter. Taking you people from your shelter to our homeland is going to be a proud thing for Australia, and for the surviving world. We're not *asking* for a reward from you. Just for things we can use that your hemisphere won't produce for decades, and till mining's safe. If you see what I mean?"

Vance smiled now. "We have the refined metals in exactly the amounts and purity-states we've broadcast. And you are more than welcome to them. More than welcome! Don't you realize they mean nothing to us here?"

"Oh, yes, righto, of course. Fine! Our scientists, metallurgical works, and so on, will be very pleased. Now, the last bit of information. The *Capricorn Queen* is in the Atlantic, some three hundred miles south of Long Island. She will anchor, offshore, before morning. We'll leave her in shielded helicopters with the first light, tomorrow. Weather outlook is splendid. The *Queen's* a big ship and she's specially shielded with lead, all about. I'm afraid you'll have to remain, as we've all done coming north, below decks, till we get beyond your West Indies. After that it'll be fair sailing. A jet will pick you up, and some of us, in Panama, and take the party straight on to Melbourne. The *Queen* will return for the metal you have, and, if you don't mind, for some of the instruments. We've envied you quite a few things up there, along with our nationwide, day-to-day sympathy. Your radiation levels required shielding on our 'copters and that makes it desirable for you to travel light when you leave. Personal luggage only, and a few changes of clothing. Our Parliament, acting for the forming world government, will see to it that you have everything you need in the days that follow."

Vance tried to interrupt, to express deep-felt gratitude.

The Australian did not allow it. "That's the packet. We'll be landing on top of Sachem's Watch around 0800—8 A.M.— tomorrow. If you're packed and all set in your elevator, we'll whisk you to the *Queen* within the hour and head straight south. All clear?"

"Isn't there a way to say *some* word of thanks?"

Again a chuckle. Oliver Jenkins, who would prove on the morrow to be Sir Oliver, said, "Very well, Farr. That word, then. You've said it. Perhaps, too, you should know this conversation's being relayed to all the surviving peoples around and below the equator. They wanted to be in on the first contact. Maybe two or three hundred million human beings are listening in. Our circuit's wide open." A moment passed. The clipped voice asked, anxiously, "Something the matter? Hello there, Sachem's Watch!"

What he heard and what the *Capricorn Queen* relayed to the transfixed, surviving half of the world, was a different voice: "This is Ben Bernman," it said. "Vance Farr has been overcome by emotion and cannot speak for the moment. Any more we could say beyond our bare 'thanks' would hardly have meaning right now."

"I see." The Australian voice was more emotional, now, than voices of Britons are expected to be ever. "I quite see. All of you are welcome, Dr. Bernman. And if there aren't any further questions? . . . Right? *Roger*. See you in the morning! . . . Over and out."

In twos and threes they moved to the Hall. Some stood; most sat down. Ben found himself thinking that Faith, whose hand he still held, deserved an offer of release from her just-made commitment. He looked down into her wet, transfigured eyes, and she read his thought. "Don't say it!" she whispered. "Don't *ever* say it! My husband is going to be sure of my love!"

"Yes," he whispered. And added, "He will be."

Lodi and George stood face to face and merely looked at one another, smiling softly, not even touching hands—a strange but moving thing. Ben momentarily thought: Oriental, maybe. Then he upbraided himself for his habit of analysis and classification; he and Faith were doing about the same.

He saw Valerie sitting shiny-eyed beside Vance Farr and saw that Vance, his purpose fulfilled, his brave, imaginative mission completed, looked gray and drained and aged. Ben reflected on the selflessness that had led the man to build the refuge that had saved them, when Farr had realized, the whole while, his own chances of being sheltered from sudden holocaust were never very good.

Except for a few sobs, the quietude grew oppressive. We should be gay, Ben thought. Even hysterically gay. But who could? Who, here and now, could rejoice? The relief was too incalculable, and that from which they were to be saved had been too titanic in its terrible extinctions, for swift or selfish jubilance.

A murmur came—oddly, Ben first felt—from Paulus Davey. Then the murmured words became distinct, and were not odd. The white-grizzled ex-butler spoke softly but with resonance.

" '. . . is my shepherd. I shall not want. He maketh me to lie down in green pastures. He restoreth my soul . . . My cup runneth over. Yea, though I walk through the valley and shadow of death . . ." Paulus choked up.

The silence deepened and sobs were more urgently strangled.

Vance, looking at his daughter and then at the man he now surely knew would be his son-in-law, felt the return of his custom of command. Then it ebbed and he felt older, content, and in stark need of rest. He cleared his throat. "Say a few words for us, will you, Ben?"

The scientist nodded. Heads turned. Streaked faces lifted. Ben spoke.

"No use to say much. No likelihood I'll say it well. An hour ago we thought we would perish here together. Now we shall be saved together." He faced Farr. "Thanks to the selfless courage, the refusal to conform, the vision and energy and poured-out wealth of Vance, we survived. But our survival, however great an example of the spirit of mankind, of his determination to endure and live and continue, depended, actually, on still another factor. I have often thought of that other factor lately.

"The name of it is love. Love that does not consider *being loved* as its necessary adjunct. Love, merely, that is offered, tendered, inexhaustibly given, without any asking price. Love of people. Love, that built the glimmering halls and galleries which saved us. It was Alberto's love, again, that riskily bored our way to the outdoors, long ago. Valerie's love that forgave, and also enabled her to conquer her own self." He did not mention his own version of such "love," or that it had saved four of the present survivors, in one hot foray, and repeatedly saved them all, through the use of ingenuity, and even tried to save the self-centered and finally mad Kit Barlow.

He gave some few added illustrations and touched, particularly, on the love between Connie Davey and Pete Williams, which had "grown so great that they had relinquished one another, to avoid the possibility of hurting" and not, Ben said, *"being* hurt."

"Now, perhaps," he continued, "Pete and Connie can suitably resume their love in the world where we shall live. It seems at least possible. We, and they, shall see.

"What I mean here, however, is called 'spiritual.' And that quality, learned by the few of us in such fearful and dreary times, is what we must attempt to carry with us. We will be feted like heroes, obviously. But however thunderous the crowd ovations, however moving the celebrations, let us never forget who we are.

"Who are we?

"You know. We are the pitiful, insufficient, mixed, fortunate remnant of more than a billion human beings. They're dead. We live. We cannot hope to represent them. We must not try to atone for their self-induced extermination. What caused it? In the long nights and days of existence here, I think we have learned their error. It was simple. . . .

"They came to love *things* more than one another. They were, on one side, godly by assertion. On the other, atheist. But above and beyond that, on *both* sides, they were materialists. Marx established his materialism as a substitute worship. Our own was established by ourselves and its voice was not Marx but a nonexistent slot in rubble once called Madison Avenue, where we wrote a new theology of things also. We can remember that, and help the world, perhaps, to remember it forever. The *use* of things can lead to man's salvation, as it has led, in our small, pitiful cases. But things as man's *end* become—became—the end of man. Such is my confession, as a physicist. And such is the small insight I can add to the confession: merely a word I cannot define but that I do *know* and hope to *embody* always. *Love.*"

Ben looked at Faith.

Her head had been inclined, but as he ceased to speak she lifted it and straightened, offered her lips, and they embraced.

Vance stared a moment, sharing with Valerie the satisfaction of responsibility abdicated for a yet more able successor. Then, knowing there was much to do in a night that would be their last and seem short, knowing the time had come to stop this condition of stricken bliss before it became conscious and sentimental, and even attitudinizing, Vance leaped forward with twinkling eyes and outthrust hands to congratulate Ben Bernman and next to hug Faith.

The leading helicopter of the rescue party swung over Long Island Sound. Its pilot, a much-traveled man, let his imagination follow his eyes and soon, run beyond the visible perimeters.

Long Island was out of shape, with bays and bights the bombs had made, long ago. Greater New York was a black-and-gray tumble of indecipherable ruins, at the edges of which the greens of encroaching vegetation could be seen. The Hudson had a slightly altered course where a vast reach of the Palisades had pitched into its waters.

His mind went westward on a once-familiar journey, now envisioning what he had learned was there. . . .

The blackness of burned forests over the Appalachians. The malformations of shore line in the still-blue, quiet Great Lakes, where not even flotsam moved with the wind any more. The naked ash of prairie that here and there was being reclaimed by weeds and grasses, of which some, botanists had said, after studying high-altitude photographs, were new species, adapted after mutation and by the remorseless process of selection for survival in the still-toxic emptiness. Beyond, the Rockies rose and then the Sierras, nude as the glaciers had left them, smoked-up in empty chaoses, snow-bearing, and without life that could chirrup, call, sing to the warmest sunrise, or howl at the strange urges of rising moons. Only that bizarre, new, insidious vegetation in patches, here and there. Farther beyond, the trampled, burned, jagged insanity of cities, of San Francisco, Los Angeles, and the rest, first buried in the death of isotopes, then sea-buried, and now awaiting reburial by time's descending dusts.

The man at his side brought back his attention by pointing. The pilot saw a smoke signal rising on a slight slant and, soon, the upturned faces of thirteen people standing in the morning light on their elevator, with little packages and cases at their feet.

He was used to upturned faces, as 'copters came down. These seemed at first no different—these thirteen. Yet they did differ in some way. The Aussie puzzled over it as he manipulated the controls, while his colleague called out the slight but bearable rise of radiation. Before he touched down, he understood the difference. These thirteen didn't wave very much. A hand now and then, lifted and drawn back quickly, almost self-consciously. Why? People always waved at 'copters, and the Yanks weren't known for reticence. This was their great moment.

And there lay the clue.

They *were* Yanks. Americans. Specifically, North Americans. Citizens of the United States. All who remained alive in that enormous nation.

The Australian then understood a solemnity which, perhaps, the nearing survivors did not quite understand themselves.

He, and his following companions, would very soon take all thirteen away. They would leave the United States of America forever.

And when they had gone, the place would have no name.

END